HADRIAN AND SABINA

A LOVE STORY

REGINA KAMMER

VIRIDIUM PRESS

Published by Viridium Press, Friday Harbor, Washington
ISBN-13: 978-0-9978893-1-4 (paperback)
ISBN-10: 0-9978893-1-4 (paperback)
ISBN-13: 978-0-9910166-2-4 (ebook)
ISBN-10: 0991016629 (ebook)

Acknowledgments

Thanks go out to my family and friends for their enthusiastic support of my writing. Thanks to the Office of Letters and Light for inspiring authors across the globe with National Novel Writing Month. Most of all, thanks to my husband for his encouragement, advice, patience, and love.

Preface

The field of Hadrianic studies is immense, despite, or perhaps because of, what at first glance seems like a dearth of factual information about the Roman emperor Hadrian (76-138 CE). We have information about his career – the honors, the politics, the travels, the campaigns – we even have a physical description of him. And, of course, we know of Hadrian's great love for his favorite, Antinous, the youth who died too early and for whom the emperor's grief knew no bounds.

But we know very little about the emperor's wife, Sabina, and their relationship. What we do know is clouded by the socio-political agendas of the writers whose opinions have come down to us over the centuries, especially the anonymous writer of the *Historia Augusta*. These writers contend that Hadrian found his wife "moody and difficult"; that she refused to carry his child; that he would have divorced her had he been a private man; that she had a slave lover; that an "informality" or "familiarity" involving her led to the disgrace of the imperial secretary Suetonius and guard prefect Septicius Clarus; that Hadrian himself caused her death by poison.

Yet, at the same time, Hadrian affectionately called her "my Sabina", she traveled the lengths of the vast empire at his side, and the emperor deified her after her death. Nor is there is any record of a contentious relationship between her and the emperor's beloved Antinous.

What I seek to accomplish is to offer an alternative interpretation of the ancient writers without nullifying their statements, and, indeed, incorporating these intriguing morsels of information. What if outsiders were meant to believe that Hadrian and Sabina had a unhappy marriage? What if, instead, their relationship was, like many political unions, complex?

Historians may balk at the recontextualizing of the Hadrian saga as a work of erotic fiction, or that some liberties have been taken. Some names have been modified from the historical record to promote readability; the timeline has been changed very little, but may diverge from historical record for the convenience of plot; and, in some cases, a choice between historical interpretations has been made.

I do hope the reader enjoys reading this book as much as I enjoyed writing it.

Brief Bibliography

Anonymous (2nd-3rd century CE). *Historia Augusta: Hadrianus*. (Loeb Classical Library) London: W. Heinemann; New York: G.P. Putnam's Sons, 1922.

Birley, Anthony Richard. *Hadrian: The Restless Emperor*. London; New York, NY: Routledge, 1997.

Boatwright, Mary T. "The Imperial Women of the Early Second Century A.C." *The American Journal of Philology* 112.4 (1991): 513-40.

Cassius Dio (c. 229 CE). *Roman History*. (Loeb Classical Library) Cambridge, Mass.: Harvard University Press; London: W. Heinemann, 1914-1927.

Lambert, Royston. *Beloved and God : The Story of Hadrian and Antinous*. London: Weidenfeld and Nicolson, 1984.

Opper, Thorsten. *Hadrian : Empire and Conflict*. London: British Museum Press, 2008.

Syme, Ronald. *Roman Papers*. 7 vols. (1979-1991).

Yourcenar, Marguerite. *Memoirs of Hadrian*. London: Secker & Warburg, 1955.

PROLOGUE

Germania Inferior, Colonia Agrippinensis, early February 98

"The assassins came out of nowhere. Or so it seemed."

Hadrian sat on the dining couch, his fingers linked behind his neck, his elbows on his knees. He was exhausted. After the attack, he had walked several miles before he found a peasant with a horse, then, with all his might, had had to urge the pathetic nag to budge. It was the final push to complete his mission, and he had already traveled over one hundred miles without stop. Now at his destination, the initial exhilaration had dissipated to enervation. Yet, he had been the first to arrive at the governor's palace to announce that, with the death of Nerva, General Trajan had become Emperor of Rome.

"Are you harmed, cousin?" Trajan asked with genuine concern. The two were more than cousins. Twelve years earlier, Trajan had been appointed guardian for the ten-year-old Hadrian after the death of the boy's father, Aelius Hadrianus Afer. Having no children of their own, Trajan and his wife Plotina had treated their charge with affection.

"'Tis but a scratch. My aide-de-camp Marianus was severely wounded. Our horses were stabbed and drowned and our carriage smashed as we forded the Mosel. I was able to subdue my assailant but his companions fled. The scoundrel finally confessed to being in the service of my brother-in-law."

"Servianus?" Trajan said with only a little surprise. He peered into his wine cup pensively.

"I stopped at the governor's palace in Moguntiacum just after leaving camp. I stupidly told him the news of your advancement." Hadrian took a long draught of strong wine to steady himself. "He would have preferred Nerva to have chosen him as successor. It seems Servianus felt that if he could not be emperor, he could at least garner the new emperor's favor by being the first to deliver the news."

A loud knock on the door to the private dining room startled the occupants. Trajan and Hadrian glanced at each other. Hadrian reached for his sword. The emperor raised his hand to calm his young companion.

"Yes?" Trajan called.

"An urgent message from Moguntiacum, my lord. From the governor of Germania Superior."

The voice was familiar to the emperor, and he smiled briefly. "Come."

A boyishly handsome soldier entered carrying a sealed scroll. He glanced quickly at Hadrian, blushed, then handed the missive to Trajan and bowed. The emperor lingered on the youth's hand as he took the scroll, the hair on the soldier's strong forearm bristling at the thrilling touch.

Hadrian was a little startled at the revelation of intimacy between the two men, master and servant, officer and soldier. He himself once had to fend off Trajan's solicitations, but once he refused to play the role of the passive, the older man had relented, since then treating his ward almost as a peer. Hadrian diplomatically kept his emotions in check.

Trajan unrolled and glanced at the note. "You may go," he said to the soldier, leering at the youth's strong legs bound in tight winter leggings.

There was a fleeting smile on the young man's delicate lips before he bowed again and left.

Trajan read the note one more time. "Apparently there is news from Servianus that I am the new emperor. He sends his most sincere felicitations." He looked up at Hadrian. "He says nothing of you."

"Playing it safe in case I survived?"

"Most probably." Trajan drew in a deep breath. "Servianus is excessively ambitious, a quality that makes him untrustworthy and unpleasant. Sometimes I feel for your sister. She cannot possibly love the man." He shook his head. "He has tried to set me against you by complaining of your extravagant spending and numerous debts, you know."

Hadrian started at this. "On what am I supposed to have spent money?"

"Hunting dogs, fast horses," the emperor eyed his former ward. "Perhaps pretty boys at the local spa."

"My lord—Caesar, believe me, I have not been prodigiously indulgent."

"No, no, of course not." Trajan rose to pour himself another cup of wine. "Hadrian, my boy," he began, sitting down next to his cousin and taking his hand. "Graeculus," he said softly using Hadrian's familial nickname, "there will always be people who want to harm us, to kill us, and even to harm our close friends and loved ones. You must be ever vigilant and alert." He took a draught of wine. "But, son, you must not be overly suspicious. You must not be disagreeable to your own family and intimates. This is what killed Nerva's predecessor, Domitian, and what would have quickly killed Servianus had he been named successor. Don't be an arrogant fool like your brother-in-law."

Trajan stared blankly at the floor, his expression of victory tempered by a sigh revealing his realization of the overwhelming task before him.

"And, in the midst of it all, in order to succeed, you must learn to trust and to love. Both require acts of courage, but both offer substantial rewards." The emperor's lips twisted in a wry smile as he looked up at the closed door. "Especially love."

PART ONE:
TEMPUS VERNUM

Rome, Imperial Palace, November 100

"The ceremony went well, I think," Salonia Matidia had said after the wedding. "Now Vibia, be a good bride and wait for your husband to come to your bed."

Vibia Sabina lay on her back waiting for her husband as her mother had commanded. The wedding had been exciting, all the people dressed so colorfully, she herself draped in a flame-orange veil. She knew her husband Hadrian was an important man. As a boy he had been the ward of Trajan, perhaps even to be his successor on the throne one day, although one really never knew what was to be in Rome. Only the gods knew. And as Sabina waited in her bedroom she just hoped the gods were watching over her.

She thought about her husband, quite a bit her elder, by ten years at least. A man really, not a boy. He was handsome, tall, bearded, a soldier, a senator. She hoped that he would take her to some far off place in the empire – the east would be grand – where she would be his dutiful wife, welcoming him home when he returned from battle.

A female slave appeared and said she should position herself on all fours. Sabina did as bidden; the slave raised her tunic and uncovered her bottom. The slave rubbed oil on her privates sending unfamiliar sensations through her body. As the slave continued, Sabina felt lightheaded, her mind removed from the physical fondling which certainly was not unpleasant. Her toes tingled. Sabina wasn't quite certain what was happening to her but her body was climbing, spiraling upward. She exhaled a moan. The slave suddenly stopped. The sensations lingered in mid-air waiting for her body to reclaim them.

The door to the bedroom opened and a slight commotion ensued. *He* was there. Her husband had arrived to consummate their bond. She tensed, not knowing what was to follow.

She heard him approach, felt his heat near her, heard him shed his armor, heard the woolen tunic drop to the floor.

He was standing behind her now.

As was only the husband's right, he untied the knot of Hercules at her waist, and pushed the now-loosened tunic further up her body, his fingers only skimming at her ribs and missing her breasts entirely. He touched her left buttock, his hand warm, strong, caressing subtly but not desirously. He hummed a thoughtful moan then grunted and placed himself between her legs.

Sabina had been told what to expect, but she did not expect this.

He was large, thick, hard. He entered her slowly, deliberately. She winced, trying desperately to keep silent as she had been told. But then he pressed against her, against some barrier inside her. She felt it stretch, felt it hurt, and could no longer hold her tongue. She cried out.

His arm snaked around her waist. "Shh, shh," he calmed. "It will be finished soon." His voice was deep, soothing, convincing. His other arm wrapped around so his hand could touch her privates in the same place the slave had done. He massaged gently until her body relaxed in his arms.

And then he pushed in, tearing her apart. She screamed.

One hand clamped over her mouth, the other continued its sensual ministrations between her legs, his body now slamming forcefully against hers, riding a wave to its desired climax. She was completely and utterly controlled by his needs, secured in his grasp. He was breathing heavily, quickly, more rhythmically. His culmination came with a clipped groan. He remained inside her for a few seconds, spasming, still holding her in his arms, his breaths slowing to composure.

Then, just as quickly as he arrived, he left. She never actually saw his face. He never kissed her, nor told her he loved her.

That was what she had thought should happen when one got married. But then again, those were girlish fantasies, the dreams of a child. She should have known better upon entering womanhood.

Sabina slumped onto her side as the slave cleaned the blood from her broken barrier. The fact that her husband had not lavished her with sentimental affection did not detract from the experience. No, in fact his behavior had presented her with something rather unexpected. His command over her body, his possessive aggression had been exciting, thrilling, and, only now after the fact, did she realize how much more wonderful it had been than her childish illusions.

Hadrian exited his wife's bedroom satisfied that he had done his duty. How many times would he be expected to do as such, he did not know. Women were useful politically, strategically. It certainly did not mean he had to become emotionally involved with them in the least. And he only had to bed them a sufficient number of times to keep up appearances.

Outside Sabina's bedroom stood two guards, soldiers placed there by her great uncle Trajan less as a measure of security and more as a reminder of her regal position. One was older, plumper, the lines on his face exhibiting how he had become hardened by years of service. The other was young, green, experiencing, quite probably, his first palace assignment. His features were intriguing, a square jaw, sharp cheekbones, and pointed nose contrasted with his luscious, red, bowed lips. He stood rigid, his muscles taut and ready. The presence of Trajan's adopted son made him nervous.

He will do just fine.

"Soldier," he said officiously. "You are to come with me. Your cohort can guard the Princess Sabina for the time being."

The guards exchanged glances, the younger with uncertain concern, the elder with a nod of expected duty. Both men knew full well the reputation of the young Roman, his arrogance and his decadence. But the younger guard hardly knew what all that could possibly mean. He followed his master a pace behind, realization washing over him when he was summoned into Hadrian's bedroom.

Rome, Imperial Palace, early June 104

"You have not bedded your wife in how many years?"

The question was annoying, but as it came from Trajan's wife, the Empress Pompeia Plotina, Hadrian had to answer. "Four, I believe."

The two sat with Matidia, Sabina's mother, and Marciana, Sabina's grandmother, enjoying the fruits of early summer as they lounged in Matidia's private garden in the Palatine complex.

"Vibia talks about you from time to time, you know," commented Matidia. "Much less so now than when you were first married. She thinks you hate her and wonders if she should simply do the same."

"Why don't you two have some children?" suggested Plotina.

Like you and Trajan? Hadrian wanted to respond as he bit into an apricot. The emperor and empress got on fine, yet there had not been any issue from the union, and, given her age, there was not likely to ever be. "Children just get in the way of appointing an advantageous heir and successor, don't you think mother?" he responded. "I think Germanicus would have agreed with me considering Gaius Caligula turned out to be such a failure."

Plotina ignored her adopted son's insolence. "At least, dearest son, you should stop cavorting with boys so publicly."

"Like the emperor has?" Hadrian countered, this time out loud, as he finished his fruit. "Ah, yes, but at fifty he has slowed down somewhat. There are far fewer *pueri* in his bed these days."

"That's my brother you're insulting, you arrogant fool," Marciana snapped. "You should honor him. He has high hopes for you." She narrowed her eyes at her nephew. "Only the gods of Olympus know why."

Hadrian crossed his arms over his chest sullenly.

Plotina shook her head in acquiescence, unwilling as she always was to argue with him, knowing all too well he was correct. "Hadrian, I am only asking you to have the veneer of conviviality with your spouse. It's good for politics, it's good for your career, and it's good for Rome." She stood up and draped a thin linen shawl around her and motioned to her sister-in-law to join her. "Women are not so bad. I dare say you've already slept with one or two." She glanced briefly at Matidia, before she took Marciana's arm in hers and strolled away.

* * * * *

Matidia watched her aunt and mother leave, then rolled onto her back on the couch. "Sabina's a lovely young woman now, Hadrian. She might attract. You should have dinner with her. She *is* your wife." She tugged at and adjusted her clothing.

She knew Hadrian was watching her as she settled herself and made sure the diaphanous fabric of her tunic and stola clung provocatively to her breasts and belly. At thirty-six, she looked as good as her eighteen-year-old daughter. If he was bedding the mother surely he should have no compunction in bedding his own wife.

Matidia looked up and met his eyes. One side of his mouth was curved into a half-smile. "You look like a hungry wolf."

He raised an eyebrow and nodded once. "And what would you do to stop me from eating you?"

Matidia felt a rush of heat pulse to her head. She sat up with intention and beckoned a servant. "Leave me and take the rest of the staff. I need to speak with my son-in-law in private." She watched as the slaves and servants exited the garden. She turned to Hadrian. "I invited you here to discuss your relations with my daughter, nothing else."

"And I should take marital advice from you?" he queried imperiously as he got up from his couch. "And which husband are you on this month, Matidia? Number three, or is it number four?" He stood behind her and leaned over. "I simply cannot recall."

"You cur," she hissed. "You will listen to me because I will tell Trajan that you are inconsiderate and disobedient. And I will have Sabina attest to that before her grand uncle." Matidia looked up at her son-in-law. He was quite handsome, despite his arrogance, an attribute that had made her think her daughter would eventually become attached to him. His dark curls framed his angular face and set off his gray, almost blue, eyes. His beard, a feature Matidia thought she would never come to appreciate, was soft, not wiry, and invited touch. She reached her hand up to do just that, and stroked the dark hair on his cheek. She licked her lips in anticipation of what could possibly transpire next, since it always did seem to happen anyway.

Hadrian lowered his head and kissed her half-opened mouth, plundering her aggressively with his tongue as his hand found its way under her neckline to cup and squeeze her excited breast. Already she was panting like a dog in heat, wanting what she knew she should not have. With a twinge of disgust, Hadrian broke off and stepped away from the couch, turning his back to her.

Matidia stood up, adjusting her shear dress and overdress from Hadrian's rough handling before she went to him. He was wearing a sleeveless tunic on this warm day, baring his tanned and brawny arms. She trailed her fingers lightly from his shoulder down to his forearm, feeling the powerful muscles and tendons under the supple flesh. A tingling chill of desire swept through her. She was only eight years his senior. It was a shame to waste his fully-developed masculine attributes on such a child as was her daughter.

"Is she as wanton as you?" Hadrian asked, still not looking at her.

She dropped her hand. "You will have to discover for yourself." Her tone carried with it the disappointment of failed consummation.

Suddenly, Hadrian swung around, grabbed her arm, and flung her against a nearby garden stele carved with the laughing, drunken face of Bacchus. She gasped when her back hit the cool marble slab. He held both her hands in one of his just above her head, as his other hand lifted the hems of her long garments. His knee forcefully separated her bared thighs and he tucked the fabric behind her buttocks. Keeping his hips pressed against hers, his hand sought and found the folds of her feminine flesh. She was dripping wet.

Matidia let out a little whimper as her son-in-law commenced his sensual ministrations.

"You're wet, you little whore," he breathed. "You want to fuck me, don't you?"

"Hadrian, please," she sighed. She was lightheaded, his touch driving her inexorably toward a depraved climax.

He released her long enough to raise his own tunic and reveal his erection. He opened her thighs wider with his own and stooped to position himself.

She let out a moaning exhale of relief as his hot, hard flesh penetrated her. Instantly she came, clenching him, encouraging him to continue his demanding thrusts. She was dissolute, delirious, beyond ecstatic and racing toward oblivion.

Hadrian kept his control, his presence of mind, as he always did. She wanted him and he was willing to give her what she needed, especially if that meant she would keep her mouth shut where his marital life was concerned. She knew he did not need Trajan's enmity; the emperor had already passed him up for several deserved promotions. Hadrian pounded into her, coolly observing her twisted expressions reflecting every single convulsing contraction choking his prick below. She could sense he too was on the verge.

"I won't give you the pleasure of carrying your own grandson in your womb," he whispered wickedly before pulling out and spraying his seed onto the ground.

Matidia slumped against him, and he dragged her back to her couch.

"Don't involve yourself in my affairs, mother," he said with caustic cruelty as he let her fall on the cushions. "Sabina is my wife. She will obey me and do what I wish her to do. You, despicable woman, should attend to matters of your own hearth and home." He turned and stormed away.

* * * * *

"Where is my wife?" Hadrian bellowed to the first servant he saw in his palace apartment.

The frightened servant bowed. "She is in the garden, my lord," he answered without raising his head.

With long strides, Hadrian tramped through the atrium, along the passageway, then into the garden. He spied his wife near a glittering glass-encrusted fountain reading a scroll. A few female slaves attended her with music and trays of cut fruit.

This should be easy. He changed his pace to a sauntering stroll.

She looked up when she heard him and blushed a little.

"Good afternoon, husband." She did not try to mask the annoyance in her voice.

"Sabina," he greeted with a nod. "What are you reading?"

"Poetry," was the curt answer.

He scanned her body extended full-length on a garden couch. The fabric of her dress draped and clung to her shape exaggerating and emphasizing her feminine curves. He hadn't realized until that moment that his wife was no longer the girl he married; she was an astonishingly beautiful woman. Her flame-red hair was coifed in simple plaits surrounding and framing her lovely face. Her eyes were not green, not brown, but somewhere in between, like an exotic polished stone. Hadrian smiled to himself. Once or twice a month in her bed might actually be a pleasant experience.

With a wave of his hand, Hadrian dismissed the servants waiting on his wife.

That drew a scowl from her. "What do you think you are doing?"

He sat on the edge of the couch, his hip deliberately touching hers. He pulled the scroll from her hand and placed it on the side table. With one hand placed behind her head to steady her, he took his wife in a deep and demanding kiss.

She gave in to his rapacious mouth and tongue, opening for him, letting him explore her, letting him lead her. She reached up and dared to thread her fingers through his curls. He had never kissed her before, and she had certainly never been kissed like this.

But it didn't end with her mouth. He trailed nibbles and pecks down her neck while his hands worked at the clasps of her stola. He could feel her heart race, her breaths become labored. He slipped the delicate linen of her tunic from her shoulders and exposed her breasts to the warm summer air. His lips covered her nipples, first one, then the other, the tip of his tongue tickling the now-hardened peaks. Sabina let out a moaning sigh, then drew in a long calming breath.

Hadrian was surprised that his wife's most assuredly feminine form was arousing him. He was utterly hard, his skin sensitive to her every touch. He wrapped his arms around her to pull her close as he continued pleasuring her yearning breasts.

It was only then that he realized that his wife had stopped touching him. And, what was more, her body was shaking, convulsing. He pulled back. Sabina was crying. Not just crying, she was sobbing.

"Dogs of hell," he muttered. "What is it now?"

"*You pig,*" she screamed as she pushed him off her.

"Sabina—" he started and reached out for her.

"*Don't touch me!*" She turned from him, sliding her legs to the other side of the couch. With shaking fingers she fastened the fibulae at her shoulders.

Hadrian tried to compose himself. "What did I do, Vibia?" he asked as gently as he could muster, using her familiar name.

"You know what you did. You smell like my mother."

"What?" He turned to face her.

"She wears a particular oriental perfume given her by her husband. The fragrance is quite distinctive, and I smell it all over you." She glared at him. "You've just fucked my mother and now you dare touch me?"

Hadrian sighed. "Vibia, love—"

"Don't call me that. You don't mean that." Fresh tears fell from her eyes. "What were you thinking?"

"I saw you in the garden, I thought you looked beautiful." He leaned in a hair's breadth. "I thought we should make love."

She faced him once again, this time with hate in her eyes. "What about all your slave boys? Are they not satisfying enough? Is your appetite so voracious you need to start in on the women of the imperial household?" She spat in his direction.

Incensed by her vituperation, Hadrian recoiled to strike her. He flinched, stopping himself, knowing abundantly well that he would be admonished harshly by the emperor himself.

Hadrian turned away and put his face in his hands. This was not going to be as easy as he had thought. He swallowed his pride. Honesty with his wife was probably the best course of action.

"Vibia, love," he began softly. "Plotina and your mother would like us to be friendly to one another, for the emperor's sake, so Trajan does not have to worry about petty affairs in his household. The best way, perhaps, to display this harmony is through fecundity. Ours."

"You want me to have your miscreant children?"

"Vibia, please," he pleaded. "You don't have to be so harsh."

"Hadrian," she responded with tears welling in her eyes. "I've wanted you ever since our wedding night. I've yearned for your attentions for four years. But for four years I've had to put up with the knowledge that you've dallied with soldiers and slaves, my own mother even. I don't understand that, really. I can only imagine it is to keep her as an ally." She sniffled and wiped her eyes and face. "Now you're here, not because you want to be, but out of duty to your emperor. Well, I'll sleep with you out of duty to my uncle and my family. I cannot guarantee marital harmony and I cannot guarantee fecundity."

Hadrian sat in silence. He had assumed his wife would comply with his demands as any good Roman wife ought. Of course, Sabina was not just any Roman wife; she was the emperor's kinswoman, and Hadrian would have to act accordingly. "I have been horrible to you," he admitted.

"Yes, you have."

Gods, if Trajan hears about this… "Vibia, I'm…I'm sorry. Will you find it in your heart to pardon me?"

"Treat me as my station demands and I will consider it. I'm not like my mother, Hadrian. I won't forgive you just because you are handsome and have a nimble prick."

"Thank you," he said quietly. He slid his hand along the couch cushion until he met her thigh. He reached further and found her hand in her lap and intertwined his fingers in hers.

They sat silently for a while until Sabina said, "You're going to be elected praetor soon, before you are thirty I mean, are you not?"

Hadrian started. "How did you know that?"

She grunted. "I'm Trajan's grand-niece, you fool. I hear things. I pay attention. And," she hissed at him, "I am your blood link to the imperial succession." She reconsidered her harsh tone. "I can be very useful to you, you know," she said softly.

Hadrian felt a cold chill creep up his spine. She was completely correct. Sabina was a woman now, an adult member of the imperial household. She would begin to wield her own power, have her own allies. He would do well to maintain congenial relations with her. She was much more important to him now than Matidia. "I'm just beginning to realize that," he admitted.

Sabina sighed. "You may come to my bed tonight, Graeculus," she said. "I will bear your little monsters."

Hadrian smiled. That she had called him by his boyhood nickname pleased him. He squeezed her hand. "I will sup with you first, Vibia, my dear wife. We have some catching up to do." He stood. "But before then, I shall visit the baths."

Dinner was elegant, simple, and in Sabina's private bedchamber. The servants had been dismissed, and she waited on her husband with genuinely-felt deference. Over oysters and guinea fowl they discussed everything from philosophy to poetry to politics. With pastries and wine, they swapped stories and gossip about senators and other officials. She even listened to tales of his soldiering. Hadrian was pleasantly surprised by his wife's wit and astute observations, especially for one still so young. He *had* been a fool for four years. She was going to make a very good mate.

Of course the only thing she could not fathom was his passion for hunting.

"The animal has not attacked you, and yet you wish to kill it?" she asked.

"It's all about the chase. It's thrilling, exhilarating," he rolled onto his back on the dining couch and gazed at the coffered ceiling. "It's a competition. When I win, I get to kill the animal."

"But you said you toy with it first sometimes." Sabina had had her fill of food hours ago, yet continued to poke at and organize the leftover morsels on the trays set between them.

"Yes, yes. If I know I have it cornered, I might let it think it can get free." He looked over at her. "Really, Vibia, you should come sometime."

"I think not, Graeculus. You take one of your slave boys whose job it will be to praise you and fawn over your conquest. I would only scold you."

Hadrian smiled at her. The gods had blessed him with a wife who felt no compunction toward his predilection for young men. She was astonishing him at every turn.

He reached out his hand and she took it. She cast her eyes down, unable to look at his wolfish gaze.

Still holding on to her, he got up, as did she. She stood before him, shy, nervous. He tucked a strand of copper back into her plaits. He bent down and brushed his lips against hers, softly this time, not demanding but encouraging. She opened for him, and their lips and tongues explored to mutual satisfaction.

He pulled away to catch his breath and pressed his forehead against hers, now holding both her hands in his. At that moment she seemed so utterly innocent, a virgin once again.

"You've not been with another since our wedding night," he said, surmising her fears.

"No," she answered, a quiver in her voice.

"I'll be gentler," he promised. "It must have hurt."

"No. I mean, yes, but it was wonderful." She finally met his eyes. "Don't mock me, but I have thought about that moment almost every day for four years."

"I would only mock you because you said 'almost'."

She giggled. With boldness flashing in her eyes, she stood on her tiptoes and kissed her husband on his lips.

"Vibia, come," he said and took her by the hand to lead her just before her bed. He stopped and stepped back to observe her, his eyes skimming up and down her body. Her pale blue cotton stola was girded just under the bust, emphasizing her youthful, buoyant breasts. Only then did he realize that was all she was wearing. She had prepared for his seduction by forgoing undergarments. Hadrian grinned at her, then chortled when she blushed. He bent down and one after the other, took off her sandals, tossing them aside. As he stood, his hands felt along her legs and hips, intermittently squeezing the flesh through the fabric. He untied the belt and unfastened the fibulae at her shoulders. The thin garment floated down and pooled at her feet on the floor.

Out of instinct or modesty, Sabina crossed her arms over her chest. Hadrian placed his hands on her shoulders and took in her form with an indulgent gaze.

"Ah, my *Venus pudica*. Do not cover yourself."

"Am I pleasing to you, husband?" she asked ingenuously. "My body is nothing like a boy's."

Hadrian started at that. "Indeed not, love! Yours is very definitely a feminine form. You have the most beautiful breasts, a gift from the gods." Hadrian stood behind her and cupped his hands under each fleshy orb, as if weighing them, and teased the nipples with his thumbs. He felt Sabina tense at first, then relax in his arms. "Yes, give in to the pleasure," he encouraged.

One hand continued massaging a breast while the other slid down her waist, over her belly to her mons. He threaded his fingers through the hair there, flame and copper-red as on her head. He pulled at the strands until just before the moment of pain, feeling her flinch against him, then continued snaking his way to her pudenda. She was sticky wet as he knew she would be. His finger coursed through the pliant folds to her entrance, then returned, drawing more slickness to her clitoris.

As he massaged the nub, Sabina gasped and once again flinched, but this time Hadrian's arm held her close to his body. As he pressed harder on her pleasure spot, deftly rubbing it toward climax, she wailed, struggling harder against him. Her weak tussles were no match for his thick arm. He restrained her facilely until she cried out and jerked against him, then went limp over his forearm.

Sabina raised her head, her breath still labored. "What was that?" she asked ingenuously.

Hadrian chuckled. "I am a failure of a husband for not providing you the experience earlier," he said softly in her ear. "That was your crisis, and I promise there will be many more to come." He urged her toward the bed. "Now let's make a little monster."

Sabina giggled as she climbed onto the mattress and burrowed under the covers, poking her head up to watch her husband strip off his clothing. She was riveted, fascinated.

"I've never seen a man utterly naked before," she said with a touch of awe.

"And am I pleasing to you, wife?" he teased, concealing self-assured vanity.

She knelt before him on the mattress. "Skin so tanned," she said as she caressed the solid flesh of his shoulders and arms, "means you are out of doors, half-clad," she looked up at him provocatively and licked her lips, "working in the hot sun amongst sweaty soldiers." She glided her palms down his rippled torso, threading her fingers up through the dense brown curls on his brawny chest, then followed the downy trail to his groin. Her hand stopped above her husband's extraordinary attribute, her eyes widening in anticipation and trepidation.

"Touch me," Hadrian intoned, his voice gravelly from need.

She wrapped her small hand around his erection, her fist barely covering the long and thick shaft, then rubbed her thumb over the smooth, tumescent tip. She moved her hand along the hardness, her face registering curiosity and intention, absentmindedly chewing on her lower lip.

Hadrian growled his approbation, but he could take her innocent playing no longer. In one swift move he maneuvered their bodies side-by-side under the sheets. Sabina gulped air, then remained still as if stunned and uncertain what to do. Hadrian realized that the one time they had been together she had been on all fours, as was the custom. He kissed her mouth as his hand smoothed over her body. When he reached her legs he urged them apart then moved to lay on top of her, their hips touching.

He lifted himself up on his arms. "You're so small," he said. "I fear I might crush you."

He could feel the heat rise in her flesh. Something about what he had just said was enticing, thrilling to her.

Hadrian bent his legs and poised himself between her thighs, first spreading the sticky slickness at her delicate entrance and then on himself. *Gods, but this is going to feel good.* Tight and unused like a virgin passage, but eager and willing. "Are you ready, love?"

Sabina bit her lip again, uncertainty clouding her expression, but clearly wanting to say something. "Graeculus," she blurted impulsively, "hold me down. Hold me like you did earlier. When I had my…crisis."

Hadrian's mouth opened in surprise before a grin spread across his face. His wife had enjoyed being restrained. The gods were truly on his side; surely this was too much to ask? "With pleasure, Vibia."

He placed her arms above her head on the pillow and held them with one hand, one very large, strong hand. The other arm he wrapped around her waist. She was tiny, easy to circumscribe. He felt her heart beat in excitement, heard her breaths pant rhythmically.

As if to test his conviction, she struggled against him. He responded by holding her tighter, his lips curling in a wicked smile. His fingers felt the fragile flesh of her wrists bruising from the force of his grip. She gulped air at the pain, but her face melted into wanton desire. When he pulled even more on her stretched arms, he swore he saw delight flash in her eyes.

And then he entered her.

She let out a wailing gasp at the shock and her body jerked. Hadrian mashed his mouth against hers silencing her with his probing tongue. His body gripped her more tightly as he thrust mercilessly inside her. Her pitiful attempts to struggle excited him even further. He slammed against her, plunging deeper with each thrust. Her channel pulsed and clenched around his massive cock, driving him inexorably toward climax. He, of all men, though, knew he could hang on as long as he wanted. He was always in control.

Except this time.

Unwittingly, he erupted, his seed spewing forcefully as he held his hips between his wife's legs. He raised his face to the heavens and let out an exultant groan, his body jerking with every jet of fluid still amazingly being expelled from his spent sac.

Exhausted, he released his hold on Sabina and crashed to the mattress at her side. He looked up and stared at the flickering lamplight dancing across the ceiling and let out a long, contented exhale.

"Graeculus?" came Sabina's concerned voice.

"Vibia. I am indebted to the gods. You inflame me. I have never had such a marvelous tumble with a woman." He quickly glanced over at her knowing he had said something that could very easily be misunderstood. "I mean, not like it is ever that good with a man either. It's different with you. You're different." He stroked her cheek. "You are magnificent."

He would be a fool no longer when it came to his wife.

Rome, Quirinalis Collis, May 107

"He has no heir."

"Ah, but Balo, it is presumed that Hadrian will be his successor."

"Yes, Bestia," responded the Dacian to his host. "This is true, although Trajan has not named him as such. So, with his removal before such an announcement of an heir, we would have an empty throne and should move quickly to make the most of it."

Balo of the recently conquered province of Dacia, and Vartan of the Parthian kingdom in the east were the guests of the Roman merchant Sextus Quintilius Bestia in his extravagant villa situated on the downside of the Quirinal – one of the famed seven hills of Rome – slightly prominent, slightly obscured, like the owner himself. The two foreigners were natural enemies against the Roman empire. Bestia was always an opponent of whomever held power as there was great profit to be had in backing those who craved power. The three feasted and conspired on a dais high above a chamber in which were performed the most wondrous and exotic entertainments. Bestia was known for his extravagant displays of decidedly prurient content. At the moment, an enormous African man was fornicating with a pale, blond Greek boy. On the back of the African a petite dark-haired Syrian girl vigorously rode a dildo strapped around his waist.

"And Hadrian is now governor of Pannonia Inferior, is he not?" said Balo as he watched the Syrian girl's lithe form and bouncing breasts. "He would be too far from Rome to fill the vacuum of power. It would be easy to swiftly promote our man in the Senate."

"Should we include Hadrian in our plan, then?" queried Vartan. "Killing him as he is far away in the provinces?" He turned from the show, apparently more fascinated by his host's unusual eyes, one blue, one brown, and the scar that marred his face from eyebrow to opposite cheekbone.

"No, too risky," responded Balo, knowledgeable from his recent experience with the war. "He is adored by his troops. He's currently legate of II Adiutrix, but the men of I Minervia are still extremely loyal from his Dacian campaign. It would be difficult to move against him." He vigorously chewed on a mouthful of sumen, a delicacy rare in the provinces. "However, I hear he beats his wife and cavorts with boys—"

"And fucks the Empress Plotina," added Vartan, finally glancing at the lustful exhibition below.

Bestia grunted. "I heard it was his mother-in-law Matidia that he screws. Along with a few senators' wives."

"We may be able to discredit him as unworthy of succession," concluded Balo.

"Trajan dallies with boys as well," said Bestia, sipping at his wine thoughtfully. "Apparently the patrician ranks forgive their emperor his weaknesses and proclivities." This was not always the case amongst the conniving patricians themselves. "I had not heard about Hadrian and his wife though."

"She's been seen with cuts and bruises," offered Balo.

"That does not mean he beats her. He may have unusual sexual appetites." To prove his point, the merchant waved his hand over one of the scenes before them. A female slave lay naked on a carpet, spread-eagle, her arms and legs bound tightly to four posts with leather straps. A dog lapped at her crotch as another slave poured fish oil on the writhing girl's genitalia.

Vartan turned away from the scene in disgust and picked at the glossy cherries in a silver bowl before him. He dropped one of the succulent fruits in his mouth and chewed deliberately. "We absolutely cannot fail this time, gentlemen," he said, spitting out the seed as he shot a look of censure at his Dacian colleague. The assassination attempt against Trajan the previous year had been an abysmal failure ending with the suicide of the Dacian king Decebalus and the annexation of the whole province as a client of Rome.

"And we won't, Vartan, we won't," said Bestia with a calming gesture, trying to avert confrontation between his two guests. "The war had its benefits. I have Roman legion deserters and newly enslaved Dacian men in the provinces as well as here in Rome, all at the ready to act when the time is right." He sipped his wine as he watched the display of bestiality, his own particular letch. Today's performance was mild compared to what he preferred his girls do with horses. "What about the Parthian front?"

"We have some split loyalties," answered Vartan, once again riveted by his host's unusual face. "But I think it best we rely on Osrhoes's men. He already has some spies established in Rome."

A commotion below drew the attention of the three men. All the performers had exited and in their place were a dozen or more robust and athletic young men of different tribes each with his hands tied behind his back. All were nude and in various states of arousal.

"Ah, the insemination."

The foreign guests exchanged bewildered glances. Neither had seen anything like the spectacles put on in their honor by Bestia. The acts were decadent and grotesque – to their sensibilities. Like Rome herself.

"My female slaves are required to produce offspring. I select my best boys to perform the task of impregnating the girls. We confine the boys with their hands behind their backs for two days and feed them oysters with garlic and other such virility-enhancing foods. My astrologers and a midwife assure me the girl is at her fertile peak."

The chosen female slave was led into the chamber, staggering drowsily as if drugged, and followed by several nude girls. Each girl moved to stand next to her appointed youth, a few actually touching their men and rubbing seductively against their bodies. The female slave to be impregnated was lifted into a hammock, her legs spread and tied to the suspension ropes. Another girl massaged the slave's clitoris with warm oil, delving her fingers deep inside her now-pliant passage. The bound slave moaned and writhed.

One by one, the nude girls masturbated the strapping youths almost to climax, then positioned them before the opened legs of the waiting slave. As each stood in place with an aching erection, his hands were untied, the signal for the young man to copulate until he spent his seed. Once unbound, their actions were wild, frenzied, each one coming with a vigorous grunting cry.

One by one, ten men filled the girl on the hammock. The eleventh, holding on desperately to the moment before the peak, did not succeed. He exploded the second he saw the slave's well-used cunt, his semen dripping futilely onto the floor.

Irritated by the youth's lack of discipline, Bestia called out to a guard below. "Kill him," he commanded. "He is useless to me."

Vartan and Balo both shook their heads at their host's depraved impatience. Neither could continue watching as the rest of the parade of youths finished doing their duty.

Zuester sat in his cell eating his gruel, his thin woolen tunic no comfort against the damp of the underground prison. He had endured much since being enslaved in his native Dacia and sold to the corrupt merchant Bestia, but today's death sentence against his friend Skiare was the final straw. He was determined that the first chance he got, he was going to escape.

It was difficult to form any sort of congenial relationship in the bowels of the villa of a perverted madman, and now his one friend was being sent to the slaughter for acting like the seventeen-year-old boy that he was.

The other slaves had been uncertain as to what was transpiring, until Zuester explained it to them. Zuester was the only among them who spoke and understood Latin, and he had had to struggle to maintain his composure when his master pronounced the fate of his friend. Bestia did not know of Zuester's talent for languages, and Zuester did not ever want to reveal it. His master would simply use his ability for evil. That afternoon, Zuester had overheard quite a number of things he wished he hadn't.

Skiare cried silently at his friend's feet. Of course he had no interest in eating, which meant more for Zuester that night. It had been heart-wrenching to listen to Skiare's sobs and regrets. Zuester had regrets of his own, the least of which was wondering if he would be leaving behind his own flesh and blood. It was ironic that he and the slave girl in that afternoon's exhibition had once been in love, had once planned their wedding and named their unborn children. It was another reason he needed to escape. He had felt a twinge of guilt when he said he would convey declarations of love to Skiare's parents and sister. Zuester probably would never see his own family again, much less that of a fellow prisoner.

The clanking of metal against metal sent an almost crippling chill up Zuester's spine. The guards were here. Would they kill Skiare on the spot and clean up his body in the morning, or simply take the lad away screaming and do their dirty deed elsewhere? Zuester shook his cellmate to his senses. When he glanced up and saw who was coming for them, he shook some sense into himself.

Bestia had sent Brutus and Draco to do the job, both former gladiators who had been caught in a disgraceful act with one another. The merchant had purchased them fully intending for the pair to use their deviant wantonness in his private exhibitions. That was many years ago, and now too old for Bestia's particular tastes, they had been reassigned to guard duty.

As Zuester watched, he formed his plan. The guards would be armed, yes, but there were only the two of them. Surely, he and Skiare were strong and cunning enough to take them on?

"Ski, listen to me," Zuester said. "We're going to get out of here, you understand?"

"W-what?" sniffled the boy.

"Look, you're skilled in wrestling. You're nimble and quick. All we need to do is to slip outside of the cell. The first opportunity you get, run. I'll do the same, but don't think about me. You need to get yourself out of here."

The glimmer of hope perked the youth up from his morose mood. "Yes, Zoos," he said compliantly, wiping his nose, pronouncing his friend's nickname rather like "Zeus".

"Skiare, you dog! Up!" Brutus called out in Dacian.

"We're here to kill you," said Draco in Latin. The two men laughed.

The door to the cell opened and the guards entered. Skiare plastered himself against the back wall.

"C'mon. Make it easy on yourself," taunted Brutus.

"No," said Skiare. "You have to come get me."

"I'll come get you, you little bastard whoreson," said a very irritated Draco as he lumbered across the straw-strewn floor.

With thought as fast as Mercury's boots, Zuester dove for Draco's legs, grappling the massive calves and swiping the feet out from under the burly man's body. The guard came crashing to the stone floor. Zuester reached for the man's dagger and keys, then turned on Brutus, dodging and dancing, feinting and threatening until his back was toward the entrance side of the cell and Brutus was further inside.

"You pile of dog shit," the guard sneered at Zuester as he grabbed his own weapon.

The moment of distraction was long enough for Skiare to dash out of the cell.

"Get back here, son of Hades!"

The additional distraction was long enough for Zuester to wound the guard. Brutus clutched at the gash in his waist as he watched the Dacian follow his friend and close the door of the prison cell behind him.

Pannonia Inferior, Aquincum, Governor's Palace, May 107

Hadrian stared up at the coffered ceiling in his bedroom. He liked coffers, they gave a room a feeling of intimacy and an element of interest. Especially when they were done the way he wanted. Trajan's architect, the damnable Apollodorus, had said Hadrian's designs were naïve and compared them to summer squash. The Governor's palace in Pannonia was no summer squash; it was a magnificent tour-de-force of classical Greek motifs that only one well-versed in the nuances of the style could have accomplished. Trajan had let him design his own palace in his own way out in the new province. Hadrian sighed. One day, it was presumed anyway, he himself would be emperor. Then, he would design all manner of monuments in Rome itself. Apollodorus was a fool.

Still, musing over such follies was merely a diversion from the tragedy at hand. Sabina had just miscarried their first child, a child conceived between battles on the Dacian frontier. She had been devastated, he had been numb. The following day, he had been angry – at himself, at his wife, at everything. Marciana, Matidia, and Sabina's sister Mindia had kept Sabina away from him for a while until he calmed down.

Now husband and wife lay in bed together, she nestled in the safe cocoon of his body. If he should be angry with anybody, it should be with the gods, not his precious spouse. He pulled her more closely to him.

"Vibia, I'm sorry."

"Graeculus, love, I've told you before, mother and our midwife Zosime say this sometimes happens naturally. It's not your fault." Sabina took a deep breath. "I keep having to tell myself it's not my fault either."

Hadrian nuzzled against her neck.

"We shouldn't worry. We'll try again," she continued unconvincingly.

Moved by her self doubt and fear, Hadrian caressed her through her night tunic. Over the several weeks she had been pregnant, her breasts had grown fuller, although still a perfect handful. He wanted to feel them now. He pulled up her hem and maneuvered his hands underneath.

"The gods have blessed me and will continue to bless me," he said, gently kneading her warm flesh. "They know best when the time is right." He felt his erection growing. Hers was the only female body that could do that every time. He kissed her hair and pressed his fully-aroused cock between her butt cheeks.

Sabina twisted her head and sought his mouth with hers. As he kissed her deeply, passionately, he moved her beneath him and spread open her legs.

Sabina stopped his eager prick with a grab of her hand. "Graeculus, we can't yet. You know that." She let go of him. "I have to wait until after my next menses is complete."

"And when will that be?" he asked. There was urgent irritation in his voice.

"I don't know," she responded with annoyance. "Zosime says I have to expel the undesirable humors that have built up in my body otherwise another baby might never take hold. It could be another month or more."

"I can't wait another month!" Hadrian blurted.

"Then have a boy!" she shot back. "Or use your damn hand." She pushed him off and curled up on her side of the bed away from him.

Hadrian hated these little squabbles they had, husband and wife equally headstrong. This time, though, it would have to be he who recanted and made peace between them. "Vibia, love, I'm sorry. I just so want to be with you. I enjoy being with you." He reached out for her, touching her arm, but she flinched. "Please, love, let me just hold you. I promise I won't make any more demands of you."

Sabina turned to face him, only then revealing the tears in her eyes. "I miss you too, you know." She wiped her face with the sheet.

He pulled her to him. "Vibia, Vibia…"

"I have needs too. Sometimes I envy those damn boys of yours."

"I feel absolutely nothing for them," he reassured.

"But they make you feel pleasure. And you give them pleasure in return."

Hadrian stared up at the coffered ceiling once again, thinking. What she said was true, and in the same way there was no reason he and Sabina could not make love. He found pleasure with young men in various ways. One of the ways, however, he refused to do with her. The mere thought of oral copulation with a woman was repulsive to him. She seemed to have no knowledge of the act and he hoped she would never request it. There were limits to what he would do to a woman. Still, they could enjoy conjugal relations. They just couldn't do it in the usual way for a husband and wife.

"Vibia, please don't be angry—"

"Graeculus, I know you have at least one or two boys a day. You're a bull."

"—but what if you and I could do that. I mean, have relations like I do with…boys."

Now it was Sabina's turn to stare up at the ceiling, uncomprehendingly. "I'm not sure I understand."

"Vibia, when I'm with a boy…" How could he say it but plainly? "I make love to them in their arseholes."

Hadrian felt his wife stiffen and thought for a moment she had stopped breathing. Finally she asked, "Is it nice?" There was the slightest touch of curiosity in her voice.

He let out a silent sigh of relief. "It is very nice. And I promise to make it extraordinarily pleasurable for you."

Hadrian reached for the unlit lamp on the bedside table, removed the linen wick, then set the ceramic well on the mattress. In the dimly moonlit room, he could see his wife's curious anticipation.

His wife… He wanted very much to witness her reaction – her pleasure – to the act. She would not be set on all fours like a boy sent in to amuse him. No. He would make love to her face to face.

"Vibia, lie on your back – as you are now – and put some pillows under your arse. I need you to be raised up a bit."

She did as requested.

One special talent of a woman was that she made her own sensual moisture. Never truly enough for such decadent acts, but it was always a sign that she was at least enthusiastic. Hadrian tentatively touched his wife and found her beyond agreeable.

Sabina drew back slightly from his touch. "Not inside, Graeculus. I told you we should wait."

"Shh, shh. No, don't worry," he reassured. "Not inside there."

He trailed the sticky slickness from her feminine folds to the puckered hole just behind. She gasped when he circled his finger around the entrance; when he inserted the tip, she emitted a clipped whine.

Hadrian poured some oil from the lamp into his palm, then dribbled the liquid onto Sabina's cleft. His free fingers worked the viscous fluid into the tight orifice, delving as deeply as he could, massaging the tight ring of muscles near the entrance. He did not want to cause pain when he breached the virgin passage.

Sabina's labored breaths assured him she was feeling some enjoyment from his actions. He smiled. She was ready.

He smeared the rest of the oil in his palm up and down his now fully erect cock, playing briefly with the prepuce. He grabbed her hips and maneuvered her just right, then spread her cheeks apart.

"Love, it may feel strange, like being stretched to fullness, at first. I'll go very slowly." He knew precisely what to say. How many young boys had he deflowered in exactly the same way?

"I'm ready, Graeculus."

Hadrian positioned himself at her snug entrance and slowly eased in. At the same time, his thumb worked his wife's clitoris.

He could see the confusion of experiencing two very different sensations reflected in his wife's face. Pain and rapture confronted her at once, twisting her expression into worried relief. Until Hadrian tried to push further to a point where he clearly could not fit.

"Graeculus!" she pleaded. "Please, no, it hurts." Her hands moved to free her body from him.

Hadrian grabbed her hands and placed them over her head. "Shh, shh," he said once again trying to alleviate her fears. He stopped for a minute and waited for her body to relax and accommodate his presence inside, all the while vigorously massaging her excited clit.

Sabina climaxed with a sharp moan. Her body's natural jerking reaction caused him to slip in further.

"No!" she cried.

But it was too late. He was fully embedded inside her.

"Wait for a moment, love," he said calmly. His thumb continued its delightful torture, and when he felt her relax once again, he began to move in and out of her deliciously tight passage.

He proceeded slowly. Intercourse with a man gave the receiving man pleasure inside. Such intercourse with a woman was a wholly different experience. Sabina would need constant stimulation during this her first time.

He curved over her and kissed her lips. "Is it good?" he asked.

"Yes," she said haltingly. The confusing sensations were causing her to fall into euphoric delirium. He could tell she no longer knew which was pain and which was pleasure.

Hadrian understood her soft whimpers and straining breaths to mean she was fully caught up in the act. He increased the rhythm of his thrusts, groaning instinctively from the delicious friction.

"The gods have blessed me with you!" His head bent back facing upwards to his benefactors. His hand worked frantically at his wife's soaking crotch.

Sabina's moans became louder, her hips rocked, inviting her husband to plunge in mercilessly. He battered against the second ring of muscles deep inside her channel.

"Graeculus!" she screamed. He knew she had lost her grip on reality, her mind descending into an abyss of swirling pleasure and pain. Her orgasm ensued amidst screams and flailing arms.

Hadrian could no longer hold on to his own peak. He came forcibly, holding himself as far inside her as he possibly could, hot jets of semen surging into her depths.

He held himself upright until he felt his body ease, his prick diminish. Pulling out would also be a shock to his very accommodating wife, he did not want to hurt her needlessly. When he did so it was met with a sharp cry on her part.

He lay beside her and enveloped her in his arms.

"So that's what you do," she said quietly.

Hadrian chuckled. "It's one of the things, yes. I might show you other acts one day."

"Your boys are lucky," she said before drifting off to sleep.

Rome, The Forum, June 107

Zuester and Skiare had been able to evade capture for the week or so since their escape. They were uncertain how much longer they could remain beyond Bestia's insidious reach, so they planned and schemed every day about their next move.

Skiare wanted very much to return to his native Dacia. "I suppose the best way would be to attach myself to a legion heading for the frontier, don't you think?"

Zuester had agreed. He would miss his friend when the time came, but knew his life belonged in Rome. Of course, they would have to somehow determine how to do this. They were making contacts and gleaning information at every moment they could, but with Skiare's lack of Latin and their general anxiety about whether or not they would be caught this proved to be slow going.

The first night, and whenever they were able thereafter, they had bathed in the Tiber. They could not use the public baths because of their master's mark branded on their backsides, a mark most likely recognizable by many despite their attempts at scarring it. They offered themselves to whomever wanted something done, finding, of course, that prostituting their bodies by night was often more lucrative – although far more dangerous – than running errands and providing manual labor by day. But with their first earnings they had been able to purchase tunics and subligacula to go underneath, taking them thusly one very small measure away from their former lives by changing their appearance ever so slightly. At nineteen, Zuester could grow some facial hair, identifying him as possibly Greek and therefore not a former slave. Skiare tried his best, but it only resulted in an imperceptible downy fuzz.

When no work was to be had and Zuester had given up for the day – sometimes earlier rather than later – he invariably found himself in the Forum at the Curia, the building where the Senate met. Why, he really did not know. But he did like overhearing the senators talk. Their Latin was eloquent and a lesson just to hear it. But the information ascertained was also rather revealing. From observation he knew who was Trajan's friend and who was not such an energetic supporter of the emperor. He also had time to reflect on what he had overheard his master telling his guests the night he had escaped.

From such attention, Zuester had ascertained that an ambitious young senator, one Messius Aemilius Papus was an avid follower of the emperor Trajan, and not only that, a proponent of the succession of Publius Aelius Hadrianus, commonly known as Hadrian. If Zuester was to change his lot in this life, he knew he would have to attach himself to Papus. Every day he watched the man, getting a sense of his personality, his activities. Zuester even followed him one day as far as he could to see what he did. Papus was utterly above suspicion and led a perfectly respectable life from what Zuester could tell. Perhaps the man was also generous and charitable. He would have to take his chances.

Approaching the senator would be difficult. Zuester played out the meeting in his head over and over again until he thought he had imagined every scenario. He would use his absolute best Latin accent and would make sure the clean side of his tunic was showing. Of course every time he started to put his plan into action, within minutes doubt and anxiety invariably took over and the young man was left fretting.

Until one afternoon. Zuester practically bumped into Papus in his enthusiasm when he saw the senator exit the Curia. Zuester gathered up every ounce of his courage knowing this would be his best chance.

Papus should have considered the dark-haired young man who nearly tripped over him as a potential assassin, but there was something endearing about the lad.

"Messius Aemilius Papus," the boy said clearly struggling with his accent. "My name is Zuester. I have been following your career and I commend you. I would like to offer my services in whatever way you need. I have not only a quick wit, but a sound body and so can help you with both intellectual pursuits and odd jobs of physical labor. Of course I expect remuneration, but this can be bed and board rather than a monetary payment."

Papus stood for a moment, nonplussed, staring at the exuberant boy before him, searching his brown eyes. "You are not Roman," he finally responded. "How do I know you are not out to cheat me?"

Obviously as sharp as he claimed, this Zuester was prepared with a surprising answer. "I will be honest with you. I am Dacian. I was enslaved in the last war and was brought to Rome. I was sold to a man, a very horrible man. I escaped. I have discovered that despite my location of birth, I am enamored of Rome and everything she stands for. I have even taken the time to learn her language, her customs. I am fascinated by her system of government and so have spent many hours observing you and the other senators. I would be honored to serve Rome, but as a freeman, not as a slave."

Papus considered this speech with a smile. The boy seemed earnest enough and his Latin was rather good for a Dacian slave. As an ambitious politician himself, he knew well that the boy's professed determination meant something, although what was unclear. Papus, however, was no fool. "And you trust me enough that I will not simply return you to your master?"

"When you hear what information I have for you, you will realize what an asset I am," responded Zuester.

So that's what it is. The boy had something he perceived as valuable. "Well, son, can you provide me with at least a glimmer of what I might find of use?"

Zuester pondered this in silence for a moment. Of course the boy would know the game was always to not give away too much, but he would have to reveal something. "My master, whom I will not name for the moment, has been scheming with a Parthian lord and a former Dacian official about the fate of our emperor Trajan."

"Ah," responded Papus coolly. Conspiracies flourished in Rome. It was a decided skill to determine which among the threats was the more serious.

"And why should I be convinced that the emperor should be worried about this?"

"Because the Dacian in question was second only to Decebalus, the king."

This is interesting news. He knew the name of Decebalus's second in command and wondered if this clever boy did as well. "And his name?"

"Balo," answered Zuester.

Yes, it is Balo. This boy had enough Latin and enough intelligence to possibly be of use. And if he were bluffing, at the very least Papus needed someone to tend the garden at his new villa in Tibur. Surely a provincial lad such as he knew some farming? If not, he could be easily trained.

"All right, my boy. Why don't you come home with me and we'll discuss the matter over dinner." His eyes skimmed the skinny youth up and down. "You look like you could use some dinner, son."

Zuester blushed but quickly recovered. "May I bring with me my younger brother?"

So now there's a brother. "Is he half as cunning as you?"

Zuester smiled. "No, sir. He is rather innocent and longs to return home. He knows no Latin, but he is a hard worker."

The senator laughed. "And how is it that *you* know Latin, my boy, and not your brother?" he asked, dubious of the actual familial relationship of the two.

"I learned it during the war, from the soldiers in Legio I Minervia," replied Zuester.

"I Minervia!" Papus exclaimed with a touch of satisfaction. During the Dacian wars it was the legion under his friend Hadrian's command. He knew the soldiers under Hadrian were intensely loyal to their commander and to Rome, and they might very well have passed this sentiment on to the young man. "And you know that Dacian gibberish as well?"

"Yes, sir." The response carried with it a slight irritation at the idea that Dacian was anything but a fine, albeit difficult, language.

"Well, you could be very useful, boy. What did you say your name was, son?"

"Zuester, sir. And I am at your service."

Tibur, Trajan's villa, July 109

"I think my husband is bored," admitted Sabina to her visiting friend Julia Balbilla. "I'm grateful for the company of you and your brother. Hadrian so likes to learn of Athens, and Philopappus is a good story teller."

"Yes he is, but my brother also likes to be the center of attention," laughed Balbilla. "That's why we call him 'King'." The two lay on couches, head-to-head, in Sabina's garden on a fine summer afternoon. Balbilla leaned in more closely. "We've heard the rumors that your husband's love of things Greek includes a particular way of relating with boys," she said boldly. Since spending so much time with Sabina, the two had grown intimate, sharing many secrets and intrigues.

Sabina blushed, then giggled and rolled onto her back on the couch. "Since his term ended as Governor of Pannonia, Hadrian really has nothing to do. I wish he had your talent for poetry. He makes sketches of buildings and monuments and such. But without an official job, it can be a tedious life. I do empathize with him, though. I'm bored too sometimes." A wicked smile spread across Sabina's lips. "In fact, I have a secret."

"A secret! Oh, do tell," Balbilla pleaded.

Sabina held out her hand beckoning her friend to lie with her on her couch. The two friends often found themselves in that position, napping in each other's arms in the peaceful garden. It seemed so natural on a sunny and warm summer afternoon.

"I had nothing to do so I watched him one day," Sabina confessed. "I watched him seduce a boy in the stables. I had followed him out there, he didn't know. I suppose I've always been curious, but even more so after he had done to me what he does to the boys."

Balbilla opened her mouth in shock and surprise. "No!" she said. "Was it nice?" she asked with genuine curiosity.

"Yes, indeed. I very much enjoyed it. We've done it often since. If it weren't for my mother and Plotina urging us to have children, I'd so much prefer to do *that* sometimes." Sabina bit into a juicy ripe peach and handed it to her friend. "They think because I'm not pregnant that we don't ever have relations," she said quietly. "But I think it's because Hadrian has spent all of his seed inside these boys by the time he sneaks into my bed at night."

Balbilla handed the now dripping peach back to Sabina and licked her fingers. "Why does he have to be secretive about going to your bed?"

"I don't know. We like to play, I think. He hurt me a few times – I won't say how, but it was an accident – and so somehow that sparked gossip that he dislikes me, that he hits me." Sabina sucked on her bite in the fruit before handing it back to her friend. "We squabble a lot too, that's also fed the fires of rumor. We've been married for nine years and have no children. It is easier for people to believe we hate each other than for them to think Hadrian is not man enough to produce offspring." Sabina raised a suggestive eyebrow. "But I know differently."

She took the last bite of fruit proffered by Balbilla then tossed the pit into the garden. She licked her fingers. "I don't know how old this boy was, but he was tall and skinny, a little too skinny for my tastes, wearing only his subligaculum and brushing a horse. Hadrian began to talk to the boy – I don't know about what, but from their gestures I think it was about the animal and its grooming. The boy was stroking the horse with his brush, and Hadrian must have indicated that the boy was not doing it correctly so he takes the brush away and does it himself, all the while talking to the boy."

Balbilla looked down at her friend and saw the signs of excitement register on her face. She brushed aside a coppery curl from Sabina's forehead, then continued to caress her friend's flushed skin, trailing a finger down her cheek and neck.

Sabina just smiled. "Then he somehow gets the boy to stand ever so close to him and take the brush, while Hadrian also holds the brush but on top of the boy's hand. Together, they brush the horse, and, you know how tall a horse is, they have to bend their bodies to brush the full flank."

Balbilla drew tiny circles on Sabina's chest, and gently ran her finger along the neckline of her stola.

"So here they are, bending together, their bodies practically mashed up one against the other. While behind the youth, with his free hand Hadrian loosened the boy's subligaculum. The boy did not even struggle. And when the cloth fell to the ground I could see his prick was stiff."

Sabina shifted her body so her companion could have better access under her dress. Balbilla slipped her hand inside her stola and pulled out a firm breast. She bent over and delicately licked the already taut nipple.

Sabina sighed at her friend's attentions. "All activity with the horse was forgotten the second Hadrian wrapped his hand around the boy's cock and began to masturbate him. The boy was breathing hard and arching back against his master. Hadrian kept pumping and whispering into the boy's ear."

Balbilla pulled up the fine linen of Sabina's skirts, exposing her friend's legs. Sabina helped by raising her hips. When Balbilla scrunched the fabric up around her friend's waist, she was surprised to see Sabina was not wearing underclothing, and not only that, had been plucked. Depilation was a Greek custom and sometimes done by Roman women, and clearly with Hadrian's love of things Greek, he had enticed his wife to follow the fashion. Balbilla stroked Sabina's thighs, urging them apart, then slipped her hand in between to touch the hairless mons.

Sabina gently rocked her hips against her friend's insistent hand. "Then suddenly he stopped touching the boy. Hadrian was saying something and the boy was nodding his head but looking a little afraid, that's all I could tell." Sabina moaned as the finger finally touched her excited clit. "The boy grabbed onto a stall post and bent over. Hadrian pulled out a tiny unguent bottle from his bag, and poured the contents on the boy's backside. With his thumb, he massaged the liquid into the boy's arsehole all the while talking to him. The boy trembled at my husband's touch on his most intimate of places. I think he was crying."

Balbilla nestled herself against Sabina's body and continued massaging her friend's soaking flesh, teasing the vulva and clit just enough to keep Sabina on edge.

Sabina's panting breaths did not prevent her from continuing with her story. "Hadrian stripped off his tunic, revealing a body to rival Jupiter himself. He too was hard, his prick almost double the size of the boy's. It's a good thing the boy did not turn around to take a look. Hadrian grabbed onto the boy's hips and pulled apart his butt cheeks. Then he pushed the head of his cock inside the boy's arse."

Balbilla quickened her ministrations ever so slightly, eliciting the desired sighing moans from her friend.

"The look on the boy's face! Utter pain and confusion, until Hadrian reached around and grabbed his cock, tiny in my husband's hand. He pumped the boy's cock and at the very same time pushed in to the hilt into the boy's arse. That was the one time I heard anything from the scene as the boy cried out, but it was a cry of satisfaction not one of protest."

With two fingers in Sabina's cunt, Balbilla rocked her own hips to the same thrusting rhythm. "More," Sabina whispered.

Balbilla knew precisely what she meant. She turned her friend onto her back and raised her knees, then pressed them down to splay open. Balbilla tested three, then four fingers, stretching Sabina and feeling her muscles soften inside.

"My husband is very aggressive, and he did not spare this young man. He brutally slammed against him – I'm almost sure I heard their bodies slap together – all the while pulling at his cock. When the boy came, Hadrian cruelly continued stretching his prick, milking the boy until all his sperm had been spent."

Balbilla tucked her thumb against her palm and reached her whole hand into Sabina's compliant channel. With the thumb of her other hand, she deftly massaged her friend's clit. Sabina arched up encouragingly, willing her friend to move her fist and wrist in and out of her yearning passage. Balbilla felt the muscles inside Sabina clench and relax around her.

"My husband could now think of his needs. He pounded his hips against the boy mercilessly. I knew when he was going to come. I know my husband. He pulled the boy against his body, digging his nails into his young flesh, as he threw his head back and—*Oh!*"

Sabina cried out in ecstasy at Balbilla's ministrations. Her body spasmed in climax for a full minute before she melted against the couch cushion, the signal for Balbilla to slowly pull out.

"Thank you, thank you," Sabina said quietly.

Balbilla felt Sabina drift off to sleep nestled in her arms. It was indeed a lovely way to spend an afternoon in the countryside of Rome.

"...not like the weather in Rome is dreary and cold, my friend, more like stifling and unbearable really, but a summer in Athens should surely be experienced."

The Athenian Caius Julius Antiochus Epiphanes Philopappus, the descendant of the kings of Commagene and known familiarly as 'King', and his sister Julia Balbilla dined with Hadrian and Sabina in their luxurious apartment in Trajan's Tiburtine villa. The two women giggled and talked secretively on a couch opposite the men.

Hadrian tugged thoughtfully on a braised and peppered partridge thigh. "Someday I will go. And not just to experience a glorious summer, but to learn. I love your philosophers' outspokenness, King. They seem to have an honored place in your culture. Our own Roman thinkers often find themselves being assassinated."

Philopappus considered the delicate cabbage heart before stuffing the whole thing in his mouth. "Socrates was executed, Graeculus."

"True," Hadrian nodded with a grin.

"And what is it that is keeping you here in Rome? Politics or family?"

Hadrian glanced over at Sabina. "I don't really know. Nothing, I suppose. Vibia would follow me anywhere."

"How do you keep yourself busy these days?" Philopappus nodded in the direction of a handsome young serving boy and raised an eyebrow at his friend. "Besides that, I mean."

Hadrian chuckled. "Well, since my term as Governor of Pannonia has ended I now enjoy the title of speechwriter to the emperor," he said soberly.

"Doesn't Pliny already do some of that?" Philopappus was amused by a bite-sized pie decorated with a pastry cut-out of a leaping hare.

"Ha!" Hadrian barked sardonically. "Trajan prefers my succinctness, I think, although Servianus obsequiously praises Pliny's turn of phrase." He stared into his golden cup. "It is certainly not demanding work, and that is my only office." He took a swallow of wine. "I am favored for the succession and yet I feel useless. I spend my days drawing and writing – the pursuits of a retired man, really. Sometimes even the boys do not necessarily please," he said quietly.

"And Sabina?" Philopappus inquired just as softly.

"She seems to be spending quite a bit of time with your sister. She's even given to quoting Sappho."

"I have heard rumors that the two of you do not quite get along."

"I see no compelling reason to dispel the rumors, King. But they are not true. We get along quite well. Just not as of late, I admit."

Philopappus sipped his wine and contemplated the two women across from them. His sister Julia Balbilla was in her late thirties and unabashedly enjoying the energetic charms of her much younger companion. But Julia had confided in her brother that Sabina was, like her husband, somewhat bored with her life in Rome. "Graeculus, perhaps you should look to your wife for amusement."

Hadrian flashed a glance at his wife over the rim of his wine cup. "In what way do you mean, King?"

"She's young, lively, and quite possibly not just learning Greek poetry from my sister." Philopappus contemplated another tiny pie before he popped it in his mouth. "I think you should do something about alleviating that boredom, and involve her. I can come up with some ideas, if you like."

A look of surprise flitted across Hadrian's face before he suppressed it into a knowing grin. "Yes, perhaps that would be fun."

Philopappus adjusted his tunic to lean in more closely to his friend. "Presumably, from the gossip about her screaming in your bed, she is rather…energetic?" He lowered his voice even more. "Have you tried, um, how shall I say? 'subduing' her?"

Hadrian looked up in surprise, glanced again at his wife, then turned back to his friend. "Not beyond what a man might naturally do."

"And is it always just you and your wife, or do you sometimes include others?"

"I'm beginning to wonder what goes on in your own bedroom, King."

Philopappus chuckled. "As I lack a wife, I lack your problem. But, the consideration of all the sensual possibilities one might pursue in a marriage should prove quite distracting, my friend. And as both of you are sufficiently bored, the results can only be mutual satisfaction. What are her limits?"

Hadrian regarded his wife once more. She was lying between Balbilla's legs, her arms draped languidly across her friend's thighs, her mouth open and tongue reaching as Balbilla fed her a cabbage dripping with pepper sauce. "None, I should think," he said.

"Good," Philopappus smiled. "And, you should really think about coming to visit us in Athens," he said, this time not so quietly. "I'll help plan your journey."

Sabina looked up at that. "Oh, Graeculus, can we?" she said, her eyes bright.

Philopappus continued. "I know a route where you'll meet one of our great philosophers."

"And I can tell you what women are wearing these days, so you'll be quite fashionable," Balbilla chimed in.

Hadrian smiled at his wife and raised his cup to her. "Of course, Vibia. I've always wanted to see Greece and now is the perfect opportunity."

Philopappus grinned at his friend. Of course in the interim, the two men would conspire on ways the couple could pass the time.

Sabina lay on her bed thinking over the day's events. She and her mother had taken Balbilla on a tour of the sites of Rome, and, at Balbilla's insistence, done some shopping. It had been remarkably fun, plus she was most satisfied that Matidia and Balbilla got on famously. After dinner, she found herself exhausted, so pleaded her excuses and went to bed earlier than usual. Her husband had been most accommodating.

She smiled and curled up, clutching a pillow between her legs. Since Balbilla and Philopappus had arrived, she realized she and her husband were not spending as much time together. Each was preoccupied. She herself was discovering new feminine diversions with Balbilla, although she knew Hadrian was not doing the same with Philopappus – theirs was an exclusively intellectual relationship. Hadrian was so good to allow her her amusements, she thought as she drifted off to sleep.

She jumped up with a yelp when she heard the door to her room crash open, then watched in panic as several very large men filed inside, their swinging lanterns casting confusing shadows. She gripped the sheets, covering herself, and cowered against the headboard as her panic turned to fear. The men stood silently at the entryway. *In Jupiter's name, where were the guards?* "What do you want?" was all she could muster.

"Close the door," a man directed.

It was the unmistakable voice of her husband.

She wanted to feel relief at his presence, but there was an ominous aura hanging in the air. In the pale lamplight, she regarded the other men. They were large, exceptionally so, with thick hands that could crush her neck in one squeeze. There were two Africans and two northern barbarians. From their blonde hair, she supposed Germans.

"Take her," her husband commanded with a wave of his hand. "You know what to do."

Sabina gasped as all four hulks strode toward her, the flickering lamplight heightening the light and shadow of the powerful muscles underneath the sheer fabric of their short tunics. An African single-handedly pulled her off the bed, then divested her of her flimsy night tunic even as she flailed and kicked. He held her naked body easily with one massive arm around her waist.

"What is the meaning of this?" she cried. "Hadrian, stop them this instant!"

Her husband did nothing but shout clipped commands to the men. As directed, the African threw her back onto her bed, then each brawny servant took a fragile limb and, amidst her struggles and screams, tied it to a bedpost, binding her spread-eagle.

Upon Hadrian's order, one of the Germans knelt between her legs. She shrieked and thrashed against him when he placed a hand under each of her butt cheeks and lifted her ever so slightly, then bent over and pressed his wet mouth and tongue to her genitalia. Hadrian had never done such a thing to her; Balbilla had only hinted at it. The sensations were strange – pleasurable and disgusting at the same time.

"What are you doing?" she wailed, tears streaming down the sides of her face. She tried to twist her body in an effort to get away from the

German, but he held her firmly. He seemed to enjoy his assignment immensely and lapped at her with gusto.

"I still need an heir, my dear. We must not lose sight of that point to our marriage. I felt the urge to procreate tonight. I really do not care what your mood is." Sabina watched as Hadrian regarded the hulk of a man enthusiastically licking her. A wicked smile twitched across his lips, yet his crinkled brow registered distaste.

She tried desperately to not want to enjoy what was the most wonderful stimulation of her privates she had ever encountered.

"I could have simply used oil to lubricate you," Hadrian explained. "Or if I were a cruel man I would not use lubrication at all. This seems so much more arousing to you, wouldn't you agree? You will be well-prepared for me when I enter you." Hadrian pulled off his tunic revealing his erect prick. Holding Sabina's gaze, he stroked the enormous shaft gently as she spiraled deeper into unwanted ecstasy.

She came with a howl, unwittingly thrusting her pelvis into the slobbering mouth of the German. The man continued his frantic licking as she lay defeated on the mattress, her eyes screwed shut against the sensual assault.

"That will be enough!" Hadrian barked, as he grabbed the German's tunic and pulled him off her. Hadrian got on the bed and positioned himself on his knees between her legs, stroked her aroused pudenda, then wiped his fingers against her thigh.

"My, my, how wet you are, my sweet. I see you have enjoyed your ravishment." He positioned his prick at her too-willing entrance. "Perhaps I should have my men service you more often." He entered her slowly, holding his body above hers.

Sabina had not realized how much she wanted him until he slid in and out of her hot, moist passage. She contracted around him with every stroke. He pressed against her, his hands wandered across her body, feeling her heated flesh, his mouth biting and kissing her neck, making love to her as if they were alone.

Yet they were anything but alone. Sabina looked up and around at the four men still standing guard at each bedpost, their erections visible under their short tunics, tenting the filmy fabric.

Her husband noticed her distraction. He reached down and pressed his thumb against her clit and massaged in gentle circles. Sabina moaned and clenched his cock with short pulses, forgetting just for an instant that her pleasure was witnessed by an audience.

Hadrian bent over her ear. "Shall we let my men have their enjoyment too?" he whispered lasciviously. "I know how you sometimes like to pamper your own slaves, my love."

Sabina froze, not knowing quite what her husband meant by that.

Hadrian looked up at the man who had just orally pleasured his wife. "Go on," he ordered gesturing his face toward the prick of the hulking man. "You may take your pleasure with your hands."

In unison, the four hulks stripped off their tunics and grabbed their magnificent cocks. Each one pumped in his own individual rhythm, each face remaining expressionless and stoic, each body driven to do its master's bidding.

Hadrian continued to slam into her. He pulled back until he was seated on his knees, raising her torso as much as possible against the bindings at her feet. She knew he was almost at his climax.

He glanced around at his men, each one ready to burst but waiting for his command. He leered lewdly at Sabina. "You may spend on my wife, but I do not want to feel a drop of your spunk on my body."

"*What?*" Sabina shrieked. "No! You monster!" she screamed. "Get off me!" She thrashed against him, only causing him to delve deeper within her.

"Don't worry, my sweet. Only my seed will be inside you. You can be assured that the child is mine." He plunged into her with purpose now, building his speed, not caring if he hurt her against her bindings.

His thrusts were like jabs of hot iron inside her. She felt his length at the entrance to her womb, slamming into her cervix. Unbelievably, she came again.

With one wicked stroke Hadrian emptied his sac inside her, keeping himself deeply embedded until every ounce of semen had left his body.

He then leapt off her before the four slaves began coming themselves, jetting their hot liquid onto her face, her breasts, her stomach, and her thighs. Sabina kept her eyes and mouth tightly shut. When she was certain they had finished, she let out a long and loud scream.

Hadrian clamped his hand over her mouth and bent over to whisper in her ear. "I dare say you enjoyed yourself, my love. I challenge you to dispute this."

"You despicable man!" she hissed and spit on him.

Hadrian laughed. He pressed his lips to her ears more closely. "We will discuss this later."

Hadrian pulled back, then dressed. "You may untie her now," he said. He watched as his men carefully freed her.

Sabina rubbed her sore wrists, while a rush of relief spurred tears to smart in her eyes. She grabbed the sheets to wipe her face and cover herself.

Hadrian waved the men out of the room.

He sat beside her on the bed and waited for her reaction. He had never before incorporated others in their private acts and had taken quite a chance that night. She knew she should lash out, hit him, spew profanities, spit on him again.

Instead, she reached for him, wrapping her arms around him, snuggling against his belly.

"It was exciting, Graeculus," she said softly. "Let's do that again sometime."

Bithynia, Claudiopolis, 27 November 109

"Here he is, my lady, fed and washed. I think he wants his mother now."

"Thank you, Magas." Apollonia took the squirming bundle from the wet nurse to gently cradle the precious form in her arms. She gazed down at the face of her newborn son, his full lips still pursing from having taken his fill of milk. As she rocked him she began to softly sing.

"He's beautiful," said Magas, in awe of the perfect features of his face already apparent on his first day of life.

"Yes, he is," Apollonia had to agree.

"He will touch power one day, mistress," said the nurse.

Apollonia glanced at her midwife skeptically. She knew Magas claimed to have powers of foresight, and at times her predictions came eerily true. "Of course he will. He will attend Roman magistrates in the courts like his father." She looked down again at her son. "Perhaps become an official himself. Maybe even go to Rome."

"Yes, yes, he will go to Rome, my lady." Magas reached down and tucked a bit of blanket behind the boy's head to better reveal his comely face. "But not as an official, no. Something higher, something sacred. I have foreseen that a man will take your son away, but you will release the boy willingly."

"No one will take my son away from me." Apollonia clutched at the boy more securely.

"It will be a good thing. You will see. He will become immortal."

"Immortal?" Apollonia laughed. "I would only wish him to be intelligent and cheerful. To have many friends, to find joy in his family and work, to marry a fine woman." She tilted her head in admiration. "Well, perhaps it would be good if he were a swift hunter as that skill is highly prized."

"Yes, mistress." Magas nodded in acquiescence. "And what shall you name him?"

"He will be named after his grandfather. He will be called Antinous."

Rome, Quirinalis Collis, October 111

All the pieces of the plan are finally in place.

Bestia sat in the dark, an audience of one in his personal theater, smugly satisfied that his strike against the emperor would be successful. As his reward he was treating himself to a private spectacle of virgins with a stallion. Three nude nymphs – it took at least that many – were stroking the animal's enormous prick, moaning and encouraging the beast. Another girl straddled the horse's back riding a dildo strapped to the saddle. She writhed rhythmically, mewling her own pleasure, her long ginger hair precisely matching the color and flow of the stallion's mane.

It was the sort of display his guests often did not appreciate.

Bestia snorted at that. His guests were usually barbarians, or common merchants, even criminals at times, none of whom would ever understand the finer things in life. Only a true patrician had such understanding in his blood. And, despite having had to purposefully estrange himself from his family, Bestia was a true patrician, of a blood line that reached back to the two triumvirs Cnaeus Pompeius Magnus and Marcus Licinius Crassus, and beyond that to the great Republic.

It was times like this, enjoying an exclusive show for his own amusement, that Bestia often reflected on his life. "Sextus Quintilius Bestia" was not his given name. No. He had been born a bastard child of the ancient and respected aristocratic family, the Licinii Crassi, the product of an affair between his mother and a gladiator. He was his mother's sixth child and his father's – the gladiator, not his mother's husband - fifth, hence his name. When he was able to speak and comprehend the world around him, he was informed, in no uncertain terms, that he could not publicly acknowledge his heritage. However, the Licinii Crassi were a proud clan, and did not utterly ostracize even the illegitimate of their line. Bestia had never wanted for money or connections. Introduced as a "close friend" of the Licinii Crassi was often just as good as being recognized as a kinsman. He kept in touch with family members still living, family members who had not been murdered by emperors of Rome for the supposed threat to imperial power that their high positions posed. Some of these relatives lived quiet lives in their lavish villas. Others had been exiled.

Amidst the brilliant light of a hundred lamps, he could see the enthusiasm on the girls' faces as they fondled the red, glistening equine member. He pulled up his tunic and stroked his own engorged cock in rhythm to the virgins' ministrations. Watching the movement of their hands was mesmerizing. His eyes glazed, staring trance-like, at the magnificent scene.

Bestia's cousin, Gaius Calpurnius Crassus Frugi Licinianus, consul under Domitian, had been exiled by Trajan. And for what? For plotting against Nerva? The former senator had been a foolish old man, chosen to be emperor because he was safe, unencumbered by corrupt perversions or political aspirations. Or was the punishment for supposedly plotting against Trajan himself? The paranoia of the Caesars ran deep against the descendants of Pompey the Great. And for that, Calpurnius Crassus, scion of the patrician class older than the empire itself, had been banished to the backwater town of Tarentum in southern Italia. It was an insult beyond insult. Why the princess Sabina herself was related to him via her mother's marriage to a distant relative. It may have been a third marriage – or was it a fourth? – but a marriage nonetheless. Bestia had initiated a correspondence, under the pretense of commercial enterprise, with his cousin, and in Bestia, Calpurnius Crassus had found, not just a relative, but a confidant, a kindred spirit in the fight against the injustice of Rome.

The girl on the saddle vigorously rubbed her clitoris. She no longer needed to bounce up and down on the back of the horse as the creature was himself shifting and weaving excitedly, striking his right front hoof on the ground as the virgins cooed and coaxed him toward his culmination. One girl in particular, a raven-haired Syrian kneeling before the beast, was so sweet, so gentle, so naïve to the perversion in which she was participating. Bestia wanted her.

She had been a gift from his Parthian connections, and far too young when he first got her to be useful. She had blossomed under his tutelage. He would have to thank the Parthians, but at the moment he could not remember precisely which faction had delivered the prize. He had hedged his bets with all players in the civil war. Surely she had not been from Pacorus, he was a little geriatric to have thought of such a present. Possibly it was the pretender Vologaeses, but most likely the girl had been a gift from the powerful Osrhoes. Bestia knew the latter had a daughter himself, and wondered briefly what she would be like. Beautiful, of course. Parthian women were always beautiful.

Yes, Bestia's plot to finally kill the Roman emperor was perfect. There was still no successor. The only contender, the general Hadrian, was in Greece, and not with his legion. He was on holiday with his spoiled, bored friends, probably making use of the boys in the local gymnasium. Rumor had it he did not use his wife, except to beat her. Poor stupid fool. Little did he know of the wondrous pleasures of women. Rome did not need such brats in power. Why not act against him as well? Bestia certainly had the men already stationed in Greece. With the downfall of Trajan and no successor in sight, chaos would ensue, the Senate would assume power. The Republic would be reborn.

The horse was restless, whinnying, about to climax. The girl in the saddle screamed her orgasm and slumped against the back of the beast. Bestia was near his own crisis, driven by the thought of fucking the black-haired Syrian girl in the arse as the horse spewed its seed on her back. The idea took him over the edge, at the very moment the stallion gushed ejaculate, bathing the three nymphs in the warm, milky fluid.

Bestia exhaled. At that moment he knew he was invincible.

Rome, Imperial Palace, October 112

Having a private dinner with one's wife when one was emperor of a vast empire was a rare event, and when one's wife was the ever-accommodating and diverting Plotina, that event was a rare joy.

Trajan sipped his wine and nodded as he listened to his wife's gossip and stories. Sometimes it was the only way he would know what was going on in his own household. He regarded her thoughtfully in the dancing lamplight. They were the both of them past their prime, his golden hair now white, her plaits also interwoven with silver strands. After over thirty-five years of marriage, they were simply friends, but, he realized, the very best of friends.

"I've been told she screams sometimes when he goes to her bed," Plotina said of their niece. "I'm worried about the two of them."

"Vibia Sabina has turned out to be a passionate woman, much like her mother," Trajan commented. "And Hadrian's tastes are quite probably frustrating for such a one. I seem to recall you also berating me at the top of your lungs when you discovered what I was doing with the servant boys."

Plotina shook her head. "You may very well be correct, dear husband. Still, now that Matidia is *Augusta*, her daughter needs to act with more decorum." She eyed him. "And, I hate to remind you of your own mortality – or shall I say, future immortality – but Sabina will be empress one day, am I correct?"

Trajan grunted his non-response. "Sabina needs to take a lover," he said instead before biting into a wedge of salted cucumber. "Who has Hadrian taken with him to Greece? Any candidates?"

"You can't arrange a love affair," Plotina laughed. "Marriage can be arranged. A love affair must come naturally."

Voices outside the triclinium drew the attention of both emperor and empress. There was a rap on the door.

"Who is it?" Trajan bellowed.

"It is I, my lord, Phaedimus," came the voice.

Marcus Ulpius Phaedimus was Trajan's trusted freedman and, after over a dozen years with his master, knew he should not bother him unless it was important.

"Come, Phaedimus," said Trajan.

The wooden door creaked open and the curtain was pulled aside to reveal the young and handsome servant. He bowed in the doorway.

"A thousand pardons, my lord," he said. "There is a Senator Messius Aemilius Papus here to see you. He says it is of the utmost importance. Life and death."

Trajan remained stretched out on the dining couch. He heard announcements like this every day. Sometimes, though, they were truly important, and when the messenger was Papus, a close personal friend of the family's, it was probably approaching a "life and death" scenario.

"Very well, send him in." The emperor drank deeply from his golden wine cup before setting it down.

Papus strode in and looked around at the scene. Aware he had interrupted a very intimate *convivium*, he bowed and offered apologies.

"Caesar, my most profound regrets." When he straightened he glanced at Plotina.

"She stays. Whatever you need to say, she can hear," said Trajan.

"Yes, my lord."

"Sit, fool. I'm only having dinner with my wife. You need not stand on ceremony or act in any manner other than naturally."

"Thank you, sir." Papus drew in a long breath. "There is an assassination plot against you, Caesar."

Trajan snorted. "When isn't there one?"

"True, sire, I believe this time you need to take this seriously."

"All right, I'll listen. Go on." Trajan leaned back onto the cushions.

"An escaped slave came to my attention several years ago. He had been part of the household of Sextus Quintilius Bestia."

"The merchant?"

"The very same. This young man, a Dacian, knew Latin fluently, apparently from his association with I Minervia during the war."

"Hadrian's legion."

"Yes," confirmed Papus. "He was servant to the soldiers but never met the general. After enslavement he was purchased by Bestia and put to work immediately. Once he discovered his job and the brutal conditions in the villa, he decided to hide his talent for languages and wait for an opportunity to escape. In the meantime, he learned of some very interesting plots and schemes. One of which was a conspiracy to have you killed."

"Among what parties?"

"Bestia has formed an alliance among himself, the Dacian Balo, and the Parthian Vartan."

Trajan whistled under his breath. "I didn't know Balo was still alive; I had assumed he committed suicide like Decebalus." He turned to Plotina. "Balo was second in command of the Dacian armies."

The news incited Plotina to speak up. "And how do we know this Dacian slave – what is his name?"

"Zuester, my lady."

"And how do we know this Zuester is speaking the truth?" the empress asked. "Do you have evidence?"

"That is why I am only coming to you now," Papus explained. "I have employed spies to follow Bestia for these last several years now. He seems to not simply be a merchant but has extensive contacts amongst the old patrician families. It is a tangle of associates that we have not quite figured out but includes the former consul Gaius Calpurnius Crassus Frugi Licinianus."

"He's still in exile, is he not?" asked the emperor.

"Yes, Caesar. For plotting against Nerva."

Trajan grunted. "Had it been Domitian, the fool would have been killed."

"Yes, well, Bestia's original plan was to act while Hadrian was in Pannonia, but there were some problems of coordination. Now that Hadrian is in Greece, on holiday and not with a garrison, they mean to strike. This time, however, they have included Hadrian in the plot. My men have delayed those whom we believe were hired to kill Hadrian."

"Won't that raise suspicion that we are on to them?" asked the now alert Trajan.

"I'm working with Marcus Vettius Latro, the procurator at Ostia. This morning his staff detained several men, including some of my own agents, ostensibly for a routine audit of customs documents and declarations of birth. He's prioritizing grain shipments to add to the delay. We probably can only sustain this fiction without arousing suspicion on Bestia's part for a few days. The time to act against the conspiracy is now, and we need to act as quickly as possible."

Trajan sighed heavily. "Thank you for this information, Papus. My men will be at your disposal." It was unfortunate that he had to use the services of the *frumentarii*, his special forces in the Praetorians, all too often these days. The emperor got up, and went to his obviously concerned wife. He took her hand in his and kissed it. "I apologize for ending our evening so abruptly, my dear." He cupped her face. "Do not worry. We'll settle this as soon as possible."

Athens, Philopappus's palace, May 113

Athens proved to be everything Hadrian had thought it would be, and Hadrian proved to be even more than the Athenians could have imagined a Roman could be. City and man began a love affair that would endure for a lifetime.

With the sponsorship of 'King' Philopappus, Hadrian had become a citizen of Athens and a member of the deme of Besa in Antiochis. If that weren't enough, he was elected *archon eponymous* for the Athenian year

112, which became known as 'Hadrianos'. A statue of him was erected in the Theater of Dionysos listing his achievements. He dined with politicians, writers, wits, and philosophers, and listened intently to all, heeding the words of his *magister* Epictetus, "if you are caught by chance among strangers, be silent." Stopping at the Stoic philosopher's school in Nicopolis during his journey to Athens, Hadrian had been enthralled with the man whom the emperor Domitian had exiled.

And now, after having been immersed in Greek culture and meeting its people, Hadrian decided he never wanted to leave Greece.

"Don't be silly, husband. Do you mean to rule the empire from Athens?" Sabina said at dinner one night. She could be indiscreet when they were among their friends Balbilla and Philopappus.

Hadrian gazed at his wife admiringly. She looked more lovely than ever in her eastern silks of yellow and pink, and her jewelry with exotic designs and gems. She had been so indulgent of his needs and desires during their time in Greece – even after hearing the tragic news of her grandmother Marciana's death – and for that he was grateful.

"Well, my friend, if you need a palace for your government, my humble home is at your service," said Philopappus.

Hadrian laughed. King's house was anything but humble. It was more extravagant than the palace on Rome's Palatine Hill.

"Or you could design your own, Graeculus," suggested Balbilla. "Don't you make sketches of buildings sometimes?"

"Yes, he does," said Sabina. "And he's very good."

If Sabina had been a man, he would have fallen in love with her a long time ago, thought Hadrian. There was great esteem and close friendship and caring devotion between them, without doubt. There was also an emotion that could be considered love, but he was not *in* love with her. Nor, he gathered, was she in love with him. He met her eyes and smiled. He had something special planned for that night.

In the hallway after dinner, Hadrian took his wife's arm. "Please come with me, Vibia," he murmured in her ear.

She looked up at him questioningly, but he stared straight ahead with determined intention.

Moments later, she discovered what he intended. In the middle of his room in the Greek palace was a pavilion made from suspended silk panels, sheer enough that one could see the shadows cast by the lamplight's broken illumination. Inside the tent, apparent from the play of dark and light, were several of Hadrian's men, now regulars in the couple's games of physical love.

Since the night he surprised her in her room, they had discussed the limits either would go. Sabina did not want another man inside her cunt;

Hadrian did not want to incorporate women. And except for garnering permission from their host Philopappus while in Athens, no one was to know. All participants were sworn to secrecy.

"Are you prepared for tonight's amusements, my love?" asked Hadrian excitedly but gently.

"Yes, husband," was her answer.

Sabina's final condition for such play was that she always be asked to consent.

Hadrian led her into the tent. The carpeted floor was strewn with pillows, along the side were a few tables with lamps, some lighted, some not. And standing at attention were the two burly Africans and the two brawny Germans. All four smiled and nodded their greetings to their lovely mistress. They were stark naked, their bodies exhibiting signs of anticipation of the pleasures to come.

One of the Africans came forward. As Hadrian undressed himself, the African undressed Sabina, slowly, expertly, completely. For such a large man, his touch was gentle. The other African stepped in front of her and held up a dark piece of fabric. Then with the help of his counterpart, they tied the fabric around Sabina's head, utterly obscuring her sight with the blindfold.

Sabina stood very still, getting her bearings without the use of her eyes. She was not afraid, certainly not with her husband present, but she felt keenly apprehensive about the unknown to follow.

She felt her husband's hot breath in her ear. "Ah, love. Now you will not be witness to your ravishment. But have no worries, I guarantee you will enjoy it." And then he was gone. Despite the presence of the five men, she suddenly felt alone. A cool breeze sent a chill through her body. She wrapped her arms around herself.

All at once, seemingly a dozen hands were on her body, stroking her, massaging her, playfully pinching her. The pushing and pulling was confusing. She felt imbalanced, yet somehow secure. Still, instinctively, she stepped forward to right herself.

"Relax," came her husband's voice now in front of her. "We have you. Let go." As if to encourage her, the hands lifted her slightly, reminding her of their strength.

Sabina composed herself and relaxed her body surrounded by the security of the well-muscled men. The serenity lasted a moment before her skin was awakened by moist breaths against her stomach and buttocks. The agitated breaths were followed by wet licks and kisses. The man at her stomach trailed his tongue lower, until he reached her hairless mons.

Suddenly, Sabina felt herself being lifted and her legs spread open. The man between her thighs commenced licking her vulva, alternating delving his tongue inside her yearning channel and flicking it against her excited clit. She thought perhaps it was one of the Germans. One in particular took great joy in pleasuring her that way, and she always appreciated his attentions.

As much as she could with her body in the hands of others, she pressed her cunt against the German's mouth. He tickled and sucked with frenzied delight, by now knowing his mistress's usual signals for the moment before climax. He added his fingers to the delectation, moving two very thick digits in and out of her dripping wet passage, while his lips and tongue tormented her clit. Sabina was on the edge, her body thrashing against the German's face. She exploded, clenching his fingers deep inside her, and feeling them wiggle in enraptured response. He did not let go, however, and instead continued sucking her moist and swollen lips. Her second climax was more forceful. She screamed and bucked against the hulk between her legs. Still, he did not let go.

Exhausted, Sabina went limp in the massive arms holding her petite frame. She panted to catch her breath and felt her heart pounding in her chest. The man at her cunt now stood in front of her and placed his slick fingers in her open mouth.

"Suck," commanded her husband.

Sabina sucked and licked her own moisture from the German's fingers to Hadrian's satisfied exhortations. When his fingers were clean, the German covered her mouth with his own, still wet with her juices. His tongue and lips tasted sour, his skin pungent with her acrid, musky fragrance.

The German broke from the kiss, leaving her satiated yet still aroused for what was to come. Hands gripped her body once again, mouths worked on her nipples, one mouth for each. She gave in to the sensual stimulation, relishing the double pleasure of both breasts sucked at once. It did not last long. She was lowered and positioned on all fours, her hands and knees cushioned by soft pillows.

She jumped when she felt a warm liquid dribbled on her backside. Large hands massaged the oil into her butt cheeks and oily fingers circled the rim of her anus. She gasped when a finger penetrated her, smearing more oil inside the tight orifice. Once again she felt the warm liquid poured between her cheeks, once again she was penetrated, this time with two very large fingers. The fingers slowly moved in and out, then separated to stretch her tight channel even further.

"I need you to be very relaxed, love," murmured her husband. "Are you feeling relaxed?"

"Yes," Sabina sighed. She knew what would happen next and she looked forward to it.

"Good."

Eight hands wrapped around her limbs and lifted her small body while one of the men positioned his prick at her anus. The men lowered her slowly as the enormous cock impaled her, stretching her impossibly.

Sabina let out a loud cry at the sensual assault. While Hadrian's attribute was impressive, she knew her husband was not as large as what was inside her now. It must be one of the Africans who was penetrating her slowly but determinedly.

Her guess was confirmed when the man began to grunt in a familiar deep tone as he thrusted in and out of her. Sabina relaxed against him. Two men carried on with their licking and nipping at her breasts.

The arms holding her thighs pulled them apart delicately while the African continued pumping her tight hole. Fingers toyed with her satiated feminine folds finding her once again aroused and wet. From the particular way he teased her flesh, she knew it was her husband who fondled her.

"Are you ready, love?" he asked, now in front of her, still stroking her.

"For what, Graeculus?" she moaned.

"For this."

His cock pushed inside her cunt at the precise moment the African exited her arse. With seemingly practiced precision, the two men pushed in and pulled out with opposite motions.

Sabina tensed at the unfamiliar sensations, her body surprised at each thrust, her mind concerned they would injure her.

"No, love. Vibia, let it happen," Hadrian soothed.

She felt fingers on her clit, rubbing her until she let go and her anxieties melted away.

Hadrian must have felt it, and then he must have signaled to the African. All of a sudden, both men were driving into her with the same force and rhythm. Fingers still excited her clit, mouths and tongues still tortured her nipples.

Sabina threw her head back and wailed her climax, clenching both men inside her. It proved too much for the African. He came instantly, jetting his hot fluid deep into her bowels. She rested her head on his strong shoulder behind her and felt his body jerk and his cock spasm in continued orgasm.

Hadrian pounded into his wife with heaving grunts. Seconds later, he exploded inside her, his hands gripping her waist, his mouth panting into hers. "Oh gods!" he groaned in satisfaction.

The two men remained embedded in her as their bodies wound down from the frenzy. The African pulled out first. As the men lowered Sabina back to standing, Hadrian pulled out, letting out one more sated growl. He remained in front of her, and enveloped her in his arms. The two stood holding each other, feeling their heated bodies calm together.

"Shall I remove the blindfold now?" he murmured.

"Yes, please."

Hadrian untied the cloth and tossed it on the floor. Sabina looked around. Husband and wife were alone in the tent, the other men having left probably at Hadrian's subtle signal.

"Satisfied?" he asked.

Sabina smiled. "Very much so, my love."

They lay on a mound of pillows and slept very contentedly.

Rome, Imperial Palace, October 113

Zuester sat in his room in the palace waiting to be called for the journey to the east. Because of his considered actions, the threat against the emperor Trajan had been thwarted. He was very pleased with himself. And he knew that, despite her hatred for the Romans, his mother would also be pleased that he had acted honorably.

He was to accompany the imperial expedition to the east. Trajan, his wife Plotina, and Trajan's niece Matidia, were to go to Antioch, with a stop in Greece along the way to see the presumed successor Hadrian and his wife. The destinations and personages were simply fantastical notions to Zuester at the moment, soon to become realities. He had been reviewing Roman history and the Greek language expressly for the trip.

As for his friend Skiare, he knew the future boded well. The senator Messius Aemilius Papus had seen to manumission for the both of them – a falsified freedom, but a freedom none would dispute. Neither really cared as long as they were free from Bestia and his bizarre, base demands. It meant Skiare could finally go home. He had been attached to a Roman legion assigned to Dacia, eventually hoping to return to his family. As was customary, in honor of his savior Skiare had changed his name to Messius Aemilius Skiare. While officially Zuester himself had also taken the praenomen and nomen of the senator, he knew his mother would want him to be true to himself and his heritage. He would remain "Zuester" in honor of her father.

Zuester had wished his friend well and now waited for his own future to begin.

Gallia Lugdunensis, October 113

Bestia couldn't stop looking behind him at every turn even though he was miles from Rome. He had fled weeks ago, pushing on without rest into Gaul. The Gaulish barbarians were hopeless; few knew Latin and those that did spoke it not very well, or they spoke it with crude accents, like Trajan's supposed successor. Trajan was a fool. The Senate would not approve of a Spanish barbarian like Hadrian as their leader.

The merchant was determined to keep going until he was as far from Rome as possible, to Britannia if he had to, knowing full well the barbarians there were probably worse.

Vartan and Balo had been murdered in cold blood. He cursed the Romans. Dacia had been conquered, yes, so it was a hopeless case. But Parthia? A separate peace could have been made with them. King Osrhoes of Parthia could have come to terms with Trajan – well, still could come to terms with the emperor as he yet lived – if he felt it best for Parthia. This trouble with Armenia was not worth going to war over. But Trajan was a war monger. He had proved that in Dacia.

Still, Bestia thought, war was generally good for merchants: Necessities in short supplies and exotic goods could be priced extravagantly. But this dodging and escaping when things went bad was definitely not what a simple businessman ever expected. Nor was this supposed to be the life of a descendant of eminent Romans. But with so many of his relatives in exile or murdered, Bestia should have foreseen such a destiny. He now had a taste of what his cousin Calpurnius Crassus must feel every day in his exile.

Bestia pressed on. No one need know his whereabouts back in the capital, and he would not stop running until he reached a place far enough away that whatever happened in Rome was considered unimportant. Night was falling; his legs were weary. He had to find a spot to rest very, very soon.

Athens, Philopappus's palace, end of October 113

"They are ready to meet you."

The voice shook Zuester from his daydream. The servant who fetched him was a mere boy, a good-looking youth, but surprisingly young.

"Thank you," said Zuester and stood to follow the boy who took the pathetic solitary bag he had packed for the journey. They walked through the service wing, passing numerous servants along dark corridors, then out into a peristyle, where Zuester caught a glimpse of a very pleasant garden. They seemed to be traveling quite far, finally passing through heavy doors to what he reckoned was the public part of the palace.

"I'll wait for you outside," said the servant as he indicated another set of intricately carved wooden doors.

"Thank you," choked Zuester. He drew in a breath and went inside.

Before him was a vast space, divided in three parts by rows of columns. The capitals shone with gilding, the walls gleamed with polished marble revetment, the mosaic floor was of the most intricate designs he had ever seen. He was so over-awed that he did not see the tall, middle-aged man approach him.

"Welcome to my home and our throne room, makeshift as it is for our dear emperor," said the man gently, his eyes sparkling. Zuester recognized him as King Philopappus. He had met his host and his sister Julia Balbilla earlier that day.

"My lord," Zuester said with a bow.

"Ah, here he is," came an impressive voice. "The young man who saved my life."

Zuester looked up. The clean-shaven man with squinty eyes and thin lips was wearing a purple toga, something, Zuester had heard, only the Emperor of Rome was allowed to wear. The man before him was none other than the emperor Trajan.

Zuester blushed, then knelt and bowed his head but not so much that he could not glimpse the imperial party gathered in the hall. The emperor stood next to a tall, handsome, middle-aged bearded man. Seated to the left of them were two elegantly dressed women, also older, presumably the wives of the Roman gentlemen present. A tap on his shoulder indicated the Dacian should rise. Only then did he notice a younger woman sitting on the far right. Zuester lingered a bit too long in his study of her. She was absolutely beautiful, her brilliant copper hair decorated with gold and gems, her sheer, clingy silk dress covering just enough to leave something for the imagination.

"Zoo-ster – I have that right, hmm?" asked Trajan.

Zuester blushed again. He knew he should not be staring at royalty and turned his attention to the emperor. "Yes, sire. That is correct, sir."

"Ah, good, Zuester," said the emperor with a little more facility as he indicated the freedman should come forward. "I would like you to meet my grand-niece's husband, Hadrian."

Zuester had to look up at the tall bearded man being presented to him. Hadrian smiled gently, the gleam in his gray eyes suggesting an enigmatic comprehension of what Zuester was thinking and feeling at that very moment. "Pleased to make your acquaintance," Zuester said with a bow. It was peculiar meeting a man he had heard so much about during the war then as a target in the assassination plot against the emperor. He was impressive, his importance deserved from his presence alone.

"I am pleased to make yours as well," responded Hadrian in his soothing bass tone. "I understand you have some facility with languages?"

"Yes, sir."

"And which do you know?"

"My native Dacian, Latin, Greek, Parthian. I am learning the Egyptian language at the moment, and have also embarked upon a study of Hebrew, the Jewish language."

"Very useful for someone engaged by the imperial household."

"Yes, sir. Thank you, sir."

"As you will be part of the household and not the court, I would like to introduce you to the women who will essentially be your masters."

"Hadrian!" the eldest of the women present scolded.

"That is Pompeia Plotina," Hadrian continued with a chuckle in his voice. "She is the wife of the emperor and you must do everything she says." Next, he indicated a middle-aged woman. "This is Salonia Matidia. She is the emperor's niece. You should probably do everything she says too." He put an arm around Zuester's shoulder and led him over to the woman sitting at the far right of the row of imperial seats.

Zuester swallowed hard. He was now directly before the very beautiful young woman he had just admired. She was even more lovely up close.

"And this is Vibia Sabina, Matidia's daughter and the emperor's grand-niece." Hadrian leaned over as if confiding in a friend. "She is also my wife. You should do anything she says, too." He bent down more closely and repeated in Zuester's ear, "anything."

Zuester flushed and tried his best to stop the stirrings of his arousal.

"Thank you for your service to my family," Sabina said. She smiled sweetly and held out her hand for him to kiss.

Zuester felt his heart beating in his ears. He touched her hand – her warm soft hand – and merely bent over it. If his lips were to come in contact with her skin he knew he would burst into flame before them all.

"Right, very well. We leave for Antioch tomorrow morning. I hope you women are prepared. Hadrian, let us to the library to discuss logistics."

Trajan's booming voice broke the spell the freedman was under, and he politely stepped back from his new mistress.

"Zuester, come with Matidia and me," said Plotina.

"Yes, my lady," he mustered. He stole a glimpse of the bewitching Sabina before he joined the two women. Hadrian had gallantly offered his hand to his wife as she stood up, and was now talking to her quietly. He caught the Dacian's eye and winked. Zuester blushed deeply and turned away.

Sabina found it very difficult to not watch the handsome, dark-haired Dacian as he left the hall.

"He likes you, you know," Hadrian teased as Plotina and Matidia exited with the freedman.

"Well I am to be his mistress, so I suppose that's a good thing." Sabina cast her eyes down. She could not reveal to her very perceptive husband that she found Zuester extraordinarily attractive.

"You know what I mean. He could not take his eyes off you. I fear he will now retire to lick the wounds suffered from Cupid's onslaught of arrows." Sabina struggled to not meet his gaze. "Ah, well. I see we'll have to apply to the medic for a salve for your wounds as well."

Sabina shot him a fiery look, then blushed deeply at his knowing grin.

"Vibia, love. I've never seen you act this way. Certainly never around me." He took both her hands in his. "If you are in love, then you should follow your heart."

"Graeculus, it is a bit early to be calling it love." Her cheeks were still burning and she tried very hard not to smile. "I've only just met him."

"Well, an infatuation, then. You are smitten. Call it what you want."

"Have you never been in love?" she asked genuinely.

Hadrian grunted. "I've never allowed myself the luxury." He kissed her forehead. "I'm going off to war and may never come back. You should indulge yourself while you have the chance. And as we are not in Rome, no one need ever know."

Antioch, Governor's Palace, December 114

For the better part of a year, the palace at Antioch had been abuzz with activity. The languages of every eastern culture, the smells of their foods, the rustle of their silks, the jingling of their fine jewelry, had filled the corridors and courtyards. Zuester had not been busier, or happier, than at any other time in his entire life. He was indispensable, not only for his language skills but for his newly realized organizational skills, and suddenly acquired diplomatic skills.

The Parthian king Osrhoes had sent an embassy to Athens, so the freedman had met the Parthian diplomatic corps there, then was made responsible for their well-being in Antioch, translating between masters and servants alike. At one point, there were so many foreigners at Antioch it was difficult to tell friend from foe. And yet Zuester was able to do so admirably, getting to know each servant and ambassador personally, then shooing away strangers, spies, and infiltrators. Clearly his duties were beyond merely serving the household, extending to facilitating court life. Still, he was not going to complain. He had never felt so useful, so needed, so proud of what he could and did accomplish. And at the end of the day, if he had to simply oversee the delivery of a soothing drink to the empress Plotina, that too was rewarding. His mother would be proud of him, he knew. He was serving the emperor of Rome! It suddenly did not matter that Rome had been the enemy, that Dacia had been conquered, that he had once been sold into slavery. He had lived more in the last ten years of his life than most twenty-six year olds. He was changed, different; his life had metamorphosed into something profoundly meaningful.

Yet, when there was a brief moment of stillness, a respite to the bustle and clamor, Zuester would realize that they had been preparing for war with Parthia. Another battle with a people much like his own in that their only sin was that they were not Romans. The emperor Trajan's need to extend the borders was unsettling; why could he just not make peace? Surely other kingdoms had become client states to Rome and yet had maintained their cultural autonomy? Only the general Hadrian appeared to be disquieted by the maneuvers toward combat. Zuester marked Hadrian's thoughts and movements when he got the chance. He seemed to be a promising leader for Rome, a man to watch, a man to make oneself useful to.

But then there was the general's wife…Sabina. Oh, Sabina! Every morning Zuester could not wait to see her. Yet every day was agonizingly different and Zuester did not know when the opportunity would arise. Sometimes he caught a glimpse of her sunning herself in a garden, unaware that she was the object of attention, that an admirer was privy to her intimate activities, adjusting her silky, filmy bodice, fixing an unruly copper curl. He felt a mixture of shame and arousal at such moments. When he was granted the opportunity to serve her, he did so with an uneven breath and a beating heart. Sometimes she looked at and spoke to him. At those moments, Zuester lost himself, feeling the rest of the world peel away to leave just the two of them.

Alone.

If only such a fantasy could be true! A freedman and his royal mistress coupling under embroidered sheets…even if for only a furtive solitary night – he'd take that much. Zuester longed to stroke her flame-red hair, to kiss her plump lips. At times it looked as if she returned his affection, that she longed for him as well. When they chatted she would nibble on the corner of her lower lip, and gaze at him with her moss-colored eyes, batting long lashes and crinkling her brow in expectation. In his bed at night, sometimes alone, sometimes not, he imagined she wanted him too, and imagined that it was her body beneath his, her body moaning and moving to his rhythm.

But palace gossip said she was pregnant, and although she had not yet begun to show, her appetites had definitely changed. Of course it was her husband's child, despite the rumors that they did not get along, that his tastes were for boys, and that he beat her when she came to his bed. In his diligence to see the princess Sabina every day, Zuester had spied her with Hadrian more than just once or twice. The two were not in love, but they were not indifferent to one another. They were affectionate, admiring and respectful, even playful, in their relationship. Yet there was something unspoken, something missing, Sabina often appearing as if her thoughts were elsewhere. The longing in her eyes, Zuester imagined, was for him.

Antioch, Governor's Palace, end of January 115

"How is the child?"

Sabina barely glanced up at her husband from her curled up position in bed. "I don't know, Graeculus," she said morosely. "Can the baby sense fear?"

The earthquake of two weeks ago had devastated the city of Antioch, almost every building had been utterly destroyed. The Antioch they had all grown accustomed to, had begun to call home, was no longer there. On the terrible night, Zuester once again proved his worth by helping Trajan and Plotina flee the palace from their bedroom window. The imperial household had lived outdoors in the neighboring hippodrome for several days afterwards. Only with inspections and approvals from engineers and blessings from priests did the emperor set the example and move back indoors.

Everyone believed the disaster to be a sign from the gods. If Trajan had not made the appropriate offerings and sacrifices, he had confided to Hadrian and Plotina, he might not have stayed to fight. But the auspices augured well, and he was determined to win the war against Parthia. The earthquake could have instead been a warning to the enemy, the emperor had reminded.

Hadrian sat down on the edge of the bed. He stroked his wife's hair then simply lay down next to her, encompassing her with his body. Sabina's pregnancy had been welcome news, but her agitated state and inability to eat since the earthquake had been worrisome to the imperial household. "The after-quakes are unsettling, I know." He nuzzled against her. "I feel it too, love. I feel apprehensive. It is not like battle where one can plan, even for surprises. One cannot plan for this, nor for what may unexpectedly come."

Sabina pressed her body closer to him, relaxing in the comfort of his warmth. "I thank the gods every day for sparing us," she said hoarsely.

Her voice was trembling, Hadrian knew she was crying. He would have to be brave despite his own anxieties caused by the calamity. "Vibia, be strong. Our child needs you now, as he will need you as he grows. As you needed Matidia."

Sabina screwed her eyes shut against the pain of his truth. "Yes, Graeculus." She heaved in a deep shuddering breath, trying desperately to calm her hysterical core but only succeeding in releasing new sobs.

Hadrian held his wife's shaking body tightly. "Shh, shh. I'm here, love, I'm here." He spread his large hand over her belly hoping to calm the child within as well. He waited patiently until her sobs became ragged breaths, then the ragged breaths became constant, even, and deep. Like every night since the catastrophic event happened, he held her in his arms until they fell asleep.

Britannia, Londinium, March 115

Bestia reviewed the rolled missive one more time before tossing it on the fire to join the charred remains of other communiqués. The Antioch earthquake had been fortuitous for his spies. The resulting confusion had afforded them the opportunity to infiltrate the palace at Antioch, gaining unprecedented access to the imperial family. Thusly embedded, his agents had been in constant communication with him as there was much to tell. Each dispatch sparked a little hope in his bleak life and instilled in him a little more reverence for the gods. Only weeks before, he had been despondent, had felt disowned by his own family deities, sacrilegiously disdaining their treatment of him, a poor disfigured bastard. But now he realized Occasio, the god of opportunity, had truly been watching over him all along.

Some Romans believed that Trajan's war on the Parthian front had provoked the disaster. The emperor, however, believed otherwise, or so he claimed publicly. Still, astonishingly, Trajan moved his entire household to the open space of the hippodrome for several days after the event. Imperial staff had not been able to keep precise track of who had perished in the catastrophe and who had not. It had simply been too easy for Bestia's men to infiltrate.

Bestia took in his surroundings, a sparsely furnished rented room with a hole in the roof, not for rain water as might be found in Rome, but to let the smoke from the ever-burning fire escape. Of course the hole did have the unintentional effect of letting in the cold and wet, making the fire a constant necessity. It was a vicious cycle, and one he felt himself contemplating much, much too often. He had never spent time in self-reflection, but he had felt trapped of late. It was not the newness of Britannia, the fact that he was a stranger in a strange land, that he had no established contacts, that he was meeting people of races and clans he had never heard of. No, it was none of that. In fact he loved the novelty, the unfamiliarity of it all. What he hated and what he felt oppressed by was the damnable weather. If he ever experienced drought again he would think twice about praying to the gods for rain.

However, the recent spate of missives set him back on course. He felt the thrill of possibility charge through him taking his mind completely away from the misery that was Britannia. Beyond the valuable information, two points contained in the string of messages intrigued him.

First, the lady Sabina, the wife of the presumed successor of the emperor, was pregnant. Such a revelation was a windfall, sending Bestia's mind spinning. The birth of a child would mean Hadrian would most definitely be deemed Trajan's heir, especially with the birth of a son. But Sabina's fecundity would be cherished even if the child were a daughter. If no child were produced – an occurrence that could yet happen – Hadrian's position was, as it had been for seemingly decades, unsecured. And if by chance Trajan died without having named a successor, there was still the chance of imperial chaos and the resurgence of the Republic.

The second piece of information involved the Parthian pretender – and presumed victor in the event the Romans did not conquer them – Osrhoes. Bestia had known the king had a daughter amongst his many sons – all of whom he had tried to ally with to no avail – but the girl's age had been an uncertainty. She could have been a mere infant and then of no use to him. Now his spies informed him she was about ten, old enough to be left angry and vengeful toward the Romans should something adverse happen to her father and her kingdom. He would keep her in mind for a future alliance, an alliance, he fantasized, which would entail his inevitable violation of her nubile and untouched, yet inexorably receptive, body.

Bestia held his hands over the fire, flexing the cold and stiffness from his fingers, and, for the first time in a long time, smiled. That Trajan had not given up his plans for war in the east even after such a violent harbinger as an earthquake was a comfort to the merchant. War meant chaos, and chaos was beneficial to men of his ilk. Chaos meant opportunity, meant anything could happen, and Bestia excelled at extracting opportunity from anything.

Antioch, Governor's Palace, April 115

Sabina drifted off to sleep in the warm courtyard of the Antioch palace while Zuester gently played his kithara and sang, an activity that had become routine for the two of them. As war-planning was at an end and Zuester's translation skills were in infrequent demand, Plotina and Matidia had felt Zuester's time was best spent soothing Sabina with poetry and music. She was in her fifth month of pregnancy and soon would have to endure the stress of her husband's absence while he was away at battle. Trajan and Hadrian were about to leave for the Parthian front.

With the handsome freedman being the last sight she saw before she closed her eyes, and his melodic voice being the continued sound she heard, Sabina, as usual, was destined to dream of him. She imagined what he must look like under his tunic. Sometimes she caught a glimpse of a powerful thigh or a strong arm, but he was terribly modest and never purposely showed off his prowess. Just once she wanted to slide her hands over his bared body and feel the ripples of his well-muscled torso as he grew heated with desire. She wanted to taste him, pleasure him the way her husband had taught her to pleasure a man. She wanted to serve him and let him be master over her.

She felt him sit on the couch at her side, his arms straddle her body possessively. His breath was hot on her cheek before he kissed it tenderly, setting the rest of her body on fire. When his lips finally touched hers, her flesh tingled with anticipation and need.

"Zuester," she moaned, licking her lips and reaching up to her phantom lover.

"Your dreams betray you," came Hadrian's soft bass tone.

Sabina opened her eyes in horror. Her husband's bearded face hovered above her after separating from the welcoming kiss.

"Graeculus!" she exclaimed, then glanced over at the servant. Zuester was playing his instrument and humming sweetly as if nothing had happened. Well, it seemed, nothing had happened indeed.

Hadrian laughed. "I thought as much," he said quietly, stroking her hair. "Does the youth know about your fantasies?"

"Don't tease me, you brute," she whined.

"Ah, I see he does not." Hadrian smiled at his wife. He very much enjoyed provoking her while she had a crush – a very big crush – on their freedman. He placed his hands gently on her belly. "And how is my son?"

"He's restless like his father," she said. "A warrior, no doubt."

"Ah, let us hope not," he confided under his breath. "I wish to end this business of your uncle's. War is destructive to the empire. It may expand borders, but at what cost? Rebellion is at every turn."

"Impending fatherhood has made you philosophic."

"I am nothing if not philosophic," he grinned. "And fatherhood is merely a benefit of my love for you."

A servant entered the courtyard escorting the midwife and herbalist Zosime. Plotina and Matidia followed close behind.

"So good to see you, Zosime," said Sabina. She turned to Hadrian. "She makes me drink ginger despite the end of my morning sickness."

"It is to keep up your appetite, my lady," responded the midwife. "For the health of the child." She nodded to Hadrian, then placed the tray with Sabina's herbal concoction on the table before her.

"Vibia, darling, you should do as Zosime says," admonished Matidia. "It is for your own good." She took her daughter's hand and squeezed it. "I did everything she told me to, and look what I ended up with." She kissed Sabina's hand. "The most beautiful daughter in the empire, I do believe."

"And, we've our own cups of the remedy, as a show of support," added a smiling Plotina.

The accompanying servant placed a separate tray with the older women's drink and several additional cups on a table. Matidia and Plotina seated themselves on the comfortable chairs nearby.

"Zuester," called out Hadrian. "I think we are out-numbered. What shall we do?"

The youth blushed at the attention drawn to his presence, but the glimmer in Hadrian's eyes emboldened him. "We should succor the women, my lord." He smiled at his own idea. "We shall join them."

Hadrian laughed then nodded his head in agreement.

The ginger mixture was poured and passed around. The party saluted the family gods as well as the goddess Alemonia, protector of the unborn, before they drank.

Hadrian gulped a mouthful. "It's not so bad," he said as he examined his cup.

"No," agreed Zuester. "I taste honey."

"Rather pleasant," said Matidia.

"Really?" countered Sabina. "It's awful." She took another draught and scrunched up her nose.

"My lady," insisted the midwife. "It should not be this way."

Sabina took another sip. "It's very bitter, Zosime. It is truly disgusting. Maybe it is too strong this time. Not your best effort, I must admit."

Zosime was distressed by this pronouncement. "Are you sure, my lady? I would like to taste it then. I mean, that which is in your own cup."

Sabina took one last drink before handing the cup to her servant. "Please, be my guest."

The midwife took a hearty swallow then promptly spit out the liquid onto the stone floor.

She pointed to Zuester and Hadrian. "Hold her arms!" She indicated a nearby servant. "Make her vomit!" She looked at the stunned faces around her. "*Now!*"

The courtyard was filled with panic as all rushed to do as instructed. Hadrian pulled his wife to her knees on the stone patio, and Zosime's servant forced her to vomit what she had just imbibed. Sabina remained kneeling exhausted and heaving.

Matidia fell to the ground to comfort her daughter. She looked up at Zosime. "What is it? What has happened?"

"Someone has poisoned your daughter with artemisia," she said, her eyes black with fear. "I hope we have acted in time. Otherwise, she will lose the child."

The remedy had come too late.

Sabina lay on her bed clutching her abdomen and groaning in pain, her face crusted with the salt of her tears and sweat. Servants rushed to and fro desperately trying to do something to help her.

Hadrian had sent Zuester to look for a culprit to no avail. The household had been full of emissaries and their staff; the kitchen especially had been swarming with servants attending to their masters' special dietary needs. Anyone could have done it. Anyone. Roman, Parthian, Greek, Jew. Anyone.

Amidst the chaos, Hadrian sat on his wife's bed in the dim light of the fading afternoon. He had to leave. Trajan, Rome, the war, the Empire demanded it. He had to, yet, he did not want to. He had not realized it until that afternoon: Sabina was his soul. She was a part of him. And when she was in pain, he was numb.

He looked up and saw his salvation.

Zuester.

The young man was endlessly helping the women folk, and this time was no different. Beyond doing what Hadrian ordered as soon as the poison was discovered, the young man had offered his services as attendant to the bedchamber of Sabina. Warm compresses, hand holding, towels to soak up the blood, everything; the handsome freedman had been there. Due to his helpfulness, the fact of his maleness was conveniently forgotten by all of Sabina's female servants as well as by her mother and by Plotina.

And, Hadrian knew, his stubborn wife would initially be reluctant, but would eventually give in to the young man's charge over her.

Hadrian stood and watched the activity surrounding the bed. The confusion was oppressing, disallowing him to think, to act.

"Get out," he said far too quietly for anyone to hear.

Some of the servants glanced around, wondering if he had been speaking to them.

"Get out!" Hadrian cried with a voice loud enough for all to comprehend. "Get out of here! Leave us alone."

The staff scurried to finish up their tasks one last time before exiting the bedchamber.

Hadrian exhaled deeply. In the sudden silence he could hear his wife's quiet sobs and sense her acute anguish.

"Vibia, I've failed you. I simply do not know what happened."

She sucked in a breath. "It hurts so much this time. I've never felt so much pain."

Hadrian stretched himself on the bed against her. "I'm so sorry, love." He wrapped his arms around her and felt her body heave as she tried to draw in breaths while also trying to halt her sobs. "I had no idea we had such enemies. I never thought you would be at risk like this."

"I wanted this child so much, Graeculus," she choked. "I wanted to have your son."

"We'll try again. We'll have another."

Sabina ripped herself from his clutch and from the bed. In her pain she could barely stand straight. "*No!*" she screamed, her body bent over, one hand stabilizing herself on the mattress. "I will not carry your monsters ever again! Do you hear me?! I will do everything in my power to make sure this never happens again!"

Hadrian still lay on the bed, frozen on one elbow, staring incredulously at his wife. Surely she did not mean that? She could not possibly be of sound mind. She had been through the most horrifying ordeal a woman could endure – the murder of her unborn child by an unseen enemy. She would come around eventually.

Sabina fell to the floor in exhaustion and grief. Hadrian picked her up and lay her back on the bed. He kissed her cheek, pulled the covers over her, and left.

Once outside the door he glanced around. Whispers and quiet movements made him realize that the household staff had indeed not scattered but had remained close to their mistress's chamber. And they had all heard what she had said.

Hadrian spied Zuester and beckoned to him. The young man obeyed immediately.

"I must leave, as you know. While I am gone, I am charging you with the care of my wife. You must taste all her food before she eats it, or you must personally oversee its preparation. Keep her in your sights at all times, and make sure she does nothing foolish, nor speaks to anyone unworthy of her audience." He examined the servant briefly. "She likes you. She trusts you. You are her protector now."

Zuester could only stare blankly at the floor. The whole series of events had been simply bizarre and unreal for all present. "Yes, sir," he answered.

"Good." Hadrian patted him on the back. He saw that Plotina had also been witness to the domestic scene. He went to her.

"Mother," he said, nodding his welcome.

"Hadrian come with me." Plotina led him down the corridor to his own bedchamber and indicated that they go in. He proceeded and she followed.

He stood in the middle of the marble-clad room, startled at the loud echoing noise that only two people could make.

"I heard everything," she said taking his hand and leading him to sit on the bed. "She's in incredible pain, my son, please understand this."

Hadrian was struck by a realization. "This has happened to you, as well."

"Yes, several times. Well, not by a stranger. But," she looked him in the eye, "by my own hand."

Hadrian stared wide-eyed at the woman he called mother. "Why? Why would any woman do something so monstrous?"

"Because it is best for the Empire." She squeezed his hand. "If you survive the battles before you, you will understand why a woman would choose you over her own flesh and blood. You are meant for Rome"

Hadrian sat stupefied at her revelation.

"And no, I did not cause Sabina's pain if that is what you are thinking."

"No, never. I would never accuse you of such a thing. It is I, rather, who should have been more aware of what goes on in my household. I've just been so damned busy with this Parthian business—"

"Shh, shh," calmed Plotina as she brushed a curl behind his ear. "Don't blame yourself, either." She placed an arm around her adopted son's slumped shoulders. "Graeculus, you should be aware that what has happened is more devastating than the loss of one child." She kissed his forehead. "She might never conceive again after such a trauma to her body as this. You have to accept that." Plotina bent her face down to meet his. "You might have to resort to adopting your own heir and successor."

Hadrian breathed out a heavy sigh, releasing all the pent up pain and torment. He wrapped his arms around Plotina's waist and let loose a flood of tears.

Ctesiphon, Parthian Imperial Palace, January 116

From her secret corner in the attic chamber where she sometimes went to play with her dolls, Roedogune could hear the chaos in the palace. She went to the slit in the stone tower and peered outside. The Roman *shah* had arrived with his troops. Her mother had told her to hide herself, that they would come for her when the time was right, but it became difficult to sit still, to not take action against the enemy intruder. In the palace below she could hear women scream "No!" followed by blood-curdling cries, and, suddenly, silence.

Where was her father? Why hadn't her mother come for her? Or anyone? What if she were the only member of the Parthian royal family to have survived the invasion? She hesitated a second before she opened the door and stepped outside to witness the massacre.

She was just in time to see Hyasdana running up the spiral staircase leading to the palace tower. The old servant was huffing and puffing from her exertions.

"Roedogune! Child, we looked everywhere for you! You recalcitrant girl! Where have you been hiding, my princess?"

"Mother told me to stay here," Roedogune responded. She was amazed she was able to maintain a sense of calm amidst the frenetic excitement of her nursemaid.

"Oh, child!" The old servant reached down and hugged her charge. Her body shook from sobs of relief.

"Where are mother and father? And my brothers?" asked Roedogune when the nursemaid loosened her clutching embrace.

"The Shah of Rome will not make peace with your father the king, so the king and queen were made to leave by their own guard. Your brothers the princes went another way. There is nothing we can do now but hide." Hyasdana took her hand and tugged her toward the stairs.

"I will not hide." Roedogune stood her ground.

"Oh! You stubborn girl!" the nursemaid chastised. "You must away with me." She grunted in exasperation as she followed her princess tromping down the stairs.

Through the back passageways known only to servants, the royal family, and magicians, Roedogune led the way to the throne room of the Parthian kings. Miraculously, it was eerily empty despite the clamor of war continuing beyond the walls. There in the middle on a raised dais and covered by a golden baldachin sat the *sella regia*, the great Parthian throne.

Against her nursemaid's wishes the princess went to the elaborately carved, gilded, and bejeweled chair. Her family had fled, and it was up to her to protect the kingdom. Roedogune was shah now. She sat on the throne and awaited her fate.

All of a sudden, the barbarian Romans burst through the doors at the end of the long audience chamber, the clang of their armor and stomp of their boots echoing in the deserted hall. The invaders stopped when they saw her, or rather one among them, a thin, pinch-lipped, gray-haired soldier of some rank, made them all stop. They stood quietly, whispering to each other, as they stared.

Staring at her majesty, thought Roedogune. *I am shah. I sit on the sella regia, the throne of the Parthian kings.*

In their guttural language, the gray old man called to a young soldier who came forward. Roedogune knew a little Latin, although she had not really paid her studies much mind. *'Puella,' that means girl, does it not?* They called her *puella.* Fools. She was shah.

The young soldier approached her, his solitary steps clicking across the polished marble floor. He was dark-haired and muscular, what some women might consider handsome. She was far too young to understand such things, but she knew the ways of the women of the palace. He stood before the throne and bowed.

"Good day," he said in Parthian.

Roedogune blinked. He should not speak to her unless spoken to.

"I am Neroni Maximus, emissary of the Roman Emperor Trajan. Whom am I addressing?"

His accent was terrible. The Emperor of Rome could find no other interpreter?

"What is your name?"

He was persistent, this poor speaker was. She realized she would have to respond.

"I am Roedogune, daughter of King Osrhoes. In my father's absence, I am now shah."

The soldier translated her statement to the old man who smiled. The two engaged in conversation as the old man approached. When he stood before the princess, he began to speak. The soldier translated.

"This is the Emperor Trajan," said the soldier indicating the old man. "The Emperor of the Parthian people. This beautiful city of Ctesiphon is part of the great Roman Empire, its jewel of the East—"

"No!" cried Roedogune. "We will never surrender to savage foreigners!"

"Unfortunately, my young princess" – he actually said 'small queen', but Roedogune, being highly intelligent, understood his meaning – "your kingdom has already been defeated, its people have surrendered. Your city has been greatly damaged and is not fit for your highness."

The old man Trajan took a step forward.

"Stop!" came a woman's shriek from beyond the raised dais.

Hyasdana ran in from behind the embroidered silk curtains lining the east wall of the palace hall. She threw herself at Trajan's feet, crying, tearing her hair, and begging for mercy.

"Please, please, oh great Emperor of Rome, do not harm the child. We have heard of such horrors that have befallen our people at the hands of soldiers. She is unmarried and has not known a man. I beg of you, take me if you must. Do not harm the girl. She is a treasure."

The old man blinked then smiled in admiration. He bent down and offered his hand to the old nursemaid. When they were standing side by side, he began to speak, his words translated by the soldier.

"We have no intention of harming the girl. We will treat her as we would any daughter of Rome." He turned to his troops still gathered at the entryway, then nodded to the soldier to translate what he said next. He bellowed to his men, the grave urgency of his commands coming through in his tone. The soldier did not need to interpret the intent, instead his voice was soft and reassuring to the women in his presence.

"Do not harm these women in any way. Any man who lays a rough hand on them will have that hand cut off. These women are our guests, not our prisoners. The laws of hospitality prevail, not the laws of war." The emperor of Rome then turned to Roedogune and Hyasdana. "Please come with me. We have a long journey before we arrive at your new palace in Rome."

The interpreter knelt at the lowest step of the throne and offered his hand to Roedogune. She hesitated, but a glance at Hyasdana reassured her. Roedogune stood and walked down the steps of the dais. The soldier and the nursemaid fell into place behind her.

She turned around for one last look. The soldiers were preparing to carry off the *sella regia* as the spoils of war.

Antioch, Governor's Palace, May 116

"My lady, Sabina, you may eat these figs," said Zuester as he placed a tray before his mistress. "I have prepared them myself, with pistachios and honey."

Sabina had finally grown accustomed to the young freedman's care and attention as he had nursed her back to health. At first she had been so deadened by the shock to her mind and body from losing her child that she simply acquiesced to Zuester's instructions like an obedient dog. Yet, while he seemed to understand her malaise, he refused to let her wallow in her depression. He boldly began to make his attendance on her into a game, sometimes refusing to give her bites of obviously tasty and clearly unadulterated food because he had to verify that it was safe "one more time", or just before feeding her a morsel holding it back to make sure "you really want to eat it?" The first few times, Sabina was simply annoyed. After a while though, she realized it could be a fun, flirty, harmless game between herself and the very attractive Dacian.

"And how do I know if they are good at all? How will I know I will even like them?" she asked ridiculously. Zuester, everyone discovered, was a fabulous gourmand.

"You will like them," he answered, feigning displeasure with her impetuousness.

"And if I refuse?"

"Then I will hold you down and pinch your nose until you gasp for air. Then I will plop the fig into your open mouth. You will have to eat it."

Sabina's whole body flushed with the thought of the young man holding her down. There would be no need, of course, as she would let him do just about anything to her. But the idea of being held down by him was most arousing.

"Hmmm," she said thoughtfully. "All right. I will let you feed me." She opened her mouth.

Zuester smiled at her wickedness. They were not alone. As usual, the women of the imperial household had gathered for gossip and games, sewing and fashion talk in Plotina's courtyard – the best in the Antioch palace. Because of Zuester's special position with regards to Sabina, he was always allowed to be there. He was a gracious and charming guest in the women's world, and Matidia and Plotina often fussed over him like mother hens. As Sabina grew more emboldened by the surrounding presence of her female companions, she began to flirt with Zuester. She was never chastised by her relatives for such behavior, and she was never discouraged by Zuester himself. All around knew that Hadrian, while devoted to his wife, had his own peccadilloes. Sabina should be allowed hers.

Zuester held up half a fig topped with a dollop of the honey-nut mixture and brought it to Sabina's parted lips. Locking his gaze with hers, she leaned in and took a bite of the fruit, her mouth and tongue making their motions in a slightly exaggerated way. She left a little morsel between his fingers.

She smiled as she chewed. "You don't have to actually watch me eat, you know."

"I want to watch you," he said, now with his own sauciness.

Sabina blushed and beamed, then leaned in once more and placed her open mouth around the last bit of fig and the fingers holding it. Her tongue grabbed the fruit and, in the process, tasted Zuester's honeyed skin.

Without flinching from his mistress's tantalizing solicitation, Zuester put his fingers in his own mouth and licked them clean.

Sabina giggled at their daring diversion.

The buzz of voices in the courtyard became suddenly louder, with shouts and squeals of excitement. Sabina and Zuester drew their attention to the commotion. Hadrian was home, seemingly uninjured, and Plotina and Matidia were greeting him with hugs and kisses.

Sabina met her husband's eyes. His knowing smile betrayed that he had witnessed some of her interaction with her freedman. He appeared pleased.

Hadrian shook his head as his wife made a move to get up to greet him. As he strolled in her direction, Zuester abruptly stood from his position next to Sabina on the couch, his eyes cast to the pavement. The Dacian was clearly mortified. Of course it was one thing to conduct harmless flirting amongst a woman's friends. It was quite another for the woman's husband to have witnessed the activity.

Hadrian approached and lowered his head. "Greetings, Zuester. I see you have been quite successful in restoring my wife's heath since I have been away. I heartily thank you."

"Thank you, sir," was all Zuester could manage.

"And," Hadrian continued. "I wish to speak with you briefly, alone."

Zuester looked up with alarm. "Sir?"

"Nothing you've done, my boy," Hadrian said softly, patting his shoulder. "Politics is all. Wait for me in the peristyle."

"Yes, sir," said the freedman before he left.

Hadrian sat on his wife's couch and gazed at her admiringly. Her lovely face was a welcome sight after battle upon failing battle. The women folk did not know yet, but Trajan's conquests, one by one, had revolted. The eastern portion of the empire was disintegrating.

He flicked a finger under her peach-colored silk stola, peeking at the pale flesh under the fabric. "Your dress is cut a bit lower, I see." He raised a querying eyebrow. "Is that the fashion, or are you trying to attract someone in particular?"

He continued to tickle and tease her half-covered breast. Indulging in his attentions, Sabina stretched against the cushion affording him the opportunity to slip his hand in further.

"Have you slept with him yet?" he asked.

Sabina's eyes widened. "No! Of course not," she said with a touch of indignation.

"I am sorry to hear that. You two seem so happy together." The tip of his finger had reached her hardened nipple. With two fingers, he pinched it.

Sabina gasped in surprise then tilted her head and tried to figure out the man before her. "You're not jealous in the least, are you?"

"I come home and see my wife happier than she's ever been? No, love, I am not jealous."

She reached up and stroked his beard. "There's much more gray. It was harrowing, wasn't it?"

"Not as traumatic as what happened to you before I left." Hadrian removed his playful hand from her dress.

Tears began to well in Sabina's eyes from the memory of the last time they saw each other. "I said such horrible things to you, love. Please forgive me."

Hadrian took her hand from his cheek and kissed it. "Of course, I forgive you. You endured a tragedy. We both did."

"I'm so happy you're returned to me safe and whole," she said, now crying softly.

Hadrian wiped her tears with his thumb. "And I am staying. I've been made governor of Syria. We will live here in Antioch."

"Governor!"

"It is a great honor. Syria is the edge of the empire, it seems." He gazed at her again. "Vibia, may I come to your bed tonight?" he asked gently.

"I don't think I'm allowed to refuse the governor of Syria, am I?" she said with a teasing glint in her eye.

"I could have you flogged if you refused me, yes," he countered playfully. His face softened with concern. "Darling, I miss you. I would very much like to be with you tonight. How is your health?"

"Oh," she said realizing what he meant. "Please come, Graeculus. I would very much like to be with you too."

Zuester stood in the peristyle outside Plotina's garden courtyard waiting for Hadrian. The general did not seem to be jealous at all of the Dacian's attentions toward his wife. That was confusing. A Roman man practically owned his spouse much like he owned his slaves. And then there were morality laws governing behavior within a marriage…well, for women at least. If she were accused of adultery, she could be banished and Zuester could be killed. But even if the lady Sabina convinced her powerful husband that indeed no transgression had taken place, surely a high-ranking Roman man would feel cuckolded by his wife's flirtations with a former slave and bring charges against him?

Hadrian approached looking satisfied. Zuester felt even more nervous.

"Ah, Zuester. Let us take a walk." Hadrian draped his arm around the freedman's shoulders, the latter suddenly feeling scrawny and weak next to the general's brawny, masculine frame.

"Thank you, sir."

The two walked along the peristyle, then through an open *ala* to a passageway which turned and led to the service area. Hadrian nodded to surprised servants as they passed the kitchens and storerooms, walking toward the rear courtyard with stables. Along the way, Hadrian made small talk with Zuester. Despite the pleasantries, the Dacian remained nervous.

"How have the women been faring while we've been fighting the war?"

"Well. Mistress Plotina seemed sad at times, but Mistress Matidia always seemed to cheer her up."

"Very good, very good." When they reached the stables Hadrian stopped and turned to Zuester in the courtyard. Around them stable hands and slaves were busy gathering and moving horse tack and animals. "Zuester," he said, "the war went as planned and not as planned, that's how these things go usually. One of the unforeseen incidents is the renewed outbreak of war in Dacia."

Zuester paled.

"The emperor has sent the governor of Syria, Julius Quadratus Bassus, to the Dacian front, to be governor there. I have been appointed governor of Syria in his stead."

Zuester had nothing to say to this. He was suddenly overwhelmed with concern for his family and friends. It had been more than ten years since he had been home, but he would never forget his loved ones.

"Bassus will be leaving shortly," continued Hadrian. "Hence all the bustle and packing," he waved his hand at the activity in the yard. "Now is the time to gather up your belongings and leave with Bassus if you feel that is best."

"Go home to Dacia?"

"Yes." Hadrian drew in a deep breath. "But, your proficiency in languages, especially languages spoken in the east, makes you extremely valuable to me here in Syria. I would like to offer you a position on my personal administrative staff, rather than the women's household staff. You would work under my secretary Heliodorus."

Zuester stood before his master, baffled. "But why are you giving me a choice? I'm only a freedman."

"Because you are trustworthy and loyal to our family. You have shown that repeatedly. I would like to honor and acknowledge that trust."

"What would Bassus have me do?"

"He cannot offer you a position, I've discussed this with him. He can only offer transport plus bed and board along the way. It would be up to you to make yourself useful to him and his staff. It is, at best, an uncertain future, but as you are a good and intelligent young man, you would make your way, I am sure of that."

Zuester shifted on his feet. An uncertain future heading into a war zone but a chance to see his family once again, versus an assured position on the staff of a Roman governor in a province not yet at war, but on the boundary of war. He had worked hard to get where he was at the moment. He knew his mother would be proud of him. What would she say when she saw him back home? That he had given up his ambition in favor of an unknown adventure? He was almost twenty-nine. He was getting too old for adventure.

"If you need more time, son, I understand," said Hadrian. "But Bassus will be leaving in a day or two."

"No. I've made up my mind," Zuester said quickly. He looked Hadrian square in the eye. "I would like to stay in Syria and be part of your administrative staff, sir."

Hadrian grinned. "Good, good. Well chosen, my boy," he said and patted Zuester on the back. He once again put his arm around his shoulders and led the freedman out of the yard. When they were a little removed from the hustle and bustle, Hadrian bent his head down and said in the young man's ear, "My wife Sabina will be very pleased you have decided to stay with us. It appears she likes you. Quite a bit."

Governor of Syria, mused Sabina as she lay on her bed waiting for her husband. She liked Antioch, except for the earthquakes, and she liked the palace. She most definitely liked the silks and jewels of the Orient. But, she was worried about where her mother might go – would she stay with her in Antioch? or return to Rome? or somewhere else even? She was also worried about the added intrigue being the wife of the governor of Syria might bring. They clearly had more enemies here than when they were installed at Pannonia.

The door to her room opened and the curtains pulled aside. As her husband, Hadrian did not need to knock, and as the guards posted at her doorway certainly recognized the general, they did not need to announce him.

He strode resolutely across the patterned mosaic floor. She ran to him, meeting him half-way. He took her in his arms and held her close before giving her a devastatingly needy kiss.

"The gods, I've missed you," he breathed when he broke away.

"I've missed you too, love," she responded.

Hadrian laughed. "Ah, but you've had your distractions. You've only missed the physical. You have someone else who is quite willing to provide you with all the attention you need."

"Pshaw, husband. I've missed our conversations." She stroked his shoulders, feeling the taut muscles under his tunic. He felt thicker, beefier than she remembered.

"Zuester is almost as intelligent as I but far more pleasing to look at." His large hands spanned her back. "I dare say if you had gotten the nerve up to take him to your bed, I would not be standing here right now."

"Don't be foolish," she chided. "He'll have to share me with you as I share you with your boys." She cocked her head and smirked.

"You are a good wife," he said and kissed her again, this time on the forehead. "Vibia, now with my new appointment, I do not wish it to be obvious I am visiting you in your bedchamber." He put his arm around her shoulders and led her to the bed. "I do not wish for any enemy to regard you as a target. I think it best outwardly that we appear to be cool to each other."

Sabina was perplexed. "You do not want to come to my bed anymore?"

"I do not want others to know I go to your bed, love." He sat on the mattress and patted the space next to him for her to sit. "Remember your outburst before I left?"

Sabina flushed. "Graeculus, please, don't bring that up."

"Listen. We can use that to our advantage. There have always been rumors that we do not truly get along; now I see that perception of us can be a benefit. If the staff, servants, visitors, anyone in the outside world sees we are formal to each other, believes us to be no longer intimate, and thinks we even perhaps dislike each other, there will be no reason to use harm against one of us as a means of coercing the other. Such a plan will be seen as ineffective and won't be considered as an option."

"You've thought about this," she concluded quietly.

"I've had a lot of time to think about this, Vibia." He stroked her hair. "Someone hurt you to get at me. I don't know who, but that makes you vulnerable. You are my weakness, my Achilles' heel."

"All right, I can try." She moved her hand along his thigh, pushing the fabric up to reveal the tanned muscular flesh. "It will be very difficult to hide the joy I feel when I see you. I would be afraid that eventually I would simply come to believe that you no longer love me."

He pulled her close. "That will never be true. And when we are in private, we can say and do whatever we feel."

Sabina sank into his arms, feeling his strength and warmth.

"That is why you should publicly take a lover."

She pulled back. "Graeculus? You can't be serious!"

"I've never been more serious. You know how the gossip spreads about me and my taste for boys. Once you take a lover, news of that will also spread."

"Of course you have someone in mind," she said.

"Of course," he grinned. "And I'm sure he will be easily seduced. It's obvious Zuester likes you."

Sabina threw herself backwards on the bed. "I can't seduce him! I mean, I want to be with him and I think I've done my best to make him know that. But I don't know how to seduce anyone. I've only ever been seduced."

Hadrian lay down beside her. "Shall I teach you how to seduce a man?" He trailed his finger between her breasts.

She giggled. "Yes, please."

He unclasped the pin securing her dress on her right shoulder. "First, as a man, your lover must feel he is in command of the situation. He needs to believe he is doing the seducing, despite the fact that it is actually you." He unfastened the pin on the other shoulder.

"That sounds like I should then wait for him to act." Sabina melted against the mattress as her husband slowly pulled her dress down from her shoulders.

"No, just that when you move forward to act, he does not realize that it is you directing the scene." Hadrian lay his palm on his wife's uncovered breast, kneading it gently. "It is not the place of woman to tell a man what to do. Even a man of low birth like Zuester will need to feel he is in control when he is being taken to the bed of the governor's wife."

Sabina squirmed with delight at her husband's touch. "All right. So he's in control. I think I need more specific information than that. I still don't know *how* exactly."

"Yes, my love, you do. You simply have not realized it." Hadrian languidly pulled up her skirt, bunching the sheer silk in his hulking hand. "I witnessed a very provocative scene earlier today. Whatever you were doing or saying to him was working quite well. If you had been alone with him he would have kissed you."

"I'm never alone with him," she lamented, lifting her hips to enable her husband's undressing her. "I think Matidia and Plotina do not want me to be alone with him. When would I ever get a chance to let him kiss me, then?"

"That is when we rely on the gods: *Kairos*, or as you know in Latin, *Occasio*, the god of opportunity. You must be aware of the most opportune moment to act." Hadrian smoothed his hands reverently over his wife's bare belly. "I think you know this already, however, you might not be aware of it."

"How do you mean?"

"When you play with him, you sometimes watch the others for a chance to be even more naughty when they are not looking, correct?"

Sabina blushed and looked at her husband in utter astonishment. "How did you know that?"

He chuckled. "Don't worry, Vibia, no one has seen you. We all do that, love. We are human." He drew circles with his fingertips down her thighs.

"Oh." She looked at him curiously. "But shouldn't he be the one watching for opportunity if he's supposed to be in control?"

"No. You watch for opportunity then do something to make him act."

"Such as?"

"Touch him casually while giving him the most innocent look with those beautiful hazel eyes of yours. Or, smile, bite your lip, and then look away as if you are too shy to ask for what you want."

"How is it that you know such particular behaviors of women, husband?"

Hadrian grinned and rolled on top of her. "Because I have been the object of such attacks, my love. Given my preference for youths, the art as practiced by women is obvious to me. Sometimes the younger boys do the same to attract me." He traced a finger delicately down her cheek.

"But the older ones don't smile and bite their lips when they want you?"

He laughed. "No, that is definitely women's way."

Sabina met her husband's gaze and briefly drew her bottom lip under her teeth, moistening it with her tongue. She closed her eyes and leaned into Hadrian's gentle touch on her face.

"Excellent, Vibia! That is precisely what you should do."

She smiled in triumph. He bent over and kissed her succulent mouth. But as this was no seduction, both lovers acted with equally unrestrained passion, their tongues twining and dancing in welcome reunion.

Hadrian pushed her legs apart and settled himself between them.

"No one else is to join us tonight, husband?"

A quizzical expression passed across his face.

"I like the German. He's very enthusiastic."

Hadrian laughed.

She tugged playfully at his beard scrutinizing the gray. "I've missed our games, Graeculus," she pouted.

"Vibia," he started soberly. "I think it best that it be just us two this first time."

She knew what he meant. It was uncertain what the poison did to her body. She pecked the tip of his nose. "Thank you."

"Vibia, there's something else." Hadrian felt uneasy asking the next question. "When I climax, should I stay inside you?"

"Of course, love," she purred and nestled against the pillow. "Why do you ask?"

"You had said you never again wanted to carry my monsters in your womb."

"Oh." She placed her hands flat on his chest. "I did say that, didn't I? I'm sorry Graeculus. I didn't mean it."

"No, but perhaps it is the best course of action."

"It is the duty of every Roman wife to be a mother," she reminded him.

"Yes, as Romans, we are told. However, *we* are not just simple Romans." He sat back on his knees. "Vibia, love," he lowered his voice as if they were being overheard. "If I am to be emperor, it would seem the traditional course of action would be to adopt my heir."

"Oh, I see." Sabina stared blankly at his chest as she absorbed this. "What should we do?"

She raised herself on her elbows. "I don't want to deny you," she said, running her hand under the hem of his tunic and discovering he was not wearing a subligaculum around his loins. She reached for his cock. He was semi-hard.

Hadrian did not stop his wife as she explored him, but merely looked at her expectantly.

"I've heard of things a woman can do to prevent pregnancy," she finally said. "I can ask Zosime for something."

"And tonight?"

She tugged at his now erect prick. "I want you to have your complete pleasure, husband. It is your right. I'll talk to Zosime in the morning."

Hadrian stripped off his tunic, revealing his strong body, brawny muscles flexing with desire under tanned flesh. He slid his fingers along her thigh, and dallied in the wetness between her legs, then stretched himself over her, his prick poised at her entrance.

He pushed in gently, then hesitated. "Vibia, am I hurting you?" he asked with great concern.

His hardness felt huge inside her tight, unused passage, but she welcomed it. "No, love," she said, her voice infused with complacent arousal.

He pushed in further and her muscles hugged his contours encouragingly. He increased his rhythm, measuring her reactions with every move.

Sabina closed her eyes, to lose herself in her own private world of erotic fantasy. She felt her husband but thought of another. She breathed to her lover's beat, exhaling airy sighs. Her hands gripped the arms straddling her body as her nails dug into the masculine flesh.

It felt so good, so right, for him to be inside her, to surround him with her throbbing heat. Her lover pressed his thumb against her clit. She came instantly, clenching him and bucking her hips in greedy acquiescence.

He continued to massage her swollen nub, groaning at every excited contraction as he felt his own rapture coil, then drove into her relentlessly. She flailed beneath his pounding until his weight pressed her against the mattress, his body overpowering hers, slamming toward culmination. Her moans grew to mewling cries, her cries to euphoric wails, her wails to dissolute pleas. He slapped his palm over her mouth to silence her.

"Is your freedman so good that you forget your husband?"

Sabina's eyes flew open as her body climaxed one last time, taking her to the pinnacle of ecstasy and leaving her there as Hadrian pushed against her. He held himself inside as he spent his seed, gazing down at her with wicked pleasure.

He tore his hand from her mouth. Sabina gasped for air, her chest heaving. She held his satisfied gaze with astonished eyes as she caught her breath.

"That was wonderful. I hope he's as good as you."

* * * * *

Zosime smiled in amusement as Sabina perused her selection of herbs and other remedies. There were hundreds of boxes and jars lined up on shelves in the midwife's work room, physics for an untold number of ailments and desires. Certainly something among them could be used to prevent pregnancy? she had inquired.

"Zosime," she said. "I love figs. I love pomegranates. But what do I use when they are out of season?"

The midwife chuckled. "Unfortunately for you, my lady, some fruits are in abundance only certain times of the year. For the rest of the year, we have dried fruit, herbs, and seeds."

Sabina looked at her anxiously. "Such as?"

"Patience, patience, my dear girl," said the older woman. Zosime had been with the imperial household for decades. She knew all about women who wanted to control pregnancy for various reasons, some well-meaning, some merely for vanity's sake. It was not her position to inquire as to why the wife of a powerful Roman man did not want to bear his children.

The midwife knitted her brow as she scanned the shelves. "Do you want to ingest something or use a pessary?"

"A pessary?" inquired Sabina.

"You insert it in your body to prevent the man's seed from entering your womb. I make mine out of wax or gum."

"And does the man feel it?" Sabina inquired shyly. "Will he be reminded when he is inside me?"

"Does it decrease his pleasure, you mean?" the midwife retorted. She chuckled again when she saw Sabina's stunned reaction. "No, my dear, he does not feel it. No matter how large he is." She would have to assume Hadrian was the man in question, and rumor had it that he was very well-endowed indeed.

Sabina blushed. "It should be something he does not have to think about," she admitted.

Zosime shook her head. If only men were aware of what women had to go through to prevent having their unwanted children. Women manipulated their bodies and their natural cycles for men's pleasure all too often.

The midwife walked along the shelves and began to choose from among the covered jars, smelling their contents before putting them aside. "I have preventatives such as salvias, mints, savin, and artemisia that you can mix with water or wine and drink for prevention." She considered other jars. "Some will help regulate the menses. And some herbs you can use as abortifacients."

"I don't know that word either, Zosime," Sabina said bashfully.

The midwife looked at her charge tenderly. "It releases the fetus when it is already secured in your belly," she explained gently. "Like what happened to you a year ago."

Sabina whimpered and shuddered upon remembering the incident. The poor girl had bled for days, lying balled up on her bed rocking herself to relieve the pain. "I don't want to ever have to go through that again, Zosime," she hissed icily. "I want to prevent the child from ever taking root in my belly."

Zosime needed to hear the urgency from Sabina's own lips. "I have a special plant from my native Cyrenaica, the silphium, from which the oil is used for such purposes. Mixed with water you may drink it." The midwife crooked her head and raised an eyebrow. "It is much like your fennel in look and taste, however, it is becoming very rare these days and is very expensive."

Sabina pursed her lips. "Is it effective?"

"Tremendously so," was the answer.

"Then I shall try it. If it does not work, we will try something else."

Zosime smiled in agreement. "Very well, my lady. I will provide you with what you will need. Please let me know when you need more. Or," she smiled at her mistress, "when you need something else."

Rome, The Subura, late August 117

Bestia's spy had already been paid handsomely. He would receive another reward in a few months once his missive had been received in Britannia. He shook his head. Britannia was known as the latrine of the Roman Empire: dank, cold, and unfortunately necessary. Why his master was there, he did not understand, nor did he question. He received plenty of denarii for his information, and was happy to keep supplying it, even if it was sent to a backwater province.

The kidnapped daughter of the Parthian king Osrhoes, Roedogune, had begun her captivity in Rome. She was living in comfort, even having her own Parthian maid, Hyasdana, in attendance. She was young, though, and her receptiveness to any sort of overture was unpredictable. It was best to lay the groundwork with the older maidservant. This Hyasdana watched over her charge like a hawk, so it was futile getting around her anyway to try to approach the princess. Strangely, though, the Romans were not persistent in trying to convert the princess to their race or their cause, insisting that the pair were merely the guests of Rome and not truly prisoners. The captors were even apologetic regarding the misfortune of suffering separation from their family to the point of allowing the audience of native kinsmen! Certainly by this means the young princess's apartment could be infiltrated, her loyalties swayed, and her allegiance to a mutual enemy of Rome attained? Perhaps the easiest method would be to introduce a native slave, familiar with Parthian proclivities. However, the operative recommended his master Bestia should wait a few years to be assured of loyalty from such a young and potentially fickle associate.

The spy licked his lips as he re-inked his pen. By that time the girl would be approaching womanhood. He had never met his master, but had heard rumors of his carnal appetites. The agent smiled as he wrote that Bestia would find it more enjoyable to negotiate with a budding young woman than a mere girl. He wondered privately, however, if the girl would be horrified by his master's reputedly disfigured countenance. He snorted to himself and resumed writing.

One curious thing his master should take note of in addition to the captivity of the princess, was the impoundment of the Parthian throne, the famed *sella regia*. The Romans held it in an undisclosed location, perhaps in Rome herself, perhaps not. While this might seem a trivial matter, the *sella regia* was a powerful symbol of Parthian sovereignty and national identity, so powerful that not one of the three Parthian factions fighting prior to Roman invasion would have dared tampered with it. Each would have accepted defeat from an enemy rather than the destruction of their throne. If this throne were to be located and retrieved it could prove to be profitable, very profitable, to Bestia.

The spy hesitated a moment in his missive. The next piece of information might not sit well with his master, he knew, as it pertained to a relative. Bestia was infamously unfailingly loyal where family was concerned, but he would have to know. There was a new emperor now and he had already started his reign off with some highly criticized deeds. In him, Bestia had a confirmed enemy.

Gaius Calpurnius Crassus Frugi Licinianus, consul under the emperor Domitian, exiled by the emperor Trajan, had been murdered by the new emperor Hadrian. Calpurnius Crassus had attempted to leave Tarentum, his place of exile, and had been killed on the grounds that he was planning a revolt. Of course the allegations were without merit. Still, it was recommended that Bestia lay low for a while, until the memory of the powerful Frugi had dissipated in the minds of the emperor and his court. There was a son, Piso, who had been encouraged by his mother to remain in the background, and so he had. Piso was named for his venerated ancestor Lucius Calpurnius Piso Frugi Licinianus, the adopted - albeit unsuccessful - successor of the emperor Galba who reigned at least two generations ago.

It was still early in the reign of the new emperor, Bestia's spy reminded his master. It was best to wait and watch at this point in time, but to never forget past offences, and instead to remember them, harbor them, and use the resulting anger to launch an attack so unexpected that it would catch the enemy unaware and defeat him.

The agent smiled as he rolled up his missive. A new court with new intrigues meant he would have continued – and very profitable – work in Rome.

Part Two:
Tempus Aestivum

Italy, the road to Rome, mid-June 118

Sabina gave a sidelong glance at her husband. The covered carruca for the ride back to Rome had been made as comfortable as possible for her on the mountainous journey. Hadrian had insisted that they ride together in the carriage, rather than he on his horse and she alone accompanied only by servants. That was not good enough for the new Empress of Rome. It also meant he could keep a protective eye on her.

The war in the east had been Trajan's final undoing. In late July of 117, he had suffered a stroke, and at Plotina's and Matidia's persuasion, left for Rome. The two women had accompanied him on the journey, along with his Guard Prefect Publius Acilius Attianus. They got as far as Selinus on the coast of Cilicia. A letter confirming Hadrian's official adoption as successor to the Roman emperor was received in Antioch on August 9th. Word of Trajan's death reached Hadrian two days later. As was customary, the Roman legions garrisoned at Syria duly proclaimed their general *Imperator*. Hadrian was now emperor of the vast Roman Empire.

Yet, all around them the empire was crumbling. The Moors were revolting in Mauretania; the Jews in Judaea as well as in the North African provinces. There was trouble in Britannia. But the worst was Dacia. The governor Quadratus Bassus had died and had to be quickly replaced by Avidius Nigrinus, once imperial legate in Greece. The Danubian provinces were insufficiently manned; too many regiments having been sent away to fight the Parthian war. Because of this, within hours of his accession, Hadrian abandoned the east, pulling his troops from the imperial provinces of Mesopotamia, Assyria, and Armenia. Trajan's conquests would have to be sacrificed. The new emperor had to protect what was already previously and rightfully Rome's. He left Syria in October of 117, after having installed the former general of the troops in Armenia as the new governor of Syria.

Along the way, from Antioch to Ancyra to Byzantium, Hadrian received both acclamations on his accession as well as war missives from his generals throughout the empire. His main concern was Dacia and the neighboring Moesia Inferior. He knew from experience that the Sarmatian tribes were not enemies to be toyed with. Bassus's replacement, Nigrinus, lacked skills in military tactics and, unable to strategize, only did as ordered. When the imperial party arrived in the middle of winter, Hadrian acted as quickly as he could. The Roxolani – under their easily appeased king – were established as a client state of Rome; the troops pulled from the east were positioned to secure the borders of Dacia and Pannonia. In doing so, of course, the new emperor upset many who had won favors, titles, and positions under Trajan because of his conquests. Amongst the old guard, resentment ran deep for the new emperor.

Nigrinus was one such man. He was to lose his position in Dacia, having been replaced by Quintus Marcius Turbo, a decorated commander and personal friend of Hadrian's. Knowing the new emperor loved to hunt, and also knowing he had received a gift of a swift horse from the subdued Roxolani king, Nigrinus invited Hadrian on an expedition to catch highly-prized Dacian boar. The ambush happened while the emperor was offering sacrificial blessings to the gods for a successful hunt. Hadrian barely escaped, but only due to his ever-vigilant and loyal staff. Nigrinus seemingly disappeared.

The event served to remind Hadrian that enemies were everywhere. Trajan himself had not been immune. His most favorite and trusted servant, the valet Phaedimus, had died three days after his master. But Trajan had been an old man of sixty-four; Phaedimus had been a healthy young man of twenty-eight. Enemies, it seemed, had even lived in the emperor's own house.

When Hadrian arrived in his former protectorate of Pannonia he received horrifying news. Attianus, Trajan's former Guard Prefect who had arrived earlier in Rome, decided to act in the name of the new emperor utterly without Hadrian's knowledge or authorization. Under his influence, the assassination of four consuls – four men who presided over the Senate – had been approved by the Senate itself: Cornelius Palma, once governor of Syria who had been with Trajan in the east; Avidius Nigrinus, Trajan's governor of Dacia who, rumor had spread, attempted to assassinate the new emperor; Publilius Celsus, Trajan's administrator in Latium; and Lusius Quietus, an unpopular Moorish chieftain appointed governor of Judaea by Trajan.

Hadrian had been incensed. All of the four men implicated in crimes against the empire were guilty of something – Nigrinus to be sure – but Hadrian had not been given any chance to personally review evidence or cases, their killings did not have his imprimatur. He had to avoid more questionable murders. From the Danubian province, he dismissed Attianus although ennobled him for his years of service to Trajan. They heard that the old man conveniently slipped away into retirement on one of his estates.

Sabina looked at the familiar Italian landscape passing by them and felt a chill of remembrance. It was certainly a relief to be home. She did not dislike Greece or Syria; on the contrary, she had enjoyed her stays abroad. What she did not like was all the intrigue, all the running about to discover who was betraying whom and why. Sabina sighed. Were the events of the last year just the normal part of a change in leadership, or a presage of their life to come? She decided she could not possibly know what was in store for them back in Rome, but as long as she was by the side of the man she loved and admired, she would endure anything. She glanced over at Hadrian and smiled. He was still handsome despite the gray, and still hers despite their new arrangement. The new emperor and empress, she mused, had intrigue of their own.

Rome, Imperial Palace, mid-July 118

"The proceedings at the Senate reveal that resentment for the whole affair still runs deep," Hadrian said morosely.

The emperor drummed his fingers on his desk, and finding no solace in the act, got up to pace. He had been haunted by the killings of the four consuls, running the episode through his head, trying to figure out what had gone wrong. He stopped and looked around at his staff seemingly not as affected by the incident as he. The imperial secretary Gaius Suetonius Tranquillus casually reviewed correspondence deemed "most urgent". Zuester, having been appointed as an assistant to the secretary, a position he was most honored to hold, was busily registering correspondence in a logbook.

"They must have been quite impressed that you were willing to take the stand yourself, my lord," commented Suetonius to Hadrian. "I dare say your defense was very good."

"I'm still confused as to why Emperor Hadrian had to defend himself when it was the Senate who ordered the murders of the four consuls," blurted Zuester. Suetonius shot him a chastising glance.

Hadrian waved his hand dismissively at his chief secretary. "The Senate, my boy, is mortified and shamed that it acted wrongly," he explained. "They must blame someone in order to save face and keep the public's affection."

"Well," said Suetonius, changing the subject, "Trajan is to be deified and the new coinage explicitly depicts you as his rightful successor."

"Yes, but my adventus was uneventful," Hadrian growled. "Almost no ceremony except that blasted cryptic sacrifice." He began to pace again. "And I've had to give the Roman people *liberalitas* – more money than my predecessor to be sure – just so I can keep in their good graces." Hadrian slammed his fist on his desk. "Damned Attianus! What in Hades could he have possibly been thinking?"

Hadrian watched Zuester glance at his superior. Suetonius, though, was distracting himself with some scrolls.

"You are hailed as a deliverer in Judaea since the dismissal of Lusius Quietus," said the Dacian timidly.

Hadrian raised an eyebrow. "And?"

"Well the Jews put great stock in such matters," Zuester continued nervously. "They have a history of being oppressed. Anyone who frees them from tyranny is regarded as, well not a god as they only have the one, but a hero at least. Quietus was known for his over-zealous repression of Jewish dissent while he was governor of Judaea, as I have read in these documents." Zuester waved at a stack of scrolls.

The young man was rambling. Hadrian smiled at him. "I appreciate your attempt to assuage my anger, Zuester."

"And," the under-secretary added boldly. "The word on the street is that the common men appreciate your willingness to talk to them on their level. They say you act like the Prince of Citizens, rather than the Emperor."

Suetonius flashed a grimace at Zuester. The young man shrunk back.

Hadrian laughed. It was true that when he could, he tried to listen to the people directly, hear in their own words their problems and concerns. He hated putting on airs, hated ceremony. "Well, I would take the plebes of Rome on a big hunt if I could," he said thoughtfully and sat back down. "I hope that when the empire is prosperous again, the people and the Senate will realize that Trajan's practice of expansion was detrimental to Rome."

"I do believe that our citizenry will feel that quite soon, Caesar," Suetonius offered obsequiously. "I have been looking over the accounts since the waiver of the contributions to the imperial fund, and the reduction of the tax on the provinces. Despite initial resistance, it seems that increased commerce because of these actions has swelled our coffers with unintended taxes."

Hadrian nodded to his secretary. "Good, good."

"And your payments of arrears in the tax amnesty plan has had a similar effect," continued Suetonius efficiently. "Your distributions of grain have been much welcome by the poor."

Hadrian exhaled from mental exhaustion. "Well, it seems I begin my tenure with a mixture of both good and bad." He rose. "Thank you, gentlemen. It has been a long day."

"We will take our leave then, sire," said Suetonius as he motioned for Zuester to pack up their papers.

The young man did so as quickly as he could and trailed his superior as he exited the office. From the corner of his eye Hadrian saw Zuester turn around for a last glimpse of the emperor, a touch of melancholy in his expression. Yearning for the bucolic days in Antioch when he merely served the women, perhaps?

In the years since he had joined the imperial household, the Dacian had changed. He was now more mature, less boyish. Yet his intellect had only grown, as had his beard, and he had become more indispensable. His new appointment as part of the emperor's staff kept him away from Sabina. Hadrian realized he would have to rectify that situation when he could. Sabina pined for her freedman, seeing him now only in her fantasies.

Later that night, Hadrian sat on the edge of his wife's bed, his head in his hands. Enemies and their plots were everywhere. Unlike war, victories in politics were complicated, convoluted, and never decisive. And he had just barely begun his reign.

He hated that he had to sneak around to be with his wife. Now alerted to the boundless intrigues that plagued the empire, he felt it best to keep Sabina from harm's way. In secret – everything had to be in secret – he had a separate corridor built from his apartment in the imperial palace to hers, and another such passage built in the Tibur villa. Only he had the keys, so she knew it was he who opened her door. Stuck in Rome for the sweltering summer as the subject of political gossip, immediately he had put the imperial passageway to use. Sabina was the only one who listened to him, who understood him, the only one he could truly trust. And she was always there for him.

Hadrian curled up and slumped on the mattress. Sabina's arms immediately surrounded him. He had never realized that being the emperor of Rome would be this awful.

Rome, Imperial Palace, August 118

Sabina liked having the maidservant brush her hair as she stood naked before the mirror. Flora always seemed intent on her duty and Sabina could be intent on her figure. Sometimes she sensed her girl mocking her, but Sabina knew her teenaged servants would not look as good as she did when they were thirty-two. They would all have had a litter of children by that time would have the plump waistlines and sagging breasts to prove it.

And, she noticed, her hair was still as vibrantly red as when she was first married. Her mother's hair was graying and she had begun dyeing her tresses upon her return to Rome. She would probably do the same once she reached Matidia's age.

Sabina hated this pride she felt for herself. It seemed irrelevant. Hadrian loved her for who she was, not for what she looked like. He simply wanted to be with his best friend Vibia. And as he was never going to fall in love with her, it only mattered that she dress and act like the empress she was. Yet deep in her heart she knew why she cared so much for her appearance. She was still infatuated with Zuester, and, in the chaos of the events leading up to Hadrian's accession, she had never managed to seduce the freedman. There had neither been the time nor the opportunity. Clearly the god Occasio had not been on her side.

The servant finished brushing her hair and waited for new commands. But Sabina did not feel like being dressed that night. She was perfectly capable of doing such tasks herself.

"You may leave, Flora" she ordered.

The maidservant did as requested.

Sabina stood on the cold mosaic floor naked and waiting. For what, she was not sure.

"Zuester," Hadrian started to his assistant. "For the first time, I feel I have accomplished something today."

Zuester cleared papers, scrolls, and tablets from the table in his master's private office. They had worked well into the night, and the pale lamplight made continuing difficult. "Yes, my lord. It has been a trying time for you and for Rome."

"You, however, have not left me."

Zuester looked up in astonishment. "And why should I?"

"Because it is Rome. There is always something better around the corner," answered the emperor.

"My lord Hadrian, I believe I have found what I need right here," said Zuester.

The emperor smiled warmly. "Zuester, you are a man among men. I wish I could do more for you. Sometimes I wish you could be emperor in my stead."

Zuester laughed. "I find it difficult enough to be a member of your secretarial staff, my lord."

"You long for the days when you only had women folk to please?"

Zuester blushed. He often thought about Sabina and their time in Antioch, but his duties had taken him completely out of her realm. "To be truthful, my lord, the women were enchanting and I truly enjoyed spending time with them."

"One in particular, I imagine."

The freedman looked away. He could not meet his master's eyes. "Your wife is a gift from the gods," he said boldly. "She treated me with respect and equanimity."

Hadrian chuckled. "She is a good woman, yes. I rely on her for advice."

Zuester's bag was packed. He was about to leave and made for the front door.

"Why don't you go the back way?" Hadrian offered and pointed to a curtain.

"I don't know what you mean, sir," Zuester said ingenuously.

Hadrian fumbled in a box on his desk and pulled out a key. He presented it to the servant. "The back way. It's a short cut to the servants' quarters. Just take the first door on your left. No one else knows about it but my valet."

Zuester took the proffered key. "Thank you, sir."

Hadrian grasped his assistant's hand when he took the key. "Zuester," he said quietly. "My wife enjoys oral pleasures, yet I find it distasteful to satisfy her in that way."

Zuester felt a chill travel up his spine. All emperors were eccentric, he had heard plenty of stories. But this intimation was beyond eccentricity. "Thank you," was all he said as he slipped his hand away. He parted the curtain, opened the door, and left.

Then wondered why the emperor had smiled in satisfaction.

The sound of the key in her door startled Sabina from her standing daydream. "I did not expect you this evening, Graeculus," she said before turning around. The instant she saw him, she grabbed the first article of clothing she could reach and pressed it against her naked body.

Zuester stood stunned near the doorway, staring, unmoving.

Sabina clung desperately to what she now realized was merely a sheer silk stola, apprehending at the same time that before she had turned around, the Dacian must have caught a glimpse of her naked backside.

"My lady, many apologies," Zuester said with a bow of his head. "I was told this door would lead to the servants' area." He kept his eyes cast to the ground and gripped the satchel in his hand more tightly.

Sabina was speechless. Having Zuester in her bedchamber was precisely what she had dreamt about for years, yet this was not how she imagined it. The gods – and her husband – were having fun with her. *Damned Occasio!*

"I should go," he said without moving.

She had to act. "No, Zuester. Wait." She crossed the cool marble floor in her bare feet, her heart pounding in her head. *Hounds of Hell!* What should she say to him?

She stood before him, trying to steady her agitated breath. They used to play so easily together, now they seemed like strangers, scarcely looking at each other. Yet, she consoled herself, this was the first time they had ever been truly alone, with not even servants present.

"Who told you about the door?" she asked gently. "Who gave you the key?"

Zuester was clearly trying not to look at her barely clad body. "The emperor," he answered with a slight tremble, his nostrils flaring as if catching the scent of her perfume.

Sabina smiled. She would chastise or thank Hadrian later. "My husband, it seems, is playing a game with the two of us. He had this corridor built expressly for our own private communication. There are only two keys: mine and his. I don't suppose he told you any of that."

Zuester looked up. "No, he said—" he stopped suddenly and flushed bright crimson, casting his gaze once again to the mosaic floor.

Intrigued, Sabina examined the freedman, waiting a moment for him to continue. When he remained silent, she knitted her brow and sucked in her lower lip. "What did he say?" she queried softly.

Zuester's body tensed as his breathing grew more labored and the furrows on his forehead deepened. His eyes, however, traveled slowly across her body, scanning her up and down, scrutinizing her. She blushed, suddenly highly aware of her nudity and her vain attempt at concealing it. Burning with self-conscious insecurity, she tried to cover herself more fully with the silk garment.

"No." Zuester reached out and touched the hand clutching the futile fabric. In one swift movement, he pulled the silk out of her grasp and dropped it on the floor along with his heavy leather sack.

Sabina gasped, her body froze despite the pounding of her heart.

Zuester stroked her cheek, staring at her with hungry eyes. He threaded his fingers through the hair at her temple. "You are so beautiful, like Venus. My Venus." His hand cupped the back of her head as he held her steady before he bent down and kissed her astonished mouth.

Sabina let the shiver of shocked surprise course through her stunned body. For an instant, all pleasure, all feeling, centered on her lips, her tongue, as she clung to Zuester, reveling in the long-desired union. Slowly she gained awareness of his sensual exploration of her naked flesh, his hands roaming freely over her, stroking and kneading. She, too, wanted more, and reached under his tunic, around the neckline, pulling up the hem, anything to satisfy her need to feel his bare skin and thick muscles under her fingertips.

When they finally parted, panting, they stood stupefied, hugging each other, their heads pressed together, still uncertain how to proceed.

"My lady," he said timidly. "I would like to share your bed tonight."

Sabina's eyes welled with tears of joy and relief. "Oh, Zuester!" she cried and flung her arms around his neck.

Zuester pulled back. "You're crying. Why are you crying?" he asked with concern.

"I'm so happy! You don't know how happy you've made me!" she wiped the tears from her cheeks.

"Shh, shh," he calmed. His hands massaged her shoulders.

"I've wanted you for so long," she said though sniffles. "I just…with all that has happened recently, I was afraid I had lost you."

He pulled her close. "I'm right here, my lady. And I'm not going anywhere."

"'Vibia'," she corrected. "Please call me 'Vibia'."

His smile was uncontrollable. "With pleasure, Vibia." He took her hand and led her to the bed. He shed his outer tunic, then began to unfasten his belt, but she stopped his hand.

"No, let me," she said. "I want to serve you."

With nervous fingers she unbuckled the leather belt and dropped it to the floor. She lifted his under-tunic as far as she could, then forced his head down with her hand to pull it off him. He laughed at her lack of artful delicacy in the matter.

She shrugged and giggled. "I've actually never undressed anyone before." She traced her fingers over his finely sculpted pectorals, down his abdomen, and licked her lips.

"I can tell," he teased.

She blushed, then knelt before him. One by one she untied his sandals and slipped them off his feet. He towered above her wearing only his subligaculum. She reached down the front and pulled out the end of the fine fabric, then slowly unwound the cloth from his hips. She heard him draw in a sharp breath of anticipation.

The garment unbound, she bunched it up and placed it under her knees on the cold floor.

She remained kneeling before him, running her hands up the backs of his strong thighs, feeling his muscles twitch and tense at her touch. His erect cock bobbed excitedly in front of her face, the prepuce already cowled back in hopeful expectation. She looked up at him with a wicked smile before turning her attention to the locus of his pleasure, gliding her tongue over the smooth heated flesh of the glans, then inch by inch drawing his prick into her mouth.

"Oh, gods," Zuester groaned, his head falling back in supplication to heaven.

She tasted him slowly and deliberately, wetting his shaft with her tongue, pulling the foreskin over the head with her lips, teasing the underside of his sensitive tip.

"Gods of Olympus!"

Having learned how to please a man from an expert in the art, she did not need to use her hands. Instead, she stroked his butt cheeks, his thighs, his hips, his balls.

"Aaahh!" Zuester cried out.

Sabina took him entirely into her mouth to let the back of her throat pulsate around his tip, her fingers gently but firmly massaging his sac. Unwittingly he began to move against her, thrusting in and out, tightly gripping her hair. He muttered expletives, losing himself in pleasure.

"Vibia," he pleaded, desperation infusing his voice.

She continued her wanton ministrations with vigor.

"Darling, please, I can't let you—*Oh Hades!*"

She grasped his butt to hold him steady as he pumped his semen in her mouth. She swallowed every drop and continued sucking while he jerked and flinched against her.

She sat back on the floor, beaming up at him in victory. "Love? Did you have something to say?" she asked innocently.

* * * * *

Zuester looked down at her, amazed that the Empress of Rome had just fellated him. And rather expertly, he had to admit.

There was only one thing for him to do: return the favor, but perhaps with a little game of his own.

"You are a witch!" he berated, feigning chastisement. He grabbed her under her arms, picked her up, and threw her on the bed. With mock anger, he menacingly crawled up the mattress until he hovered over her and grimaced.

She giggled.

He collapsed in defeat and nuzzled against her. "Vibia, Vibia. What am I to do with you?" He looked deep into her eyes. "I'm utterly spent. I can't think of anything I can do for you."

She giggled again. "I can."

"No, love. I'm sorry, I just cannot. Not tonight. I think I should just go to sleep." He stroked her hair and kissed her cheek before he closed his eyes and slumped his body on top of hers.

"Zuester!" she pouted and tried to shove him off.

At first, he pretended to be unmoved by her jostling, until she relinquished with an exasperated sigh. Suddenly, he grabbed her breasts, eliciting the hoped-for squeal of surprised delight. Within moments his mouth was resolutely sucking on an erect nipple.

Sabina moaned and settled into the mattress. "Oh, yes, please…"

Zuester moved to attend to the other nipple, his fingers still poised on the one just satisfied. His mouth covered her, his tongue flicked against the delicate nub.

"Bite me," she said provocatively.

Zuester's eyes flew open at the command. He chuckled against her then bit down gently on the sensitive flesh while his tongue teased the now-engorged peak.

"Yes, oh yes, my love," she hummed encouragingly. Sabina writhed beneath him, stroking and pulling his brown curls.

He sucked harder, squeezing the excited flesh with his lips, tormenting the peak with the tip of his tongue. Sabina undulated wildly, exclaiming her admiration in short choppy breaths growing louder and faster. To Zuester's utter amazement, she cried out in climax.

Urgently wanting to please her more, he slid down her body, licking and nipping the ivory skin of her belly, until he reached her mons. Her hairless mons. In his experience, barbarian women did not do such things, but the Roman and Syrian servants certainly did. And now he knew the Empress of Rome herself did as well. It was a lovely sight to behold.

He parted her pouty outer lips with his thumbs revealing the fleshy pink folds within. From the sound and the glistening in the dim lamplight he knew she was sticky and wet. He pushed her knees up and open and settled between her thighs. He wanted to devour the treat before him, but wanted to sustain her pleasure as long as he could.

He drew his tongue from the entrance of her passage to her clit, savoring every taste of dew, then sucked in her fleshy inner lips massaging them as his tongue pierced her yearning channel.

Sabina cried out and gently rocked against him, her fingers tugging distractedly at his hair. If this was something her husband never did for her, then he was going to give her a memorable experience.

With the thumb and fingers of one hand he exposed her excited, pulsating clit. He flicked his tongue against her at a deliberately and maddening slow pace. She squirmed and pushed her hips up demanding more.

"Zuester, please," she pleaded.

With his other hand he played in the sticky moisture, delving his fingers slowly into her heated channel. Gradually he picked up the pace, his tongue flicking frenziedly as two thick fingers plunged rhythmically in and out, feeling her muscles quiver and clench around him. She moaned encouragements as he stroked her moist walls to find her pleasure spot. Upon discovery, Sabina tensed, emitting staccato mewling cries in cadence to his touch. As her body absorbed the sensations, her muscles stretched and contracted to the same tempo of his ministrations.

All at once Zuester increased the palpitating pressure inside her while furiously licking her. Sabina cried out to the gods and thrashed against the pillow. Her hips slammed against him frantically, until with one last lift she pressed up, willing him to plunge and suck harder, while she screamed in joyous ecstasy.

Under the bed covers, Sabina curled up in her lover's arms, feeling every inch of her satiated skin touching his. He was warmth and comfort and safety. As she nestled even closer, Zuester nuzzled his nose in her hair and kissed her lovingly.

His attentions to her had been the most amazing sensations she had ever experienced. While Hadrian's German was always willing to pleasure her with his tongue, it was, like the man himself, barbaric and raw. Zuester, however, had skills and knowledge beyond her imagination, eliciting feelings and emotions beyond her comprehension. How he had learned such things she did not care; it only mattered that he desired to do them to her now.

"Zuester," she asked quietly. "Will you be my lover?"

He chuckled. "Yes, my lady. Although it appears I already am."

She smoothed along the muscles of his arm until she found his hand. Their fingers laced together instinctively, naturally. "Yes," she murmured. "And you are very good at it too."

* * * * *

The next morning was the deification ceremony for the Emperor Trajan. The formal commemoration could finally be carried out now that the new emperor had returned to Rome. It was a solemn and stately affair, but deviated from the traditional ritual somewhat. Trajan's remains were to be placed at the base of his column erected in his forum until a temple honoring the god-emperor could be built.

The palace throne room was bustling with senators, dignitaries, and their secretaries awaiting the royal party. A herald called all to order and silence fell – amazingly to be sure considering the amount of bodies present – in the marbled hall. The Augustae, Matidia and Plotina, were led in. If some of the junior senators had never seen the women in person, then it was made quite clear to them that these were eminent women. Dripping with gold, gems, and silks, the elegant royals floated on the mosaic floor and were led up to the dais where they sat on their finely-carved ebony chairs.

Outside the throne room in an antechamber, the emperor Hadrian paced restlessly waiting for his turn. He hated these sorts of things, the plodding ceremony, the ostentatious costumes, the dispassionate memorized proceedings. He was acutely aware that his subjects demanded such rituals, but would almost rather just begin a set of new, casual customs.

"Sire?" came a voice behind him.

Hadrian turned around, now awakened from his introspection. "Yes?" he said to the immaculately dressed servant.

"The empress, Caesar." The servant bowed and indicated with his out-stretched hand.

Sabina entered the antechamber. Of all the imperial women, she was dressed the most spectacularly. The flounce of her rose stola was fringed with garnet beads, and set off her honey-colored tunic. She was wrapped with a palla dyed purple and embroidered with gold to match the emperor's *toga picta*. Her jewel-encrusted gold diadem looked exquisite set atop her elaborately coifed flaming-red hair. With matching earrings and necklaces it seemed as if gold framed her entire face. Her very radiant face. Hadrian could tell his wife was extraordinarily happy, presumably because of his under-secretary's visit the previous night.

"Sabina," Hadrian said, greeting his wife formally. He took her hand and kissed her ring.

"My lord," she responded, barely containing her happiness yet knowing she had to hold her personal feelings in check on such a solemn occasion.

Upon seeing her struggle with her emotions, Hadrian let a smirk play briefly upon his lips. He held out his arm, and, as was customary, she placed her hand on his forearm. They stood in the doorway of the antechamber waiting for their cue to approach the dais.

Hadrian smiled. "How old are you, son?"

"I am thirty, sire."

"My wife is thirty-two. By your age, most people have established a reputation one way or another. Besides being publicly honored for her piety and modesty, hers is that she is married to a much older man who dallies with boys and runs around fighting wars. She has never acted shockingly; she has been beyond reproach her whole life. Now at her age, if she takes a lover, it will be seen as the normal course of a loveless marriage with an inattentive husband."

Zuester stared off blankly into space, his mind clearly elsewhere, the corners of his lips twitching to suppress a smile.

"And, I should add, it will be even beneficial to her reputation if the affair lasts a long time." Hadrian studied his secretary. "You're in love with her, aren't you, son?"

"I think so," he said hoarsely.

"Go to her tonight. Tell her so, or at least show her so. But don't take the back corridor. You should visit her bedchamber tonight, and every night hereafter, via the front door."

Sabina heard the knock on her bedroom door while she knelt in prayer at the lararium. Whoever it was did not know of her nightly routine, but she trusted her maid would keep the visitor at bay. She gave her final bid for protection and bowed before the altar. Drawing in a contented breath, she stood and turned to see who needed to have an audience with her so late at night.

She gasped when she saw Zuester.

She flushed, feeling the heat rise in her cheeks, her heart pound in her chest. He remained standing near the entryway, shifting on his feet, looking a bit uncomfortable. The maid kept her head lowered waiting for a command. She had seen the pair the morning after their first night together and knew they had been intimate. Hadrian was the only other person. He must have counseled his secretary to make the affair public.

The thought sent delight and horror to descend upon Sabina all at once. She wanted nothing more than to be with the handsome Dacian, but realized that the affair was no longer simply an expression of their desire for each other. It was a political maneuver to show the world that Hadrian and his wife cared not for each other, enough so that she would carelessly flaunt her paramour in public.

"You may go, Flora," she said to her maid.

The servant curtsied and left.

Sabina pursed her lips and looked at her lover as tears began to well in her eyes.

Zuester was before her immediately, striding across the marble floor in quick, long steps. "Vibia, Vibia," he soothed as he wrapped his arms around her.

"You don't have to be here," she sobbed.

"I want to be here."

"You're here because of my husband."

Zuester pulled back. "I used the front door because of your husband," he countered.

She sniffled. He was right.

Zuester offered her an edge of his woolen mantle, and when she nodded in acquiescence, he dabbed her eyes and cheeks then wiped her nose.

Sabina giggled.

"That's my Vibia." He draped an arm around her shoulder. "Come, at least let us hold each other," he said as he led her to the bed.

After taking off his shoes and wrap, Zuester relaxed against the pillows and stretched out his hands beckoning Sabina to join him.

She nestled in the crook of his arm, feeling his warmth, his strength, and sensing her body becoming aroused by his closeness.

"It's been difficult to get a chance to see you, much less be with you," he explained softly. "I understand the implication of having to go through the guards in your apartment, and really I don't mind." He kissed her hair. "I would rather have the freedom to be with you when I want, rather than having to suss out opportunities when no one is around."

"I suppose you can't bother Graeculus for the key every time you want to make love to me," she sighed.

"No," he agreed and pulled her close. "And I think I want to make love to you quite often, every day if I can."

Sabina looked up at him and smiled. "Every day?"

"Hmmm," he nodded and kissed her nose.

She gazed in his eyes before touching her lips to his. Their mouths met in a succulent and tender kiss, their tongues greeting slowly, sensually.

"I've missed you," she said.

"Not as much as I've missed you." He took her hand and placed it on his crotch. Beneath the layers of wool and linen, she could feel he was hard.

She bit her lower lip in anticipation, then laid back on the pillows invitingly. He followed, stretching along her side. They kissed, softly, tentatively, Sabina sensing a mutual nervousness, as if they were newly-wed virgins.

Zuester leaned on an elbow and traced a finger down her neck to her chest. "Vibia, love, I want you to be truly mine. I mean, I'm highly aware of your position, that you are the wife of the Emperor of Rome," he said haltingly. "I want you completely, but I'm concerned that..." he picked at the neckline of her nightdress, "I know that we have to act in such a way as to prevent you becoming with child." He stroked her cheek. "I know one way—"

Sabina pressed a finger to his lips. "It's taken care of," she said.

He knitted his brow. "How do you mean?"

"I mean Zosime has provided me with herbs to prevent such a thing from happening."

"Zosime knows about us too?" he blurted.

Sabina laughed softly. "Well, actually no, she doesn't. But she will soon enough. As will everybody else."

Zuester pulled her to him and kissed her again while his hand sought the sash to her robe. He untied it and loosened the garment, baring her shoulders. "Vibia," he said between pecks at her ivory skin. "You deserve a lover who can give you every pleasure your heart demands."

Sabina hummed her agreement, relishing his touch.

Zuester bunched up her skirt and reached underneath. "Unfortunately, I don't think I can be that lover tonight." His fingers traveled up her thigh and found her hips bare of underclothing. He smiled in surprise. "I confess, love, I am at bursting since being without you these last several months." He separated her legs so his fingers could continue their wanderings in the dark recesses of her femininity.

Sabina moaned and rocked her heated wetness against his hand. "I'm bursting too," she confided. She stretched her neck to whisper in his ear. "Fuck me."

In an instant, Zuester stood on the mattress and tore off his tunic and subligaculum, discarding both garments unceremoniously in a heap on the tiled floor. He knelt between Sabina's legs, his ready cock protruding demandingly, and when he lowered himself over her, his heated rod found its aim precisely.

Sabina held his gaze as he pressed in, slowly at first, making sure of her, then, in one thrust, seated himself fully inside her swollen channel. His thickness warmed her entire body as a wave of sated desire enlivened her senses. He gave her only a moment to indulge before he drove into her with purpose. She responded with a loyalty to her own passion, digging her nails into his butt cheeks as their hips crashed together in unison, each demanding gratification from the other, each intent on reaching their peak regardless of what their partner might achieve.

Sabina came first, the intensity of her wail matching the forcefulness of her contraction. She clamped around him, almost succeeding in preventing him from pulling out to continue his rhythmic stroke. But nothing would stop Zuester from taking his satisfaction from the woman beneath him, and he pounded into her relentlessly. She continued to tighten in short pulses, melting into ecstatic dissolution, encouraging him, knowing that his culmination would mean the branding of her as his own, his possession of her body and soul.

With one final thrust he plunged into her, then held steady as he emptied himself with a clipped sigh. Sabina clenched, swallowing his seed willingly, looking up at her new master with loving desire.

Zuester slumped in exhaustion on top of her, then slid off to the side, his arm still clutching her tightly. "You're mine," he said in a dark whisper. "You're mine now."

Sabina closed her eyes. She had wanted to be his for years. "Yes, Zuester. I am yours and only yours."

Rome, Imperial Palace, May 119

Hadrian loved having dinner with friends. Good food, good wine, and good company were some of the delights of being a sought-after guest. He also felt the need to distance himself from his wife, who greatly enjoyed spending long weekends with her lover at the emperor's extensive villa in the Tiburtine hills, still under construction, but usable enough. The more husband and wife were seen apart, the better. She was thoroughly captivated by the Dacian anyway, and he by her, and they needed the time together in their honeymoon period.

The emperor also enjoyed private dinners with his family, and greatly enjoyed being the center of attention amongst his female relatives. Plotina, Matidia, as well as Sabina's sister Mindia, and even his own sister Paulina, all found him charming and entertaining. Since Sabina had immersed herself in Zuester, Hadrian and Matidia had re-ignited their once passionate relationship, an affair that had been on hold for fifteen years. When Sabina was away at the villa, Matidia would install herself in her daughter's apartment in the palace, citing the better angle of the sun in the gardens. Really it was to make use of the access to Hadrian's chamber via the secret corridor.

Quiet, private dinners with family were a much welcome respite after a long day at the courts or a day answering legal correspondence from the provinces. Today's business had been attendance at a regular session of the Senate followed by ensuing discussions with a handful of senators until late afternoon. Exhilarating, yes, but exhausting. The evening was pleasant, a soft breeze drifted through the triclinium. Hadrian reclined on the dining couch with his hands behind his head. He closed his eyes and listened to Matidia and Mindia describing a salacious incident involving a gladiator, laughing and tripping over each other's words in their race to tell the story. He smiled. Sometimes he wished he could be a private man and experience such times as these more often.

He must have dozed off a bit, he realized, when he felt Plotina prodding him with her foot.

"Graeculus!" came the dowager's voice

"Hmmm?" he said, propping himself up.

"You work yourself too much, my son."

"Or he's drunk too much wine," said Matidia.

"Don't worry, Salonia," he said to his mother-in-law. "I'm still quite sober and can perform any task if called upon." He winked at her.

Matidia blushed and distracted herself with a bowl of dried apricots.

"I hear you have some plan to visit the provinces," said Plotina. "What say you to this?"

Hadrian cleared his throat. "Well, now, mother, I think that won't be for some time now. There's plenty to do here in Rome."

"Yes, I know. You have Matidia's brick factories working overtime with your building campaign." The dowager was not harsh, just matter-of-fact.

"I don't think Salonia minds much, do you?" Hadrian insisted on calling his mother-in-law by the more familiar name given their renewed intimacy, which was not unknown amongst the close circle present.

"Not at all, Graeculus," Matidia responded.

"I think the temple to all gods is a wonderful idea," interjected Mindia. "And I've seen the plans. Graeculus is a wonderful architect."

"Yes," Plotina agreed. "The Pantheon will be a marvelous sight to behold if it is constructed as you wish it to be."

Hadrian bowed his head. "Thank you, mother."

"Now, when is it that you plan to go to the provinces? You know I'm too old to travel and I want Matidia near me."

"I don't expect you to go, mother," Hadrian chuckled. "I don't expect either of the eminent Augustae to travel far anymore," he said glancing up at Matidia. "And," he sighed, "like I said, it won't be for some time. I'm working on military reforms that I wish the garrisons to adopt." He picked at a bowl of pitted cherries before plopping one in his mouth. "I'm also worried about Falco's reports from Britannia. There's been some revolts in the northern part of that province that he's had to spend a great deal of energy putting down. We need a new military strategy there as well."

"You'll go all the way to Britannia, then?" said Mindia.

"Yes," Hadrian replied. "I'll visit the western provinces first. Gaul, Germania, Britannia." He took a sip of wine. "But, I feel very strongly that right now Rome needs her emperor, needs an imperial presence. Trajan was absent from the capital for five years. I don't want the Senate thinking Rome can manage without an emperor."

"And since you began your reign with so much antagonism with that esteemed body, they might look for a way to do exactly that," said Plotina. "The senators don't like you, Graeculus."

Hadrian eyed his adoptive mother. Only she was allowed to say such things to him, she who had been the wife of an emperor and knew the workings of politics intimately. "I'm trying to change that mother," he said glumly.

"And what about your own household, son," the dowager continued. "I hear your wife has taken a slave lover. It is about time, given all your perverted affairs."

Hadrian glanced up at Matidia who had paled. He shook his head. Plotina, Hadrian supposed, had also had a bit too much wine. They both knew she had been the one who orchestrated his adoption and succession. Because of that, Hadrian had to allow her great liberties.

"He's a freedman, Augusta. And you know him. It is my under-secretary Zuester."

"Those two haven't had enough of each other yet?" said Plotina with surprise.

Matidia caught Hadrian's eye, and he nodded his head.

"They never made a connection in the past," explained Matidia to the dowager.

Hadrian sighed and rolled onto his back. He had wanted to have his family be privy to his and Sabina's scheme, but he realized he could not. Only Matidia knew the truth. No one else knew, not even Sabina's sister.

"Well it's the least you could do for her after all those palace page boys," remarked the dowager.

Hadrian wondered if Plotina was really scolding him, or if she was merely remembering Trajan's notorious behavior. Besides, Hadrian had recently forgone his taste for page boys to take up with a young – and politically very well-connected – Roman aristocrat, Lucius Ceionius Commodus. The youth's sexual appetites were not only voracious, they were refreshingly adventurous.

"Come along, Plotina," said Mindia, holding out a hand to the intoxicated matron. "Let me escort you to your rooms." She motioned to two slaves to help her get Plotina to stand.

Hadrian watched the women leave, then glanced at Matidia on the opposite couch. "Leave us," he commanded to the servants.

The servants bowed and left, some with empty trays and dishes.

"Come here, Salonia. Sit by me," he said to Matidia.

He moved back a little to give her room. She sat down and drew her fingers through his curls.

"Sabina's happy, Graeculus. And so am I. At least until you leave to subdue your barbarians." Her fingers trailed down to his beard. "Plotina's drunk; don't listen to her. Sometimes I think she misses Trajan. You should involve her in politics more, you know, ask her advice and opinion occasionally."

Hadrian took her hand and kissed it. "Come, lie with me," he said, smoothing the space on the cushion alongside him.

Matidia lay next to him, burrowing against his sheltering arm.

"You are looking well," he said under his breath. "Positively glowing. I trust my secretary performed his services to your satisfaction?"

Sabina choked and suppressed a smile. "I hope he was not too late to his morning offices, my husband."

"His tardiness was made up with fresh energetic enthusiasm for his duties," answered Hadrian.

They exchanged amused conspiratorial glances before they set out with dignified expressions. The multitudes of Roman officials should not know that the emperor and empress shared a private, indelicate joke.

Hadrian led his wife to her throne on the dais.

"I am happy for you both," he said with a twinkle in his eye before she sat down.

Sabina nodded in gracious thanks for her husband's services, then stared straight ahead as if she had not had an exhilarating tryst with her lover the night before.

As for Hadrian, watching his wife relive her amorous experience in her head and try not to show it made for a most diverting time during an otherwise boring morning.

Britannia, Verulamium, September 118

Bestia stood in the atrium of his house and glanced around. He had been in Britannia for almost five years, a length of time that seemed somehow longer in the barbaric province. His lodgings did not match the riches of the extensive villa he had in Rome, but the amenities one could muster in the outlands were surprisingly adequate. Thoroughly Romanized settlers from the capital and the provinces had staked their claim in the far-flung island with atrocious weather. Entrepreneurs and adventurers along with soldiers and conquered natives had made the backwater somewhat civilized and livable.

The merchant missed the money, the exotic goods – spices, silks, jewels – the slaves, especially the women, that could be had when one held sway in the center of the empire. He had established contacts amongst the northern barbarians with connections in the east – the Suiones, the Suebis, the Saxones and their brethren the Frisii among them. They had no allegiance to Rome, but, as every man had, they had allegiance to wealth and power. They were accommodating to a certain extent, but drove a hard bargain at every turn. And everything took longer and cost more money than in the capital. If he were allowed to raise his own army, to be able to use some force, he knew he could easily acquire wealth. Of course he would share it with his overlords, after he took his own fair percentage.

When he had heard Trajan was dead and Hadrian was made emperor, it had come as no surprise. What was astonishing was that Hadrian had foolishly given up on the east. That was where the real wealth was! Not in Dacia, and certainly not this far west. Still it did not appear the new emperor would be acting anytime soon to solidify his power in the backwater that was Britannia. Hadrian had sent Quintus Pompeius Falco to be governor of this place forsaken by the gods. Falco had rebuffed Bestia's initial solicitations – casual introductions made via expatriate intermediaries of course, for Bestia knew he himself to be a wanted man. Falco was a fool for ignoring proper Romans. Bestia would make sure he knew that during his tenure.

Bestia had established contacts with the barbarians in Britannia to secure his local power, remnants of conquered peoples and tribes who refused to be subject to Roman rule: the Brigantes, the Selgovae, the Novantae, and others of the Caledonian race. They would have no quarrel with any move he made against their common enemy. It would be a very useful alliance.

More contact meant more choices where his sexual appetites were concerned. Most girls of Britannia were easily led astray and some even relished the unusual physical freedoms that life in his villa offered them. But the boys were a different story – untamed savages that required discipline and training. In the meantime, Bestia had imported more accommodating youths from Gaul.

One of those Gaulish youths – a magnificent creature – came running in from the entrance toward him.

"A dispatch from Rome, my lord," he said as he handed a folded note to his master.

Bestia took the missive, noting a curious spark in the boy's eyes as he did so. An invitation, perhaps?

"Suck me," he commanded.

The boy dropped to his knees excitedly and pulled up his master's tunic. His mouth and tongue worked enthusiastically on his cock.

Bestia groaned his approval as he opened and read the note. It announced the unexpected deaths of the consul Gnaeus Pedanius Fuscus Salinator, Hadrian's nephew-in-law, and his wife Julia Paulina, Hadrian's niece. Salinator had been considered by some to have been Hadrian's heir apparent. The void meant that the couple's son, Pedanius Fuscus, a boy of five, was now Hadrian's closest blood male relative. However, the writer noted, this did not mean that Fuscus was destined for the throne. The emperor's brother-in-law, Servianus, was still a strong contender for the succession. Servianus and his wife Paulina, Hadrian's sister, were reportedly now taking care of Fuscus.

The calming effect of the attention to his cock enabled Bestia to easily follow the chronicle of the family lineage. It was always good to keep track of such things; one never knew who was going to be easily influenced. An innocent boy of five could easily be swayed into becoming a competitively ambitious young man. He tugged on the hair of the youth between his legs, and slammed his cock into his mouth, quickly reaching his peak. The boy grabbed on to Bestia's buttocks, sucking and swallowing, seemingly wanting more.

And to think this Gaulish boy was painfully shy just a week ago. That was how easy it was to turn an impressionable youth.

Rome, Imperial Palace, November 118

Hadrian had been watching his under-secretary all day. Zuester performed all his tasks with diligence and efficiency, yet it was clear his heart was not in any of it. He was distracted, distant, pining, Hadrian surmised, for Sabina.

Hadrian had been with her several times over the last few months, but it hadn't been until recently that he had realized she had only been with him. When finally prodded, Sabina had let loose a flood of tears. She wanted Zuester, but he avoided her, didn't look at her when they were in the same room together, was polite and formal when they were required to speak. Hadrian's plan of having Sabina take a lover had not been as successful as he had intended.

Suetonius and his page boy were packed up and ready to go. The master secretary bade his good night to the emperor and nodded to his staff to leave.

"Zuester," said Hadrian. "I would like you to stay a moment longer." The emperor smiled at Suetonius. "It is a personal matter regarding a friend from when the lad was a member of our household staff. You understand, don't you?"

"Yes, Caesar," said the secretary. He bowed and left leading his small entourage.

Hadrian waited a moment until he was certain the nosy Suetonius was indeed far down the corridor. "I'll get right to the point."

Zuester shifted on his feet and looked around uncomfortably.

"I understand you have been avoiding my wife."

Zuester gasped. "No, no. Not at all, sire."

"I mean in the bedroom," Hadrian clarified.

The young man flushed. He clearly had no idea what to say.

Hadrian perched on the edge of his desk and indicated the secretary should sit before him, which he immediately did. "Zuester, Vibia likes you a great deal. She's told me about your brief encounter."

Zuester muttered an oath to himself and looked as if he were about to faint.

"She would like it to continue." Hadrian bent his head down. "*I* would like it to continue, too. For the sake of the empire."

The Dacian perked up at that. "How do you mean?"

Hadrian cocked his head to one side. "Remember when Vibia was given something to drink and lost her child?"

Zuester nodded grimly. "That was a horrible day, my lord."

"Yes, yes, it was. And I've had at least one assassination attempt levied against me since as well. Even Trajan's death was suspect. Intrigue and plots abound." The emperor crossed his arms and drew in a long breath. "I do not want to jeopardize the empress's life. I do not want anyone to know we get on well, that we are friends, that we love each other. I think it best the world sees us as having a cordial marriage at best. If possible, though, I would like to create the fiction of a privately antagonistic relationship."

Zuester stared at the emperor in disbelief. "Why would you want to do that?"

"Don't misunderstand me. I love Vibia and would do anything for her. I just do not want anyone using that against her. I do not want our enemies to think that harming her can be used as a weapon against me."

Zuester sunk back in his chair, trying to process the information. "With all due respect to your experience and philosophy, that doesn't make sense, my lord. The emperor Trajan and Plotina Augusta did not use such a strategy. She fared well, I believe."

Hadrian grinned. "I admire your willingness to speak your mind, my boy." He grunted. "Yes, my mother and father did not have to construct such an elaborate ruse. However, to my knowledge, no one ever made an attempt on the dowager empress's life or health."

"Yes," Zuester agreed. "You have a point." He swallowed hard. "And how do I fit in?" he asked quietly as if already suspecting the answer.

Hadrian looked him square in the eye. "I would like you to continue your affair but to conduct it in public."

The young man paled. It seemed as if he were going to be sick.

Hadrian put his hand on Zuester's knee. "Vibia likes you a great deal, son. She's probably really in love with you. I like you too." He leaned back. "Zuester, lad, she deserves the best. She deserves to be with you. If I could, I would set her free to be with you. But I cannot."

Zuester inhaled deeply. "Have you discussed this with your wife, sire?"

"Yes," Hadrian answered. "Vibia has agreed."

"She has?" he blurted, his face flushed with surprise and hope. He swallowed hard. "My lord," he began softly. "As you are well aware, the act would be criminal. As an adulteress Vibia could be banished."

Hadrian smiled. His secretary was far too intelligent for his own good sometimes. "And technically, if anyone knew of this conversation I could be guilty of *lenocinium*, of pandering my wife for my own gain, even if that gain is only peace of mind." He grunted. "However, I am the emperor. I am above the law."

Zuester fidgeted in his chair. "And what of her reputation?"

Hadrian smiled. "How old are you, son?"

"I am thirty, sire."

"My wife is thirty-two. By your age, most people have established a reputation one way or another. Besides being publicly honored for her piety and modesty, hers is that she is married to a much older man who dallies with boys and runs around fighting wars. She has never acted shockingly; she has been beyond reproach her whole life. Now at her age, if she takes a lover, it will be seen as the normal course of a loveless marriage with an inattentive husband."

Zuester stared off blankly into space, his mind clearly elsewhere, the corners of his lips twitching to suppress a smile.

"And, I should add, it will be even beneficial to her reputation if the affair lasts a long time." Hadrian studied his secretary. "You're in love with her, aren't you, son?"

"I think so," he said hoarsely.

"Go to her tonight. Tell her so, or at least show her so. But don't take the back corridor. You should visit her bedchamber tonight, and every night hereafter, via the front door."

Sabina heard the knock on her bedroom door while she knelt in prayer at the lararium. Whoever it was did not know of her nightly routine, but she trusted her maid would keep the visitor at bay. She gave her final bid for protection and bowed before the altar. Drawing in a contented breath, she stood and turned to see who needed to have an audience with her so late at night.

She gasped when she saw Zuester.

She flushed, feeling the heat rise in her cheeks, her heart pound in her chest. He remained standing near the entryway, shifting on his feet, looking a bit uncomfortable. The maid kept her head lowered waiting for a command. She had seen the pair the morning after their first night together and knew they had been intimate. Hadrian was the only other person. He must have counseled his secretary to make the affair public.

The thought sent delight and horror to descend upon Sabina all at once. She wanted nothing more than to be with the handsome Dacian, but realized that the affair was no longer simply an expression of their desire for each other. It was a political maneuver to show the world that Hadrian and his wife cared not for each other, enough so that she would carelessly flaunt her paramour in public.

"You may go, Flora," she said to her maid.

The servant curtsied and left.

Sabina pursed her lips and looked at her lover as tears began to well in her eyes.

Zuester was before her immediately, striding across the marble floor in quick, long steps. "Vibia, Vibia," he soothed as he wrapped his arms around her.

"You don't have to be here," she sobbed.

"I want to be here."

"You're here because of my husband."

Zuester pulled back. "I used the front door because of your husband," he countered.

She sniffled. He was right.

Zuester offered her an edge of his woolen mantle, and when she nodded in acquiescence, he dabbed her eyes and cheeks then wiped her nose.

Sabina giggled.

"That's my Vibia." He draped an arm around her shoulder. "Come, at least let us hold each other," he said as he led her to the bed.

After taking off his shoes and wrap, Zuester relaxed against the pillows and stretched out his hands beckoning Sabina to join him.

She nestled in the crook of his arm, feeling his warmth, his strength, and sensing her body becoming aroused by his closeness.

"It's been difficult to get a chance to see you, much less be with you," he explained softly. "I understand the implication of having to go through the guards in your apartment, and really I don't mind." He kissed her hair. "I would rather have the freedom to be with you when I want, rather than having to suss out opportunities when no one is around."

"I suppose you can't bother Graeculus for the key every time you want to make love to me," she sighed.

"No," he agreed and pulled her close. "And I think I want to make love to you quite often, every day if I can."

Sabina looked up at him and smiled. "Every day?"

"Hmmm," he nodded and kissed her nose.

She gazed in his eyes before touching her lips to his. Their mouths met in a succulent and tender kiss, their tongues greeting slowly, sensually.

"I've missed you," she said.

"Not as much as I've missed you." He took her hand and placed it on his crotch. Beneath the layers of wool and linen, she could feel he was hard.

She bit her lower lip in anticipation, then laid back on the pillows invitingly. He followed, stretching along her side. They kissed, softly, tentatively, Sabina sensing a mutual nervousness, as if they were newly-wed virgins.

Zuester leaned on an elbow and traced a finger down her neck to her chest. "Vibia, love, I want you to be truly mine. I mean, I'm highly aware of your position, that you are the wife of the Emperor of Rome," he said haltingly. "I want you completely, but I'm concerned that..." he picked at the neckline of her nightdress, "I know that we have to act in such a way as to prevent you becoming with child." He stroked her cheek. "I know one way—"

Sabina pressed a finger to his lips. "It's taken care of," she said.

He knitted his brow. "How do you mean?"

"I mean Zosime has provided me with herbs to prevent such a thing from happening."

"Zosime knows about us too?" he blurted.

Sabina laughed softly. "Well, actually no, she doesn't. But she will soon enough. As will everybody else."

Zuester pulled her to him and kissed her again while his hand sought the sash to her robe. He untied it and loosened the garment, baring her shoulders. "Vibia," he said between pecks at her ivory skin. "You deserve a lover who can give you every pleasure your heart demands."

Sabina hummed her agreement, relishing his touch.

Zuester bunched up her skirt and reached underneath. "Unfortunately, I don't think I can be that lover tonight." His fingers traveled up her thigh and found her hips bare of underclothing. He smiled in surprise. "I confess, love, I am at bursting since being without you these last several months." He separated her legs so his fingers could continue their wanderings in the dark recesses of her femininity.

Sabina moaned and rocked her heated wetness against his hand. "I'm bursting too," she confided. She stretched her neck to whisper in his ear. "Fuck me."

In an instant, Zuester stood on the mattress and tore off his tunic and subligaculum, discarding both garments unceremoniously in a heap on the tiled floor. He knelt between Sabina's legs, his ready cock protruding demandingly, and when he lowered himself over her, his heated rod found its aim precisely.

Sabina held his gaze as he pressed in, slowly at first, making sure of her, then, in one thrust, seated himself fully inside her swollen channel. His thickness warmed her entire body as a wave of sated desire enlivened her senses. He gave her only a moment to indulge before he drove into her with purpose. She responded with a loyalty to her own passion, digging her nails into his butt cheeks as their hips crashed together in unison, each demanding gratification from the other, each intent on reaching their peak regardless of what their partner might achieve.

Sabina came first, the intensity of her wail matching the forcefulness of her contraction. She clamped around him, almost succeeding in preventing him from pulling out to continue his rhythmic stroke. But nothing would stop Zuester from taking his satisfaction from the woman beneath him, and he pounded into her relentlessly. She continued to tighten in short pulses, melting into ecstatic dissolution, encouraging him, knowing that his culmination would mean the branding of her as his own, his possession of her body and soul.

With one final thrust he plunged into her, then held steady as he emptied himself with a clipped sigh. Sabina clenched, swallowing his seed willingly, looking up at her new master with loving desire.

Zuester slumped in exhaustion on top of her, then slid off to the side, his arm still clutching her tightly. "You're mine," he said in a dark whisper. "You're mine now."

Sabina closed her eyes. She had wanted to be his for years. "Yes, Zuester. I am yours and only yours."

Rome, Imperial Palace, May 119

Hadrian loved having dinner with friends. Good food, good wine, and good company were some of the delights of being a sought-after guest. He also felt the need to distance himself from his wife, who greatly enjoyed spending long weekends with her lover at the emperor's extensive villa in the Tiburtine hills, still under construction, but usable enough. The more husband and wife were seen apart, the better. She was thoroughly captivated by the Dacian anyway, and he by her, and they needed the time together in their honeymoon period.

The emperor also enjoyed private dinners with his family, and greatly enjoyed being the center of attention amongst his female relatives. Plotina, Matidia, as well as Sabina's sister Mindia, and even his own sister Paulina, all found him charming and entertaining. Since Sabina had immersed herself in Zuester, Hadrian and Matidia had re-ignited their once passionate relationship, an affair that had been on hold for fifteen years. When Sabina was away at the villa, Matidia would install herself in her daughter's apartment in the palace, citing the better angle of the sun in the gardens. Really it was to make use of the access to Hadrian's chamber via the secret corridor.

Quiet, private dinners with family were a much welcome respite after a long day at the courts or a day answering legal correspondence from the provinces. Today's business had been attendance at a regular session of the Senate followed by ensuing discussions with a handful of senators until late afternoon. Exhilarating, yes, but exhausting. The evening was pleasant, a soft breeze drifted through the triclinium. Hadrian reclined on the dining couch with his hands behind his head. He closed his eyes and listened to Matidia and Mindia describing a salacious incident involving a gladiator, laughing and tripping over each other's words in their race to tell the story. He smiled. Sometimes he wished he could be a private man and experience such times as these more often.

He must have dozed off a bit, he realized, when he felt Plotina prodding him with her foot.

"Graeculus!" came the dowager's voice

"Hmmm?" he said, propping himself up.

"You work yourself too much, my son."

"Or he's drunk too much wine," said Matidia.

"Don't worry, Salonia," he said to his mother-in-law. "I'm still quite sober and can perform any task if called upon." He winked at her.

Matidia blushed and distracted herself with a bowl of dried apricots.

"I hear you have some plan to visit the provinces," said Plotina. "What say you to this?"

Hadrian cleared his throat. "Well, now, mother, I think that won't be for some time now. There's plenty to do here in Rome."

"Yes, I know. You have Matidia's brick factories working overtime with your building campaign." The dowager was not harsh, just matter-of-fact.

"I don't think Salonia minds much, do you?" Hadrian insisted on calling his mother-in-law by the more familiar name given their renewed intimacy, which was not unknown amongst the close circle present.

"Not at all, Graeculus," Matidia responded.

"I think the temple to all gods is a wonderful idea," interjected Mindia. "And I've seen the plans. Graeculus is a wonderful architect."

"Yes," Plotina agreed. "The Pantheon will be a marvelous sight to behold if it is constructed as you wish it to be."

Hadrian bowed his head. "Thank you, mother."

"Now, when is it that you plan to go to the provinces? You know I'm too old to travel and I want Matidia near me."

"I don't expect you to go, mother," Hadrian chuckled. "I don't expect either of the eminent Augustae to travel far anymore," he said glancing up at Matidia. "And," he sighed, "like I said, it won't be for some time. I'm working on military reforms that I wish the garrisons to adopt." He picked at a bowl of pitted cherries before plopping one in his mouth. "I'm also worried about Falco's reports from Britannia. There's been some revolts in the northern part of that province that he's had to spend a great deal of energy putting down. We need a new military strategy there as well."

"You'll go all the way to Britannia, then?" said Mindia.

"Yes," Hadrian replied. "I'll visit the western provinces first. Gaul, Germania, Britannia." He took a sip of wine. "But, I feel very strongly that right now Rome needs her emperor, needs an imperial presence. Trajan was absent from the capital for five years. I don't want the Senate thinking Rome can manage without an emperor."

"And since you began your reign with so much antagonism with that esteemed body, they might look for a way to do exactly that," said Plotina. "The senators don't like you, Graeculus."

Hadrian eyed his adoptive mother. Only she was allowed to say such things to him, she who had been the wife of an emperor and knew the workings of politics intimately. "I'm trying to change that mother," he said glumly.

"And what about your own household, son," the dowager continued. "I hear your wife has taken a slave lover. It is about time, given all your perverted affairs."

Hadrian glanced up at Matidia who had paled. He shook his head. Plotina, Hadrian supposed, had also had a bit too much wine. They both knew she had been the one who orchestrated his adoption and succession. Because of that, Hadrian had to allow her great liberties.

"He's a freedman, Augusta. And you know him. It is my under-secretary Zuester."

"Those two haven't had enough of each other yet?" said Plotina with surprise.

Matidia caught Hadrian's eye, and he nodded his head.

"They never made a connection in the past," explained Matidia to the dowager.

Hadrian sighed and rolled onto his back. He had wanted to have his family be privy to his and Sabina's scheme, but he realized he could not. Only Matidia knew the truth. No one else knew, not even Sabina's sister.

"Well it's the least you could do for her after all those palace page boys," remarked the dowager.

Hadrian wondered if Plotina was really scolding him, or if she was merely remembering Trajan's notorious behavior. Besides, Hadrian had recently forgone his taste for page boys to take up with a young – and politically very well-connected – Roman aristocrat, Lucius Ceionius Commodus. The youth's sexual appetites were not only voracious, they were refreshingly adventurous.

"Come along, Plotina," said Mindia, holding out a hand to the intoxicated matron. "Let me escort you to your rooms." She motioned to two slaves to help her get Plotina to stand.

Hadrian watched the women leave, then glanced at Matidia on the opposite couch. "Leave us," he commanded to the servants.

The servants bowed and left, some with empty trays and dishes.

"Come here, Salonia. Sit by me," he said to Matidia.

He moved back a little to give her room. She sat down and drew her fingers through his curls.

"Sabina's happy, Graeculus. And so am I. At least until you leave to subdue your barbarians." Her fingers trailed down to his beard. "Plotina's drunk; don't listen to her. Sometimes I think she misses Trajan. You should involve her in politics more, you know, ask her advice and opinion occasionally."

Hadrian took her hand and kissed it. "Come, lie with me," he said, smoothing the space on the cushion alongside him.

Matidia lay next to him, burrowing against his sheltering arm.

"I wonder what Plotina thinks of my affair with you, mother," he said into her ear, knowing she hated it when he called her that. "Perverted, no doubt."

"You're despicable," she said, clearly hiding her amusement.

"Yes, I am, and you admire that quality in me, do you not?"

She turned her face to his. "It's good for politics, I suppose."

He kissed her, long and hard, pinning her body against his. She tried to push free, only to be held down more assiduously with one strong hand, while the other nimbly tugged up her skirts.

"Here?" she said when he loosened his grip.

"Um-hm," he hummed. "I think the wine was not mixed properly tonight." He pulled at her subligaculum, unraveling the cloth. "Too strong." His hand stroked her now-bare bottom and thighs, massaging the soft plump flesh.

"Graeculus—"

"No, no. Hush." He pulled up his own garments. "I want you," he murmured. "Here and now."

His erection nudged between her butt cheeks. He pressed his hips against her and pulled hers to him with his hand around her waist. His cock rubbed against her anus.

He reached down and touched her mons, sliding his hand across the hairless flesh until he found what he wanted.

"You obviously had the same thing in mind," he said, gently stroking her deliciously wet vulva. He drew a finger along the sticky moisture to manipulate her excited clit.

She closed her eyes and moved against him to the rhythm of his hand, purring softly. When his hand disappeared, she opened her eyes. "Finished already?" she teased.

He placed his hand between her thighs from behind. "Lift your leg."

She did as directed and bent her leg, resting her foot on the opposite knee.

With better access he could now touch all of her. His hand wandered amongst her folds touching, rubbing, delving his fingers in her swollen and yearning cunt. She moved against him, demanding more, taking what he gave her. She came as his fingers plunged inside, his thumb grazing her clit.

His hand scooped along her, drawing moisture back toward her tight puckered hole. He circled the opening, wetting it thoroughly, then delicately pushed a finger in.

She clenched around him, her body stiffened. "Graeculus, what are you doing?"

"Is it not pleasurable, Salonia?" He kissed her neck. "Just relax. Trust me."

"I'm trying. I'm—"

"Touch yourself."

She reached down and masturbated herself gently as Hadrian's finger pushed in further. She jumped when he tried to insert a second digit.

"Shh, shh. It'll be fine in a moment. Just relax. Pleasure yourself against the pain."

He moved his fingers in and out, excruciatingly slowly, but enough for her to whimper a little. He pulled out completely, then reached his hand to cover hers on her clit, shadowing her movements.

"That was not so bad, was it, love?"

"I suppose not."

"Good." He once again drew moisture from her cunt to her crinkled orifice. When he pressed the tip of his cock to her tight arsehole she jumped.

"No!" she hissed.

"Shh, shh, love. Trust me." He pressed in further, until the swollen head was embedded inside her.

With a frantic shove, Matidia pulled away from him, freeing herself from the connection. Both his arms grabbed at her, bringing her down against him.

"I will not be one of your page boys!" she seethed struggling against him.

"Yes, yes," he relented trying to calm her. "All right. I understand." He clutched her closely and swayed gently until she had calmed down in his embrace. "I would never do anything against your wishes, Salonia. Please believe me."

Their uncovered privates were still touching, his erection still insistent between her thighs. With one arm still holding her body against his, her back to his front, he directed his cock inside the more willing hole. His hips rocked against her, pulling and pushing his length in and out. Matidia relaxed on top of him.

He held her steady as he slammed inside her, each thrust building toward his inexorable satisfaction. He resumed tormenting her sensitive nub, his masterful ministrations quickly bringing her to climax.

Her fantastic contraction around him sent him over the edge. Hadrian did not pull out, knowing he need not anymore at her age. He pressed their bodies together, shooting his seed deep inside her, letting his cock empty completely.

He held onto her, feeling her breath rise and fall in time to his. "Thank you, Salonia. Thank you. I don't know what I would do without you."

Eight months later, Salonia Matidia was dead. A sickness inside her, the doctors had said, grew slowly until it had spread to her chest. Sabina had been at her bedside every moment in her last days at the villa in Tibur. Hadrian had sat with his wife when he could.

When her mother died, Sabina was beside herself with grief. No one could take her place, could fill the emotional void. Only Matidia had understood the depths and true nature of Sabina's love for her husband, for she had loved Hadrian herself. It had not been a competition, but a sharing, selfless and joyful, between mother and daughter of the same man.

Sabina hid herself away from the world at the Tiburtine villa. Even Zuester was banished for a spell, until she realized she could not handle her grief alone. He did what he could. He simply listened to her memories, or held her sudden grief-stricken body. He was there for her when she needed him.

Hadrian longed to mourn with his wife. But he was the emperor and had to demonstrate his emotional strength to the people of Rome. He gave the funeral oration requesting his fellow citizens join "my Sabina" in mourning the loss of such a modest, tender, and chaste beauty. In honor of his "most beloved" mother-in-law, the woman who was also his cousin through his adoption by Trajan, he held gladiatorial games and gave gifts of spices and perfume to the people of Rome. Salonia Matidia was accorded all rightful honors as a loyal member of the imperial family. Her daughter Sabina was granted the title Augusta, and she herself was made Diva – a goddess.

Because of their self-imposed agreement, husband and wife, Hadrian and Sabina, suffered separately during the time when they most needed to grieve together.

Britannia, Verulamium, July 121

"You wanted the report on the imperial party, sir?"

"Yes. Go ahead." Bestia did not look at his steward Comuxus, a pretty youth with the blond hair and blue eyes of his native Dobunni, but instead kept his eyes on the exhibition before him and his Germanic guests. A young Britannic girl lay in a swinging hammock, her legs spread open. As two youths fondled and licked her breasts, another young girl pleasured her orally. It was the first sexual experience for the girl in the swing. The mixture of fear and desire on her face was a delight to behold.

"As you know," reported Comuxus glancing briefly at the guests, two Caledonian chieftains and a Suionine leader, "the emperor Hadrian and his administrative staff left Rome in the late spring to tour the western provinces. Among his staff are the Guard Prefect Septicius Clarus who oversees the personal Praetorian Guard, and the chief secretary Suetonius Tranquillus who heads up a large staff of under-secretaries and pages. They are in Gaul now, but we assume Germania is their next stop before they arrive in Britannia."

"Their mission, Comuxus?"

"A review of garrisons and military strategy, our sources say."

"Yes. That is not surprising given his own career as a general," the younger Caledonian, Tharian, commented, obviously trying hard not to stare at his scarred host. This was not too difficult as the sexual performance was most riveting. He had told Bestia earlier that they certainly did not have the luxury for such exotic displays up north in Caledonia.

"And with the amount of administrative staff, it appears, perhaps, significant policy changes are being considered," added Bestia. He picked up his cup and regarded it pensively before gulping down the strong local wine. "What about that blond noble he had been spending time with. The libertine?" He looked up at his steward with raised brows.

"Lucius Ceionius Commodus, my lord?" Comuxus was the only servant unafraid to look into the unmatched eyes of his master.

The girl in the swing began to thrash about and moan loudly. All three guests turned abruptly to observe her.

Bestia himself returned his attention to the display. "Yes, that's the one. With his family background it would seem the emperor is not just using him to dump his seed. Is he with the party as well?"

"No, my lord," responded the steward. "Our reports have him in Rome. He has not been seen with the emperor for quite some time."

"Ah." It was said with a note of comprehension.

The elder Caledonian, Galdus, looked sidelong at Bestia. "What does that mean?"

"I had assumed this Lucius was being prepared for the throne by his pederast lover."

Comuxus cleared his throat. "Lord Bestia, our sources say there is as yet no successor named, nor anyone being groomed for such a role."

"Ah-ha!" Bestia barked. "And so we find ourselves in a most beneficial situation once again, my Caledonian friends."

The girl pleasuring the girl in the swing was now being penetrated from behind by one of the youths, and she wriggled against him whenever he plumbed her depths. The other youth masturbated while standing near the head of the girl in the swing, his cock aimed at her face.

"What about your Senate? If there is no emperor, there is still your Senate. It is too difficult to destroy your empire," said Sweor of the Suiones, a wealthy tribe from the extreme northern climes. His people knew Rome's reach well, for they had extensive contacts both inside and outside her borders. He was most pleased in lending financial support to Bestia's schemes.

"I'm not out to destroy Rome. Just cause a little chaos for my friends the Caledonians," Bestia's lips curled conspiratorially. "The Senate is filled with old men who want nothing but to retire to their farms and estates. There's not a viable military man left," he said to Sweor before turning to his other guests. "You'll have your opportunity, Tharian my lad, to despoil her fertile valleys and prosperous citizens."

Comuxus shifted on his feet. "Lord Bestia, if I may, there is one more piece of information some of our sources found surprising."

The girl being penetrated screamed in horror as the youth entered her unused anus.

"Yes?"

"The emperor and the empress, it seems, are no longer enamored of each other. We have reports that she has taken a lover and he has resumed his perversions with page boys."

Bestia grunted. "That is not so unusual. Most marriages cool after a few years."

"Again, if I may, my lord, I think some of our sources thought it interesting that the empress Sabina is a member of the imperial party."

"Hmmm," the merchant intoned thoughtfully. "That is interesting. She could be useful, perhaps."

On stage, both youths roared at once, climaxing in unison, one pushing his cock deep inside the bowels of the struggling girl, the other ejaculating onto the spitting mouth of the girl in the swing.

Bestia smiled in satisfaction.

Germania Superior, Moguntiacum, Governor's Palace, March 122

"The Gaulish legions took well to your new codes of conduct, my lord," remarked Suetonius as he went over the usual imperial correspondence with the emperor. "Let us hope the soldiers in Germania do as well."

"I think they will," responded Hadrian. "I'll work them hard, get them fit. My plan is to construct a palisade joining each of our fortifications and rebuild the watchtowers in stone. The palisade will define Rome's borders and give our soldiers a sense of who they are and what they are defending."

"Yes, of course. And Roman soldiers will do as their leaders require."

"Hmmm." Hadrian liked Suetonius; he was efficient and professional. But what he didn't like was the secretary's obsequiousness and disdain for personal chit-chat. He always suspected Suetonius was covering up for what was probably a love of gossip. "How is that book coming along, by the way? The biographies of all my predecessors."

The secretary started and blushed briefly. "I am grateful for the opportunity to explore all the imperial libraries in the provinces. It is most enlightening." Suetonius spoke rapidly, excitedly, clearly enthralled by his subject matter. "I have finished the drafts for the Life of Julius Caesar and the Life of Augustus."

"Oh?" Hadrian responded. "I should like to read the account of Augustus."

"With pleasure, my lord. I look forward to doing more research here in Germania. You know, both my next subjects, Tiberius and Gaius Caligula, as well as Caligula's father Germanicus, spent quite bit of time in Germania. And, I must admit, I am thrilled to go to Britannia where my next subject, Claudius, put down an uprising."

Hadrian grinned at his secretary. He had never heard the man speak so much before and all at once. Suetonius clearly enjoyed his extracurricular work. "Well done," he said.

The emperor looked at the pile of documents on his desk, then at the small staff busily writing at a table across the room. Someone was conspicuously missing.

"Where is the secretary Zuester, Suetonius? He should be here given the amount of foreign correspondence we must deal with."

"My lord," Suetonius started hesitantly. "Due to Zuester's frequent absences over the last couple of years, I've had to train a few new secretaries."

"Absences? What absences?"

"When we are in Rome, he often leaves for long periods of time. I believe he goes to the villa at Tibur."

"Yes, yes. I do know that," Hadrian said dismissively. "He has work there, as well."

Suetonius shuffled papers distractedly, as if afraid to voice what was on his mind. "Sire, you're fond of Zuester, are you not?"

"Of course. He's bright, capable, and very pleasant. I like having him on my staff."

"Yes." Suetonius briefly considered what he had to say next. "My lord, it appears your wife, the empress Sabina, has been seen, uh, cavorting, shall we say, with the secretary Zuester. My lord, it is unseemly. He is a former slave—"

"He is a freedman," corrected Hadrian. "And a very intelligent young man," he added.

"With all due respect sire, he is your wife's lover. Your wife, sir, need I remind you, is the Empress of Rome."

Hadrian grunted. "Ah yes, and if I were a private man, I would divorce her. She's clearly in love with him, and when not otherwise preoccupied she can be moody and difficult. I see no need to put an end to the affair. It simply means she stays out of my bedroom, which is really no place for a woman anyway."

Hadrian scrutinized his secretary for a reaction. It was obviously not the response Suetonius was expecting. He certainly knew about his emperor's proclivities, and, given the tastes of Hadrian's predecessors, the secretary should not have been surprised. He was probably not prepared, however, for Hadrian's casual detachment from his wife's personal behavior.

"Don't try to protect me, Suetonius. I want Zuester back on my staff."

"Yes, Caesar," he said with a bow. "I will fetch him presently."

Hadrian lay on his bed thinking about what had happened earlier that day in his office. Suetonius needed to hear the indifference in his voice about his wife's conduct. And Hadrian was confident that whatever the gossipy Suetonius knew about the emperor's personal affairs eventually would be spread about, dropped offhandedly in conversation, albeit under the pretext of "only hearsay". But word would get out in the provinces. Hadrian hoped his enemies abroad would eventually pick up the information and resist including Sabina in any nefarious schemes.

He felt restless. He needed physical release, but had no taste for a boy that night. He craved Sabina. They had dallied furtively a few times over the last couple of years. Their forced abstinence from one another meant his body was set on edge every time he saw her, every time he was in her presence, or simply heard her voice. He tried not to act like a lovesick school boy when someone talked about her – what she did that day, what she wore, ate, laughed at. He could sense his wife felt the same way, although her urges were tempered by her adoring lover.

Her rooms in the Governor's Palace were not far from his, but as there was no secret corridor, he would risk someone seeing him go to her. He could hide himself in his voluminous pallium, but it was common knowledge that he wore the Greek garment instead of the toga, and it would be a dead giveaway to his identity. He threw the covers off his nude body, got up, and stood in the middle of his room, staring blankly at the bed…the bed covered in a soft, lightweight woolen sheet, something common enough in the imperial household. He tore it off the mattress and wrapped it deftly around himself, creating a hood to hide his head. He stepped out of his room and into the hall, then followed the corridor to his wife's rooms. He knew his loyal guards would make note of his midnight journey but would be highly discreet about his destination.

He had made sure the two Germans and the two Africans employed years ago in his marital escapades had always been Sabina's door guards. Over the years the four men had been unwavering in their devotion to their mistress. But they also respected and highly regarded their master, and as the wedded husband of their lady, knew he would always have unquestioned conjugal rights. When Hadrian stood at the doorway to his wife's bedroom he briefly lifted his makeshift hood. With no expression, the German opened the door silently, then closed it after his emperor had entered the room.

Hadrian stood behind the entryway curtains. He did not know what to expect. He had hoped Sabina would be alone, but knew there was very definitely the possibility that she would not be. From his secluded alcove, he heard the breathy urgent moans of his wife and her lover. Every pore on his body tingled as the blood rushed to his cock. He opened the drapery just enough to spy the bed at the back of the room lit in the dim lamplight.

The sight was both astonishing and spectacularly arousing. Sabina was straddling Zuester, riding him, her body undulating in time to her rhythmic movements. Her breasts, still wonderfully buoyant at her age, bounced and swayed gently. Zuester, lost in a delirium of erotic delights reached up and fondled the pale demi-orbs briefly before he was overtaken by the sensations he was feeling below. He gripped the mattress and rocked his hips against his love.

No Roman man would allow such a degrading act in his own bedroom. No man would allow a woman to dominate him thusly, unless she were a prostitute and it was at a brothel where he could act out such deviant fantasies.

But Zuester was a Dacian with different sexual customs, and, it was obvious, a man utterly and completely lost in love. His hands held on to Sabina's thighs as she changed her movement slightly, thrusting her hips forward on the up stroke and relaxing them on the downward release. She bent over him, one hand on either side of his head. Hadrian could hear her soft murmurs and encouragements and the secretary's deeper groans in response.

Their impeccable rhythm, the way their heads drew together, the way one's hands touched the other's body, every move said the two were deeply enamored with each other, that they considered their relationship as one between equals, not freedman and empress. Hadrian felt a twinge of regret that he could not be that man for his wife. He loved her passionately, but he could never let her ride him like that, let her be in control of his pleasure. He relished being the one in control, holding her as she futilely fought and struggled, then submitted to his every wish.

Sabina was doing something wicked, Hadrian could tell. She was poised above Zuester, whispering in his ear, the tip of his surprisingly well-endowed shaft buried inside her, but the rest exposed to the night air and Hadrian's lascivious view. *She must be clenching him.* He began to stroke his erection, then grasped the glans and squeezed in what he remembered her rhythm to be. He almost cried out at the pleasure, but caught himself. He had never been so on edge before. Her control over him was driving him mad.

Their voices grew louder, but still indistinct. She was taunting him. Zuester said "yes" and perhaps "please". She continued her verbal provocation while she once again began to move her hips, sliding up and down Zuester's erection slowly and deliberately. Hadrian stroked his cock to the same motion, his hand gripping his length as he knew she was gripping the Dacian's prick.

In one swift downward movement, Sabina slammed against her lover. Hadrian pumped his cock as he watched his wife bounce on Zuester like a soldier riding a horse. She was frenzied, ecstatic, but utterly in control. Zuester was powerless, moaning blasphemies to the gods and thrashing against the sheets. As he pumped himself harder, Hadrian let himself relinquish his senses to the scene before him. Just as Zuester let himself be taken to the brink, then over the edge, Hadrian let himself explode onto the sheet wrapped around his body.

Sabina threw her head back and laughed in delight, then crashed down on her spent lover. She was still smiling and giggling and wiggling when Hadrian donned his hood, opened the door behind him, and returned to his room.

Zuester lay breathless, panting, smiling at the joyous woman at his side.

"I made you come! I made you come!" Sabina giggled in glee as she snatched and grabbed playfully at her lover.

"Yes, yes you did, my little hetaera," said the thoroughly slaked Dacian, laughing and trying to fend her off.

Zuester finally succeeded in trapping her in his arms. He held her close until she calmed down from her triumphant fervor. With their bodies entwined, their breaths kept time in peaceful satisfaction.

Zuester inhaled deeply. "If it could be otherwise," he said softly. "I would make you my wife. I would give you sons and a daughter. I love you, Vibia. The gods know and now I want you to know." He nuzzled against her. "I love you."

Sabina tried to stop the tears from falling. "I love you, too, Zuester. I love you so much," she sniffled. What she could not tell him was that she loved two men – two very different men – one as much as the other, and could not live without either.

Britannia, Londinium, Governor's Palace, beginning of July 122

"I do hope you are comfortable in our humble accommodations here in Londinium, my lord Hadrian," said Quintus Pompeius Falco.

"Thank you, Falco," responded the emperor. "And thank you for your service to us in the last war."

"Thank you, Caesar," said Falco. "It was hard won." Falco, the governor of Britannia, had been the general in charge of the legion IX Hispana who fought back the Brigantes and other tribes from the north of Britannia. The barbarians were fierce and many Roman lives had been lost.

The two men stood at an oak table in the library reviewing drawings that the emperor had made just prior to landing in the province.

"I think the fortification will keep the tribes at bay. Our similar plan in Germania appears to be working."

"It's an excellent plan, sire."

Hadrian was proud of his design: A grand wall with mile castles and towers to stretch the length of the northern frontier to both define and defend the border. Instead of timber, with which most of the one in Germania had been built, the Britannic fortification would be of native stone. Hadrian had brought with him Legion VI Victrix from Germania to supplement and succeed veteran troops under Falco. The governor himself was to retire and be replaced by Aulus Platorius Nepos. But first, Falco was to be tour guide for the emperor.

"As an island, Britannia has more easily defensible borders," commented Hadrian. "Unlike Parthia with simply more land and more kingdoms beyond for the unrequited conqueror to pursue." He glanced around and lowered his voice. "As one soldier to another, Falco, I do believe it is time to establish our borders and defend what we have. This business of expansion leads to far too many revolts and rebellions."

Falco looked his old friend in the eye. "I agree, Graeculus," he said quietly. "The Brigantes would give you nothing but trouble. Best to keep them out altogether."

Hadrian patted the governor on the back, then bent over his designs to review them one more time before they were to leave for the north.

"You have a fine city here, General Falco." The voice was imperious and very feminine.

Hadrian raised his head to see his wife standing in the doorway of the library. He had to try very hard not to smile. As always, she looked deliciously ravishing.

"Thank you, my lady," said Falco with a slight bow. "Are you to travel north with us?"

"Oh, by Castor, no!" she exclaimed. "Please forgive my frankness, but reviewing troops and building fortifications sound thoroughly boring. And I'm certain I would be the only woman for miles." She glanced demurely at her husband before she sat on one of the large oak chairs surrounding the table. "I've had my tour of Londinium, and now I believe we are to go west to Aquae Sulis."

"Ah, the baths!" proclaimed Falco. "You will love it there. Very extensive facilities with everything you could want. Positively relaxing."

"The empress will be accompanied by our sisters, Mindia and Paulina, and chaperoned by my Guard Prefect Septicius Clarus and my secretary Suetonius," added Hadrian. "My under-secretary Zuester, a Dacian polyglot, will accompany me." He nodded at Sabina, his only way of telling her publicly that he knew she would miss her lover terribly.

"I'm sure I will hear endless stories about our forebears from your secretary, husband," said Sabina as she adjusted her dress. He knew she was not happy about traveling with the two men whom she found dull. She had said, however, that she looked forward to the magnificent baths, about which she had heard wonderful things, and gossiping with the female members of the imperial household.

A page knocked on the partly opened door.

"Yes?" called the governor.

A young soldier stepped into the library. "General Falco, sir, you are wanted by General Nepos," said the youth timidly. He was trying very hard not to look at the bearded man next to the general, the man he of course knew was the Emperor of Rome.

"My apologies," stated Falco to his guests. "I must attend to this." He bowed to the empress and left with the soldier.

Sabina finally let the smile she had been hiding spread across her lips, her eyes glowing with eagerness as she watched her husband close the library door. Instinctively, he looked around, then, certain they were alone, he pulled her up out of her chair and into his arms.

"You're playing with fire, Graeculus," Sabina giggled, playfully tugging at his beard.

"The fire burns inside, Vibia. Only you can quench it."

"Here?" She glanced around, her eyes widened wantonly.

Hadrian lifted her onto the table and pushed up her skirts. His mouth plundered hers as he separated her knees with a strong thigh. His fingers explored the feminine flesh between her legs until they were covered in sticky moisture.

He released her from the kiss to stick his wet fingers in her mouth. She sucked hard, her lips curled in a lewd grin, and raised an eyebrow as he pulled up his leather skirt and tunic. He was bare underneath, having hoped for a furtive opportunity such as this, his cock at full stand, aching to be inside her. He positioned himself just right, then pulled Sabina toward him, impaling her in one swift move. She gasped in relief, looking up at him, her loving expression softening as he moved in and out of her welcoming passage.

Hadrian gazed down at his wife. Her open mouth, her eyes black with lust, her choked-back moans were compelling. He dipped his head and kissed her, his tongue tangling with hers, as he tried to steady her on the table top. He drove into her, grateful for the unexpected chance to possess her body.

"Vibia, darling," he panted. "I love you. I love you and I can't stand not being able to scream this to the gods every day."

Sabina was on the edge, breathing heavily. "Graeculus, I—"

Sensing she was about to cry out in climax, Hadrian pressed his mouth against hers, swallowing her moan. He jerked his own orgasm, jetting his hot seed inside her clenching channel. As their passion abated, he held her tightly, feeling her body shake with silent sobs. Their love-making had been far too hasty.

"Tonight you will be with your lover," Hadrian said gently. "Say your good-byes. I don't know how long we will be gone. Probably several weeks." He pulled back and wiped her tears. "And don't cry."

"I'll just say they are tears for my mother."

"Very well." Hadrian pulled out feeling a sense of loss as he did so. He helped his wife off the table and made sure her dress was straightened and smoothed. For a brief moment they stood facing each other, holding hands, unwilling to part. Hadrian kissed her on the forehead and directed her to the exit.

When she had left, he leaned back against the carved oak door and drew his hands down his face in an effort to compose himself. The emperor should never show emotions of love and regret.

It was a curious scene that Suetonius had just witnessed. He had entered the library in the Londinium palace through the annex door – most of the scrolls he needed were tucked away in the history section of the small room. As he browsed through the cubicula, he heard low voices and a slight commotion coming from the main library chamber, separated from the annex by heavy woolen drapes. The secretary decided to take a quick peek before making himself known. He made a chink between the curtains with his stylus. He almost dropped it when he saw what was going on.

The emperor and the empress were engaging in coitus on the large oak library table. Once he spied the sight Suetonius was riveted and could not take his eyes from it. The emperor had certainly not forced his lady, as one might believe given their rancorous relationship. She was indubitably enjoying herself, as was he. It was clearly an act of love, not the base physical release needed by a powerful man.

Suetonius had watched until the end, then watched as the Empress Sabina left. Realizing he had only a bit of time before the emperor himself would leave, the secretary hurried noiselessly out the annex door. He retreated to his own room, where he sat at his desk cogitating pensively about the whole affair.

Britannia, Aquae Sulis, Bath House, mid-July 122

Sabina could not have been more relaxed. She lay on a slab in the tepidarium, a masseuse kneading her warmed muscles as she breathed in the lavender-scented oil. Taking the baths at Aquae Sulis while her husband and lover slogged about the mist and muck at the northern garrisons was a wonderful idea. And spending time with Mindia and Paulina was really quite fun. The unmarried Mindia found the men of Britannia rather handsome, constantly chirping her approval about the local serving boys and flirting with elites. Paulina, with a disinterested husband thirty years her senior, was fascinated by Mindia's boldness, clearly wanting to join in her sister-in-law's games.

Sabina was just about to fall asleep when a young servant girl requested she get up from the slab in order to be scraped.

"It is a wonder my brother still amuses himself with boys when he could have a woman like you, my dear," said Paulina as she too stood for the strigil. "You've got a beautiful figure."

"And at your age too, Vibia!" teased Mindia.

Sabina could only smile at her sister-in-law. She had to keep her true relationship with Hadrian a secret from Paulina because of the ambitions of her husband, Servianus. Otherwise, she really liked Paulina and would have loved to have confided in her.

"I suppose your attractions do not go to waste with that foreign lover of yours," commented Paulina.

"Oh, no, they do not!" laughed Sabina, before feeling the sting of absence in her heart for her Zuester.

"He is a handsome one, isn't he?" said Mindia. "I wonder if your husband has taken him away up north out of jealousy?"

"Of course not. Zuester is very useful to him." Sabina shot her sister a warning glance. Mindia was one of the very few who did know that the emperor and empress shared a bed from time to time.

"Why don't you take a lover, Paulina?" Mindia said to change the subject. "Would Servianus mind, really?"

"Ha! He's so wrapped up in politics he would probably not notice, nor even care," Paulina sighed. "But, I would hardly know how to do such a thing."

The servant girl indicated it was time to bathe in the hot waters of the sacred spring. Sabina wrapped a fine linen robe around her nude body and slipped into wooden sandals. She linked her arm through Paulina's as they followed the girl to the next room.

"Perhaps we can find a matron with a bored younger brother," she intimated. "You too have a fine figure that should not be wasted by your elderly husband's indifference."

The women laughed as they passed through to the grand, vaulted bath hall. Except for the local serving staff and designated members of the elite, Sabina had the complex to herself. Septicius's Praetorian Guard stationed outside the bath house made sure of that. Plus, her husband was never content with just the Guard. Her two Germans and two Africans also hovered about outside. The concern for her well-being while separated from her husband was a constant reminder of his deep love and regard for her. Even with him so many miles away, Sabina felt protected and safe.

* * * * *

"This is marvelous, Septicius," commented Suetonius as the two relaxed in the hot bath. "Britannia is ever so much more frigid than Italia that I never thought I would be warm again."

"I heartily agree," said Septicius. The Guard Prefect felt almost guilty taking the waters while his charge, the empress Sabina, was left with practically only her ladies-in-waiting to watch over her. However, she had attended the baths the day before and had insisted he enjoy the experience for himself.

"I hope we are not disturbing you gentlemen?" came a deep voice from above the pool.

Suetonius looked up to see a middle-aged man, his face disfigured by a scar, standing with an attractive younger companion. The two had just been scraped with the strigil and now were ready for the hot bath. "No, not at all. Please join us," said the affable secretary.

The two men took their places along the adjoining side of the pool. "As everyone in Aquae Sulis is from somewhere else, may I inquire as to your origination?" asked the older man.

"We are from Rome," said Suetonius noticing the eyes of the older man were of two different colors. He found it difficult to not look at the man's intriguing face.

"Rome?" the man exclaimed. "I've heard that the emperor himself is in Britannia. Are you with his party?"

Suetonius glanced at Septicius who nodded. "Yes," he said.

"Is the emperor here in Aquae Sulis?" queried the pretty blond youth who was clearly the intimate of the older man. The youth spoke with the accent of the native Britons.

"Ah, no," responded Septicius. "He is reviewing troops up north where there has been some fighting of late. There is to be a new fortification of sorts."

The two companions looked at each other with surprised glances. "He is not like his predecessor is he, this Hadrian?" commented the elder. "He seeks to fortify our borders rather than expand them."

"Yes, but his preference for young boys is the same," laughed the attractive youth.

The party joined in his mirth.

"Shouldn't you be with him in the north?" queried the man with the scar.

"We are here with the Empress Sabina who has elected to take the baths," remarked Suetonius.

"Ah, his wife," intoned the disfigured man with a sigh. "I hear she is beautiful. However, I am sure the emperor can do without her for the time being, as he'll have soldiers to enjoy. Their unmarried state incites desires, even unnatural ones." His laugh held a hint of depraved comprehension.

Suetonius guffawed. "Well, yes, I suppose his particular appetite is well known. However, you would be surprised at his enjoyment of women as well," he remarked.

"Women?" exclaimed the older man. "I had no idea he knew they existed."

"From all accounts he hates his wife," said the youth.

"Well, perhaps not as much as one might think," said the now utterly relaxed Suetonius. "Why I even saw them enjoying a marital moment the other day."

"How do you mean?" asked a surprised Septicius.

"I mean they appeared loving together, as if they actually meant it."

"'Loving'?"

Suetonius drew in a deep breath, then glanced around as he revealed his secret. "They were copulating in, of all places, the palace library at Londinium. It was not an unwelcome act on either of their parts."

All the men present blew out a collective grunt.

"I would not have thought it, I mean, that the Emperor Hadrian enjoyed his wife's company," said the older man running his hand across his scarred forehead.

"And not only that, they appeared to be quite in love really," revealed Suetonius.

A servant approached the party to indicate that Suetonius and Septicius should proceed to the frigidarium once again. The two men bowed politely as they exited.

Bestia watched as the two imperial councilors sauntered away to their next activity in the bath. He glanced around surreptitiously before speaking.

"The emperor is in love with his wife? And the empress is here in Aquae Sulis? This is too much to imagine, Comuxus. The gods have simply dropped opportunity into our hands."

The steward only responded by draping his long, well-muscled leg across the thigh of his master.

The two men exchanged expectant glances before continuing their relaxation in the hot bath.

Britannia, Pons Aelius, end of July 122

"The veterans appreciate your personal presence at the edge of the empire, sire," commented Falco after Hadrian had addressed the retiring troops.

"They have served the empire well and deserve to marry and ply their trades," responded Hadrian. "I understand many are native to this land, and others who have chosen local girls as brides will stay here in Britannia. This is good. Rome is strengthened by the presence of contented subjects in her provinces. Too many of our people are rebellious."

The two men, along with their respective aides, rode their horses at a slow pace and observed the building of the Pons Aelius, a bridge and fort dedicated to the emperor at the eastern end of the proposed wall. Hadrian's swift hunting-horse, Borysthenes, a gift from the king of the Roxolani, seemed annoyed at the leisurely review of the project. The emperor leaned over and soothingly patted the animal's neck.

"And now that you have restored discipline, mutinous thoughts will not penetrate the legions."

"I never considered my own men would revolt against me, Falco. However, their dishonest business practices do not reflect positively on the empire. Let the barbarians gain the reputation for cheating and deception."

Zuester rode up alongside his master.

"Ah, Zuester. It is a wondrous site, is it not, to see such civilizing activities out here at the end of the empire?" said Hadrian to his aide.

Zuester nodded. "I've just been delivered a few items of correspondence, my lord. The construction a bit further west of us is proceeding as planned."

"Good, good," Hadrian exclaimed. "Anything else?"

"A missive from our party in Aquae Sulis, sire," Zuester said knowing the emperor would understand his meaning.

"Ah, I see," Hadrian said dispassionately to Zuester. He turned to Falco. "General, I must confer for a moment with my secretary. Please go on ahead."

"As you wish, Caesar," said Falco. He turned his horse and rode up ahead.

Hadrian pulled the ever-restless Borysthenes closer to Zuester's rather tranquil mount. "What do the letters say, son?"

"It seems Suetonius and Septicius are mixing with all the right people, attending literary parties, taking the baths."

"Fucking Hell, man! I don't care a whit about what Suetonius is doing! How is *she*?"

"The imperial secretary says your wife appears to be enjoying herself," Zuester commented. "She takes the waters daily and is absolutely glowing for it."

Hadrian's lips curled in a sly smile. "And what does my wife write to you?"

Zuester blushed. "I don't think I should repeat it, my lord."

Hadrian guffawed. "Any of it?"

Zuester opened the letter to him from Sabina. "She writes you can build your damn wall all you like, she is enjoying the spa, but she wishes I were there to enjoy it with her."

Hadrian beamed at his secretary. "You miss her don't you?"

"As do you," Zuester replied impertinently. "I wish I were with her right now," he sighed. "I don't understand why you chose me to attend you on this trip."

"Because Suetonius is useless when it comes to practicalities," admitted Hadrian. "And, no, it was not to keep the two of you apart, if that's what you're thinking. I'm not jealous, I have no right to be jealous where she is concerned." Hadrian regarded his wife's lover admiringly. "You are good for her and she deserves you. You'll have plenty of time with her when we return to Londinium." He patted Zuester's thigh. "That is my only source of jealousy. That you get to be with her openly while I do not."

"She is safe, my lord. And contented. She says to tell you that. And," Zuester hesitated, then read directly from the letter, "'tell Graeculus that I love him.'"

Hadrian pursed his lips. "Thank you," he said hoarsely. "Anything else?"

"No, Caesar."

Hadrian turned the impatient Borysthenes around and rode off to meet up with Falco.

Britannia, Aquae Sulis , beginning of August 122

Sabina listened to the poet recite his lines and tried to keep from dozing off in the warm courtyard of her rented villa. The last several weeks had been pleasant enough, with parties, tours to the lush green countryside, and the ever-present mineral baths. She, Mindia, and Paulina had made a few women friends, most of whom had never been to Rome or the east, and were always interested in hearing about customs of far-off places. But throughout it all, Sabina had felt a nagging emptiness inside. She missed Zuester and his loving attentiveness. She also missed her husband and even their false antagonism. As she had expected, Suetonius and Septicius had been accommodating but dull.

"My lady," came Suetonius's grating voice. "We'll leave tomorrow for the return journey to Londinium."

"Oh?" said Sabina, shielding her eyes from the pale sunlight as she looked up at the secretary. "I had forgotten it was so soon."

"You need do nothing. Your maids have taken care of everything."

"Will my husband's party be there when we arrive?"

Suetonius smiled and Sabina could have sworn she saw him wink. "They have further to journey, but yes, they will meet up with us in the capital."

Sabina settled back against the couch. "Good. Then I believe I will visit the baths this afternoon for one last dip before we depart."

"The empress Sabina leaves tomorrow, Bestia."

"Thank you, Comuxus."

Bestia had waited for their opportunity for days. Now all he needed to do was to separate the empress from the Praetorian Guard. They protected her like a treasure. His spies were also concerned about the four very burly men – barbarians, two of whom were black Africans – who shadowed the empress and her Guard.

Any fool could see that the emperor truly cared for his empress, otherwise he would not look after her with such diligence.

But guards usually only protected doorways and obvious entrances. They did not watch rooftops or windows.

Sabina still couldn't sleep. She had asked for a sedative before she had gone to bed that night, and Zosime had given her a concoction made with chamaemelum, a local herb. She had taken the remedy, seemingly to no avail. Her mind raced at the promise of seeing Zuester and her husband again. It had been over a month since their separation.

She lay on the bed fantasizing about the moment of reunion, what she would say, what her lovers would say. She knew Hadrian would be cold initially, but he would find it difficult to maintain a veneer of indifference for very long. She loved watching him seethe with desire in her presence. It enflamed her as well. Poor Zuester! Sometimes he was the victim, rather than the object, of her own libidinous needs.

But Zuester did not seem to mind. The concept of being cuckolded was somehow not a part of Dacian culture. He was just content to hold Sabina in his arms, to whisper honeyed words, to hold her down as he had his way with her…or was that Graeculus? She couldn't remember which lover did what at that moment…the two became one…it had been too long…

As she felt herself falling deeper and deeper into slumber, she wondered if the man climbing through her window was supposed to be there. He didn't look like anyone she knew. A chill went through her… something was not right… she should get up and call the guard. She tried to get out of the bed… she was certain she was out of the bed and that she was walking across the floor… she tried to move her hand then realized she was still lying in bed… frozen… she hadn't moved at all.

She tried to scream but no sound came out. She couldn't even move her mouth. What *was* it that Zosime had given her?

The man was at her bed now…his eyes were filled with hate…terror gripped her…he reached down to pick her up…with all her might she tried to escape…she was being lifted…she tried to struggle…was she struggling? She saw the floor beneath her…spinning…the room was upside down…her head began to hurt from the blood rushing to it…all the pressure…

She gave in to the strange feeling and blacked out.

"She's awake, sir."

The moment Sabina opened her eyes she knew she was not where she should be. Despite her blurred vision and confused brain, she knew that the twenty or so men surrounding her were not party to a game of her husband's. From what she could tell the men were in rags if they were wearing clothes at all. They seemed to be in a stable. The stench of the strange place was stifling.

She tried to move, and immediately felt a painful tugging on her wrists, her ankles, her whole torso. She lifted her head and a muscle in her shoulder cramped, sending an agonizing jolt down her spine, just before she was able to catch a glimpse of her shocking predicament.

That's when she tried to scream and realized she could not. She was gagged.

She was strapped into a hanging contraption, a sort of swing, her legs grossly spayed open and tied. She was utterly naked, her body on display for the dozens of men in the room.

She broke out in a cold sweat of realization and thrashed against her bindings, ignoring the pain.

She felt the sting of a strong hand strike her face, but only just barely, as if her cheek was already numb from previous blows. She did, however, feel the cold trickle of blood run down her neck.

A man pressed his head forward, directly in front of hers, displaying a face she would never forget. A deep scar as from a knife marred its entirety, unkempt graying stubble barely concealed pock-marked skin, his eyes of two different colors. He began to speak, his voice low and grotesquely intimate. She struggled again, but he held her firmly, indelicately, and spoke more resolutely.

"…you'll know how to rid yourself of any unpleasant consequences. Remember in Antioch? I showed you how effective artemisia can be."

Sabina's eyes widened in horror. It had been him. This evil man had killed her child.

She pulled at her bindings and tried to scream again. This time the blow to her head was stronger.

She did not feel what happened next.

Britannia, Vindolanda, mid-August 122

"Borysthenes, go! Forward!" Hadrian raced after the wild boar the moment he spotted it. The poor creature never had a chance. The emperor deftly stabbed the unlucky beast with his spear as Zuester and Falco caught up with him.

"Ha!" cried Falco and motioned for the servants to come bag the catch. "I have only heard about your skill in the hunt, Graeculus. I have never witnessed it firsthand. You are very good."

"Thank you, my friend," responded a panting Hadrian. "Tonight we shall enjoy a hearty pie made from what the gods have given us." The three men laughed.

As they trotted back to the garrison in the fading sunlight of the late summer evening a messenger approached riding hard. He stopped before them, an urgent expression on his face.

"What is it?" asked Falco.

The messenger bowed. He knew precisely who his audience was. "I have a very important missive for the secretary Zuester," he puffed.

Hadrian and Zuester exchanged glances. It could only mean one thing: Sabina.

"I am he," said the secretary.

The messenger handed Zuester a document and then bowed. "I was told to not wait for a reply. The gods be with you, gentlemen." And he sped off.

Zuester read the note, paled, then quickly recovered.

"Is it important?" asked Falco.

Zuester considered the slowly dimming daylight. "It is nothing that cannot wait until the morrow."

"Good!" said Falco. "Then we shall enjoy our pie."

At dinner that night Hadrian waited for a chance to take Zuester aside. They excused themselves on the pretense of studying the position of the stars in the provincial sky.

"What is the news?" Hadrian asked as soon as they were alone. "What has happened to her?"

Zuester took in a deep breath. "I don't know. The note did not specify. Only that she has been injured but is being cared for, and that we should return to Londinium as soon as we are able."

Hadrian looked up at the summer stars. "Now, I only imagine the worst."

Zuester boldly slipped his fingers against his master's palm. "Don't say that, my lord," he said quietly. "Whatever it is, there are two of us to support her."

Hadrian squeezed the friendly hand holding his in the dark, and prepared himself for the worst.

Britannia, Londinium, Governor's Palace, mid-August 122

As soon as he arrived at the palace yard in Londinium, Hadrian slid off his horse and called for his staff. He instructed Zuester to seek out Sabina immediately. Both men were still not certain what precisely had happened.

Suetonius and Septicius appeared directly, followed the emperor into a private bureau, then stood before him nervously, watching him pace with agitation. Hadrian bombarded them with questions, leaving little chance for the councilors to respond.

"She was kidnapped, my lord," Suetonius was finally able to interject. He glanced up at his master but quickly looked away, avoiding the emperor's panic-stricken countenance. "They came via the roof at the villa in Aquae Sulis and entered through her window."

"Were there no guards?" Hadrian was incredulous.

"Not on the roof. It had not been considered," Septicius responded, trying hard not to be defensive.

"She was gone for several days. We think she was held at Verulamium." Suetonius drew in a long breath, bolstering himself. "She was raped, repeatedly—"

"Gods above!" Hadrian murmured in disbelief, reaching for a chair.

"—her battered body was dumped here at the palace a week ago."

Hadrian stared wide-eyed and disbelieving at his secretary. "Why her?" he asked darkly. "Why? Sabina has done nothing to deserve such violence." He stood and paced again. "Why would the gods allow this? She is faultless." He turned to his secretary and his guard prefect, his eyes flashing realization. "They knew who she was. They knew it was her. She was targeted," he roared before he collected himself. "Why?"

Suetonius glanced nervously at Septicius. "We're not sure, my lord," answered the latter.

"You're not sure? How is it that the chief of my personal guard is not sure?"

"We are continuing the investigation, Caesar," Septicius responded meekly.

Suetonius glanced nervously at his friend. "My lord emperor, the lady Sabina did mention something of importance."

Hadrian looked frantically at both men. "What? What did she say?"

"One man, the leader she believes, was the one who killed your child several years ago, the child in her womb. In Antioch."

Hadrian dropped his jaw, incredulous. "Who is this man?"

"We believe him to be a Roman, possibly related to the Frugi. If you recall, the consul Gaius Calpurnius Crassus Frugi Licinianus escaped exile and was killed upon your ascendancy."

"Gods be damned," he muttered, drawing his hand down his face. "Why Sabina? Why not me?"

Septicius stepped in. "The man seems to think you and Sabina have a connection, that you are attached, perhaps in love."

Hadrian glanced back and forth between the two advisors. "And why would he think this? I have never declared any emotion but indifference to my wife."

Suetonius looked uncomfortable. "My lord, it was an accident. I saw you with her. I divulged this intelligence offhandedly."

Hadrian took a step toward the secretary. "You saw me with her?" he hissed.

"In the library here in the Londinium palace."

Hadrian pressed his fingers to his temples. He remembered the incident; he had copulated with Sabina. It happened in the space of five minutes. Yet his imperial secretary had decided that the scene showed he was in love with his wife. He grunted to himself. What other conclusion could an observer have drawn?

"Your carelessness and indiscretion have led to an abomination," Hadrian condemned. "The Emperor of Rome should not be the subject of gossip by his own officers, especially not with strangers. I expect your resignations in my hands tomorrow." He looked at Septicius. "The both of you."

The imperial secretary and the guard prefect briefly looked relieved before they were hit with the reality of their situation. They both knew the emperor was being very generous: Neither man was to be executed. Previous emperors would have done just that.

"Yes, my lord," was all Suetonius could say.

Hadrian stormed out of the office, calling for his Praetorian Guard. Several appeared instantly. "Put my two Africans on the roof," he instructed. "Your men will relieve them at the expected intervals."

The guardsmen did not question their emperor and went to do as they were told.

Hadrian walked the corridors until he saw Sabina's room up ahead. He stopped and checked himself. He was incensed, wanting to kill whomever it was who had harmed her, but knew that was not the state of mind he should be in when he entered her room. He drew in a deep breath then walked calmly down the corridor and stopped in front of her door. He glanced at the guards before he entered. The two Germans stood stock still as they had been trained to do. Their bloodshot eyes, however, reflected the pain buried beneath the brawn. The emperor grabbed both their arms for comfort – his or theirs he wasn't quite sure – and went inside.

Sabina's bedroom was dim, reflecting the dark mood cloaking the place. Women in mourning garb padded about, doing meaningless chores. Zuester sat in a chair at his lady's bedside, his head in his hands. Hadrian dismissed the staff but motioned for Zuester to stay. Then he saw her, a small, tightly curled ball completely covered by the sheets and blankets. He sat on the edge of the mattress. She did not move.

"Vibia, are you well?" It was all he could think of to say at that moment.

She remained as she was.

Hadrian glanced at Zuester with questioning eyes. The secretary shook his head, unsure how to proceed.

The emperor was at his wit's end. He turned down the covers, revealing his wife's battered face. He choked down his shock and sorrow at the sight.

She looked up at him. "I am recovering," she said, her voice rough from crying.

Overcome with emotion, in one swift move Hadrian pulled her to him. "Vibia, I am so sorry! I should have been there to protect you." His tears were unstoppable.

Sabina shook with sobs. She clutched desperately at her husband.

"Please forgive me," he said softly, then motioned for Zuester to join them. "Darling, Zuester is here. He will take care of you."

Zuester sat on the bed tentatively, then at Hadrian's invitation, lay himself alongside Sabina. Hadrian tried to get up but Sabina continued to cling to him.

"Vibia, Vibia. Zuester will stay with you for the night. I've put the Germans at the door and the Africans on the roof. No one will ever harm you again. Ever." He held her face in his hands and looked deeply into her eyes. "Darling, I will find them. Believe me."

She relented amidst tears and turned to her lover. Zuester held her gently but firmly.

Hadrian got up and left his wife's bedroom determined to go seek out her attackers. Although he had sworn he would never use them, the remnants of Trajan's secret police, the *frumentarii*, would quite possibly be of service to him now.

Zuester wrapped his arms closely about Sabina, reminding her that she was not alone. She was still crying, but had slowed down to intermittent sobs spurred on by a sudden memory of what had happened. Every time she had such an emotional break, he made sure she knew he was there for her.

He did not tell her everything would be all right, that she would get through this, because he of all people knew that being forced into acts against one's will was not simply demeaning and dishonoring as outsiders might think, but a soul-crushing experience that utterly shattered one's world as one had understood it to be. Never would her life be the same, never would her relationships be the same. If she were ever able to trust anyone again it would not be for a very long time. If she were ever to feel safe in the world again it would take great effort to squelch her fears.

And if she were ever to talk about what happened to her, it would have to be on her own terms. It could not be forced out of her. Zuester would have to explain this to Hadrian. Luckily, the emperor was very accommodating when it came to matters concerning his wife, and would certainly comply.

The summer night was getting chilly, as the Roman party had learned was the norm in Britannia. Zuester realized that if he was to stay with Sabina all night he would have to be under the covers.

"Vibia," he said softly, tentatively. "It's getting cold in here. With your permission I would like to be under the covers. I am wearing my tunic and subligaculum. I also have my cloak. I can wrap myself in that instead."

Sabina turned over. In the pale lamplight he could see her eyes were puffy from crying, her face bruised and cut.

"I would like you to be with me, Zuester," she sniffled with a tremble in her voice. "Please get under the covers. It will be warmer."

Zuester was moved by her consent, knowing that it was the very first indication of being able to trust again. Tears welled in his own eyes as he joined her under the sheet and blanket.

They lay in silence for a moment, neither able to sleep.

"Zuester, I'm scared," she finally said.

"I know," he said.

"How would you know?" she snapped bitterly.

He ignored her acrimony knowing it came from pain and was not directed at him. "Because it happened to me. Many years ago, before I met you."

"You?" she questioned. "But you seem so…so…as if nothing bad ever happened to you."

"Like I said, it was many years ago. Fifteen years or more." He was gentle in his tone. "I will tell you if you feel you need to hear it."

Sabina paused a moment. "I didn't know. I would like to know. I think."

Zuester drew in a long breath. "After the war with Dacia, many Dacians were brought to Rome as slaves to be bought and sold, I among them. I understand that most of my people went into households to do menial and laborious tasks. But a few of us – all very young, all very handsome and pretty – were bought by a man who owned a grand villa. It was explained to us that we would lead a life of luxury if we did what we were told.

"Of course what youth would not want that! At first we lived in beautiful rooms with mosaics and frescoes. We ate to our hearts content. We enjoyed the sunshine in the courtyard, playing music and singing. And, as youths and maidens are wont to do, we fell in love.

"It was what our master had expected, and what he had wanted to happen. When he saw a pair looking moony he took them aside, then they would disappear. The rest of us had no idea where they went but imagined that the lovers were treated with even more extravagance. Rumor grew that they were taken to our master's even finer villa in the Bay of Naples.

"And then it happened to me. I fell in love with a girl, I must have been seventeen, she much younger. She was a virgin; I, however, had been with maids before in my homeland. The master took us aside and asked if we would like to be married and consummate our love. Of course we said yes.

"That night we were put in a room together, a wonderfully decorated room, with erotic scenes on the mosaic floor and bright red draperies covering the walls. A bed was in the center. We were told to not touch each other and to remain separated. We were elated, filled with anticipation of starting a new life in a luxurious villa in the south. I remember looking into her joyful eyes from across the room and mouthing, 'I love you.'

"Suddenly the drapes were raised. We were not alone, but in some sort of private amphitheater. There must have been a hundred or more men – and possibly some women – seated and watching us. My love was terrified. She screamed. Instantly several strong men strode in and picked her up, ripped off her clothes while she struggled and kicked, then deposited her on the bed, holding her down with thick, harsh hands. All the while I was held back by equally strong men. My master appeared at my side. I was to deflower my 'wife' – as he called her – before the audience, and if I refused I would be severely beaten and forced to watch as anyone who wanted would violate her.

"How does one react to that, what does one do? Especially when one is a youth, a slave, and suddenly aware that one was purchased to be the private sexual plaything of a wealthy madman? I said I would comply. I owed that to my love. I knew she would never forgive me if I were to leave her to any and all present.

"I was stripped of my clothing. There was to be no preparation, I was to simply enter her. I hesitated and immediately felt the consequences in the form of a whip across my back. I did it. I felt horrible. She was crying and flailing against her bondsmen. The crowd cheered when I broke her barrier, cheered when I myself climaxed, and cheered when the blood on the sheet – and on my penis – was exhibited.

"That night we were separated and put in what was to be our permanent home: an underground warren of cells, much like I understand prisons to be. From thence forward, we were expected to do anything and everything, and with whomever and whatever was available.

"As a man I do realize I was afforded a great many advantages and was not as abused as the women at the villa. Still, I was made to do acts with other men, other women, as well as animals. If I hesitated, I was whipped. If I had refused or did not perform well, the result was death. I witnessed many of my friends tortured and some I never saw again. I myself was beaten and whipped several times."

Zuester lay in silence alongside Sabina, feeling her breathe unsteadily.

"What happened to your girl," she finally asked. "Your betrothed?"

"I saw her sometimes, but in such an environment one is inured against all emotions. We never felt the same about each other. We learned to never feel any emotion akin to friendship toward anyone. Such feelings simply turned to pain. When I escaped she was still there."

"So that's what happened. You escaped."

"One day I overheard that the master's men were going to kill a boy I had foolishly become attached to, my cell mate. That night in our cell I knew I had had enough. The gods must have been with us. We found opportunity and escaped together."

Sabina moved her hand to touch Zuester's. "If you ever saw the master again, what would you do?"

"I would kill him," said Zuester categorically.

Sabina drew in a long breath and exhaled unsteadily. "I, too, would kill my attacker...I think. I've never felt such an emotion." The tears welled again. "I cannot get his face out of my mind. His eyes were...I can't explain, they were each a different color. A gruesome scar ran the length of his face. The memory has become more vivid because he was so distinct." She shook with sobs as she buried her face against the pillows and pressed against her protector.

A chill surged through Zuester's body enlivening every pore with horrific realization: The man who had assaulted Sabina had been none other than his former "master," Sextus Quintilius Bestia. The absolute delight in feeling Sabina reach out to him physically and emotionally was overshadowed by the hate-filled anger pumping through his veins.

Hadrian stared at the two men standing before his desk in his private office in the palace. Because of their idle chatter, Suetonius and Septicius had put his wife's life at risk and had marred her reputation. The emperor had no replacements for the men; he simply wanted them out of his court.

"You are to speak not a word of this to anyone," Hadrian said caustically to his former officers. "If I hear that you have divulged this information to any person – casually, purposefully, poetically, however – I will make life very unpleasant for you." He looked up at them. "Do I make myself clear?"

"Yes, my lord," they muttered in unison.

"You may go. I have your resignations. I expect you to simply explain to the curious that you have completed your service to the emperor and are welcoming your retirement with open arms."

As the two men exited, two Praetorians arrived at the door.

"Yes," said Hadrian perhaps a little too harshly to the young men.

"My lord," said the taller of the two, bowing. "I have news which is of interest to you concerning the welfare of the empress."

Hadrian studied them. They were both towering, athletic, handsome. They were *frumentarii*, the select of the Praetorians.

"Close the door."

"My lord emperor," continued the taller guard in the secluded office. "The men in question have been found. There are ten of them. We await your orders for their fate."

Hadrian knew exactly what he wanted done to the bastards who had assaulted his wife. He wanted to personally sever the cocks and slit the throats of each and every one of them. That, however, would appear as an act of madness. Nonetheless, he had no qualms about exacting personal justice in such cases as this.

"Is the leader among them?"

"No, my lord. He remains at large and has possibly left the island. But from information supplied to us by the empress, we know his physical appearance, and from information supplied by the secretary Zuester, we now know his name."

Hadrian raised his eyebrows at the latter. With such leads, surely his Guard would be able to track the villain down. Until that time, a message would have to be sent to this evil man, a very strong message.

"Kill all ten men. No mercy. Leave no trace of who has committed the deed."

"Yes, sire. We know of certain local practices of murder which will deflect any suspicion of our own involvement."

"Very good," said Hadrian. "Tomorrow we leave for Gaul. Have it done after that."

Part Three:
Tempus Autumnum

The Mediterranean to Asia Minor, 122-123

Through Gaul and Hispania, on the boat in the Mediterranean sea, and along the coast of North Africa, Zuester was there for Sabina. She had refused to return to Rome. She was determined to be with her husband as she had originally intended during his grand tour of the provinces.

Hadrian had been worried at first. She was not fit to travel, he had said privately to Zuester. But the under-secretary respectfully disagreed, stating that the empress needed distractions and needed to see that the world was not utterly filled with villains and criminals. It would soothe the emperor's nerves, as well, seeing his wife in good hands.

Once in Gaul the party received the sad news of the death of Plotina. Hadrian deified his adoptive mother and founded a temple in her honor in her hometown of Nemausus when they passed through. He would not let grief immobilize his administration, so while in Gaul announced the appointment of Lucius Julius Vestinus, the former governor of Egypt, as Imperial Secretary. Vestinus was a veteran of several emperors, and, despite his advanced years, was willing to join the royal party to Hadrian's satisfaction. Of course, this freed up Zuester to pay more attention to his ladyship.

Misfortune seemed to follow the imperial assemblage, however. An assassination attempt was made upon Hadrian at Tarraco in Hispania. The attacker, a slave, was pronounced a madman. Certainly he was not politically motivated, nor connected to the conspirators from Britannia. Only slightly shaken, the party continued their journeys.

After briefly reviewing Legion discipline and other administrative matters in the north African provinces, the party headed east. War with Parthia was once again a possibility. First stopping in Crete, they finally sailed into Antioch.

Sabina breathed in the salty air. "Antioch is a second home for me, Zuester," she said. "It feels good to be in a familiar place."

Her spirits were up, she slept better, she laughed. The journey to exotic locations had worked miracles for her soul. Of course Zuester's constant care had also been a great help. After a year, she had let him kiss her, let him touch her naked flesh, but had still withheld sexual intimacy. She was still afraid. The cramps and pain had gone away, but the deeply entrenched fear had, ultimately, not.

And when they continued on their travels across Asia Minor, Zuester continued to do whatever was needed to be done for the sake of his empress, his love.

Bithynia, near Bithynium-Claudiopolis, September 123

The deer were swift in Bithynia which made them more of a challenge to hunt. Of course, as the emperor preferred boar meat to venison, he also enjoyed the pursuit of the relatively more lackadaisical wild boars. However, the most prized prey was the Anatolian leopard, and for such a hunt, even an expert like Hadrian needed local men.

A team had been gathered from nearby Bithynium-Claudiopolis, a small city between the Black Sea and the forested hills where the leopards lived. Twelve men, ranging in ages from youth to middle-age, assembled around the emperor as he performed the proper sacrifices and rites. When the gods had been suitably thanked, the team went out to seek the precious fauna.

Hadrian, skilled hunter that he was, was also an adept student of observation. He hung back, watching the locals track and signal, feeling the anticipation and desire for the catch build and ensnare all involved.

The leopard had eluded the party, had avoided even being seen. To flush out their prey, all assembled took a respite to remain still and quiet. It worked. The animal popped its head up above the brush to see if its way was finally clear. Like Pegasus galloping with beating wings, the local men reacted fleetly, more swiftly than the poor leopard. The beast was shot with at least three arrows.

A meaningful smile spread across Hadrian's lips as he regarded the victors. One was a mature eccentric who had snagged the leopard in the rear left leg. Another was a still-young family man who had engaged the emperor earlier in conversation about his six children. The third, however, had somehow gone unnoticed by Hadrian up until the moment he shot the creature with an arrow to the heart. He was the most beautiful youth the emperor had ever laid eyes upon.

The golden-haired Apollo had been utterly focused on his goal. His movements with the bow were second nature, as if the quiver and arrow were simply extensions of his supremely athletic body. His horse, as well, was one with him. It proudly carried the magnificent youth to the now-inflamed Hadrian.

"The leopard still lives, my emperor," the youth said in heavily accented Latin. "It is yours to kill." He bowed.

The lyrical quality to the youth's voice diverted Hadrian with a shameless fantasy. "Thank you," he said with as much charm as he could muster.

Hadrian dealt the final blow. The leopard would have died shortly from the youth's deed, but etiquette and custom demanded that the Emperor of Rome be the ultimate victor.

"The youth and his compatriots shall be my guests at dinner tonight," Hadrian said to a servant in attendance.

Until he was to see him again, Hadrian would have to be content with daydreams involving himself and the beautiful boy.

"He will have his fourteenth birthday in a little over two months, my lord," said Zuester quietly in Hadrian's ear at dinner that night.

Hadrian drew in a breath. He himself was forty-seven. Would a youth as spectacular as that even look at him? "It is too fantastical a notion to imagine myself with such a one as he."

"Well, I needn't remind you, you are the Emperor of Rome, and may have whatever you wish," Zuester baited. "Besides, from what your wife tells me, you are in rather excellent condition."

Hadrian shot Zuester an annoyed look, then softened after seeing his secretary's smirk.

"I've been too obvious tonight, haven't I?"

"No, my lord. Except to those who know you intimately."

Hadrian smiled and patted his secretary on the back. "I am lucky to have such devoted friends," he said.

"And if I can be of service, sire, simply let me know."

Hadrian knew Zuester was genuine in his solicitation. And as he hadn't quite figured out the best way of approaching the youth in question, perhaps the Dacian *could* be of service.

"At the very least, tell me his name."

"Antinous. He is a native of these parts, hence his skill with the leopard. He's been hunting since he was a child."

Hadrian took a draught of his wine and glanced at Zuester. "How is it you know all of this?"

"I am reluctant to tell you, Caesar, for fear it may embolden you."

"Zuester," Hadrian said, warning dripping from his voice.

The secretary smiled. "He inquired about you, and as I was the only one amongst the courtiers who spoke fluent Greek, we struck up a conversation. He finds you charming and kind, and perhaps even a little bit handsome."

Hadrian inhaled deeply, then shook his head. "Jupiter be damned. I'm no longer a naïve prince, I'm the bloody emperor. He's merely flattering me to satisfy his own ambitions." He put down his wine cup. "Which, I suppose, I should at least take notice of since he has such ambitions at this early an age."

"I'm not so sure that is a correct estimation of his character, my lord," replied Zuester. "When you converse with him in person you will see. He's quite beguiling and leaves one with a warm glow inside, but I don't think his charm is meant to deceive."

Hadrian grunted. Deep inside he felt like a nervous, insecure youth who had fallen head over heels but was afraid of being rejected if he revealed his feelings to the object of his affection.

Zuester seemed to understand. "I will set up a meeting tonight if you wish. You can discuss his hunting techniques. It will have the veneer of innocence and practicality. And afterwards, if you are still concerned about his motives, then I'll help you mend your broken heart."

"All right," Hadrian agreed. "Alone, but not too far from the dining hall." *I don't want to be left in the cold.*

Antinous had been told to wait on the balcony of the villa where the feast was taking place. It was night, but he knew the view over the forested hills would be spectacular during the day. It was a shame he would never have a chance to witness the sight.

He felt nervous. The man from Dacia who spoke Greek had told him the emperor wished to converse with him about the leopard hunt and his local techniques. But deep inside Antinous didn't want to discuss the hunt, he wanted to learn about the man himself. There was something about the emperor Hadrian that drew him in, that mesmerized him.

Antinous had known for the last few years that he was not interested in taking a wife and leading a familial existence in Bithynia. The other local boys, not much older than he, were beginning to do just that. But he felt indifference toward the female sex. He had never had crushes on local girls, like his friends had, but he had had crushes on some of his male friends. They had played around physically a bit, but most of his friends felt that they were now too old to continue such childish games. Until such time as he would have to take a wife, he wanted to fantasize about handsome men with beards and a taste for the hunt.

"Antinous," came a soft, deep voice behind him.

The youth jumped in surprise and turned around. It was the emperor himself and he was alone. Antinous flushed then worked up the courage to speak. "Good evening, sire."

Hadrian must have noticed the tremor in his voice. "You needn't be nervous son. It is really I who should be nervous of your precise aim and agility in dealing a blow."

"You speak Greek!" Antinous exclaimed gleefully.

"Fluently," said the emperor with a smile.

"I had expected a translator to join us and was concerned he would not know all the proper vocabulary."

Hadrian laughed. "I see my reputation does not precede me here in Bithynia."

"I don't understand, sir."

"I am well-versed in Greek culture and philosophy, as well as the language." He strode out to the edge of the balcony and beckoned the youth to join him. "What a grand vista this will be in the morning light."

"I was thinking just that, my lord," Antinous exclaimed, placing his hands on the railing.

"Really?" Hadrian said, turning to look at his companion.

Antinous blushed again knowing he was being scrutinized in the dim light of the lamps and the moon. "I apologize, sir, if I spoke out of turn. I fear I tend to babble in my nervousness. I've never been around an emperor before."

Hadrian guffawed and placed his arm around the youth's shoulders. "I don't bite. And as it is simply you and me at the moment, then you may babble all you want. I think my officials will expect you to behave with decorum when you are amongst them, though."

Antinous looked up at Hadrian. *His beard seems so soft.* "Thank you, sire," he said with a smile.

"Now let's talk about your hunting," said Hadrian with a pat on Antinous's back. "You and your party had some interesting techniques and I want to hear all about them."

Zuester had been looking for his master all morning. Hadrian had apparently not been in his bed all night. No one else seemed to be concerned, however, including the secretary Vestinus and the Praetorians. But as Zuester had spent the night with the empress, he was not aware of what was going on. Against Vestinus's protests, he went to seek the emperor.

He found him where he had left him the night before, out on the balcony but in rather different circumstances. Hadrian and Antinous lay wrapped up in blankets on couches on either side of a bronze cauldron with a warming fire. They were chatting amicably, as if they were old friends.

Hadrian looked up when the under-secretary made his appearance. "Ah, Zuester! I suppose if you are here then my evening's amusements must be over." He began to shake off his blankets. "I guess there will be correspondence to sign and people to meet today. Does Vestinus have my agenda?"

"Yes, my lord," said Zuester a little distractedly. The golden-haired Antinous had gotten up and strolled to the balcony. With a blanket around his shoulders he stood staring out at the view.

"We've been exchanging hunting stories all night," Hadrian said as he stood up. "I'm surprised there's an animal left in Bithynia after hearing about Antinous's exploits." He looked over at the youth as he stood at the railing. "He's marvelous," he intimated, as he stared at the object of his affection. "Very bright. He shares my interest in philosophy." He turned to his secretary. "Come," he beckoned as he went to join his new friend at the railing.

"It's a beautiful sight," Hadrian said, casually draping an arm around the boy's shoulders. "You have beautiful country here, my boy."

"I've never seen my home from such a place as this. It is as if the villa were placed here in order to take advantage of this view."

Hadrian laughed. "Yes, Antinous, that is precisely what has been done. That is what people who build villas on hills do."

Zuester realized the youth was genuinely awestruck, and from the comfort displayed in their pose, that he and the emperor had formed a close bond overnight.

Hadrian turned to the boy and placed both hands on his shoulders. "Antinous, how would you like to join the imperial party in our travels? I'll show you lots of views and you can try your hand at hunting strange beasts. Of course, I also have my work to do, as the emperor's job is never finished. But I will make a point to see you every day."

Antinous stood before Hadrian wide-eyed, disbelieving what he had just heard. "Do you truly mean that, sir? I can join you?"

"Certainly!" effused an enamored Hadrian.

"But first," interjected Zuester, "you must attend the imperial school in Rome where you'll improve your Latin and learn the ways of the court."

Hadrian chuckled. "Of course. My under-secretary knows far more about this sort of thing than I do." He gazed at the youth. "Would you like to go to Rome?"

Antinous's eyes widened. "Rome?"

Zuester smiled to himself. Clearly the youth thought Rome to be a magical, wondrous metropolis and not the squalid den of urban iniquity it often was. He could almost see the fantasies flash through the youth's mind.

"I must ask permission from my parents," Antinous said with a touch of uncertainty.

The emperor nodded at Zuester. "My secretary will arrange that."

Suddenly overcome by the invitation, Antinous threw his arms around Hadrian's waist. "Thank you, Caesar, sir! Thank you!" he exclaimed.

Zuester watched as Hadrian wrapped his arms around the youth and gently caressed his back. The emperor seemed temporarily lost in the embrace as he casually threaded his fingers through the youth's golden locks. Antinous softly sighed.

Zuester walked away knowing it would not be long before the man and the youth would find solace in another kind of embrace.

Suebia, May 124

As he pulled the fur bed-clothes closer around him, Bestia kept reminding himself that he had once thought Britannia was cold. But Suebia? Suebia was *fucking* cold. Why the gods allowed humans to live in such a forbidden wasteland, he could not guess. Perhaps it was only to instill desire for a better way of life, a voracious, blood-thirsty, marauding desire. These Suebis were truly animalistic, uncivilized barbarians. No wonder the Romans built fortifications to keep them at bay.

The warm naked body of a youth fidgeted at his side, not realizing, however, he was privileged to be in Suebia and not further north, across the water. Bestia had just endured the most horrific winter – his second – amongst one particular tribe, the Suiones, a tall, blond race that lived on what seemed to be another island in the cold northern seas. If Suebia was fucking cold, then the damned island of the Suiones was *bloody fucking* cold. For the first time in his life Bestia had felt sorry for the servant boys sleeping on the cold stone hearth before night's fading fire. He himself had only had a mattress stuffed with straw, yet, as it was raised from the floor, it shielded the chill from his bones. The servants had complied readily when beckoned to his bed. And they did not complain about his violation of their young bodies at night and again in the morning.

It had been almost two years since he had fled his home in Britannia, after his attack on the empress. He had expected the emperor to act, but not in such a swift and decisive manner. His men had been slaughtered, including the sweet Comuxus, and his estate near Verulamium had been overrun by a mob incited by the prospect of looting the riches of an enemy of Rome. Once he had crossed the Oceanus Germanicus, word awaited for him that his villa on the Quirinal Hill had been searched and plundered, his slaves set free. He could never go back to Rome. He was a man on the run. But with his powerful connections, his labyrinthine network of spies, his cruel yet generous reputation, it did not matter. He would start again.

Bestia reached for the oil lamp still warm from its recent flame. He loved starting again. Too often men in his service would become overly ambitious, would offer their own opinions when not asked, would even act against his orders. It was always good to cleanse oneself of such odious upstarts. Killing them could be difficult if they had formed their own alliances. Having a common enemy murder them, as had the Roman emperor this last time, was always preferable and kept allegiances open to every possibility. Even in the barren hinterland that was Suebia, he was gathering an entourage based on the strength of his personality, the notoriety of his erotic spectacles, and his hatred toward Rome.

Bestia poured oil onto his palm, then stroked his eager cock, slowly, thoughtfully. During his stay across the Mare Suebicum, it seemed to him every enemy of Rome had a representative in the court of the Suionine king.

Refugees, expatriates, and ambassadors were forming alliances in the unlikely frozen island of Scania. Germanic tribes such as the Chatti, Caledonians barred from Britannia by the emperor's new wall, Sarmatians chomping at the bit near Dacia, Parthians loyal to the dethroned Osrhoes, even radical Jews unhappy with the emerging policy of assimilation. All were friends because they shared an enemy. The naval strength of the Suiones facilitated assembling such an alternate empire in the north.

The Parthians, unbelievably, had been a part of this northern empire since their conquest by Trajan ten years earlier. Several occupied positions in the court of the Suionine king, lending a cosmopolitan air to the otherwise barbarian outpost. It was from these courtiers that Bestia learned of the plans of the imprisoned Parthian princess Roedogune. From her guarded villa in Rome she had made contact with any who would seek to return her family to the palace at Ctesiphon. She had not specified that she wanted to do away with the Roman emperor, but Bestia had sent word to her that if she would be part of his ambitions, he would help her in hers.

He toyed with the tight arse of one of his bed mates. He did not need help really. He was quite capable of arranging an assassination from beyond the borders of empire, an assassination on the other side of the empire even. Just a few months ago, the emperor had been hunting in the mountains of Mysia – it was simply too easy to attack the man while he hunted – and Bestia's men had arranged for Anatolian locals to ambush the imperial party from the trees. Unfortunately, the men had been paid in advance, had wasted their money on women and drink, and only one of their group was sober enough to continue with the assault. Hadrian had been clearly disquieted, especially with the attack on his wife still fresh in his memory, but the local had been merely punished and dismissed. The assassination attempt had failed miserably, not, Bestia reminded himself, from anything he did, but because of the foolish incompetence of others.

Bestia pulled the younger of the two boys in his bed against him and poised his now rock-hard prick at the lubricated anus. No, he did not need help in attacking the emperor. No. But now that he was effectively banished, he needed access to Rome. A princess in captivity in the heart of the capital could do wonders.

The boy struggled just a bit at the invasion. Bestia groaned in satisfaction as he pushed deeper inside the tight orifice of the youth and wondered if the Parthian princess would be as delicious a conquest.

Athens, Imperial villa, September 124

Hadrian watched his wife sun herself in the rooftop patio of their villa in Athens. It had been two years since her attack, and two years since they had been intimate. Zuester had protected her loyally, for which Hadrian was grateful. His wife deserved all the attention the Dacian lavished upon her in this dark time. Hadrian knew he couldn't be there for her for as much as she needed. They saw each other infrequently, but when they did they both knew the bond of love was as strong as ever.

One of the ladies-in-waiting noticed the emperor standing with his arms crossed, gazing at his wife. She nudged the empress awake.

"Ah, my husband has found time in his busy schedule to visit me," Sabina joked affectionately.

"Vibia," Hadrian nodded his greeting. "I see the Athenian air is to your liking."

She scooted over on her couch and patted the space next to her. Away from the court, from the crowds, she could be bold and exhibit her true emotions. "Sit, husband," she said.

The ladies-in-waiting bowed as the emperor came forward, then retreated to allow husband and wife some privacy.

Hadrian smiled and took his wife's hand in his as he took his place at her side.

"You may kiss me, you know," she teased, her eyes bright with regard for the man before her. "They won't tell," she whispered, indicating the servants now busily sewing in the corner of the patio.

Hadrian leaned over and at first pecked her lips tenderly. Overwhelmed by a passion he had not felt in a long time, he kissed her again, his lips and tongue tangling familiarly with hers.

"That's better," she said when they parted, biting her lip playfully.

Hadrian laughed at his wife, still flirting with him after so many years of marriage. "I cannot tell you how much it warms me to see you in high spirits." He smoothed her hair then held her cheek for a moment. "Zuester has done his job keeping you company exceptionally well."

"And somehow still has time to deal with your correspondence," she giggled. She played with his fingers, tugging them distractedly, threading hers in between. "I hear you've banned knives at the Eleusinian ceremonies this year."

"Yes," he said glumly. "It's for our safety, love."

Sabina changed the subject quickly. "Tell me about the boy," she said patting his hand. "I suspect you've no hunting opportunities in Athens or else you'd be off with him and not here with me."

"Uh-oh, you feel neglected. I can tell," he bantered.

"I'm happy for you, Graeculus," she said. "Really."

"Unfortunately, your lover sent him away."

Sabina looked at him with astonishment. "Whatever for?"

"The imperial paedagogium. Training to be a palace page."

"Ah, well, that's for the best, isn't it? You certainly know how to seduce page boys."

Hadrian laughed out loud. He gazed at the wonderful woman at his side. He was bursting to divulge his feelings to his wife, his best friend. "I know I can say this to you because I've seen you with Zuester, I've seen how the two of you act in private with each other." He drew in a breath. "Vibia, I think I'm in love. I've never felt this way for anyone. Not even you, and I love you dearly. It's frightening to lose control over one's emotions like this."

"It's wonderful as well, Graeculus," she rejoindered.

"But to not know if he reciprocates…to be so far away from him…to not know when I will see him again…it's maddening. And what if he is repulsed by the attentions of an old man?"

"You're not just *any* old man, Graeculus. You're the Emperor of Rome."

Hadrian shot her a perturbed look.

"And, love, you're not an old man. You're a man in your prime, really. I think the youth will be flattered." Sabina touched his bare thigh under his tunic, massaging the lean muscles delicately. "To think you have been burning for a year. That is not like you, husband. I would imagine that you would have rushed off to Rome by now."

"I've never been in love before!" He stood up and paced before sitting back down. "How do I begin? What do I do?"

Sabina smiled. "I seem to recall I had help in the form of a very devious husband who made sure the object of my desire entered my room when I was most opportunely naked."

Hadrian grinned. "I never knew that. You were naked?"

"He couldn't resist," she said.

Hadrian turned serious. "And now?"

"We haven't, well, engaged in coitus yet. I'm still wary, even though I'm certain I'm completely healed. He pleasures me. But even he is afraid to let me pleasure him with my mouth. He thinks it's too, um, 'dominating' is the word I think he used."

Hadrian gazed at his wife lovingly. "Vibia, let us make a pact. I will seduce my boy if you seduce your lover."

"And then we can compare notes?"

He kissed her forehead. "That is why I love you so much, my darling wife."

Zuester plopped down on Sabina's bed that night. "Ugh," he groaned. "I'm exhausted."

"Has my husband been working you too hard, my sweet?" asked Sabina.

He noted a coquettishness in her tone that he had not heard in a long time. Perhaps she was testing the waters again? He decided to not play with her just yet, and instead string her along.

"Remember that wall we started in Britannia? There've been some problems with that, on top of all the correspondence from the other provinces. Now that Rome's subjects have personally met their emperor, the petitions seem endless." He stretched his spine along the mattress.

"Including from your mother," Sabina reminded him.

He chuckled. They had visited the northern provinces of Dacia and Moesia on their journeys, and the secretary had been granted leave to visit with his family. When the emperor appeared, quite unexpectedly, Zuester's mother had berated him for keeping her son too skinny.

Sabina knelt on the bed next to her lover. "My husband is lucky to have such a hard worker as you." She placed a hand on his thigh and slowly moved it upward. "Especially since he is so distracted by the youth."

Zuester felt his body react to Sabina's touch. Every pore was on fire. "Antinous, even hundreds of miles away, is good for him. I think Hadrian in love is more focused sometimes than Hadrian the politician."

Sabina moved her hand between Zuester's thighs, caressing the down-covered skin, her thumb tugging impatiently at his subligaculum. "I think you may lose his focused mind when he finally beds his Antinous."

Zuester looked at her perplexed. "Is the boy here?"

She smiled as her teasing hand finally decided to pull loose the linen wrapped around his groin. "No," she giggled. She smiled once more before bowing her head and taking his cock into her mouth. He was already semi-hard from her playful caresses.

"Vibia," he protested weakly. "Are you ready, love?"

She lifted her head to look up at him. "Are *you* ready, my love?" she asked, biting her lip.

"Oh, yes," he moaned. Zuester leaned back against the pillows as Sabina licked and sucked him, remembering how she used to do it. He closed his eyes and beat back tears. She was his again. And that night they would celebrate the occasion with every part of their bodies.

Rome, Caelius Mons, Caput Africae, April 125

The imperial paedagogium proved to offer much more than instruction in how to be a page in the Roman court. For a naïve boy of the provinces, it was an eye-opening experience that quickly bore him to manhood.

Boys as young as twelve from wealthy families across the empire were brought to the Caput Africae on the Caelian Hill for their training. The younger ones began with instruction in the duties of running the emperor's household. As they grew older, the boys learned administration and complex finances toward their eventual careers in the civil service and estate management. All learned proper literary Latin and Greek, courtly customs and manners, and partook of a regiment of calisthenics for strength and agility.

The master of the school, a formidable freedman from Gaul, instilled obedience with both fear and love. Defiance and insubordination meant punishment in the dank, dark basement. Disregard of the rules and forgetfulness of the lessons often produced merely a rap on the knuckles or a sharp smack on the head. But tasks perfectly done and verses beautifully recited were met with privileges at dinner, a special outing, or, perhaps, extracurricular instruction in the master's quarters.

Truly obedient and intelligent boys were allowed to visit the homes of important and wealthy Romans. These boys came back with stories of being treated to rare pleasures of the flesh – tasty delicacies, perfumed baths, the latest gossip, and the sight of girls and women, all of which only served to inflame the youths' burgeoning desires.

As they progressed in the school, and as they grew from boys to young men, their bodies awakened to new carnal cravings. With no one but themselves and their companions, the boys experimented, some more willingly or more adventurously than others. Such activities were neither encouraged nor discouraged; they were tolerated as long as they were not disruptive.

As the very special favorite of Hadrian himself, Antinous was treated much differently from the other pupils. He was not pampered, but he was not mistreated. Most seemed to know he had been hunting with the emperor, had discussed Greek philosophy with him, and had been handpicked to attend the paedagogium. Such knowledge would seem to cause jealousy or even feed ambitions amongst the sons of the provincial gentry, but Antinous was not one to instill such negative and petty emotions. Even at his young age he was kind and patient. He was, simply, *good*.

Yet, because of his special status, Antinous was lonely. As they found him so comely and alluring, some of the older boys were able to form fleeting attachments with him. But not one of them could match the intelligence and wit, nor instill in him the exciting twinge of lust, as the enigmatic yet magnetic Hadrian. Antinous hoped beyond hope that he would meet the emperor – *his* emperor – again. At least he had had that one night, a memory he relived countless times in his bed alone.

Thespiae, Boeotia, April 125

They had been away from Rome for four years, Hadrian reminded himself. It was time to go back. Time to make his presence known and felt in the capital, to act as emperor before the Senate no matter how much that chamber despised him, to reacquaint himself with his native subjects who still adored him.

Time to return home, where there now lived a certain youth, a beautiful young man who was utterly unaware that he had conquered the heart of the emperor of Rome.

Hadrian could not stop thinking about Antinous. Zuester had been right to send the youth away so that the emperor could concentrate on doing whatever it was an emperor was expected to do amongst the people of his provinces – restore roads, dedicate temples, hear petitions. In addition to his work, Hadrian had tried to distract himself with page boys to no avail. Even dalliances with the more youthful of his courtiers had become rote physical release. Sabina was compliant and patient and offered him a tantalizing hint of what it was like to be with the person with whom one was utterly enamored, yet he found this more frustrating than fulfilling.

In a few months, they would be back in Rome, where waiting for him was the possibility of true love.

And on the return trip, Zuester had suggested, Caesar must avail himself of the wonderful opportunities for hunting in the forests of Boeotia. Hadrian, his secretary offered, might find temporary solace in this exhilarating activity.

Hadrian often wondered how it was the Dacian freedman knew him so well.

Game was plentiful in the lush mountainside, but the magnificent vistas of the Greek landscape were distracting, reminding Hadrian of his night with the youth in Bithynia. From his swift horse, the emperor killed a bear not far from Thespiae, a town devoted to the worship of Eros, the son of Aphrodite, the goddess of love. As he watched his men carefully remove the skin from the animal, Hadrian found himself overcome with emotion, remembering the leopard hunt with Antinous. He suddenly felt restless, he needed to walk, to run, to think, to attempt to comprehend this gift from the gods. Mount Helicon, the home of the nine Muses, loomed before him. He set off alone, the ursine pelt tucked under his arm, and told his attendants that he would return in the morning.

He chose a ledge with a view of the verdant forested surroundings, a vista which heightened his awareness of being a man – not Caesar – alone in the wilderness. As he sat outside his tent watching birds rustle through the tops of trees, a smile tugged on his lips. He could easily become accustomed to being a private man, to living by his wits day to day, hunting his food, pitching his tent. Still, it would be better if he had someone with whom to share his world.

When the sun began to set, he prepared his offering to Eros. He unfurled the bear skin, crisscrossing newly-cut myrtle boughs at the head, placed a myrtle crown on his own head, then lit seven lamps. He poured a cup of fermented honey and lifted it to the purplish sky, now dotted with the faint light of emerging stars.

"Oh Eros, archer son of the sweet-tongued Cyprian, who dwells at Heliconian Thespiae nearby Narcissus's flowering garden, breathe your quiet grace upon me, that grace which is given to you from heavenly Aphrodite Urania..."

Hadrian sipped from the cup.

"...so that I may know her favor."

Once again he drank the liquor, this time finishing the contents of the gold vessel. He closed his eyes, lifted his face and breathed in the night air.

"But, Graeculus, I am the goddess of spiritual love. Are you certain that is what you desire?"

Hadrian's hand flashed to the hilt at his side as he turned toward the voice.

Before him was the most magnificent sight. There stood a woman of uncommon beauty, larger than life, glowing with a light from within. She was clad in shimmering cloth that seemed to disappear when it touched her body, revealing a form so profoundly feminine that all womankind must have sprung forth from her.

He instinctively recognized her as Aphrodite Urania – Celestial Aphrodite – the goddess of pure, spiritual love.

Hadrian sank to his knees. "My lady!" he exclaimed bowing his head.

"Get up, foolish man. You are the emperor of Rome. I am merely a goddess."

Hadrian opened his mouth to protest but saw Aphrodite was smiling. She offered her hand. When he took it, the world fell away and he was in the clouds.

"You've never wanted anything from me, Graeculus. Why is that? Has age mellowed you?"

"On the contrary. Youth has inspired me."

"Ah. Clever man." Aphrodite spread her arms wide scattering the clouds. "You can have anything you want." She walked to a curtain billowing white in the dissipating fog, then pulled it back. Half a dozen naked youths sprawled amidst a cloud, their limbs intertwined. Delicate fingers stroked taut thighs, insistent fists pumped eager cocks, moist mouths sought mutual satisfaction.

Hadrian exhaled a sigh. The youths were exquisite, enticing. One boy caught the emperor's eye. He dismissed his fondling mate to approach the new object of his desire, his hand reaching out in solicitation. The instant his delicate fingers touched the emperor's chest, Hadrian's tunic disappeared, revealing his potent erection which the youth proceeded to tug. Hadrian sucked in a breath and stilled the boy's hand.

"Do boys no longer please you?" Aphrodite asked ingenuously.

"They can please me physically. Yet the act is no longer the same since I met him. I now know what could be."

The goddess dismissed the youth. "What *could be*?" she challenged, circling the emperor. She stopped before him, her body a hair's breadth away, her lips poised above his. "What about a woman?" she breathed. "What about a goddess? *What…about…me*?"

Every pore on his flushed skin tingled with anticipation. Her seductive powers were no match for his weak human flesh. Hadrian pulled the goddess to him and kissed her open mouth, feeling heated shocks pulse through him where his body melted into hers.

"You are arousing, yes," he murmured against her lips. "Provocative to be sure. But it is only fleshly desire; there is still an emptiness inside. Even with the goddess of love."

She pulled back from him, amused. "What is it that you think could be with your Antinous?" She stretched out her hand indicating the very youth seated amongst the clouds.

A spark ignited inside Hadrian, quickly flaring to rapturous desire. He started toward his passion. Aphrodite put up a hand.

"No," she said plainly.

"My lady, please," he begged. "I don't understand."

"You must know what you want."

"I want him," Hadrian said frantically, pointing to Antinous. "What he does to me. How he makes me feel."

"This is not enough."

"It is not libidinous. It is not base." Hadrian paced back and forth, gesturing wildly. "It is like pure joy rushing through me when I think about him. All at once I feel comfortable, secure, yet aroused and inflamed. I simply cannot express it. I've never felt such an emotion. It is beyond my comprehension, as if a gift from the gods."

She smiled. "Is it like this?"

Aphrodite pointed behind the emperor. He spun around, finding himself in his wife's bedroom in Rome. It was night, the scene before him lit only by lamp light.

It was Sabina and Zuester in an earnest embrace.

"I—"

"Like this?" the goddess asked calmly.

Suddenly, Hadrian was on top of his wife, making fervid love to her, thrusting in and out of her clenching passage, their bodies undulating as one, their breaths and moans uniting in an amorous chorus. Yet something was very, very different. The act felt strange, unfamiliar, nothing like it usually did; it was far more profound and intense than he had ever experienced. The heat of passion boiled in the pit of his belly radiating pleasure throughout his body, exciting every erogenous nerve. His heart filled with an expansive warmth, his head danced with dizzying giddiness.

He studied his wife's face. She returned his gaze with an expression he had never before encountered, an expression of unguarded and utter abandon, an expression of pure joy with an expectation of more.

Hadrian glanced at the mirror propped up near the bedside. His eyes widened in astonishment.

He wasn't Hadrian. He was Zuester.

He looked back down at the woman moaning beneath him. This was what Zuester and Sabina experienced together.

His climax was unearthly.

He rolled onto his back, laughing in jubilant hysteria. "Yes, yes," he panted squeezing his eyes shut. "This is what it is. Not just the physical, but something beyond. I am…I feel…transported."

With a gulp and a gasp, Hadrian opened his eyes. It was dawn. He lay on the bearskin, his hand holding his cock covered in his emission. He sat up and looked around. The goddess was gone. Everything was gone except for his tent as he himself had set it up the night before. He smiled. He was in love and Aphrodite had given him her blessing.

Rome, June 125

Hadrian's entry into the city, his *adventus*, was, as it should have been after years of absence, festive indeed. Commemorative coins had been struck in his honor, public prayers were offered, and an adoring citizenry had come out to greet the royal party. Zuester had been a member of the imperial entourage and was openly exposed as Sabina's lover. Her broad smile made known her pleasure at the arrangement. Zuester was quite surprised at the attention his new status drew.

The day was very different from the emperor's entry seven years before, Zuester recalled. Of course, Hadrian had at that time returned from a failed war after the death of a popular ruler. But the most important dissimilarity this time around was that Hadrian himself was in a very good mood. He was in good health, just proven weeks prior by his climbing Aetna, the volcanic mountain of Sicily, in late May. His building campaign for Rome had progressed immensely well while he had been away. The Pantheon, his tribute to all the gods, had been completed. The Temple to the Deified Trajan and Plotina was almost finished. He had remodeled the imperial palace in the city, the residence on the Palatine Hill originally built by the despised Domitian. Plus, work on Hadrian's own estate at Tibur was progressing: From sleepy country villa it was being turned into a sprawling royal palace.

And, of course, the emperor was in love. Deeply in love. The object of his affection was not yet cognizant of this, as Zuester well knew. But it did not change the fact that Hadrian was feeling invincible and fearless. His eternal opponent, the Senate, did not know what they were up against.

It was unclear to Zuester if it had been this new-found infatuation and the intent of its fulfillment that had changed his own relationship with the emperor of Rome. Hadrian had somehow garnered a new admiration and respect for Zuester. He had exhibited of late certain familiarities, at times smiling knowingly and draping his arm around the freedman's shoulder, at other times telling Zuester to go "have his fun" with Sabina. Zuester could only imagine this all stemmed from Hadrian's own desires.

In addition, Zuester's position in the household and court at Rome seemed nebulous, perhaps, he speculated, because of his history and resulting relationships with both the emperor and the empress. While each of the dozens upon dozens of servants, slaves, and staff who worked for the emperor had a precise duty from which he or she rarely deviated, Zuester himself was given a variety of tasks, never quite the same from day to day. He usually worked as one of Hadrian's many secretaries, yet he was also called upon to supervise the personal attendants in the apartments of the emperor and empress, to confer with the imperial steward and financial administrators, and to advise Sabina in her business matters. Most importantly of all, he remained the empress's lover and companion, and was amongst the emperor's intimate friends, his *amici*, and attended the emperor far more than any mere servant would.

Soon after their arrival in Rome, Sabina retreated to the Tibur villa to concentrate on her business matters, taking Zuester with her. She had legacies left by her mother Matidia to deal with, including a brick-making business that was supplying Hadrian's building projects.

"I've left their care in the hands of accountants for too long," she explained to Zuester one night. "It is about time I get reacquainted with the sources of my income. Perhaps I have enough to found a temple." Indeed, Zuester thought, from just a glance at her books, she probably had enough for quite a few temples.

Comfortable in the arms of his lover, Zuester knew he would enjoy his life in Rome this time around.

Rome, The Pantheon, mid-December 125

It was a bleak day indeed. Rome in December was dreary and made Hadrian long for the more temperate winters of Greece. Still, he understood it was not as grim as the season in Britannia. There one really felt the sorrow of Demeter as she mourned the loss of her daughter.

Zuester had said there were preparations for Saturnalia in the new Pantheon and that the festooning and decorations needed to be seen before the crowds obscured the spectacle. Such an outing would also give the emperor a chance to be with his people, something he enjoyed. Sometimes, Hadrian felt he was only truly himself when he was secreted with his wife, or conferring with his trusted secretary, or joking with common soldiers or citizens. He took the opportunity to walk part of the way from the Palatine Hill to the Pantheon.

The Pantheon. The emperor was indeed proud of his creation. Not garish like temples made by his predecessors, but not severe either. The colored stone of the floor and aediculae was imported from all over the empire, symbolizing the reach of the gods to all corners of the earth. Its shimmering gilded coffers and gleaming polished marble were the perfect balance of opulence and solemnity reflecting the emperor's own awe and reverence for all the gods.

The imperial party approached the temple porch buzzing with activity. Freedmen called out orders to the imperial pages to wash unsoiled marble, to move wreaths and garlands to just the right place, then, suddenly, to halt all activity and bow to Caesar. Hadrian walked through the parted clump of youthful workers, nodding and smiling, amused by their nervousness as they tried, yet not tried, to look at their emperor.

Once inside Hadrian stopped, his jaw dropping briefly in amazement. Zuester had been correct; it was indeed a spectacular sight. Festoons of gilded flowers and blood-red ribbons draped along the walls. Oil lamps gave off an amber illumination, their flickering flames causing shadows to dance across statuary making them seem alive. Hadrian smiled.

"Thank you, Zuester," he said.

"I knew you would enjoy it," responded the secretary. "Would you like to meet the man in charge?"

"Of course."

Zuester indicated Hadrian should follow him and they walked to a group attending the altar to Venus. A jolly man was describing a floral arrangement to imperial pages.

"…the evergreen boughs like so …"

Zuester cleared his throat. "Sergius? The emperor would like to speak with you."

The jolly man swung his thick frame around to Zuester. "The emperor?"

"The very same," said Hadrian.

Despite his size, the caretaker jumped at the voice, then bowed, waving frantically to his youthful assistants to do the same. "Caesar."

Hadrian chuckled. "Carry on, Sergius. You are doing a stupendous job. I am very pleased with the results."

"Yes, Caesar. Thank you, Caesar."

Hadrian turned to the pages. "I thank you for your help, as well. It is good to honor the gods with displays of their bounty."

"It is a testament to the power of the gods that there is still beauty during the winter months of Demeter's mourning," came a youth's voice from the back of the group.

"It is impertinent to address the emperor, boy!" admonished Sergius.

Hadrian started. A proper Roman boy would have called the goddess Ceres and not Demeter. "No, no, it is all right," he assured the caretaker. He addressed the group of pages. "Please show yourself."

A tall, blond youth of uncommon beauty stepped forward. Hadrian's heart swelled in unexpected joy. He could not hide the smile, but hoped no one could discern the erection that had sprung forth the second he laid eyes on the body of the boy now become a man.

"Antinous! Lad! It has been some years."

Antinous smiled broadly, then collected himself and bowed solemnly. "Yes, sire. It is good to see you in vigorous health."

You have no idea how vigorous I feel at this very moment, mused Hadrian.

"Please forgive me, Caesar," began Sergius. "I had forgotten you knew the boy."

"Yes, yes. We hunted together in his native Bithynia." Hadrian knew he had to stop looking at the gorgeous youth or he would become obvious. He also had to stop talking in front of his subjects as there was suddenly a distinct shaky nervousness to his voice.

"Perhaps your highness would like to take a moment to renew your acquaintance?" suggested Zuester.

Dogs of Hell, the blasted secretary's set it all up! "Thank you, Zuester." Hadrian turned to Sergius. "May I borrow your student for a moment?" His heart was now beating in his ears.

"Certainly, Caesar," the caretaker bowed again.

Zuester indicated Antinous should follow him, which the youth did without hesitation. The three walked toward the center of the temple, to the edge of the marble drain carved in the shape of the face of Oceanus, with mouth, eyes, and nostrils gaping directly under the oculus.

"I must continue my check on the preparations, sire," said Zuester. "May I leave you alone with Antinous?"

Hadrian detected a slight deviousness in Zuester's tone. He would have to thank him later. "Yes. I'm certain the lad is trustworthy." He eyed the secretary as he walked away a little too gleefully.

He turned to the object of his unrequited passions. "It is good to see you once again. How has your time been at the paedagogium?"

Antinous shifted on his feet. "They treat me well. They know about our connection," he said boldly, finally looking into Hadrian's eyes. "I think they give me privileges because of it." He blushed and tried to hide a smile.

"And right they should." Hadrian could not stop looking at the lad's face. He wanted simply to kiss the full lips. Of course he knew he wouldn't be able to stop there. In an effort to relieve the tension growing inside him, the emperor indicated they should stroll around the marble drain. When he saw the youth move, his erection grew harder with every step.

"If I may, my lord, I think this temple to all the gods is a beautiful space. I know you designed it. I've been wanting to see it since it was finished."

"This is the first time you've been here, then?"

"Yes. We don't have much opportunity to journey out into the city."

"And what do you especially like about it?"

"I like that it is round, I mean the dome, the oculus, and how the shape of the circle is repeated in the marble tile," he moved his hand across the air as if polishing the floor, "and again in the face of Oceanus." Antinous moved beneath the hole to the sky, his legs straddling the open mouth of the water god.

Hadrian swallowed hard.

The youth continued. "It is not like our square temples back home. The circle is more natural, more organic." He once again lifted his eyes to meet Hadrian's. "It is more sensual."

Hadrian's pulse throbbed. *Gods, oh gods! How am I to restrain myself?* "Thank you. I was once criticized by Trajan's architect for that very quality in my designs. It is nice to know an intelligent youth admires the space."

"It is my pleasure to admire your work, Caesar."

Hadrian watched as a rain drop, and then another, fell through the oculus and dripped down Antinous's face. The youth licked the water when it touched his lips. The emperor tried to steady his quickening breath.

"You should not remain in the rain, Antinous. You'll catch a chill."

"But did you not design it so we can enjoy all of the gods' gifts to us? The light of Phoebus in the day, the orb of Selene at night, the stars of Phosphorus in the morning and Hesperus in the evening as they cross the sky," his hands drew a semi-circle above his head, "above the staring eyes of their master Oceanus," he indicated the marble face staring up his tunic. "And now, in the winter, the tears shed by our lady Demeter," he spread his arms letting the droplets caress his hands, "which inspire dormant seeds to burst forth from their tombs of dirt and soil, bringing back life and joy to a dark and dreary world. I want to stand here when it rains and feel the holy water bathe my skin, penetrating my psyche until I am imbued with its sacred energy."

The rain fell harder. A downpour drenched the lad. The emperor stepped beside him and into the shower, brushing the slender fingers of his delicate hand.

The rain suddenly stopped.

Hadrian and Antinous looked at each other and laughed.

* * * * *

The cold Antinous suffered for the following three weeks was worth it. He had finally seen his Hadrian in the flesh. He knew what he felt was no longer a school-boy crush, but instead the urges and desires of a fully-realized man. He yearned to be stroked by his large masculine hands, to be secure between his powerful thighs, and to return the favor with his own fervent passion. He knew he wasn't alone in his fantasy. He knew he could sense the same urgent need from his beloved.

The truth of his notion was confirmed when, a few months later, after the final touches to his training, he was summoned to the palace to serve amongst the emperor's personal and private household staff.

Rome, Imperial Palace, December 126

It took a little longer these days for the emperor to rise and perform his morning prayers, to be dressed and be made presentable for whatever appointment he might have. He was ill – his heart, his doctors told him, did not beat as it should – and he moved slowly. Added to that, his hair dresser, an ancient man who had lived through far too many emperors, had recently died. The lad who had been trained to take the old man's place had also died, of a fever. It was left to untrained servants to attend to their emperor. Sabina had long stopped disguising her amusement over his various coiffures.

"Your hair wants cutting very badly, Graeculus," she said one day. "Perhaps Zuester could cut it? He attends you every morning anyway."

Hadrian had dismissed the notion as ridiculous.

But Zuester was there every morning, directing the attendants, reporting on the day's agenda, surreptitiously checking on the health of his emperor, and even his moods. Some days the emperor was particularly cantankerous.

"My lord, you seem in a sullen state today," Zuester remarked. "Shall I send the youth in?" he asked quietly with a knowing grin. "It will do wonders for your spirits. And I know he will take good care of you."

"I don't want him to see me like this – weak and unmanly." Hadrian burned with self-denial. But he worried the perfect flesh of the youth would be marred by his decrepit presence.

"I've cared for your wife these past few years. It has only strengthened the bond of our love."

"I'm no woman, Zuester," Hadrian bit back. "Besides," he said more softly, "I don't know if there is a bond yet."

Zuester looked at his master surprised. "You've not dallied with him?"

"No," the emperor said somberly. "He's not just any page in my household. He's different. He's...*good*. Kind. I won't sully him merely for my own pleasure."

Zuester smiled. "Come. You need air and sunlight. Despite the chill, today is a very fine day." He wrapped a pallium around Hadrian's shoulders before leading him out to the courtyard.

The emperor's personal attendants – some of them functional *cubicularii*, while some of the prettier ones merely ornamental *pueri* – lined the edges of the atrium. Antinous stood among them. Hadrian nodded imperceptibly to the youth who blushed at the hint of attention.

Zuester sat his master down on a low divan and beckoned to Antinous.

The lad hastened nervously to the couch. "My lord," he said, bowing his head.

"Antinous," Zuester acknowledged. "It has recently come to my attention that you learned the skill of hair curling at the paedagogium."

Hadrian tried to not reveal his pleasure in his realization of what might possibly happen next.

"Yes, sir, I did."

"Good! The emperor needs a new hairdresser." Zuester motioned to a couple of pages who brought out a tray of styling implements and a folding table. "Will this be all you need?"

Antinous, slightly apprehensive, glanced at the tools on the table. "Yes," he said quietly. "Yes, this will do just fine."

Zuester smiled at the youth, bowed to his emperor, and left with the two pages, leaving the other attendants standing at the ready in the corridor.

Hadrian chuckled to himself. Zuester was too good to him. He smiled at Antinous standing next to him seemingly at a loss for what to do. "Please, you may proceed." He sat back, relaxing into the chaise cushions.

"Yes, Caesar." Antinous picked up an ivory comb from the tray and hesitated for a moment above the graying hair of the emperor. For far too long, he had wanted to personally attend to the man now seated before him. But now that he was granted permission to actually touch and care for him, a sudden bashfulness sent an ache of desire to throb in the pit of his stomach. *If I just touch the hair I won't reveal my emotions.* As he began detangling the strands, smoothing the surprisingly luxurious locks, he noticed the emperor had closed his eyes and was smiling, a sign, he presumed, he was confident in the youth's abilities. Assured, Antinous picked up the *calamistrum* from the dish of smoldering ashes and proceeded to curl his master's hair with the hot iron rod. He kept the implement far enough away from the skin so as not to burn. Handling just the hair helped the youth steady his breath, and eventually lose himself in the rhythm of the tasks.

When he finished curling his master's hair, he noticed the hair at the back of the emperor's neck needed a bit of trimming. Antinous picked up the scissors with his right hand and drew his left hand along the down-covered skin to gather the strands.

Hadrian opened his eyes and let out a groan of satisfaction.

Suddenly cognizant of touching the warm flesh of the man he had constantly dreamed about, Antinous blushed while his skin flooded with sensation. He tried to steady his breathing to no avail. Luckily his cock was bound in linen under his tunic. He was rock hard.

"Do the others know Greek, Antinous?" The emperor's voice was calm and quiet as he spoke Antinous's native tongue.

The youth furtively glanced around at the pages still in the corridor along one side of the atrium. Maybe a Gaulish or Germanic youth here and there, the rest were Latins. All could unfailingly recite ancient poetry but without proper understanding. "No, *Kyrie*. There is none among us who speaks Greek."

"Good. Then we shall converse in relative privacy." There seemed to be a sultry edge to the emperor's voice.

Antinous tried to steady his once-skilled hands, but only managed to drop the scissors. The *clink* on the tiles raised eyebrows amongst the pages in the corridor.

"I apologize. I fear I have caused you distress," said Hadrian gently.

"It is not every day that Caesar speaks to one so intimately."

Hadrian grunted. "Do not think of me as such when we use Greek between us. Think of us as the friends we were in Bithynia so many years ago."

The emperor's words soothed Antinous, and emboldened him. "Aye, *Kyrie*, I will do so." He commenced trimming the back of his friend's neck, stroking the skin gently, indulgently, his mind wandering in his enjoyment of the simple act.

"Your touch is reverent. You don't find my sagging skin and graying hair repugnant?"

Antinous smiled. "No, *Kyrie*. Your skin is smooth and warm, like that of a vibrant, passionate man," he said as he brushed fingers along the back of the emperor's neck. "And your hair is thick where it still holds color. As for the gray, I think it fine and distinguished," he murmured. "A sign of an early life well spent."

"You are kind, Antinous," Hadrian began quietly. "But I must be candid. I did not want you to see me this way…as a sick man."

"Me?" Antinous stopped his duties. *The emperor thinks of me when I am not present!*

"I was ashamed of appearing so weak before one with whom I have *philia*, a special friendship."

The revelation was astonishing to the youth. Antinous felt a little lightheaded, felt his stomach clench, felt his body tremble. He quickly collected himself. "My lord, such a friendship can only exist between equals."

"Ah, yes. I am the Emperor of Rome, and you, my serving boy," Hadrian chuckled. "Of course, other aspects of our relationship balance this out. Are we equals in the hunt?"

"*Kyrie*, please, I don't understand—"

"Are we?"

"Truthfully," said Antinous haltingly, "I am the better."

Hadrian laughed out loud. "Yes, you are, my boy. Yes, you are. And do you consider this a weakness in me?"

"Of course not!"

"Because, I think, you feel the bond of friendship too."

Antinous tried to steady his rapidly beating heart. "I believe I have finished," he said as he handed his master a mirror.

Hadrian regarded his hair in the polished bronze, turning his head side to side. "You have done the miraculous. You have made this ill man look presentable. Thank you," he smiled as he looked up at his attendant.

Antinous blushed. "The emperor does not need to say 'thank you'. It is my duty and honor to serve."

"As a man I say thank you. It is my pleasure to have you attend me, to enjoy your intimate ministrations."

Hadrian held out the mirror for Antinous to take. When the lad took the handle, Hadrian placed his other hand on top of the youth's. Antinous glanced up in surprise, meeting Hadrian's penetrating gray eyes as the emperor's fingers delicately and discreetly stroked his own.

Every nerve in Antinous's body sparked with excitement. He flushed, blood pumped to his cock. "You return the favor sir," he said boldly but quietly. "Now it is I who experience pleasure at your touch."

Hadrian smiled as if understanding the depths of the youth's feelings.

"I must begin my official day." Hadrian groaned as he tried to get up from the chaise only to find his muscles still aching and uncooperative. Antinous instinctively steadied his master by placing his hands on either side of Hadrian's chest, helping him to stand. For a moment the men faced each other, the youth uncertain if the emperor was covering an erotic excitation with the breathlessness of illness. Antinous inhaled sharply, blushed, and released his hold on his lord.

"I have asked the gods for strength and they give me a handsome blond youth," Hadrian murmured softly. "Will you also be my cane as I walk through the corridor?"

"It would be my pleasure, *Kyrie*."

Antinous placed one hand on the small of the emperor's back and grasped his arm firmly with the other. Touching his master, feeling the warmth of his body, incited him to want to explore more. He had to restrain his urges, and wrap them in the veneer of dutiful service. The walk to the office was delectation and torture all at once.

Once in the chamber, Hadrian released his arm and faced him. "Thank you."

"*Kyrie*," Antinous responded, bowing. "As I've said, it is my great pleasure to serve you."

"I should like to have you attend me more often."

"I am at your command, *Kyrie*." Antinous struggled to maintain his composure. Everything about the man before him was thrilling.

"Do you enjoy the role of *ornator*? Of curling my hair?"

"I do, sire. Very much," he said wistfully.

"Good. Then I will have you attend me every morning. In my bedchamber."

Antinous swallowed hard. Before he could respond, the curtains to the bureau fluttered open.

Zuester suppressed a smirk as Hadrian and Antinous turned abruptly at his entrance, looking as if they were guilty of a crime. He glanced briefly at Antinous, then lowered his head in a bow to the emperor. Zuester had heard – and understood – every word.

"Ah, Zuester. Antinous here will be attending me in the mornings." Hadrian had switched to Latin for the benefit of any staff, or others, also listening in.

"In what capacity, Caesar?"

"Hairdresser. But perhaps there are other services he may provide."

"Yes, Caesar." Zuester had to hide his surprise at the bold insinuation.

Antinous shifted on his feet nervously. The youth seemed to be both excited about his prospects but uncomfortable about the attention currently being paid to him.

Hadrian placed a hand on the boy's shoulder. "Until tomorrow then?"

"Aye, Kyr—my lord." Antinous bowed.

The emperor and his secretary watched as the youth exited the office.

"And Zuester," Hadrian began quietly in Greek. "I certainly don't need an army present at my toilet. See that the lad and I are left alone."

Rome, Imperial Palace, Spring 127

Sabina slipped into her husband's bedroom from their secret corridor, hoping to find him still lolling in bed, his morning erection fresh and unfulfilled. She had worn practically nothing, and had left her own lover still sleeping and unresponsive from the previous day's exhaustions.

Instead, she saw her husband already sitting at his dressing table, the beauteous Antinous in attendance, curling and combing his hair. Hadrian was more awake this morning than she had ever seen him. It was captivating to watch. She smiled.

Antinous was engrossed in his work, but not so utterly that he could not share a conversation with his emperor. Whatever it was Hadrian and Antinous were talking about it was in Greek. She could catch a word here and there but not enough to understand the conversation completely. The two obviously had a very good rapport. Her husband was vibrant and animated, his demeanor clearly indicating he had gotten over his illness. Antinous reacted and responded spontaneously, unaffectedly, as would a great friend rather than a hairdresser.

Sabina watched as their conversation turned, it seemed, to hunting stories. Both gestured broadly, describing their hunts with their hands, laughing uproariously in mutual appreciation. While Antinous told his tale, Hadrian gazed at him with admiration, with adoration, the youth unaware of the emperor's depth of emotion.

For the emperor was very much in love, and anyone who loved him could tell.

However, the youth seemed to be in love as well. And, from his excitement and blushing, it was with her husband.

Hadrian caught her reflection in the mirror on the bronze stand on his dressing table. Meeting his eyes she gave him a taunting smirk. He smiled and raised an eyebrow. Antinous must have noticed something. The youth turned toward the bed and saw the empress lounging across it.

He dropped the brush. Luckily the floor beneath was covered with a Boeotian bear skin, otherwise the ivory handle would have smashed to pieces against the marble mosaic floor.

"My lady," he said, genuflecting. "I apologize. I did not know you were here."

"I wasn't until just a few moments ago," Sabina said, regarding her husband's servant with curious approbation. She arranged her diaphanous morning attire around her on the bed. Had she known the youth was attending Hadrian she might not have worn something so clingy and revealing, but the look of terrified shock on Antinous's face when he saw her had been utterly precious.

"Vibia, darling, don't tease," Hadrian admonished affectionately. He motioned to Antinous to stand. "There is a private passageway between the empress's chambers and my own, for our communication," he explained.

"I see." Despite the professed comprehension, Antinous was still pale and somewhat befuddled.

"Are you well?" Sabina asked with genuine concern. "You look as if you've seen Trajan's ghost."

"No...I..." Antinous looked at the empress before blushing and turning to the emperor. "I had just heard...gossip..." he stammered. One more look at Hadrian helped him recover. "I had heard that the two of you did not get on. Well, to be truthful, that you disliked each other greatly."

"'Hate' is the word generally used, I believe."

"Vibia! Don't tease. Antinous is being polite." Hadrian beckoned his servant to lean in. "Can you keep a secret?"

"Yes, *Kyrie*," Antinous nodded.

"Vibia and I are very good friends, really. But we don't want anyone to know. When we were publicly harmonious, there were attacks upon her life."

Antinous turned to Sabina, horror-stricken. "My lady! Who would do such a thing?"

Sabina grabbed one of her husband's more concealing robes and put it on as she strolled to the pair. "You are innocent to imperial politics, I see."

Antinous bowed his head. "I prefer to remain detached from such intrigues."

"Good strategy." She smiled at the youth. Something about him made her want to twist a finger in his golden locks. He was sensuality wrapped in innocence, and she suddenly understood her husband's fascination with the boy.

Instead, she twisted a finger through Hadrian's hair.

Hadrian swatted her hand away. "Don't touch! I'm to meet with senators today. Go play with your lover!" he scolded playfully.

Sabina laughed. "And, yes, he knows about Zuester," she said conspiratorially to a fascinated Antinous.

Sabina sat down on a stool at Hadrian's feet. "I see you've cut his hair," she waved in the direction of her husband.

"Oh, yes, my lady! I've trimmed the curls – and the beard – just a bit." Antinous gesticulated about the emperor's head. "One does not want the frame to detract from the fine portrait."

"No." Sabina bit her lip to conceal her pleasure at the last. "And what do you think of the gray?"

Hadrian smirked with annoyance at his wife. She pursed her lips to hide a smile and ignored him.

"I think the gray rather pleasing. It matches his eyes."

Sabina looked more closely at her perturbed husband. "Yes, I suppose it does," she agreed. "Very handsome."

Antinous blushed.

"Enough!" Hadrian stood up, unbalancing his wife on the stool. "Did you come here for a reason, Vibia?"

"Just a social visit. We have not spoken for days, Graeculus. I can come at a more convenient time."

"No, please, it is I who should leave," Antinous interjected. "I have other duties to attend to."

"Very well," said the emperor, trying to hide his disappointment. "I will see you tomorrow morning, Kynegiskos."

The youth smiled sweetly then bowed to his emperor and empress and left.

Hadrian glared at his wife as she stood and circled him. "What was that you called him?"

"Kynegiskos."

"Which is Greek, I suppose. For what?"

"Little hunter."

"Ah."

"What is wrong with that?" he asked dismissively as he strolled to the bed.

"You have a nickname for him? And what does he call you?"

"Usually something in Greek," he said dryly.

"Besides the new hairstyle, you're looking different, dear husband." Sabina drew a finger across his chest. "Vibrant, glowing, healthy. You're over your illness, it seems." Her finger trailed down his torso until she reached his crotch. Under his tunic, he was semi-hard. "So what's he like?"

"'Like'?" he exclaimed. "Vibia, I've not laid a finger on the boy."

"What?" Sabina was truly incredulous.

"I want to. The gods know I want to," he groaned and sat on the edge of the bed. "Vibia, I'm…I'm afraid. What if he doesn't return the affection? What if he is appalled, or even worse, disgusted? I don't want to lose what we already have. He is a good friend. We discuss poetry and philosophy. And hunting."

"It's obvious he admires you. He's a little obsequious, but comfortable in your presence at the same time." Sabina tugged on her husband's cock. "He blushes at your attentions, yet relishes the time he spends serving you."

Hadrian fell back on the mattress with a groan.

"Remember our agreement to seduce our respective lovers? Yet, you've done nothing?"

Hadrian felt himself responding both to her touch and to the fantasies she was inspiring in his head.

"Take him to Tibur. Alone."

Hadrian stilled her hand. "What did you come here for?" he asked with a scowl.

"To be with you."

"What about Zuester?"

"You keep him too busy," she pouted. "He's exhausted."

"He is a very good steward. But I'll try to keep your concerns in mind."

He reached up for her, more out of a need for physical release than a need to be with his wife. Their deep kiss sent shocks of urgent desire pulsing through him, made all the more unbearable when she resumed her gentle fondling of his crotch.

He could easily take her, it would be quick and satisfying for both of them. But it would be dishonest. He knew he would only imagine the boy, imagine the smooth flesh and himself buried up to the hilt in his tight arse.

Hadrian drew his breath through his teeth. "Vibia, I…can't."

"You *can't?*"

"I mean I can, and I want to, please know this, but I'm distracted. I think I'm preserving my affections for him."

"I understand, Graeculus."

"I'll give Zuester a respite for the day. I don't need my steward to attend me while I'm being bored by senators."

"Thank you, husband."

Tibur, Hadrian's villa, 27 November 127

Hadrian knew he could not possibly have a tryst in the imperial palace in Rome.

The newly remodeled edifice had attracted several members of the extended imperial family who had either simply moved in or would stay – invited or not – for long periods of time. This included the new charge of the emperor and his wife, the orphaned Marcus Annius Verus, a distant relative and grandson of one of Hadrian's most trusted advisors. Unlike so many of the other relations, Marcus was genuinely likable, honest, and dependable, earning his nickname "Verissimus". He was something of a prodigy, engaging the emperor in philosophical debates even at the tender age of six. To such an astonishing child Hadrian suddenly found himself in the role of father with all the attendant responsibilities.

With such intense familial scrutiny, then, the palace on the Palatine Hill was simply out of the question for a romantic encounter between the emperor and the object of his fantasies.

Had he invited Antinous to his bedroom in Rome anyway, the youth might have balked at the brazen audacity of it all. So Hadrian – or rather, Zuester – had arranged a private dinner in the more private palace. It was Antinous's eighteenth birthday, and celebrating it at Hadrian's glorious country villa was an honor the youth could not pass up.

The Praetorians were not to be seen inside, but were staked surreptitiously at all entrances and exits. That way Antinous would not feel on display as the emperor's plaything. *That* was something he most definitely was not, for the emperor was truly in love.

One servant, a girl, attended them at dinner and poured the wine afterward. Conversation flowed effortlessly from hunting to Greek philosophy to Antinous's Latin studies to soldiering. Hadrian found his young guest composed and demure all at once, smiling invitingly at times. The fifty-one-year-old Hadrian, however, was unsettled and nervous.

Until Antinous took his hand.

It was clearly a casual gesture to a shared joke, but there it was: The small unblemished hand was suddenly in his and did not leave.

Hadrian caught his breath as the slender fingers sought to mingle with his own, rough and callused as they were, a gentle coaxing to a promise of what could happen next.

"Kynegiskos," the emperor began. "We've become close friends this last year. I greatly enjoy your company."

"And I enjoy yours," said Antinous without affectation. He sucked in his lower lip, then released it, glistening.

Hadrian tried to steady his breath at the provocative sight. He bent his head down to the delicate hand in his own and kissed the inside of the palm. He thought he heard the youth sigh, but he wasn't sure, because his heart was beating in his ears.

Should I speak? Should I act? What does one do? He had never wanted something as much as he did at that moment.

Still holding Antinous's hand Hadrian stood, then gently tugged the wide-eyed youth up beside him. He could hear his companion's short excited breaths inviting him, encouraging him, desiring him. In one movement, Hadrian took Antinous in his arms and kissed him.

The youth did not flinch, did not repel. No, he gave in completely, opening his mouth for Hadrian's invasion, boldly encircling the emperor's neck with his arms, pressing his needful body against his seducer's. Antinous had clearly longed for this moment as much as Hadrian.

Hadrian pulled back from the kiss, threading his fingers through the youth's blond curls. "I've wanted you this past year, Antinous. You don't know how much I've been in pain from the denial."

"Yes," panted the youth, "I do. Believe me. Sometimes I feel you are my heart, without you my body would wither away. And with you I feel my blood surging through my veins."

Hadrian smiled. "My heart." He rested his forehead briefly against his love's. "I completely understand. Mine, the doctors say, is weak, but you have strengthened it."

"Kiss me again, my lord. I've never felt a beard in a kiss before."

Hadrian softly kissed the tender lips of the youth's smooth face. Antinous moaned quietly as he reached up and placed his palms against the emperor's cheeks and stroked the short, bristly hair. The youth's mouth demanded more as his fingers clung to his master's whiskers.

"And," Hadrian began when the embrace was over. "Do you like my beard?"

"I do." The youth licked his burning lips.

Hadrian draped his arm around Antinous's shoulder and led him out of the dining room. He stopped in the hall. "Are you sure?" he asked without further description. "You are too precious to me, and I cannot proceed if you are unsure even just the slightest."

"I am sure, Graeculus," intoned Antinous.

Hadrian's heart skipped a beat. The youth had never used the familiar name before. The emperor beamed as they walked to the bedroom that had been set up for their hoped-for union.

A lamp flared dully in one corner and Hadrian set about lighting a few more. He wanted to witness every moment he shared with his lover.

The emperor unfastened his dinner wrap then stripped off his tunic, revealing himself to be naked underneath. Thusly exposed, he approached Antinous. The youth simply stared at his elder's lean muscular body while the emperor divested him of his brightly-colored mantle and tossed it aside.

Hadrian put an arm around his love and kissed him once again, plundering his mouth to distract Antinous from his other hand which reached under his tunic. He tugged at the subligaculum he found there, unwinding it, exploring the bared body, the taut bottom, the sculpted hips, the hard cock.

"I want you," Hadrian said huskily. "I want to possess you."

Antinous followed him to the bed, and at his invitation sat down.

"Let's take this off," said Hadrian as he lifted the youth's tunic from the hem. The sight of Antinous's smooth, athletic body inflamed the emperor. He stroked the sleek muscles swathed by perfect ivory flesh before him. "You glow with beauty like Apollo."

"No, Graeculus," he responded. "I am Ganymede to your Zeus."

Hadrian felt the blood pump to his cock at that. He spread open his legs, displaying his eager member. At his master's instruction, Antinous imitated the pose. Hadrian moved forward, his legs still spread, and draped them over the youth's, excitement sparking through his body the moment their balls touched. Antinous glanced up, craving and hesitancy in his eyes. To reassure the youth, Hadrian kissed him and took his prick in his hand.

The shaft was soft and smooth, and fit in the emperor's large grip perfectly as he glided his fist up and down with gentle urgency. Antinous was lost in the sensual assault, breathing faster against Hadrian's mouth as the emperor quickened his pace.

Antinous drew back. "I – I – " he cried, his hips rocking in rhythm to Hadrian's insistent hand. "Oh, gods!" He came too quickly, the thick milky fluid pouring over his lover's clenching fingers. Antinous blushed. "I'm sorry. I've been on edge. I—"

"Shh, shh," Hadrian admonished softly. "That is just the first time tonight. Remember, I was young once as you are now. I know a lustful youth can last all night." He gracefully wiped his hand on the sheet.

Antinous smiled. "I think it will be a few minutes, at least, before I am ready again," he said puckishly.

"Then I have a few minutes to admire your beauty and kiss you." Hadrian did not hide his adoration and wonder as he caressed his lover's hairless flesh, feeling the subtly honed musculature underneath. Antinous was thin but sleek, not scrawny, an athlete on the cusp of manhood. And as he touched his young lover, Hadrian sensed the youth's renewed excitement, then kissed him once more to inflame him even further.

The emperor reached behind him and grabbed a lamp from the bedside table and blew it out. The oil would be warm, he knew, and he poured some out into his palm. He smeared the liquid on the index and middle fingers of his right hand and reached under Antinous's balls, seeking his puckered hole, then gently tracing the crinkled edge.

"Have you ever been touched here?" he asked, knowing most boys never got that far in their erotic play.

"No," said Antinous in a voice that betrayed his curiosity and arousal.

"I think you will enjoy it," said Hadrian. "Tilt up a little." He poured more oil on Antinous's crotch letting the viscous liquid flow down onto his working hand. He inserted his fingers inside the youth's tight passage, moving in and out slowly as Antinous became used to the feeling. Hadrian marked the expressions on his lover's face, noting when they turned from confusion to delight, until Antinous's eyes were black with desire as he stared helplessly at the man giving him pleasures he had never imagined.

His finger now embedded up to the second joint, Hadrian crooked it slightly toward Antinous's penis and began gently massaging.

The youth drew in a sharp breath. "Oh, gods, what are you doing to me?"

"Do you like it?"

"I'm in ecstasy."

"Oh, no, you're not," counseled Hadrian. He leaned back and poured more oil on his own belly, then scooped it up with his free hand and coated first his own cock, then that of his lover. He pulled both shafts together with the wide span of his fingertips and began pumping slowly. The sensitive slicked undersides of the united pricks rubbed together as Hadrian slid his fingers along the top sides.

Antinous's body jerked against the assault of pleasure. His mouth fell open as he struggled to control his ragged breath.

"You want to come again, don't you?" Hadrian taunted.

"Yes, please," was the meek answer.

"You want me to come as well, don't you?" Hadrian pumped faster.

"Yes, oh yes, my lord."

"Lie back," Hadrian commanded, releasing his hold on their cocks.

Antinous fell back against the mattress. Hadrian's finger was still inside him, stimulating him to madness.

"Frig yourself," the emperor instructed.

Antinous grabbed his own oil-slicked cock and pumped furiously. Still with his finger massaging inside his lover, Hadrian moved until he was kneeling over the youth, then gripped his own prick and masturbated.

Antinous was on the edge again, his shoulders flailing against the bed, his moans howling to the heavens. Hadrian had more control, he observed every twitch, listened to every breath, watching Antinous climb to the peak.

With an ecstatic scream, Antinous climaxed, milking his cock onto his stomach. Hadrian worked his fingers inside the youth, watching his lover's face dissolve into incredulity as he continued to jet hot fluid.

Antinous lay on the bed spent, panting, unaware that his vulnerable beauty was driving Hadrian to his own culmination. With a clipped warning cry, the emperor ejaculated onto the youth's belly, his sperm mingling with that of his lover's.

Hadrian hovered over Antinous, marking the youth's reaction. Antinous smiled, then laughed.

"I don't think I can go again tonight," he said.

"Good," responded Hadrian stretching out beside him. He grabbed the discarded subligaculum and dabbed at Antinous's belly, kissing his cheek intermittently. He drew up the covers and pulled the youth's glorious body against his own.

"I just want to hold you the rest of the night anyway," Hadrian said as he nuzzled the ivory flesh of his new-found love.

Alpes Maritimae, May 128

Bestia awoke to the somewhat pleasant realization that someone was sucking his morning erection. He shifted in the bed, the act of doing so making him aware that he was not in his bed, but was instead on a narrow dining couch. He half-opened one eye. The room was empty but for the couches, the dying fire, the skins under which he had been sleeping, and a certain slave boy pleasuring him orally with gusto.

The visual cues sparked his memory. Since living in the Alps north of Italia, Bestia had grown fond of a certain Alpine herbal wine and had imbibed in far too much of the stuff the night before. He did recall falling asleep in a crumpled heap on a couch in the dining room after a failed attempt to find his bed. It seemed his boy servant had fetched his furs and blankets, and had probably slept at his master's feet by the fire.

He closed his eyes, feeling the boy working earnestly on his cock. There was annoyance amidst the pleasure. He really had to piss.

Bestia knew he was taking a chance by living so close to Rome, but he could no longer bear living amongst the Marcomanni, a tribe he had joined when the cold of Suebia grew too much for his tastes. The Marcomanni, however, were too willing to concede, to negotiate, to not only form alliances, but to freely assimilate and intermarry with their neighbors. They were, in short, a people willing to be indistinct, perhaps, in the long run, willing to be overrun by Rome. They had at one time even been a client state under Augustus! Who knew if the new leaders looked back on those days with a touch of nostalgia? Of course they had repeatedly said that Rome was their enemy, but argued that there was more strength when enemies were united. And, they believed, amongst this alliance against Rome, not one group should hold sway. They believed in some sort of *democratic* arrangement. The notion made Bestia shudder.

The Marcomanni, were, then, not the sort of people who would be interested or able to advance his own interests, and not the sort of people Bestia wanted to be associated with. After six months with them, he was compelled to move again. And after those six months, the frozen wasteland of the more aggressive and confident Suiones in the north did not look so bad.

It was winter when Bestia decided to seek another home further south. He ended up moving further south and west, toward the Alps. It was either lunacy to go to the mountains during the winter, or it was a brilliant bit of strategy. Really, he discovered, it was both. He fell in with the remnants of the Salassi, a fierce mountain tribe whose numbers had been wiped out by slaughter or slavery during Augustus's bloodlust for territory. The handful that was left was imbued with hatred toward Rome. Bestia and the Salassi were kindred spirits, and once they heard the merchant's story, how his own flesh and blood had been murdered by the Emperor Hadrian, the Salassi took him in. Survival in the snowy mountains of the Alps was best in concert with others, he discovered, no matter what skills he has acquired while living with the Suiones in barren Scania. The western Alps proved to be as formidable as any of the wastelands he had traversed through in recent years. Bestia cursed the gods every day for his fate, then thanked them every day he survived.

But now in spring with flowers carpeting the hillsides, the mountains did not seem so unbearable. They were, if one were inclined to think such a thing, rather beautiful. Plus he had brought with him on his journey a boy slave, half-Suebi, half-Sarmatian, a rather enthusiastic chap whose predilections mirrored his own. The cold winter doldrums had been kept at bay by the boy's willing and eager tongue and arse. Springtime, with its warm air to limber the muscles and bones, held even more erotic possibilities.

The boy was furiously frigging his own cock now as he licked Bestia's balls. He was on his knees before the side of the couch, his head firmly ensconced between his master's thighs. As he slowly roused under the boy's ministrations, Bestia became aware that he was in the most unnatural position on the couch, with his head almost falling off one side, and his legs twisted around and splayed open on the other. He would require a massage later, from the boy's nimble hands, to sooth his stiffness and aches. He wished the boy would wait until then to suck him. He did not think he had enough energy for two ejaculations today. His head was killing him. And he still needed to relieve himself.

Last night's excessive celebrations had been warranted. Bestia had been celebrating the receipt of good information. Intelligence in the Alpine region was far better than in the hinterland of Suebia. And this was precisely the type of information he had been waiting for.

It appeared that the emperor Hadrian was enamored of a certain Bithynian youth. And "enamored" in this case seemed to be such a mild word. Apparently, his sources informed him, the youth had utterly captivated the heart, mind, and soul of the emperor. This was not anything like his relationship with Sabina, which had proven to be difficult to pin down. No matter. The youth, Antinous, was known to be occupying the imperial palace – probably sharing the imperial bed – and was his emperor's constant companion. The youth was young, impressionable, and, from all accounts, religious to the point of superstitiousness. He would be easily cornered, captured, swayed, and destroyed. In the meantime, the emperor was so distracted that he had not yet bothered about a successor. Bestia had found himself in the perfect spot.

On top of this, his spies had finally made contact with the daughter of the Parthian king Osrhoes. Her name was Roedogune, and now at twenty-four, and probably still a virgin, he understood her to be the most beautiful foreigner, if not simply the most beautiful woman, in Rome. Of course to Bestia any young Parthian woman being held against her will could be nothing but beautiful. She had agreed to meet with his representatives and understood she could not meet with the great merchant until, if ever, she was freed from the city.

But she would be the one reason he would return to Rome, where he had a price on his head. Bestia thought about stealing into her luxurious Roman prison at night, having his men hold her down, fucking her virgin cunt, and coming on her mortified face. Then, he would sit back and watch each of his men having his way with her. The thought was finally making him concupiscent. Only then did he appreciate the adept tongue doing its work on his cock.

Bestia tugged at the rich black-brown hair of the boy, threading his fingers distractedly through the luxurious curls. He was awake now, his head still ached, and he still wasn't quite sure he wanted to be sucked at the moment. All he could think about was that he really should have relieved himself an hour ago.

Gods of his father, but he absolutely had to take a piss.

Bestia held his slave's head against his cock, groaning loudly in relief as he released his water into the boy's mouth, then dropping his hands to the sides of the couch. The boy flinched with the first rush of urine and pulled back, letting the salty, bitter liquid flow on his lips and down his chin. Seconds later though, the youth was relishing the new game, pumping his own cock to climax, and thrusting his chest out as his master emptied his bladder onto his nude body.

If his head did not hurt so much, Bestia would have had the boy continue to fellate him. He closed his eyes and rolled over. Maybe later.

Numidia, Lambaesis, June 128

"Go with you to review your troops? In Africa? I should think not. I simply cannot think of anything more boring. I'm staying here in Rome."

Even with the enticement of watching a legion of sweaty muscle-bound men in the throes of battle practice, Sabina had refused to join her husband on his tour of the North African provinces. It was the first time she had declined to accompany him on his journeys as emperor.

"Look, I have our work in Gabii to carry out, remember? We're restoring their ancient sanctuary of Juno. And then there are your endless extensions and remodels at the Tibur villa. Plus managing my brickworks to supply all of these projects." She had stroked his beard at that point. "Don't look so pained, husband. You'll have your youth to look after you."

He could not help but smile. There were reasons he loved his wife so much.

"Besides," she had continued, "it would be good for our charade if we spent some time apart from each other, with our respective lovers." Hadrian had to agree to that.

When the emperor requested Antinous join him, the youth had accepted immediately, saying he would be deliriously thrilled to be an official member of the imperial entourage. Hadrian's heart had jumped in gratification and expectation. It would be their first time traveling together; they would camp together, live together, eat together, sleep together. As a husband and wife might have a journey after their marriage ceremony, Hadrian and Antinous would have a similar diversion after having declared their love for one another.

It was an overdue expedition, too. It had nagged the emperor that he had not spent much time in the African provinces. Six years earlier, during his tour of the western empire, trouble with the Parthians and, he conceded, worry for his wife's well-being, had prevented his staying in North Africa for any duration. True, he had put down a revolt in Mauretania and had spent time in Carthage, but his original intent had always been to thoroughly explore the breadbasket of the Roman Empire. Once he finally arrived, he found himself delightfully astounded.

They had left in spring to witness the lush growing season. The light, the sun, the warmth, were stupendous. Demeter had truly blessed the place with the riches of agriculture. However, he was quickly informed, farmers had not seen nourishing floods for five years. Then, as if to show her appreciation for the appearance of the emperor in her favored lands, the fertility goddess sent rains to drench the parched earth. The timing did not go unnoticed and Hadrian was exalted for his god-like gifts.

Hadrian responded with more benevolence and munificence. Five ancient municipalities were granted the prestigious status of *colonia*; ten native towns dotted along the fertile valleys were elevated to *municipia*. In addition, he freed up unused imperial lands to be cultivated by citizens who would eventually be allowed to take possession of their hard-won plots.

By the middle of June, the emperor was in the military province of Numidia, home of the legion of III Augusta. There the imperial legate, on behalf of the legion, had dedicated a pair of altars, one to Jupiter Best and Greatest the Lord of Divine Rainstorms, the other to the Winds that Have Power to Bring Beneficent Rainstorms. All of Africa was filled with gratitude for their emperor.

Next, the imperial party journeyed to the new military base at Lambaesis where work on the fortress was still in progress. Hadrian found himself in his element. It was a unique opportunity for the amateur architect to review the dedication and hard work of the soldiers and to discuss fortifications and construction techniques. He reviewed cavalry, tactics, training, and weaponry and was greatly satisfied with his men.

Best of all, Hadrian loved relaxing with the common soldiers, being regaled by their war heroics, singing songs of battle adventures, swapping bits of advice, listening intently to their complaints and regrets. The soldiers appreciated the personal attention of their emperor. He was a man, a soldier, just like them. No better, no worse. And for that he garnered their undying respect.

He was no different…except at night when they went back to their austere barracks, and Hadrian went back to his own tent. There he found the beauteous Antinous waiting for him, lying nude under furs and silks, his body supple and smooth, pliant and willing. A youth, a relationship, a future open to all possibilities.

Antinous had spent the day watching his beloved intermingling amongst the sweaty and scarred bodies of soldiers and veterans who loved the fight and never forgot the glory. He knew his Hadrian to be a virile and courageous man, but had never seen him in such surroundings, a milieu so comfortable he was no longer his sweet Graeculus, but before his eyes became the potently masculine and powerful Publius Aelius Hadrianus, the Roman general and Imperator. It was exhilarating.

Ostensibly brought along as one of the emperor's *amici*, merely a close friend, it was difficult to maintain the fiction for very long. When Hadrian was not attending to his troops and duties, the two were inseparable. Their casual rapport revealed their friendship; their fiery chemistry alluded to something so much more.

Yet, in their tent at night, Hadrian was cautious. Their love-making was still as tender and gentle as it always had been. Antinous, however, was craving something else, something he had not yet tasted, something he wanted to give, but, it seemed, something Hadrian was not ready to take. Hadrian had over and again denied them the mutual pleasure, saying that they had to wait for the right time. Yet when was that to be?

"Graeculus," he finally started one night as they drank wine after dinner. "You know I love you…you know I love being with you…when we're alone…I'm just, I guess, confused, I don't understand why, my love, why do you not," Antinous looked Hadrian directly in the eyes, "*have* me?"

Hadrian appeared briefly flustered then exhaled long and deep. He glanced beseechingly at the youth. "You're simply not like anybody else."

"I don't understand," Antinous responded with a touch of despair.

"You're not flesh to be corrupted. You're different. I feel different when I'm with you. Not like with…the others."

"But," he touched Hadrian's hand, "Graeculus, I *want* you. I want to feel you. I want to give myself to you."

Hadrian looked away.

"It won't be like the others because I give myself freely to you. Please accept my gift." Antinous stood up. "I've felt so strongly for you since I've met you. It has only been as I've become more of a man that I realize what it is I want us have together, to do together. Graeculus, when is it going to be the perfect time?"

Hadrian held his hand to his mouth, then turned to face his beloved. Antinous saw that he was crying.

The youth fell to his knees before his master. "I'm sorry, I'm sorry, love, please forgive me." He took his lover's palm and held it to his own smooth cheek. "I only thought that since we were alone, so far away from Rome…" He trailed off, choking back emotion.

Hadrian released his hand and ran his fingers through the youth's mass of golden curls. "The gods know I have burned for you every day since I met you," he said softly tipping up Antinous's chin.

Antinous looked at the pained man before him. "And I, you."

"Yes. I know that to be true. I know that in my heart." Hadrian bent down and kissed the boy's plump red lips. Inflamed, Antinous, wrapped his arms around Hadrian's neck, pulling him closer, hoping against hope their bodies would unite.

But Hadrian pulled back. "Not quite yet, Kynegiskos." The emperor released himself from the embrace. "I have a confession, a secret perhaps."

He got up and walked to the bearskin on the floor before their bed. He picked it up and lay it carefully on the mattress, the head of the bear at the foot of the bed.

"When I first met you, I knew something was different, *I* was different. I experienced feelings, emotions I never had before. I sought solace and answers, went hunting and slew this creature." He stroked the fur reverently. "It was in Thespiae, where Eros is worshipped. I made an offering and prayed to him for guidance." Hadrian chuckled. "Instead I was visited by his mother, Aphrodite Urania."

"The goddess came to you?" the youth exclaimed incredulously.

"She showed me what could be, a love born from mutual respect, friendship, and desire." Hadrian walked back and took Antinous's hands. "It has been frightening to see all that she has shown me come true. Yet, I'm still afraid. I don't want to ruin what I have, what we have now."

Antinous saw a glimmer of hope. "No, you won't. We'll make it better. Let us honor the goddess of love with our bodies." His arousal gave an impatient edge to his tone.

"Yes, it is right to honor the gifts the gods have bestowed upon us." Hadrian led the youth to their bed, then kissed his forehead. Antinous lifted his face wanting more. Hadrian only smiled. "Take off your tunic and your underthings," he directed.

Antinous quickly and excitedly divested himself of his garments.

"Sit on the skin."

Antinous did so with alacrity. He crossed his legs and watched his love.

Hadrian went to the lararium, knelt before his household gods, and said a quick, quiet prayer. He took the small jug containing perfumed lamp oil from the altar. He held it over his head, closed his eyes and gave a benediction to bless the liquid, then brought the jar down and pressed it against his heart once again invoking Aphrodite. When finished, he got up and placed the jug on the bedside table.

Hadrian stripped completely, then knelt on the bearskin toward the foot of the bed. Antinous felt the mattress bounce and sink under the weight of his love, sending a thrill of anticipation through him.

"Lie down."

Antinous did as instructed, looking up at the tent roof and trying to steady his heavy breaths. The scent of crushed wildflowers filled his nostrils when Hadrian poured the cool consecrated oil on his chest near his heart. Hadrian recited a litany of prayers as his warm hands rubbed Antinous's pectorals, sending shocks of arousal to his nipples. The emperor continued his quiet orisons as he dribbled the oil down the youth's torso, spreading it across the rippled muscles with a light but urgent touch.

Antinous gasped when Hadrian reached his groin, his slick fingers sliding silkily against the depilated skin.

Hadrian touched a finger to his lips to silence the youth, then continued his poetic incantations while he massaged Antinous's penis, thoroughly coating it in the sacred oil. Antinous sputtered breathy moans as the expert hand glided up and down his hardening shaft. He looked up in protest when Hadrian suddenly stopped.

"Spread your legs," his master said softly, a smile twitching on his lips. "And bend your knees."

Caught up in the anguish of anticipation, Antinous moved quickly into position, his stiff, lubricated cock bobbing between his thighs. He propped himself on his elbows.

Hadrian smiled at his impatience, a soft, knowing smile. He placed his hand under the youth's scrotum, barely brushing the tender sac, sending a shiver up Antinous's spine. The emperor tipped the jar and poured out another libation. With that offering he thoroughly lubricated Antinous's anus, spreading the thick liquid not only around the snug, puckered opening, but as deeply inside as he could reach, repeating his motions carefully and attentively, one finger, then two, working the oil in thoroughly. Antinous let his head fall back and moaned at the sensual intimacy. When Hadrian stopped, Antinous looked up, impelled to know what would happen next.

The emperor then slowly and deliberately coated his own fully-erect cock, stroking the magnificent member up and down until it glistened, all the while holding the youth's gaze with his penetrating gray eyes.

Antinous salivated in anticipation, nibbling and licking his lips. The moment he had longed for, the moment Hadrian had denied them for far too long, had arrived. This night appeared to be, finally, the right time.

Hadrian put down the jar and lifted his lover's hips and buttocks, keeping them raised with his bent knee until he slipped a silk pillow underneath. The emperor positioned his formidable cock at the tight orifice. Antinous could scarcely contain his excitement.

Hadrian pressed inside Antinous but a hair's breadth. The youth sucked in air. It was quite different from when he used his fingers.

"Repeat after me," Hadrian said, his eyes holding those of his lover. "I offer myself on the altar of Eros…"

"I offer myself on the altar of Eros…" Through his excitement Antinous could barely speak the words.

Hadrian pushed in a little more. "And supplicate myself before heavenly Aphrodite…"

"And supplicate myself before heavenly Aphrodite…" Antinous choked, denying the pain.

"To bear witness and bless this integral union of mortal souls." Hadrian pushed in further until half his cock was buried in the youth.

"To bear witness and bless this integral union of mortal souls." Antinous felt his skin tingle with perspiration, his breath exhale in bracing huffs. He tried to concentrate on relaxing, to think about the pleasure.

In one excruciatingly slow movement, Hadrian entered his love. Antinous cried out in agony. The emperor gripped the boy's oil-slicked cock, gently pumping it back and forth as he held himself steady inside, letting Antinous's body soften and accept the invasion.

"We are one," Hadrian said in a voice trembling with profound emotion.

Antinous let out a tremulous breath. He had no idea what to expect. His body was in shock, but the pain was exquisite. And Hadrian's hand masturbating him only heightened the pleasure. He wanted more, and he wanted it now.

"Make me yours, Graeculus."

But Hadrian did not move, remaining embedded, simply still, the desire in his eyes betraying his reticence.

"Please."

The absolute urgency in his tone must have sent Hadrian over the edge. He pulled out all the way, then pushed in, still carefully, cautiously.

Antinous was beyond loving gentleness. The overwhelming ecstasy empowered him. He removed his lover's hand from his cock. He wanted his undivided attention.

"Fuck me."

Hadrian's mouth fell open.

"Fuck me hard, Graeculus."

It was what they both wanted, what they both needed. Hadrian slammed inside the boy, bending his back to meet his lover's face, taking him in a deliriously deep kiss, their tongues twisting and twining in abandon.

Antinous thrust up as Hadrian pushed in, encouraging an increasing rhythm. Hadrian drove into him, frantically, wantonly, as if catching up for the lost pleasure he had been denying himself.

"Touch yourself," he commanded. "I want you to come when I do."

Antinous reached between their bodies to stroke himself, finding his prick extraordinarily sensitive. He knew his climax was imminent. He slowed his hand.

"Don't hold back. I'm on the edge. Do it, my love, do it."

With two more strokes, Antinous came, and when he did, Hadrian placed his hand over his, gripping his cock even tighter. Antinous gasped, feeling a surge of ecstasy, a second climax, another emission.

With a violent jolt and a clipped cry, Hadrian emptied himself in the youth, twitching and shuddering over and over as jets pulsed within.

When his body had calmed, Hadrian snuggled against his lover, their satisfied breaths slowing in unison. Antinous felt the cock inside him soften.

Hadrian kissed his cheek. "You're crying, Kynegiskos. Did I hurt you?" His sensual tone conveyed concern.

Antinous had not noticed his tears. He turned his face to wipe them on a pillow. "I weep in joy, Graeculus."

"I know how you feel," was the gentle response.

Antinous could feel the soft hairs of Hadrian's beard against his neck and shoulder. His own arms were still clinging intently to the emperor's back. He loosened them, sliding his hands along the musculature, feeling the potency and strength of the man above him, the man who made him think, made him laugh, made him smile, made him dream. The man he loved. Then, suddenly, as water rushing over a bridge after winter's rains, Antinous let loose a flood of emotion, sobbing and shaking.

Hadrian kissed his neck. "Shhh, shhh," he consoled.

But Antinous would be silent no longer. "I love you, Graeculus. I will love you forever."

Tibur, Hadrian's villa, end of July 128

Sabina looked up from her poetry at the sounds of her husband's footsteps on the tessellated garden walk. She wasn't really reading anyway. The summer sun's warmth was far too hypnotizing. "And did the youth please you?" she asked.

"Wicked woman. You've not seen me for months and that is the first thing you say to me?" Hadrian sat beside her on the couch.

"I've been married to you for twenty-eight years, Graeculus. I can almost read your thoughts."

"Frightening, isn't it?"

Sabina glared at him impertinently. "Well?"

"He pleased me. Very much so."

"Good. Now that you have consummated the affair you will be far easier to live with."

"I think it is within the law for the emperor to discipline his wife when she is insolent."

Sabina laughed. "I would only enjoy it, Graeculus, and you know that."

He grinned. "And I would enjoy it far too much as well."

Sabina bent forward and kissed her husband's cheek. "Welcome home. What did you come to tell me?"

"We're going to the East again. This time I would like you to come with me."

"All right. Who will keep me company this time?"

"Zuester of course."

"Of course. I would simply have to act the bitter, betrayed wife without him."

Hadrian ignored her. "Mindia, Paulina—"

"Paulina? Your sister?"

"My sister, yes."

"Is her interminable bore of a husband coming too?"

"Servianus, no. But her grandson Fuscus will be joining us."

Sabina turned sober. "He's your only male flesh and blood. He is technically your heir," she said confidentially. "Still, I don't like him. He's ambitious, obsequious, superstitious, and gambles to excess. And he's not even sixteen yet."

Hadrian grunted, then glanced around. The servants, however, were not within earshot. "I don't like him either; everything you say about him is true," he said quietly. "I would like to spend some time with Paulina, though, and she requested that he join the imperial party. Look, you don't have to have anything to do with him."

"I do like Paulina. Maybe we can find something for Fuscus to bet on and leave us alone." Sabina glanced sidelong at her husband. "You're not making him your heir, are you?"

Hadrian drew his hands down his face. "I would hope I have some time left to make a considered decision."

"You have someone else in mind?"

"Yes," he answered in a low tone.

Sabina sat silently, wondering if Hadrian would continue with the thought.

Instead, he inhaled deeply. "And Lucius Ceionius Commodus will be joining us later," he said before smiling provocatively. "In Egypt."

"Egypt? We're going to Egypt? How exciting!" The question of his successor was completely forgotten with the delightful news.

"Yes, and with that I will have circled the empire. It is my duty as emperor. I wonder that my predecessors had not thought of such a thing."

"Too busy creating the empire, I should think."

"You really are cheeky, aren't you?"

"Ah, but you married me nonetheless."

"As you recall, it was all arranged. I barely knew you." He kissed the tip of her nose and grinned. "Had I known you were as fiery as this I probably would have chosen you myself anyway."

Sabina laughed and stroked his beard.

Hadrian took her hand. "Vibia," he started gently, "did you feel secure in my absence?"

"Yes, husband. Very," she said smiling and looking beyond him toward the peristyle colonnade.

The emperor turned around and saw his very able secretary and chuckled. Despite his efficient conduct and humble manner, the younger man was heroic in his protection of the empress, something Hadrian was most grateful for.

"Vibia?" Zuester called in an overly-familiar tone. He stopped when he saw Hadrian. "My lord," he said as he bowed to the emperor.

Hadrian stood and put his arm around the Dacian's shoulder. "You sleep with my wife. Perhaps it is time for some familiarity?"

"Yes, my lor—Graeculus." Zuester looked down sheepishly.

"Ha!" Hadrian released his friend and walked to the divan opposite his wife. "'My lord Graeculus' will do fine," he said as he lay down, folding his hands behind his head.

"Don't tease the man, husband," scolded Sabina. "You're arrogant and have a terrible temper sometimes. He's only trying to keep his head."

Zuester sat on the couch next to Sabina. She put her arms around him and squeezed. "We're going to Egypt, love."

"Egypt?" Zuester glanced back and forth between the imperial couple.

"Yes, eventually," Hadrian answered. "But first we're going to Greece for the initiation ceremony for the Eleusinian Mysteries. I've been invited to be advanced to the second stage. This is truly a great honor. And," he said eyeing the lovers across the courtyard, "I would like both of you to attend."

"Us?" queried Sabina.

"Me too?" asked Zuester.

"Yes, yes, the two of you. Besides it being politic for the Empress of Rome to attend, I think you will find the ceremony exhilarating, enlightening perhaps. Antinous will be there as well. Sharing such an experience will bond us all together. And remember, he is my companion now. Like family."

Sabina smiled at her husband, as she leaned her head on her lover's shoulder. "I'm glad you consider Zuester that way. As family."

Hadrian regarded the couple, playfully pecking and cooing. He was relieved Sabina would have someone to make her happy after he was gone.

He sighed. He had to tell them.

"Vibia, Zuester," he started without looking at either of them, "the doctors say spending some time in the deserts of Egypt will be good for my health."

Sabina sat up straight and looked at her husband in shock. "Graeculus, what's wrong?"

"Nothing, or rather, the same. I sometimes have difficulties breathing. I'm sure it's just the foul air of Rome. I had no problems in the African provinces."

"And the nose-bleeds?" Sabina asked with concern.

"Seemingly only when I am around senators," he chuckled morbidly.

"When do we leave, then?" asked Zuester. "It sounds like the sooner the better, Graeculus."

Hadrian glanced over at his freedman and friend, and smiled. He had used his familiar name without compunction. "Yes, we leave very soon."

Eleusis, Greece, the Telesterion, September 128

Antinous wrapped his fingers around Hadrian's hand and sighed, knowing that whatever befell them over the course of that night would bind them together irrevocably. Hadrian looked down at his companion and smiled in encouragement.

It had been constant activity for Antinous and the other initiates and the youth was exhausted. In Athens, they had received instruction at the Eleusinion and had made offerings to the pantheon of gods on the Acropolis. They had fasted and barely slept. They had gone to the sea near Phaleron, stripped naked, and chased a small pig into the water where they finally caught it. Amidst chants and songs the piglet was sacrificed, laid on a bed of barley stalks, and cooked in a clay casket in the middle of a bonfire. Not long afterwards, the hot casket was pulled from the flames and smashed, the animal's succulent flesh torn limb from limb by the hungry mob who ate the meat voraciously.

That was just the first four days.

Hadrian had insisted his beloved be initiated into the Eleusinian Mysteries alongside his most intimate friends. They were all there together: Hadrian, Antinous, Sabina, Zuester, even Sabina's sister Mindia. It was Hadrian's second time, a very important time, when he would be initiated into the higher level of the Mysteries. The emperor had been personally invited by the powerful high priestess herself.

Together they and thousands of others had experienced the opening rites and ceremonies in Athens. On the fifth day the initiates, the *mystai*, had gathered at the Kerameikos, the cemetery of that great city. There they had been crowned with laurel wreaths and given myrtle branches to wave. Across their backs they had slung baskets containing sacred objects, the mysteries of which would be revealed to them that night. Led by hierophants, they had walked in procession to Eleusis, some 12 miles away. At the head of the cortege had been carried a statue of Dionysos Iacchos, son of the earth goddess Demeter, crowned with a wreath of gold, as the mystai sung and chanted songs of his joyful reunification with his mother at Eleusis.

They did not stop during the entire length of the journey, but had continued walking, driven to reach the destination of spiritual revelation. If one initiate stopped and fell behind, he or she was exhorted – or berated – to continue by a hierophant. When night fell, they walked by torch light. When they had reached the bridge at Cephisos, masked men in black robes hurled insults and pebbles at those who were known to be patricians. It hurt Antinous to hear the name of his beloved Hadrian mocked, and on the very bridge that the emperor himself had recently rebuilt for the people of Greece! Could they not show respect and admiration for their emperor?

No, they could not. There was no emperor, there were no aristocrats, there were no senators, no land owners, no wealthy merchants. Neither were there slaves, women, simple freedmen, the old, or the infirm. There was not one individual, they were all one, all the same. Antinous was the same as Hadrian. He felt proud walking beside his best friend, his comrade, his lover, his equal.

They had reached Eleusis and the outer courtyard of the place of the Mysteries at night on the fifth day. But they did not make camp. Instead, despite having walked all day and all night, they had continued singing and dancing in honor of the goddess Demeter, their unrested minds and bodies energized with expectant elation.

It was for Demeter that the elaborate ceremonies took place. The goddess of fertility, the goddess of death and rebirth, without whom nothing would grow. Without whom there would be no food, no sun, no wine, no warmth. There would only be death, interminable winter, and endless sorrow.

Demeter's beloved daughter Persephone had been desired by Hades, god of the underworld. One day, he kidnapped the girl as she wandered through the fields of Enna, picking flowers, trusting the world around her to be good and kind and beautiful. As she struggled in the arms of her captor, she watched in horror as the ground split open and Hell was revealed. She screamed as the black carriage descended into the underworld, then watched in disbelief as the fissure in the ground above her sealed shut. She was trapped in the black, cold underworld as the wife of Hades.

Demeter looked high and low for her beautiful Persephone, her only child. She asked who had seen her daughter? Who had witnessed the disappearance? No one could answer her.

She wandered the earth for four months, fasting, tearing her hair. For those four months there was no sunshine, there was no warmth, the ground remained barren, rain poured from the heavens, snow covered the mountains, rivers iced over. Mankind was beginning to die as the goddess of fecundity and life mourned the loss of her sole progeny.

Finally, Helios, the god of the sun, revealed to Demeter that he had witnessed the despised Hades take the goddess's precious daughter. Helios also knew the lord of the underworld had performed carnal acts upon the girl's virgin body. Demeter demanded to speak with Hades.

"Return my daughter." She was livid.

Hades laughed in her face. "I have made her my queen. She is compliant. She endures the bed chamber. It is quite alluring."

This only enraged the goddess of fertility, to know her innocent daughter had been molested by the hideous lord, hated even by the other Olympian gods and goddesses.

Zeus had to intervene. Without plants to green the earth, animals to tame the land, grain to eat, wine to drink, mankind would not survive. If mankind did not survive, then there would be no offerings to the gods. The situation was untenable.

"You must return the maiden to her mother," the god of all gods had told his despised brother Hades.

"She is a maiden no more," said the lord of the underworld.

Zeus understood the implications. "How many times has she been in your bed?"

"Four."

"Then she shall share your bed for only four months during each year."

Hades knew he could not object. Besides, that meant for four months every year he could please himself with a beautiful girl who would be otherwise unsullied during the rest of the year. During the first month of her annual captivity it would be as if she were a virgin once more, tight and unused.

"I accept," he said readily.

Demeter protested. Her daughter was an innocent who did not deserve to be in Hell for four months every year.

"He has claimed her as his wife, sister," explained Zeus. "You know the law of the Fates."

Demeter did know the law. She had to comply.

Persephone was led out of Hell by Hermes, the messenger god. The destroyed, beleaguered girl was pale and wan, new lines of distress in her face revealing the horrors to which she had been subjected against her will.

But when she fell into the arms of her mother, she instantly became the beautiful youthful lass she had been before being dragged into the mouth of Hell. Mankind rejoiced at the reunion. Crops grew, animals gave birth, women's monthly courses flowed. Life had been restored, resurrected. Demeter herself bore a son, Iacchos.

Antinous knew the story by heart. He had, of course, heard it as a child, over and over again. But when he was a boy the story had been that Persephone had eaten four pomegranate seeds in Hell, and for that she had to remain queen for so many months. That she shared Hades's bed once a month for four months had not ever occur to him. It was revelatory. After days of instruction, it had made sense that women's bodies – their sexuality, their menses – would be tied into the story of fertility and fecundity and the beauty of mother earth.

The celebrations had continued for three more days. During that time, the mystai had attended plays where the tale of Demeter, Persephone, and Hades, and the themes of death and rebirth were performed by actor-hierophants. Animals had been slaughtered, their meat cooked over burning braids of dried barley stalks, and, as they watched the bonfire, the initiates had roared with pleasure at the popping sounds of sacrifice in the midst of the conflagration. They had fasted, bathed each other, washed their clothes.

They had meditated, the relaxed state lulling the more exhausted to their first sleep in days.

Then on the afternoon of the third day, they had donned their pure white himations amidst joyous chanting, the men in low hums, the women in rich soprano tones. Hierophants had swung censers filled with incense, splashing their clothes with sweet perfume. Antinous had found himself mesmerized by the lush sounds, the magnificent sights, and the intoxicating smells.

Now he stood in his himation, holding his lover's hand, anxiously waiting in the courtyard before their entrance into the Telesterion, the vast hall where the mystery of life would be revealed to them. It was dusk, and the final ceremony was still an hour away. A palpable giddiness spread amongst the initiates, once again wearing their baskets containing the sacred objects, anticipating the revelation of what lay within. At the appointed time, each initiate was given a gold cup filled with *kykeon*, a strong beer of barley and pennyroyal. For the more experienced among them – the second initiates like Hadrian – it was the first sustenance they had imbibed for days. Antinous found it very bitter, but it was thick and warm. He had never appreciated drink so much as at that moment.

As night fell, the hierophants took up gongs, marking a beat as the priests chanted and the initiates filed into place. Despite the solemnity, Hadrian and Antinous could not contain their happiness. They grinned broadly as they were led into the Telesterion, overjoyed to share the hallowed occasion together. As the initiates entered the space, each was kissed on the forehead and crowned with a new laurel wreath, the symbol of victory over death heightening their expectations. The hall was dimly lit, only enough to see where to go. In the middle was a high platform, the Anaktoron, the place of the high priests, where the mystery would take place. The initiates knew to watch that space, that sacred space, for a mystical revelation. Once all were inside, they sang an uplifting song, filling the air with ecstatic rapture. It was a song about Persephone, about her innocence, her love of flowers, her joy when with her mother. The very joy shared by all at that very moment.

Antinous felt the euphoric inspiration pump through him, but as he sang the high notes he became aware of a lightheadedness, and as he sang the low notes, he felt a little queasiness in his stomach. Flashes of heat prickled his skin, his pores opening for relief, seeking cooling air. He looked down at his free hand, barely discernible in the pale light, and saw it shaking. He glanced up at Hadrian. His lover was solemnly singing, perspiration beading on his cheeks and brow. Antinous himself was now dripping with sweat, but at the same time he felt very, very cold. He looked over at their companions. Zuester stood next to Sabina, a look of concern on his face, his arm wrapped around her, supporting her as she swayed, clearly unsteady on her feet. Antinous pressed his hand to his temple, realizing he was dizzy as well.

Then suddenly he was oppressed by darkness.

What had been a transcendent moment of unified fervor had in an instant changed to a frenzy of abject terror. Initiates, both men and women, screamed in panic, the heavy blackness only heightening their own physical discomfort. Realizing he no longer held Hadrian's hand, Antinous reached out for his love. There was nothing. He was alone in the dark with the cries and wails of death all around him. He fell to his knees in prayer.

A light appeared in the center of the vast dark hall. A light where the Anaktoron had just been minutes before. Instead there was a sunken black pit.

"Open your baskets," a loud voice bellowed.

The frightened initiates did as told, each one opening their baskets, knowing the secret of life would soon be revealed to them.

Antinous opened his basket and saw a snake. Now free, the creature hissed at him in anger.

He dropped his basket, as all the other initiates had done with their own.

The snakes slithered amongst the feet of the screaming congregation. Paralyzed by fear, Antinous could only watch his own serpent wind its way to the pit. The rest of the snakes were doing precisely that. The room was filled with cowering, wailing people forming a circle of fear around the now writhing mass of serpents in the pit.

The light became brighter at one edge of the circle. A girl appeared in the light, dressed in gold, wreathed with circlets of barley and flowers, her long flowing locks draping delicately about her shoulders. The sweetest smile broke upon her lips, a smile Antinous knew was for him alone. He felt a glimmer of hope to combat the fear. He smiled back.

In an instant, she was grabbed from behind by a masked man dressed in black – one of the men who had hurled insults from the bridge days before. She screamed and struggled against him, but he held her firm. He carried her to the edge of the snake pit then threw her in.

The initiates gasped in horror.

She thrashed and wailed as the snakes covered her, the mass of them seemingly swallowing her, pulling her downward into the pit. Her cries were smothered by the reptiles. Moments later she was silent.

The throng of initiates surged forward. Antinous tried to push backwards, to no avail. He was being forced forward, toward the snakes, toward the girl.

Toward the fissure into Hell itself.

Fear overtook him, fear of the unknown, fear of death, fear of pain, fear of nothingness, all that which was happening to the girl who could no longer be seen or heard.

Antinous fought to beat back the throbbing crowd, screaming at them at the top of his lungs. Yet no sound came out. He had been rendered mute. In desperation, he covered his head with his hands. He would have to suffer his impending fate.

Blackness fell across the hall again, stilling the mystai into silence. For how long they remained this way, Antinous could not tell. It seemed as if forever, as if he would never see again, he would never hear again, never speak again, never touch his lover, never feel pleasure. Never live again.

Suddenly, a light seemingly brighter than the sun appeared above him, pouring forth from the Anaktoron. From beneath the platform came the most wondrous sound of harmonious singing. The priests, priestesses, and hierophants were chanting sacred words, sacred words of life, of birth, of rebirth.

The high priest appeared at the top of the stage. He was naked, his cock engorged, pointing straight out unabashedly. In one hand, he held a sheaf of bound barley above his head. Draped across his other arm and shoulder was the limp form of the golden girl from the snake pit. The crowd of initiates howled mourning laments for her unmoving body.

The high priestess came to the side of the priest and took the girl, holding her delicately in her arms, as a mother holding a newborn baby, while a beautiful nymph approached the priest and began masturbating his swollen cock, his face revealing he was at the precipice of his climax. In less than a minute he moaned his satisfaction. The nymph held his prick as he sprayed his seed onto the limp body of the girl and the priestess.

The golden girl woke instantly. She threw her arms around the neck of the high priestess, crying tears of joy.

The crowd cheered her awakening, her rebirth. She had survived Hell and had been brought back.

The girl smiled again, the sweet innocent smile she had revealed when she first appeared. Once again Antinous could swear her smile was for him alone.

The initiates burst into spontaneous song. Each turned to the other and hugged their neighbor. A woman put her arms around Antinous. He was surprised to feel as if he had never been touched before. He could feel every inch of her arms around him, every pore on his body was enlivened by her touch, pumping blood to his hardening cock. The woman began tearing at his himation, tugging it off his body, until it fell to the ground. Others around them were ripping off their clothes. Antinous had never wanted a woman before, but suddenly could not think of anything else but coupling with the stranger before him.

It was not to be. Behind him he felt familiar arms grasp him around his waist, freeing him from the temptation of the lustful woman and the ecstatic fervor of his own cravings. Hadrian pulled Antinous close to him, and kissed him full on the mouth, their nude bodies pressing together wanting to be melded as one. Antinous lifted himself up and wrapped his legs around Hadrian's waist.

"I've never wanted to fuck you – to fuck anything – this much before in my life!" the youth panted into his lover's ear.

"Hmmm," Hadrian grunted in satisfaction as his cock bobbed against Antinous's scrotum. It seemed he could not stop smiling. "Kynegiskos, you've just shared the most profound religious experience of my life…of our lives. You need to wait before we share carnal salvation, my love. Patience."

"But Graeculus—"

Antinous did not finish his protest. He was abruptly pulled off his lover by forces unknown. Just before a blindfold was placed over his eyes, he saw Hadrian regard him with expectant joy.

As he watched Antinous being taken away for the final rite, Hadrian realized he had learned a great deal of patience during the years of his infatuation for the boy. His cock now ached for satisfaction, but he knew he could wait. Their coming union would be transcendent for the both of them.

The high priestess appeared before him, and held out her hand. "It is time, Caesar."

"Yes, my lady. I am ready." As he took her hand, Hadrian quickly glanced over his shoulder. Zuester and Sabina were pawing at each other frantically, and even Mindia was copulating with a handsome Greek boy.

It was to be expected after the strong narcotic they had all imbibed. Hadrian himself had had to undergo rigorous training to accept the mind's hallucinations and the body's instincts and not react to perceptions but instead to true knowledge and desires.

And once he had accomplished that discipline, he was accepted to be initiated in the higher level of the Mysteries as an *epoptes*, or, "one who has seen".

Hadrian and the priestess walked through the ecstatic coupling in the Telesterion to an ante-chamber on the edge of the hall. They entered the small space through a heavy black curtain.

"Stand," commanded the priestess as she pointed to a spot in the middle of the dim room.

Hadrian obeyed her bidding. Before him a youth offered a golden cup with a dark liquid.

"Drink."

Again, the emperor obeyed the priestess and drank the contents of the cup, a palatable sweet wine.

"Remain."

Hadrian did not flinch as two youths lifted his arms to bind him to chains hanging from the ceiling. With even breaths, he calmed his body in preparation to what was to happen next.

The whip's sting was not unexpected, but its abrupt timing did cause him to flinch. He felt it one more time across his shoulder blades before he recited his prayer.

"The soul remains in misery while in subjection to the body," he intoned. His voice, he realized, betrayed the very anguish his body was experiencing.

The whip fell again, a little lower, across his middle back.

"Mankind must be purified from the defilements of our material nature." Unwittingly, he felt his cock spring to life. Hadrian tamped down his quickening breath.

The whip cracked three times against the emperor's back. Each time he flinched a little less. His erection, however, seemed to have a mind of its own. *The drink.* Whatever had been in the cup was doing this to him.

"Denying the body elevates us to the actuality of spiritual vision." He was unable to suppress the confusion in his voice.

One last time the whip struck its mark. Hadrian stood firm.

"I release my body from this earth."

A tortured wail pierced the room from against the wall. It was Antinous. Hadrian only then realized his lover had witnessed the whole proceeding. He closed his eyes to the building anger and sorrow and tried to exhale his distress from his body.

It was part of the rite, he reminded himself. They had involved the youth to test Hadrian's resolve.

This time the whip was wholly unexpected. Hadrian felt his skin tear at its lash. He held himself steady, blinking back the tears forming in his eyes.

"No!" Antinous screamed. "Please! Do not harm him! Take me! I will give my life for his!"

The youth's frantic pleading swelled Hadrian's heart. He could no longer control his tears. He could not free his soul from his body, the needs of the body were too strong. He had failed. The acceptance released him to give in to the delicious feeling of his hardened cock. A choking sob escaped his throat.

Lamplight focused on the corner of the small chamber. Hadrian saw his love seated and tied, surrounded by several nude nymphs. Agony was etched in his beautiful face.

"My love," he gasped, struggling against his bindings. "Please," he called out to those in the room. "Please, he has done nothing. Release him."

The nymphs slowly began stroking Antinous, their hands straying across his smooth chest down his taut stomach to fondle his prick unaroused from his misery. One girl put the flaccid member in her mouth and slowly began licking and sucking. Against his will the youth grew hard.

"Who are you?" came the priestess's voice from the dark.

"I am Antinous, friend to this man." His voice cracked trying to steady himself against the onslaught of pleasure.

"You offer your own life, to deliver him from his fate?"

"I do." There was such anguish and earnestness in his response.

"Who is Hermes?" It was a question asked of all initiates during their instruction period.

"He is the messenger of the gods and the guide to and from the underworld."

"When Persephone is kidnapped and held by Hades, how does she live?"

"In darkness."

Hadrian could see his love's face soften into ecstatic dissolution as the girl expertly used her tongue and lips. He swallowed a protest.

"And man, when Persephone is in Hell, how does man live?"

"In darkness," Antinous responded, struggling to keep his composure.

"Who shows Persephone the light?"

"Hermes, the messenger god."

"Hermes delivers those in darkness to the light?" the priestess prompted.

"Yes, he is a deliverer." His breaths were unsteady. Hadrian knew his lover was almost at his climax.

"Who is this before you, man or god?"

"He is a man." The last word was said with breathless assurance.

"What are you now offering?"

"To deliver him from his darkness. To deliver him from his death."

Antinous's pelvis jerked up toward the mouth of the girl pleasuring him. He pressed against her as she sucked and swallowed, and she continued to hold him there until she had drawn every last drop from his body.

Hadrian flinched, this time because his heart had been thrashed.

When the nymph pulled back, Antinous remained sprawled against the bench, spent and ashamed.

The priestess appeared in the dim light of the chamber dressed in a long hooded robe embroidered with sheaves of barley in gold thread. She motioned for the youths in attendance to free Hadrian from his bindings. But she motioned for the emperor to remain where he was.

"There are two types of darkness. The darkness of the soul and the darkness of the earth. To conquer the darkness of the soul, we must give ourselves completely to another." She indicated the youths should untie Antinous and bring him before Hadrian. The lovers stood face to face, not touching as commanded, tears of joy, relief, and shame streaming down their cheeks.

"When we have conquered the needs of our own flesh and offer ourselves to others we have freed our souls from the darkness." She took the hands of the lovers and joined them together. "You two have proved that you have conquered this inner darkness. You have offered your own selves to one another."

The priestess turned to Antinous. "You are Hermes. You have brought this man out of the dark."

She turned to Hadrian. "You are epoptes. You have now seen the light."

Hadrian could not contain the emotion welling in his heart. "With you, my love, my Antinous, my Kynegiskos, I am reborn."

Antinous smiled before breaking out in joyous laughter. "I did not know my true path in life before I met you, *kyrie*, my Graeculus."

"The union of true souls is a gift from the gods. Yet darkness still covers earth as long as there is sorrow and mourning. To conquer the darkness of the earth, we must unite your pure souls to the earth." She regarded the happy lovers. "We must infuse the earth with your spirit, your seed."

From beneath her robe, the priestess pulled out a stalk of six-row barley carved from stone, larger than life, with plump ripe kernels each polished to a smooth sheen. Hadrian recognized it as a fertility dildo used in other rites of the Mysteries.

"Your fecundity, your seed will rejuvenate the earth, as releasing the seed rejuvenates the flesh."

On her cue, one of the youthful attendants spilled a bag of dry, loose soil onto the ground at the feet of Hadrian and Antinous.

Hadrian saw one of the girls behind Antinous and watched as she poured oil in her hand and massaged his lover's butt. Behind him another girl was doing the same thing, drawing the viscous liquid into his anus, preparing and relaxing him for the next rite.

The girls held Antinous steady while they turned him around and made him bend forward slightly.

"Your seed will mingle with that of the youth's and be expelled onto the sterile soil. The union of your souls will feed the earth."

One of the girls guided Hadrian's cock to Antinous's lubricated hole. He pushed in, feeling a rush of relief. His groan of satisfaction was countered with his lover's sigh.

"Give him your seed."

Hadrian thrust in and out of the tight channel, deliberative at first, then building toward abandon, losing himself in the desired and much needed act, until he felt something warm and hard nudge against his own puckered hole.

It was the dildo wielded expertly by the priestess. It had been over thirty years since he himself had been penetrated. His body clenched against the invasion.

"Calm yourself, let go," the priestess counseled gently. "Give in to the pleasure and the pain will disappear."

Hadrian clasped Antinous closely to him as he moved in and out of his lover's body. He softened and opened himself for the sacred stone, feeling each nub reach the pleasure zones within, untouched for decades. With a gratified sigh, he moved in unison to the priestess's rhythm.

Instinctively, he reached for Antinous's cock but found it was already being attended to by the expert hands of one of the nymphs. The youth was lost in his own sensual bliss.

Awash in pleasures he had denied himself for too long, Hadrian let go utterly, now driven by a fervent need to feel release. Unfettered from his prejudices, he slammed into Antinous, hoping the dildo would slam into him. It did, unbearably yet deliciously so.

"Fill him. Fill the youth. Let your seed mingle with his."

He could not hold back. With a final thrust, Hadrian pushed forward, spewing his ejaculate deep inside Antinous. The dildo remained inside him, massaging him, forcing him to come in abundance. With each twitch of his sated body, the nymph pulled Antinous's cock, pumping in rhythm to Hadrian's bursts. Amidst Antinous's cries of release, unending jets of milky fluid drenched the soil at their feet, his cock gushing the emissions of two men. When he was spent, the nymphs had to hold fast to the youth's collapsing, slaked form.

"The light of your unified souls now rejuvenates the earth, rendering it sterile no longer. Your seed will perpetuate the fecundity of our lands."

The priestess slowly removed the dildo from Hadrian as two youths helped him pull out of his lover. He felt satiated yet spent, energized yet enervated. A physical experience so tremendous, he felt spiritually reborn, his soul renewed, transcending the body, like a god himself.

The priestess smiled at the emperor. "In my years I have initiated the ancient heroes to the Mysteries. Now I have brought to the light the master of the vast earth and the infinite sea, the sovereign of innumerable mortals, Hadrian, who has poured out indescribable riches on all cities and, above all, on our famous city of Kekrops, our Athens. Now he has poured out his own soul to nourish our fields."

The exhausted lovers fell into each other's arms, laughing with exuberant delight.

Pontus, Byzantium, January 129

Roedogune sat in the window seat of her temporary quarters overlooking the sparkling sea. The city of Byzantium was beautiful, like a jeweled gateway to the east, but it was still Roman. Nothing that was Roman could have value or beauty for very long. It was an upstart empire, filled with merchants and farmers and men of ill-breeding who could, horrifyingly, become king.

Still, Rome's subjects were useful for some things. She was to meet with one of them, one who had begged and pleaded for her audience, a man who knew how to properly address and flatter a woman above his station. A man who had as much of a reason to hate Rome as she did. She would meet with him, she had said. In the meantime, she sent her spies to check up on him.

The Parthian princess sighed. After twelve long years the Roman emperor Hadrian had finally released her, supposedly as a gesture of good will. She had never met this Hadrian, but he was probably much like the soldier-king Trajan she had come face-to-face with in Ctesiphon – meaning paternalistic and common. This Hadrian, though, exhibited a glimmer of being a shrewd strategist. He had retained the great throne of the Parthian shahs, the *sella regia*, as war booty, stating that it might one day be returned if the Parthians became a client kingdom of Rome. Roedogune snorted at that. It would never happen.

Perhaps this Roman she was to meet would be able to help her retrieve the throne. He wanted use of her contacts in Egypt for some scheme of his. The first reports of her spies had said this Roman had made several failed assassination attempts against both of the emperors Trajan and Hadrian. She knew of the emperor Hadrian's planned trip to Egypt. She had quite a number of contacts there, from traders and local administrators to priests and astrologers, the latter of which would work best. From reports she understood this Hadrian to be a religious man and even constructed his own astrological charts. Killing him would be fairly straightforward. It would be in the stars.

She chortled at her own joke and lay back against the pillows.

Soon she would be going home, and the realization of this fact always sent her mind reeling. Her mother and father would be waiting for her, her brothers too. Her father, King Osrhoes, was still alive she knew, the Romans and her spies had confirmed this. He had been made Shah again after the succession of the Emperor Hadrian. She did not know the fate of the other members of her family; she would be glad to see any and all of them.

But she was twenty-four now, quite old for an unmarried princess. The reunion would be brief before she would be gifted to the most politically suitable royal mate. It was always possible that this chosen husband would be handsome as well. Thoughts like that always made her feel giddy. Fantasies of sharing the bed of a handsome Parthian prince had been one of the ways she had distracted herself during the boredom and frustration of captivity. She had first noticed a fascination with her Roman guardsmen, some of whom had been quite attractive. They wore short skirts exposing their strong muscular thighs, as opposed to the concealing long pants of the Parthian guard. After her nursemaid Hyasdana had died, Roedogune had been given Roman maid servants – not one of whom, however, was in actuality a maid. Hyasdana had been there for Roedogune's transition into a woman, but it was the Roman maids who had taught her what she could do with her new womanly body.

They had also been able to sneak her into the servants' baths when the men were bathing. From behind screened windows, Roedogune had watched with lustful eyes as naked men were massaged and oiled, paraded shamelessly while displaying their bodies and flexing their muscles in boastful camaraderie. Her maidservants showed her how to relieve herself of the hunger for male flesh with her own fingers. And when that hunger drove her to the brink of madness that her own ministrations could not assuage, they initiated her into the world of women pleasuring women with their hands and tongues.

She had to admit that some parts of her captivity had not been without benefits.

A knock on the chamber door startled her.

"Yes?" she called.

"A thousand pardons, my princess, the information you had wanted about the Roman merchant has arrived."

She had been waiting for this. The meeting was the following week. "Enter."

A servant, hunched from obsequiousness and not age, entered ceremoniously and handed a missive on a platter to the princess.

Roedogune glanced at the seal. It was indeed the much-awaited second report of the spies on the Roman who wanted to meet with her.

She waved at the servant. "Please leave me."

He did so amidst bows and praise for his royal mistress.

Roedogune opened the report and read. Her eyes widened at some parts, and she grinned ear to ear then laughed at others. This Roman, this Sextus Quintilius Bestia, would be far too easy to manipulate.

Bestia was finding his audience with Princess Roedogune not only valuable; it was quite gratifying. She was as beautiful as he had imagined, more so even. Raven hair and golden – yes, golden – eyes, an exotic color somewhere between green and brown. And she spoke Latin with the most alluring accent. He was enthralled in her presence, growing hard at every syllable she spoke, but reminded himself they had serious business to discuss.

And discuss business they did, finding they did indeed have goals in common. Roedogune hated Trajan and Hadrian for warring with Parthia and imprisoning her, and Bestia hated the two for exiling and murdering his cousin. Assassinating Hadrian would be a joint effort, Roedogune providing support in Egypt where Bestia did not have many local contacts, and Bestia providing the scheme and seeing the plan through to the bitter end.

But she wanted something in return, something odd to him, although he understood the symbolic value. The princess Roedogune wanted the Parthian throne, the *sella regia.* It apparently sat in Rome somewhere, perhaps in the imperial resident on the Palatine Hill. She really did not know. She described it in great detail. Surely he could find it for her?

Surely, he had said, he could indeed. But perhaps his tone or expression had conveyed otherwise?

It was the only thing he could think of once he found himself tied to a chair. And now that she was forcing the issue, he was not so sure he had any other choice but to look for the throne.

She had lured him into a compromising position, had dismissed her servants and asked him to sit next to her on her pillow-strewn divan. She had engaged him in demure conversation, nibbling on her lower lip, gently drawing circles on the cushion next to his thigh, offering alluring giggles when he spoke, staring unshaken at his disfigurement. She was at least thirty years his junior, and was clearly indicating her interest in him. And then she said the words that took him over the edge.

"I have remained a virgin during my captivity," she murmured with a breathy edge to her voice. "It was difficult with all the handsome, young, virile Roman soldiers watching over me, but I managed."

He found himself utterly hard at those words.

"To keep my innocence, I learned how to pleasure myself."

That knowledge only excited him more.

He had decided she was definitely flirting with him, wanted him to be her first, perhaps to seal their agreement. He had inched closer, until their knees were almost touching, and had leaned in for a kiss, a chaste, exploratory kiss, when he felt strong hands grab each of his limbs and pull him away.

He hadn't even touched her.

He was hoisted bodily from the divan, dragged down a corridor into a dark room, his clothes torn from him, vigorously pushed into a chair, and forcefully held down. His mouth was gagged to silence his protests as he was tied – rather expertly he had to admit – to the chair, his hands behind him, his legs spread. When they reached for his balls he had struggled, then watched in fascinated horror as a metal cuff was placed around his sac. When he realized there was a hole in the seat through which his balls were to be hung, the cuff attached to weights bound down to rings embedded in the floor, he struggled some more. It was utterly futile.

He wasn't quite sure he did not like it, but being the submissive victim was a new experience for him.

A curtain was drawn and before him, wonderfully presented with theatrical lighting, was a couch upon which a young girl was lying, utterly nude, her legs splayed open. She began touching herself, quietly purring to the pleasure she felt. At first the delicate pink flesh before him was soft and velvety. Moments later, after her deliberate ministrations, she was sticky wet, ready for more and moaning loudly. The blood in his cock was pounding.

She kept going, urging herself to climax. Bestia could not take his eyes off the spectacle. He strained at his bindings, trying to free himself. When he realized it was pointless, he tried to reach for her, tried to move his chair in her direction, tried to bend forward to taste her.

That was utterly futile as well. His chair was somehow fastened to the floor. He could lean forward, but the sudden searing pain to his testicles prevented him from getting too close.

And then she stopped, at least her hand had left her dripping cunt to fondle the pert breasts of a beautiful ebony-haired, golden-skinned girl who had joined her, the licking and moaning sounds of their deep kissing tantalizing Bestia. His cock was harder and more swollen than it had ever been in his life.

Until the new girl began to finger her playmate in full view.

Bestia was panting now, his hands frantic to release themselves, to frig himself. Anything, he would do anything, to get his cock jacked.

"You foolish man," he heard the princess Roedogune admonish from the dark void behind him. "Did you think you could get what you wanted so easily?"

He squirmed, trying to turn to the sound of her voice, but he was in no position to move. He imagined her naked and touching herself.

The thought was driving him mad.

He heard the sounds of jangling chains to his right and turned his head. It was his slave boy, the half-Suebi, half-Sarmatian whose sole desire in life was to pleasure his master. He too was bound, in chains, a collar around his neck, his cock wrapped tightly in linen. He lunged for Bestia, grunting and straining, his tongue stretching to satisfy his lord's cock. He could not reach. It was frustrating for the both of them. The boy was mere inches away.

As his cock twitched in desperation, Bestia felt more fully the weights tethered to his balls. The sensation had turned from painful distraction to erotic urgency.

The ebony-haired girl had two fingers, no, three, inside her friend's cunt, pushing in and pulling out, the sounds of wet smacking against wet making Bestia frantic. She pulled out all the way and murmured honeyed praise to her friend as she poured scented oil on the exposed labia, spreading it generously around the fleshy pink folds. Bestia began salivating. He licked his lips.

And when the dark-haired girl poured the oil on her hand, covering it completely, Bestia sucked in a breath of anticipation.

Balling her oiled hand into a fist, the golden-skinned girl bent over and licked the yearning clit of her friend as she slowly inserted her hand into the well-lubricated passage. Amidst more words of praise from the dark girl, the oil-slicked fist pumped in and out of the now-pliant passage. The girl on the table howled a glorious moan in reaction to the overwhelming pleasure she was receiving.

If someone did not relieve the pressure building inside his cock, Bestia knew he would pass out from the exquisite pain. The slave boy kept stretching, straining, seemingly now closer to his master despite the sheer improbability. Bestia tried to tilt his hips, emitting a clipped bark of agony as the weights pulled down.

Behind him in the dark, Princess Roedogune laughed wickedly.

The girl on the table screamed her orgasm.

Bestia broke out in a cold sweat.

The dark-haired girl pulled her fist out and scrambled on top of her companion, kissing, licking, and stroking every inch of the satiated girl's flushed skin. Desiring her own satisfaction, she rubbed her wet clit against the belly of her friend. She reached below to a small table holding all manner of erotic supplies, and retrieved what looked like an extremely long cock. As Bestia studied it more, he realized both ends of the device had tips shaped like fully exposed glans. A two-headed dildo. He knew what to expect.

The agitated dark-haired girl frantically shoved one end of the dildo inside her, letting out a moan of relief as she did so. Her companion on the table reached around and grabbed the other end, placing it inside her spent cunt. The girl on top moved up and down with gusto as her friend underneath rubbed her engorged clit.

Instinctively, Bestia tilted his hips, once again feeling the pain below, but this time hoping the pain would release the building tension within. The slave boy seemed closer still. There was a spark of hope that the boy would actually be able to reach his master.

If only he could stretch his tongue just a little further.

The cold sweat on Bestia's body had turned to a heated flush. Perhaps he could try to not look at the girl before him bouncing up and down. No, that wouldn't work as he would still hear her moans of ecstasy, still hear the murmured words of encouragement, still smell the scent of perfumed oil and female musk, still know what was going on before him, just out of reach.

Then suddenly, miraculously, the slave's tongue was touching the tip of his cock, its wet heat shocking him to exhilarated ecstasy, while the pain of the weights pulled him back to reality. Bestia relaxed to relieve the pain in his balls, and tried to control his breathing to calm himself within. Now that the slave had somehow been able to reach him he could endure the spectacle before him torturing his senses.

The tongue on his prick, however, was not calm. In his utter excitement, the boy frantically flicked at the shaft and head randomly. If anything the effect was confusing to the senses. Bestia tried to hold on to every shred of erotic stimulation, channeling it into the well of excitement growing inside him. He was on the edge; a bead of semen trickled from the tip of his cock. With considered concentration, he knew he could control his orgasm.

Except this time; he was not in control of anything. With no warning, the slave boy was jerked backwards by forces unseen, his task left frustratingly unfinished. Bestia let out a muffled wail of discontent.

The Parthian princess chirped with glee.

As if on cue, the dark-haired girl shrieked in orgiastic delight, expelling the dildo, spraying her ejaculate onto Bestia, the sudden shock surprising him to come unwittingly in a disappointing ooze.

He heaved a sigh of defeat. His orgasm had happened without fanfare, without full release. He felt an overwhelming sense of annoyance and failure.

He heard the rhythmic clicking of delicate boots behind him. His gag was brusquely removed from his mouth. Immediately, he opened and closed his jaw several times, loosening the tense muscles. He knew better than to speak just yet.

"You will look for the *sella regia*, then, the throne of the Parthian kings." It was not a question.

"Yes, my princess," Bestia responded. "I will do whatever you say."

Egypt, Alexandria, early August 130

Hadrian buried his nose in the mass of golden curls on the pillow next to his, breathing in the masculine fragrance. He adored that Antinous fell into a deep slumber after they had made love. He found himself always still preoccupied about some matter – a provincial policy or a threat to Rome – but thought it quite endearing and refreshing that his Kynegiskos could simply fall asleep. He knew he should really follow his companion's example; fretting just made his breathing more difficult and his heart thump too rapidly. The fresh air and relaxed surroundings of Egypt should help him, he reassured himself.

After the Eleusinian initiation, they had stayed in Athens another six months, eventually moving on to Olympios for a spell. Sabina's close friend Julia Balbilla had joined them as she had always yearned to return to her grandfather's homeland of Egypt. After Greece, the party had crossed by boat to Asia, continuing along the mountainous Mediterranean coast through Pamphylia and into Cilicia. They then headed north to Cappadocia and Pontus. By June of 129, almost a year after they had left Rome, they had journeyed south to Antioch.

They stayed in and around Antioch for the next six months, during which time the most curious incident happened. Hadrian availed himself of the opportunity to climb Mount Casius to sacrifice at the famed sanctuary at its peak. Climbing, of course, was his particular diversion, but this mountain was especially important as the home of Zeus who spoke in thunderbolts. The emperor and his party – including Antinous, Zuester, a priest, and a sacrificial goat – climbed at night to be able to witness the glorious dawn from the top. As the priest conducted the offering ceremony at the altar, Zeus responded in the form of thunder and lightning. The priest and the goat were killed instantly. The others were stunned into speechlessness.

No one mentioned that Hadrian had just months before been declared a god by the Greeks. It seemed too ominous, as if Zeus had something to say, but no one was quite sure what.

Hadrian nuzzled against his lover. The honorific decreed by the citizens of Olympios, "Hadrianus Olympius," effectively made him a god. With Antinous in his arms, he mused to himself, he certainly felt like a god. His weak body though seemed far too human sometimes.

After the Antiochine visit, the imperial party had journeyed south to Arabia, then looped back north to visit Judaea. They had finally arrived in Alexandria by August of 130.

Through it all, the emperor had made generous gifts to his people, restoring roads and public buildings, dedicating shrines and temples. Once in Alexandria, he announced plans to found a Greek-style city in Egypt, Hadrianopolis, to advance the ideals and philosophy of Panhellenism. With the luxury resort of Canopus so close by, he also hoped to be able to spend some time as a private citizen, to restore his health, to invigorate his passion with his beloved Kynegiskos.

The arrival of Lucius Ceionius Commodus bode well for his plans. It had been over ten years since Hadrian had bedded Lucius, but the memories of the impetuous and fiery affair still lingered, for the both of them. For that reason, the two would always remain close. The twenty-nine-year-old Lucius was a well-liked senator and soon-to-be praetor, even though he courted the reputation as a flamboyant libertine who lived and loved to excess. Still, his political connections were impeccable, and the emperor needed his support. The moment he had arrived in Alexandria, he and

Hadrian had fallen into their former teasing rapport. Hadrian truly enjoyed being around such old friends.

But tragedy came fast on the heels of celebration. Hadrian's beloved sister, Paulina, died suddenly. It was not unexpected, as she too was in ill health like her brother, but it had been hoped that the cleansing airs of Egypt would aid her. Her grandson, Pedanius Fuscus, had accompanied her and was beside himself with grief. His grief soon turned to anger when his grand-uncle Hadrian did not immediately elevate the flawless Aelia Domitia Paulina as a goddess.

There were no honors; Hadrian was in too much anguish over the loss of a close member of his family to partake of such formal exercises. He had let that stand as the official statement. In private, however, he had confided in Sabina that he could not possibly make Paulina a goddess. Such an act would have given her husband Julius Servianus more ideas and pretense to power. It was maddening enough that the eighty-three-year-old had the audacity to consider himself Hadrian's rightful heir. Had he not simply learned his lesson when Nerva, then Trajan had denied him such a distinction?

Hadrian hugged the youthful body of Antinous more closely to him. He wished he too could simply fall asleep and dream and not be bothered by the ugly affairs of state.

Pedanius Fuscus brooded in his apartment in the Alexandrine palace, tearing at his hair. The Egyptian sun did not beckon him as it had everyone else that morning. No, he was fuming, he was not of a mind to play. He could simply not believe the slight.

His late father, Gnaeus Pedanius Fuscus Salinator, had held the office of *consul ordinarius* in 118. His grandfather, Julius Ursus Servianus, still living at the incredible age of eighty-three, had been governor of Germania Superior and consul twice. His grandmother, the recently deceased Aelia Domitia Paulina, wife of Servianus and mother to Salinator, had also been the sister of the Roman emperor, Hadrian.

And yet, where were the honors for this august woman? Where was the respect accorded to and deserved by his noble family? There was nothing. No imperial funeral, no elevation to Diva, no speeches, no games. Paulina had accompanied the emperor on his eastern journey because brother and sister had wanted to spend some time together. With such familial connection as this, one would think the emperor would have expressed his sorrow with, well, with *something*.

Instead, the emperor preferred to dally with his boy-lover, the foreigner Antinous. Not only that, the foppish aristocrat Lucius Ceionius Commodus had joined their party. Rumor had it that he had once enjoyed the sexual favors of the emperor as well. Lucius's libertine manner in the presence of the imperial party embarrassingly flaunted that lurid past. That he was a well-respected senator and skilled politician stood in utter contrast to the frippery of his powdered and painted scantily-clad entourage. It was unclear why he had even bothered to come at all.

Hadrian had deified the empress Plotina. Of course rumor had it that it was she who had arranged the marriage between Hadrian and Trajan's grand-niece securing his place in the empire, and that it was she who had forced Trajan to name Hadrian as successor. Hadrian had even deified his mother-in-law and had held games in her honor. Well, rumor had it that he fucked her anyway, so why not?

But the emperor did nothing for his very own flesh and blood. Fuscus knew his mother had been an honorable woman, unblemished by scandal, immaculate in her relationships, a woman who thought of nothing but family as was the sole concern of a proper Roman woman. She deserved the title Diva. At least she should have had a funeral.

Fuscus's only solace was that it was he alone who was heir to the emperor. The empress had remained barren. There had been no adoption, not even an obvious political grooming. Servianus was certainly far too old to be considered heir to the throne. Fuscus was the only proper choice. And when he was emperor, he would deify his mother and damn the memory of his uncle.

He rose from his pillow-strewn divan. It was time to seek an astrologer to find out when precisely he might expect his deserved fate to befall him. And Egypt had the best astrologers in the world.

The moment they arrived in the delta of the Nile river, the imperial party had been bombarded with petitions from the Egyptian people. The Nile had not flooded for two years. There were food shortages and the people were anxious that supplies would not last another year. Surely their god-emperor Hadrianus Olympius could do something about this?

In their anxiety, the people had recounted an ancient custom, practiced since the days of the pharaohs, to re-awaken the Nile gods and encourage the fertile flooding. The drowning of a youth, one pure of heart, could appease the river gods.

Hadrian was shocked to hear this. Human sacrifice of an innocent? He would not condone such an act in modern Rome. He sought out the Egyptian priests at the temple of Nilus, questioning them about their beliefs and rites in this matter. He would rely on their counsel.

With a certain uneasiness, the emperor discovered the array of sacrificial victims in the past. A pharaoh, a pharaoh's daughter, the sons of "pure" parents, all had been killed to appease the Nile gods.

"How were they chosen?"

"The priesthood can make such an appraisal of the appropriateness of an offering."

Incredulous, Hadrian had stated that this was unacceptable.

"And if one youth wishes to be the sacrifice, Caesar?"

He hadn't thought of that possibility. Still, "I cannot allow such a thing."

The priests remained calm and patient. "We have known of times when animals were used, sire."

"That I will allow."

The priests had acquiesced to this.

One priest, however, offered another solution. "There are stories that suggest some of the victims were accidental."

Hadrian eyed him with suspicion. "By which you mean…?"

"They fell into the Nile by accident. The river gods do not seem to mind if the victims are intentional or not."

Hadrian could not imagine hoping for such an event, nor that such an occurrence would truly be accidental. "I shall consult the astrologers. Perhaps the stars can elucidate the future."

As he left the priests, Hadrian had fretted. While he loved the mystery and the rich history of the Egyptian cults, he did not want to cross a line beyond what was acceptable in Rome. Death as punishment was sanctioned; death to appease the gods was no longer practiced. He would learn as much of the ancient religion as he could and hope to infuse it with his own power. Perhaps the Nile gods could be persuaded by gifts of love.

Marmarica, Libya, early September 130

One petition received in Alexandria had been a rather curious one. In fact it was really not a petition at all, rather more of a challenge, a dare to the god-emperor, and one which Hadrian was delighted to accept, a feat he knew he could accomplish, thus solidifying his status in the eyes of his Egyptian subjects.

The fearsome Mauritanian Lion had long ranged over neighboring Libya and terrorized the inhabitants, killing not just a few who dared get, or unwittingly found themselves, in its path. The Libyans knew their emperor was a hunter, they had also heard of the prowess in the chase of his intimate friend Antinous. The entreaty was to the both of them. Hadrian kept the hunting party small, with only the most skilled of his associates present.

Antinous's horse, much like the young man himself, was swift, nimble, and lean. The youth's job was to ride around and confuse their prey as if he were a dozen men on horseback. With such a strategy, the wary lion did not know from where to expect an attack. After the trick and taking cover by obscuring brush, Antinous sat in wait for the deadly animal, his breathing matching that of his steed. He held in his left hand the bridle-rein and in his right was poised an adamant-tipped spear.

But the kill was Hadrian's to make; Antinous knew this. When he saw his lover from the corner of his left eye, he hoped the lion could not sense the blood pumping faster in his body, heating his flesh and quickening his breath. Hadrian, erect on his horse, wielding a bronze-fitted spear, was a dashing sight indeed.

Then Hadrian loosed his spear, hurling it at the deadly beast, but only wounding it on the thigh. Incensed, the lion roared in anger, and spun around in the direction of the emperor.

It was not like Hadrian to miss. Antinous took a split second to glance at his master, enough to see Hadrian offer a slight nod and a raised brow, an invitation to the youth to finish the quest with his sure aim.

Antinous had no time to act. The beast had felt his presence and, no longer seeking to attack Hadrian, had veered to the right and was upon him instead. Sharp claws frantically ravaged the ground, sending up clouds of dust, obscuring the young hunter's line of vision. Only when the lion's open foaming mouth was before him, did the youth catch a glimpse of the animal. Now with Antinous in his sight, the lion gnashed its teeth, spraying spittle, its mane bristling from the anger and rage within.

Trying to entice the agitated beast away from his lover, Hadrian lurched forward, readying his bow and arrow. But the lion was unstoppable. It lunged at the youth, its jaw meeting the neck of Antinous's horse, toppling the little hunter to the ground with just enough time to thrust his spear into the lion's shoulder.

Hadrian unleashed an arrow, then another, this time meeting his mark with deadly aim. The first arrow penetrated the neck, and as the animal reared, the second sunk into its heart. The lion crashed to the ground.

Having recovered quickly from his fall, Antinous let loose one of his arrows, hitting the beast in the eye, the tip pushing deep into the brain. The lion lay on the ground, struggling to get to its feet, to regain control, to fight back. It was Antinous's horse, however, that felled the next blow. Enraged by the scent of its own blood gushing from its neck it trampled the lion, crushing it into the dirt.

The imperial party held still for a moment. Hadrian approached the beast first, gripping his sword in his hand in case the animal yet lived. He prodded it guardedly with the sharp bronze tip. The animal did not move.

The emperor beckoned for his beloved to join him, and placed his arm around his shoulder when the youth came to his side. They stood together, their feet on the lion's neck, panting, regaining their composure as the rush of adrenalin dissipated. The circle of blood oozing from the dead animal's wounds widened, covering the ground at their feet, its edges spreading in a lobed pattern, like a deep red flower to mark the grave of the conquered beast.

"I should never have put you in such grave danger. It was foolish of me," murmured Hadrian to his Kynegiskos. "It will never happen again. I am your protector, your guardian, and I love you beyond belief. I simply do not know what I would do without you."

Egypt, Canopus, late September 130

The pleasure resort of Canopus was alive with luxurious delights during the day, but notorious for its decadent revelry all through the night. The canals were lined with boats filled with party-goers, chiefly beautiful young men and women, but all who wished to partake of the opulent pleasures were welcome. Music and dancing, eating and drinking, flirting and love-making, all were done to excess.

Moored along secluded quays, the imperial party was treated to private entertainments and dinners. The emperor, in Egypt for his health, needed proper rest and relaxation, and could not endure the din of festivities throughout the night. To ensure this, the area was heavily guarded after dark.

That did not stop Sabina from venturing out to visit her husband's barge one night. Zuester had fallen asleep hours before, but the empress was restless with curiosity. The open licentiousness amongst some of the young men earlier that day had incited her, one youth with golden hair and sleek muscles engaged in the erotic play had inspired her. She had seen her husband with page boys before; watching his masterful command over them was always arousing. But she had never seen him with his beloved Antinous. She needed to see her husband with his own companion of incomparable beauty.

She wore a common black cloak, something any older servant might don as she threaded her way unnoticed along the quays in the cool night air. Guarding the emperor's boat were two of the forever faithful slaves, one of the Germans and one of the Africans. A matched pair guarded her own barge. As she approached, they instantly knew who she was. She expected they would; they knew her intimately.

When he saw her face, the German looked at her questioningly and sympathetically. She nodded her hello to him. "I know," she whispered.

She knew that her husband had abandoned her bed to be with the youth. He was happier than he had ever been, and because his happiness meant a great deal to her, she did not mind. She missed him, though, and needed some connection – any connection with him.

She entered the curtained annex with the German at her heels, a waiting guardsman taking his place at the door. It was pitch black inside. A kithara player was stationed in the dark annex to provide musical accompaniment for the emperor and his lover, yet afford them their privacy.

A sliver in the curtain to the main cabin of the barge beckoned. She peered in, able to see quite clearly from the illumination of a dozen oil lamps the richly furnished room with furs and rugs scattered on the floor, embroidered and jewel-encrusted hangings, and silk pillows bolstering divans. She smiled when she saw Hadrian and Antinous.

They were talking, as any couple enamored of one another might. Hadrian gesticulated wildly while Antinous was doubled over laughing, tears streaming down his face. The story ended, their mutual mirth turned to comfortable joy, which eventually itself turned into romantic cuddling.

Then Hadrian leaned back against a stack of pillows and pulled Antinous against him, deeply kissing his succulent mouth, gently caressing his muscular back. In his youthful enthusiasm, Antinous was not as casual. He crawled on his master, tugged on his tunic and beard, nibbled his neck and shoulders. He was playful and very determined. Minutes later he had Hadrian's cock in his mouth. The emperor let his head fall back against the pillows. Sabina drew in a sharp breath. She knew she was wet.

The German sensed her arousal. He knelt down at her side, lifted the hem of her stola, and tucked it up under her girdle. With a delicate massage of her thighs, he urged her to spread her legs just enough for him to draw his fingers through her sticky slit and briefly torment her engorged nub. He pressed his face against her hairless mons and flicked his tongue through her fleshy folds, licking slowly. She had to hold her hand to her mouth when her sucked on her clit. She rocked her hips against the German's mouth, mirroring Hadrian's movements against his own lover in the next room.

She did not hear the African come in, but felt his strong hands and knowing touch as he removed her cloak and kissed her neck. He untied and ungirded her stola and lifted the filmy fabric over her head, baring her to the desires of her slave lovers. The German still feasted on her, thrashing exuberantly, noiselessly. The African cupped her breasts and pinched her nipples. She leaned against him in invitation, but he moved his hands away. Her disappointment did not last long. She felt him pour warmed oil at the base of her spine, letting it run between her butt cheeks, then stopping it at her anus. He massaged the tight hole, lubricating it inside and out.

Antinous had stripped off his tunic, his fantastic form still bent over her husband's crotch. Hadrian gently encouraged him up, smoothing his hands across sleek shoulders. Enraptured, the youth sat on his heels and watched as Hadrian removed his own clothes to reveal his brawny physique. Chattering inaudibly and grinning in anticipation, Antinous eagerly danced his fingers across the masculine chest sprinkled with gray before him. Sabina, however, could not take her eyes off of Antinous; his body was breathtaking to behold. His muscles were sensuously sculpted, his skin unblemished and smooth, hairless like a woman's. His generous erection bobbed wantonly before her husband. Sabina undulated her hips against the dual assault of the African's fingers and the German's tongue. She imagined the youth penetrating her. The African placed a hand on her mouth stifling a needful moan.

Hadrian grabbed an oil jar and poured some of the liquid on his own magnificent cock, rubbing it seductively up and down, all the while watching his lover gape at his deliberate movements. Impatient for the pleasures that awaited him, Antinous leaned back, spread his legs, and tilted his pelvis. Hadrian poured more oil in his palm and spread it generously, his hand disappearing under the hips of the youth. Sabina could see the enraptured expression on Antinous's face at the emperor's invasion.

Hadrian leaned in and kissed his lover deeply as he moved to lie between his legs. He broke away from the kiss, murmured encouraging words, then held the youth's eyes with his own as he languidly entered Antinous.

Sabina felt the African's cock nudge her slick anus then push in slowly, all the while keeping his hand over her mouth to muffle her moans. She knew Antinous's lost, dissolute expression mirrored her own, each of them penetrated in the most intimate way. Hadrian proceeded with soft strokes; the African matched the even rhythm of his imperial master. Sabina watched the spectacle before her, feeling everything Antinous felt, but knowing his relationship with her husband was vastly different. With Antinous, Hadrian was soft and gentle, a man clearly in love. He wasn't aggressive or dominating. His position on top was encouraging, not demanding. As she watched Antinous descend into lascivious pleasure, Sabina realized she did not feel a whit of jealousy toward the youth. She had her Hadrian and Antinous had his. She very much preferred the side of her husband she saw, commanding her actions, controlling her pleasure.

The German licked her frantically now, willing her toward orgasm. Antinous pumped his cock in youthful frenzy, delving deeper into the abyss before his crisis. She could see the tell-tale signs in Hadrian's body hurtling him toward his own culmination. As if on cue, the African jerked against her, emptying himself at the very moment Hadrian thrust vigorously into Antinous, holding himself in place as he spent his seed, laughing with delight as his lover came on his taut stomach. Shaking the sweaty, damp hair out of his eyes, Hadrian turned his head toward the curtains at the entryway of the boat. As she peaked in climax, Sabina met his penetrating gaze. As if knowing she were there, he smiled, his gray eyes twinkled. The African had to stifle her longing moan.

Hadrian awoke to the kiss of sunlight across his face, feeling his legs tangled in Antinous's. His lover lay across his body in a deep sleep, unaware that he was in the most unnatural and surely most uncomfortable position. *Ah, the pliability of youth,* Hadrian smiled to himself. His old body would have protested had he slept in such a manner. One day his Kynegiskos would discover this, when he himself grew old.

Old.

Hadrian gently stroked the soft downy hair beginning to sprout on his lover's chest, the physical sign that Antinous was growing up, getting older, becoming a man. An adult male. *Damn the gods!* They simply could not keep this up. A pang of deprivation shot through him.

The Greek custom of mentoring a boy meant the older man would release his disciple when the boy came of age. Now a man, the former novice would take his own boy to advise and train. Men remained friends, associates, allies, but never lovers. It was considered unseemly for two adult men to carry on in such a manner.

But that was the Greek way. Perhaps Roman Panhellenism could institute a new tradition? Why did their relationship have to come to an end? Morosely, Hadrian drew his hand down Antinous's tanned flesh across the rippling abdominals, then spread his fingers at his groin. The youth's magnificent morning erection quivered, tempting Hadrian to renewed activity. He slid his palm along the smooth rosy shaft.

For the moment they could enjoy themselves like young lovers. *Young.* With Antinous, Hadrian found a vigor he had not known for years. Not only his Kynegiskos's admiration and friendship, but their shared experience in the Eleusinian Mysteries had done that. Their mystical bonding had increased his own potency.

Hadrian sighed.

Antinous stirred.

"Why so glum?" asked Antinous. The hand lovingly stroking his cock was a bit incongruous to the dour expression on his master's face.

"I'm just thinking about us."

Antinous righted himself from his twisted position, scrambling to his knees. "And this makes you depressed?" he reproached.

Hadrian pulled the glorious youth back down to his side. "No, of course not. I've just been thinking. Convention demands our relationship come to an end. You know that. We both know that."

Antinous pulled away sharply and got up. He paced a moment with a dejected air before relieving himself in the chamber pot. "I love you, Graeculus!" he professed, his back still turned to the emperor. "Nothing will ever change that," he said with youthful defiance, marching back to the bed.

"Antinous, Antinous," the emperor soothed, patting the mattress next to him. "You're getting older. You're almost a man. You'll want to take your own boy lover soon," Hadrian teased trying to lighten the mood.

"No! Never!" Antinous's exclamation was tinged with sorrow. He plopped on the bed in a huff.

"Sweet, I don't want you exposed to gossip about what might be seen as an unseemly relationship. It is not done, two adult men together."

"We can go against tradition," suggested Antinous quietly, burrowing under Hadrian's arm. "Start a new one."

"I wish it were so," responded the emperor glumly. "If we remain intimate, you will become subject to palace plots and intrigues. I don't want that. We may be able to continue in private," he conceded. "But, I'll have to take another youthful favorite to deflect suspicion. You, as well."

"What about Nero's lover? Didn't they marry as man and wife?"

"Nero castrated his Sporus."

"Oh." Disappointed, Antinous nuzzled against the older man's powerful chest and kissed him tenderly.

Hadrian pulled the youth closer to him. "I do see what you are saying. It is something I wish more than anything, but I fear that it will not sit well with the Senate. They already dislike me, they don't need more fodder for their vitriol." He smoothed the boy's silky curls. "They might fear you are in line to the succession."

"I don't want to be emperor, Graeculus."

"No, indeed you do not," Hadrian agreed emphatically, getting up to piss in the pot. As he relieved himself, a slight pain made him realize his health, despite the Egyptian climate, was not improving. In some ways Antinous made him feel invincible, but buried deep inside he knew better. Despite the trappings of godhead, Hadrian knew he was purely mortal. He felt it more so every day. He stared down at the pot filled with the evidence of his mortality.

So why in Hades should a dying man have to give up his life-sustaining joy? Merely because of tradition and convention?

Fucking Hell. He was the bloody emperor of Rome, the maker of new laws, the creator of new customs, the harbinger of new traditions.

No, he would not give up the boy or the man. Instead he would present his people with a new imperial paradigm. He would take his Kynegiskos as his consort, a dual role the youth would share with the empress Sabina. There would be an official announcement that Antinous the Greek was not in line for the succession, but his union with the emperor would signal the triumph of the new Roman Panhellenism. The founding of the Greek polis of Hadrianopolis in Upper Egypt would be the perfect time and place for the proclamation. The imperial party would return to Rome triumphant, the emperor and his two consorts. Antinous would be his forever.

Egypt, Heliopolis on the Nile, early October 130

The emperor felt energized. His new scheme for dual consorts solved his problems. Announcing it in Egypt would give the idea legitimacy; surely there was precedence in the ancient Egyptian religion? Why, their kings married their own sisters! He had confided his plan to Zuester. His secretary had, at first, been stunned, had argued a few points about impropriety, then seemed to warm to the idea. Zuester was particularly protective of Sabina, but once assured that her place would not be debased, he said he would support the plan. Everyone loved Antinous, he was good and kind and brought a new vitality to the imperial household.

Hadrian wanted to start the tour of the Nile as quickly as possible, the quicker to arrive at the planned spot for Hadrianopolis and make his announcement. The party departed Canopus at the end of September. By early October they disembarked at Heliopolis, just beyond the delta region, the famed center of worship of the sun god Re. Hadrian had been invited to meet with the priests there who practiced astrology, discussed philosophy, and, rumor had it, wielded divine magic. The temple to Re had an accompanying sacerdotal school at which it was known Plato had once studied.

It had been two years since their initiation into the Eleusinian cult and all the imperial party still talked about the profound experience. For Hadrian and Antinous the memory inspired them to seek out the mysteries of the ancient Egyptian religion. Publicly, Hadrian wanted to discover what the priests of the sun god had to say about the barren Nile. Privately, though, he and Antinous hoped the priests could give him insight into his health.

Antinous and Zuester accompanied their emperor in his visit to the renowned prophet of Heliopolis, Pachrates, who was to initiate Hadrian. Hadrian had been told to fast for the occasion, so the others did as well. They met the bald holy man at the massive temple complex, filled with acolytes and priests garbed in crisp white linen. Pachrates greeted them in heavily-accented Greek, and led them through the incense-filled halls to his private sanctuary.

The walls of sandstone blocks were covered in painted pictures depicting the story of Heliopolis and its association with Re. According to the mythology depicted, the city was the birthplace of all creation.

"If all was created here, may one experience renewal here as well?" Hadrian asked.

The priest seemed to understand the earnestness in his initiate's voice. He eyed the emperor up and down.

"It is you who wishes this renewal? You are ill," he said categorically.

Hadrian was surprised at first. But of course most knew he was there for his health. "Yes."

"But there is something else. A renewal of empire. You wish to somehow change Rome."

Hadrian felt a jolt of shock course through him, a slight sweat break on his brow. He glanced at Antinous then at Zuester. The secretary was staring in utter amazement.

"An emperor always wishes to advance his empire," Hadrian deflected.

"Ah, yes, of course." Pachrates smiled knowingly. "Now, you wish to experience our rites, but first you must believe. The initiate must experience fully the magical powers granted by Re to his devoted servant," said Pachrates referring to himself in the third person.

Pachrates explained that the magician-priest had four powers: he could attract and trap that which was uncontrollable, he could inflict sickness without death, he could inflict sickness with death, and he could send dreams. To accomplish these tasks he invoked powers from the condu, a magical globe.

"And how shall we know when these things have been shown to us?"

"They will appear only to you, my emperor. You will be sure of them."

Pachrates went to a cabinet and took out the globe, a ball of engraved, gilded silver on a stem base. He twisted off the top and the globe became a cup. He took a glass bottle from the cabinet and poured some of the contents into the condu. He bent over the cup and said an incantation, then turned around and offered the condu to Hadrian.

"Drink."

Both Zuester and Antinous stepped forward in the emperor's defense.

Pachrates's lips twisted into a grin. "We may all drink of the cup. I will go first."

He sipped and drank then held the cup out to whoever would take it first.

Zuester took the cup next, then Hadrian, and lastly Antinous.

"Ah, very well, then," said the priest when the cup had been passed around. "Now it is time for you to visit with the scribes at the library. They will show you our holy scrolls. I will see you tomorrow. You will believe."

"Did you hear about what happened on the river banks today?" asked Sabina as the imperial party dined that evening.

"Yes!" exclaimed Mindia. "Wasn't it amazing?"

Hadrian briefly glanced up at the two sisters. "What happened?" he asked.

"Well it was earlier today," began Sabina, "late morning perhaps, while you were still at your temple. A crocodile had breached the banks of the river near a market and tried to snatch an infant from its mother's grasp. A priest charmed it away from the child and back into the water."

Hadrian looked over at Zuester and Antinous. "Did you witness this, Vibia?"

"Yes, Balbilla, Mindia, and I were shopping. We saw it with our own eyes." Sabina turned to her grand-nephew. "I cannot recall if you were there, Fuscus. Did you see it too?"

"No," the sullen boy said curtly, not bothering to look up.

Sabina rolled her eyes knowing full well Fuscus was bored with anything and everything. "Well," she continued, "he was a little bald man dressed like a priest in white linen. I think I heard his name was Pancrates."

"Pachrates," corrected Hadrian.

"So you know him?" inquired his wife.

"I do. He is the one initiating me into the cult of Re."

"But that's not even the half of it," said Balbilla. "When the mother and child were safe, the priest then called the animal back onto the land and spoke to it. Well, really more like he berated it in Egyptian. All the market was watching. He waved his hands in the air and the animal began to thrash back and forth, then he lifted his hands and the crocodile flipped over oozing a green bile from its mouth."

"Then," interjected Mindia, "the creature rolled back onto its stomach and returned to the water so slowly it looked like it was drunk."

"It was quite amazing," said Balbilla. "Everyone was awestruck."

Fuscus grunted with disdain.

"I heard the poor animal died later," commented Sabina.

"This Pachrates is a magician with such powers," said Hadrian, still trying to convince himself.

Later that night in his bed, with an arm around a sleeping Antinous, Hadrian went over the story again and again, telling himself that it was a trick any magician could do with a trained animal.

"Yes, I suppose that's right," came the priest's voice.

Hadrian sat bolt upright in bed.

Pachrates laughed.

The priest stood in the middle of the bedroom on the emperor's boat, dressed in his heavy linen caftan, an eerie light emitting from the bright white robe.

"You should name your successor when you make your announcement about the youth." Pachrates pointed to Antinous, still fast asleep as if nothing were happening.

"Sound advice, but it is information I already know. If I am to believe you are in my dream, you must tell me something I do not know," Hadrian challenged.

"That is fair, my emperor." Pachrates lifted the hem of his garment above his knee, then turned his leg out to display his inner thigh. A long, arc-shaped scar marred the pale flesh. "It was achieved when I tried to fight a crocodile the first time."

Hadrian stared at the wound. Antinous stirred beside him.

"Graeculus?" he said with a yawn.

Hadrian turned to his love. "Shh, shh, Kynegiskos." He turned back to face the priest.

But the room was empty.

* * * * *

Hadrian paced before the priests sitting on the dais above him in the scriptorium as Antinous and Zuester watched apprehensively. Pachrates had met with the emperor alone earlier, had reluctantly, at first, shown him the scar on his inner right thigh, then realized what had transpired the night before.

"It takes a while for me to have memory of the visions when they are granted to the intended dreamer. I do recall now. You have a very luxurious barge."

Pachrates insisted Hadrian direct any further questions concerning his initiation to a panel of priests. They met seven priests gathered in the scriptorium where the scrolls could easily be referred to.

"Since I have arrived in Egypt I have heard that the Nile has not flooded for two years." Hadrian turned to Pachrates. "Can you not use your magical powers to attract the uncontrollable flood waters?"

"The flood waters are not uncontrollable. Man has built dams to bind them in," was the answer.

"It is our god, Osiris, who prevents the Nile from flooding," said Sanabares, a dark-haired priest. His accent was Parthian.

"Who is Osiris and why would he do such a thing?"

"He is our god of the afterlife, of the underworld, of the dead," explained Menches, a native of Egypt. "From time to time, it benefits him to have death amongst the living."

"Like our Hades?"

"Very much so like your Hades. But he is also like your earth goddess."

"Demeter?" Hadrian said using the goddess's Greek name.

"Yes, yes. Like your Demeter," agreed Theogenes, a priest of Greek extraction.

"But she gives us life," countered the emperor.

"Osiris has a dual role," explained the lean and ghostly Phmersis. "He controls the underworld and so is the god of death. But death can only come from life. He is also our god of the life that sustains us, the god of fertility, the god of the inundation that produces the fertile soil, and the god of the vegetation that sprouts forth. It is a cycle that repeats every year. The earth dies then is reborn after the floods."

Hadrian thought this over. "Why does your god prevent the fertile flooding?"

"Some say perhaps it is because he needs more souls," answered the Parthian.

"Yes," agreed Pachrates. "It is true that some believe a pure soul must be delivered to the god of the dead."

"He awaits satisfaction," chimed in Psenithes, a jovial, round priest. "The hope of new life will come after death."

Hadrian paced, still unsatisfied with the explanations offered.

"Perhaps if we explained the story of Osiris this would help," suggested Pachrates.

The emperor nodded.

"Osiris, a son of the god Re," began the magician, "was a great king who traveled the land to teach his people how to farm. His people loved and respected him and listened to all he taught. However, Osiris had an enemy in his jealous brother, Set, who, one night, lured him into a coffin, sealed it with lead, and threw it into the Nile. Isis, the beautiful and faithful sister-wife of Osiris, mourned and walked the earth searching for the coffin of her beloved, knowing without a proper burial he would not rest in the land of the dead. She finally discovered the coffin in the open sea and returned it to Egypt.

"Set, still jealous and bitter, found the body of his brother and tore it into fourteen pieces, scattering these across Egypt. Isis, ever the obedient and loving wife, retrieved the pieces, molding them into the body of her husband once again, then breathed life back into him. Husband and wife, sister and brother, the resurrected and the living lay together one last time before Osiris journeyed to the underworld to rule the land of the dead."

"So you see," counseled Sosos, a young priest, "Osiris is our god of fertility, of life, but also our god of the dead."

"And our god of rebirth," added Didymion, the most handsome of the priests. "All along the Nile we commemorate his death and celebrate his rebirth every year in October."

"Then I will be there to celebrate with the Egyptian people," said Hadrian. "To show my support for their festivals and to pray for the inundation."

Pachrates and the seven priests murmured their approval.

But Hadrian continued to pace.

Pachrates eyed the emperor. "There is something else you would like us to answer. You wish another renewal, yes? Your own health is faltering. There are not many years left in you."

"I thought you only made people ill," challenged Hadrian.

"Pachrates does have that power, yes," said Menches. "But we all have our skills."

Antinous jumped at that. "How may we restore the health of the emperor?" he asked exuberantly. "Perhaps we can appeal to Osiris to renew his body like he renews the earth?"

Pachrates looked at the beautiful youth, knowing it was he who had shared the emperor's bed the previous night. "Yes, there is a way. The life force of one who is stronger and more youthful can be used to lengthen the life of the emperor."

Hadrian turned to Pachrates, horrified. "Sacrifice? I have already told your brethren in Alexandria that the Romans will not stand for such barbaric practices. They had wanted to throw a youth into the Nile to appease your Osiris."

Psenithes laughed. "That is a practice as old as the Pharaohs, my emperor. If it seems to work, then who can blame the people for demanding such an offering?"

"I did not say sacrifice," pronounced Pachrates emphatically. "The youth has not just his life to give. What he can provide is far more sustaining in the way of life-giving force." Pachrates scanned the youth up and down, stopping at his crotch, then raised an eyebrow at Hadrian.

Flustered for just a moment, Hadrian glared at the priest.

Antinous blushed at the suggestion. "I would do anything for my emperor," he said quietly.

"It is known that when the old share life with the young there is a transference of energy," said Phmersis.

"Youth renews the spirit of the aged," agreed Didymion. "Simply by a constant connection. You will do right by having youthful energy with you at all times."

Hadrian considered this for a moment, then looked at Antinous. It pained him to think his beloved might believe he was being used merely to extend the life of the emperor. Hadrian was absolutely in love with his Kynegiskos; he was already the life force that pumped through his heart.

"I have no intention of ever being without a youthful companion," he said.

Sanabares sat back and watched the proceedings before him. Clearly from what was being said, the emperor Hadrian was ill and had not long to live. Perhaps, the Parthian mused, the man could simply be killed with a potion masqueraded as a medicine.

No, he knew that would not work. Based on what Pachrates had said happened the day before, too many protected what the emperor ate and drank. Including the handsome youth who was clearly enamored of his ruler, enough so he seemed willing to die for him.

But what if this Hadrian were so very weak that any stress could take him to the brink of death hastening the inevitable end? He did seem a physically fit man on the outside, so it must be something wrong on the inside.

Perhaps it was his heart. Perhaps that organ was weak.

And if the youth Antinous was as much a part of the man's heart as appearances were wont to testify, perhaps a danger to the youth could be a danger to the emperor's heart.

Sanabares smiled to himself. His mistress, the princess Roedogune, would be very pleased with the scheme.

* * * * *

Antinous sighed as he nuzzled against his love. From the deck of the barge the two watched the sun set across the river. Brilliant colors slashed the sky and danced on the water as the night goddess Nyx chased away Helios and Hemera of the day.

Hadrian gazed down at his beloved nestled in the crook of his arm. "The gold of the sun is like your shining locks, the red of the sky like your plump lustful lips."

"And the gray that descends upon them both is like your penetrating eyes," Antinous giggled. "And hair."

"Hmmph," growled Hadrian affectionately before taking his lover in a deep kiss.

Antinous reached up and stroked the bristly beard of his master and opened further for his invasion. Their passionate kisses always roused and comforted him.

"Shall we go inside?" murmured Hadrian against his mouth. "It is more private in there."

Antinous bit his lower lip in sensual expectation and took his lover's hand.

With a flick of his wrist, Hadrian dismissed the servants readying the barge for the evening's activities. The couple certainly did not need a crowd to tend to them. The emperor guided his Kynegiskos directly to the bed.

But Antinous stopped before the mattress and hesitated a moment before taking off his clothes.

"Does my love not excite you at this moment?" Hadrian inquired with concern. "Are you hungry? Thirsty?"

"No," Antinous answered softly. He gazed at his lover with sorrowful eyes. He hadn't thought it would be so difficult to express his thoughts.

"Kynegiskos," Hadrian said taking his hands in his own. "Something has upset you. What is it?"

"You know what the priest meant, Graeculus," Antinous said haltingly, "when he said I could sustain you with my life-giving force."

Hadrian stepped back. "Yes."

"I know the act would be shameful for you. To take me in your mouth as I take you. It is not customary for the master to engage the youth in such a fashion. Nor for the emperor to be on his knees before his loyal and loving subject."

The emperor drew in a sharp breath to calm himself, his twisted expression reflecting the anguish in his heart. It was no good; the tears pooled in his eyes.

"My love," he said falling to the ground before Antinous, his body shaking with sobs.

Every nerve in Antinous's body clenched. "My Graeculus, my emperor, we don't have to do this." He threaded trembling fingers through the gray-speckled hair.

"No, please, Kynegiskos, my love, I want this," Hadrian choked on his words. "Please."

His eyes smarting with emotion, Antinous tugged on Hadrian's arms wrapped around his knees. The emperor stood and faced his love. He let out an exhale, not of surrender, but of strength.

They went to the bed. Antinous, according to Hadrian's direction, sat against the headboard. The emperor spread the youth's legs and knelt between, then bowed his head.

It had been a long time since another had given him oral gratification. When Hadrian took his hard cock in his mouth, Antinous was jolted into wondrous rapture. He cried out, gripping the pillows, transported to an ethereal reality.

"Oh gods of Olympus," he moaned, his head swarming with forgotten pleasures.

It just got better. The tongue, the heat, the wetness were without end, frantically licking, sucking, as if demanding gratification, and demanding it now. Hadrian knew what another man wanted. Antinous responded with a thrust of his hips, offering his body to his lover. The pressure on his cock increased, insisting he expel his seed, the emperor needing to taste his nourishment.

And so he came, reluctantly, wishing the pleasure could have lasted a little longer.

Hadrian lifted his head, still swallowing the salty, sour liquid. He grunted, and rolled onto his back.

Antinous looked down at his lover. "That was magnificent, Graeculus."

Hadrian laughed. "Yes it was, my Kynegiskos, yes it was." He inhaled heartily. "Your response was quite exhilarating, as I hope your seed was. I would do that to you every day if it meant I would increase my life by an hour." He looked up at the youth. "Or even a minute."

Antinous laughed.

Hadrian got up, clearly energized by their new arrangement. He beamed at his lover mischievously, a hungry look in his eyes. "Darling, I want you to fuck me."

Antinous blushed crimson. "Graeculus, I...I've never..." he faltered, his breath unsteady. It was a difficult and embarrassing admission.

"Gods of my father, you're a virgin."

Antinous could only nod.

Hadrian rolled onto his back. "I hadn't thought...I mean...of course..." He trailed off.

Antinous stared off into the space before him. "So, shall I?"

"Yes," was the immediate answer.

Hadrian grabbed an oil lamp from the bedside table, blew out the flame, and handed it to Antinous.

"The oil will still be hot, so you will want it to cool just a bit." He smiled at the gawking youth. "You'll know when it is ready when you pour it into your palm."

Antinous took the proffered lamp and watched as Hadrian settled himself on all fours. He knew exactly what his master did in preparation for his own sensual abasement, but it felt strange to go through the motions himself.

He dribbled warmed oil at the base of Hadrian's spine and drew it down to the crinkled orifice below, then watched, fascinated, as his oil-slicked finger penetrated the reluctant hole. The tightness at first allowed then disallowed the invasion.

"Now two," came the command.

Antinous gasped in amazement as he watched two fingers disappear through the puckered opening, and smiled as he pulled them out. Would it be this easy?

Hadrian chuckled. "The first time is always the most instructive. For both parties."

"Have you never… ?" Antinous stopped in shock.

"Of course. But it has been a very long time. Well, with a man."

Antinous knew he referred to their initiation at Eleusis. Hadrian had talked about his penetration with the dildo as a most rousing experience, and only hoped he could match the heights of eroticism achieved on that night.

"I think I'm ready for you."

Antinous slicked his cock in nervous preparation, then placed it at his master's orifice. He pushed in just a little.

Hadrian groaned. It was a needful, desirous groan. "Oh, yes," he encouraged.

Antinous pressed on. It was more difficult than he had thought, and tighter than he had expected. And far more pleasurable.

"More," was the plea.

He pushed in, further than the tight opening suggested was possible.

"Jupiter's balls! You're huge!"

And you feel tighter than a schoolmate's clenching fist. Antinous was approaching ecstasy. One more shove—

"Ooohhhh, gods above!" the youth cried. He was in all the way. It was the most amazing feeling.

"Now move in and out, slowly, add more oil as you need," Hadrian guided, his languid tone reflecting his own state of licentious abandon.

The words were like a drug to Antinous. For good measure, he poured more oil on his enraptured cock as he slipped it out. He tossed the lamp onto the bed, forgetting his master's words and slammed into the tight hole.

It was heaven.

Antinous closed his eyes and gripped the brawny hips before him. He rammed himself repeatedly inside the snug, oil-slicked hole, disregarding the anguished groans beneath him. He had never felt such absolute ecstasy in his life. Unbelievably, his crisis verged again. He tamped it down, hoping to prolong the exquisite sensations.

He could not. He felt the peak, then let loose his seed, jerking against his lover's buttocks.

Antinous exhaled long and hard and slumped over Hadrian's back.

The emperor chuckled. "It was more than you imagined, was it not?'

Antinous grinned. "Yes, yes it was." His cock was still twitching.

"Stay inside me. Let me have all you have to give."

The youth was happy to comply. He did not want to pull out just yet anyway.

And when the youth did slacken and release himself, the lovers collapsed onto the bed.

"I'll do that to you every day, whether it extends your life or not," admitted Antinous staring up at the ceiling.

Hadrian laughed a good long laugh and pulled Antinous to him. "I love you, Kynegiskos. I love you. I don't know what I would do without you."

Egypt, Oxyrhyncus on the Nile, mid-October 130

The emperor was spending more time with his architects and planners working out the details for Hadrianopolis. Antinous sometimes observed, but mostly it was tedious, so he often availed himself of Hadrian's philosophy collection and sat by the shores of the great river to read and dream.

One day, from his vantage point on the raised bank, he saw a marvelous spectacle, a parade coming his way. At the head was a golden-haired man dressed in vibrant blues and greens followed by a scurrying servant carrying a parasol to shield his master from the sun. Behind them trailed dancers and musicians, then a dozen servants each in a matching short tunic the color of the sky, their lips and eyes dramatically painted. Antinous was awestruck for a moment, until he realized the man at the front was none other than Lucius Ceionius Commodus.

Antinous always wondered how he should feel about Lucius. He was Hadrian's ex-lover, he knew that, and really felt no jealousy toward him, although perhaps there was a little bewilderment. He wondered why his Graeculus would have become involved with the aristocrat. He was a notorious libertine who slept with every one of his servants, male and female, sometimes all at once. He was up until past dawn seemingly every day carousing and feting. Plus he had scandalously left his wife and infant daughter back in Rome. His appearance was foppish and vain, his character flirtatious and loud, and his entourage extravagant and excessive. He was everything Hadrian was not. And yet the two were extremely close friends.

Lucius saw Antinous and waved. When Antinous waved back, the senator took it as an invitation and scampered up the bank to join him. The entourage followed at his heels.

"Ah, Antinous, such a pleasure to see you. A very lovely day, is it not?" Lucius saw the scroll in Antinous's hand. "What are you reading?"

"Epictetus," the youth answered.

"Hmmph. Graeculus loves that Stoic, but he is far too critical of persons of high status for my tastes. It is no wonder Domitian exiled the old man."

"You've read him then?"

Lucius beamed. "Of course!" He laughed, truly amused. "You think that because my servants match I can't know philosophy?" It was said in an engaging, teasing tone.

Antinous was too much in awe of the man before him to answer. He was physically attractive, to be sure, with piercing blue eyes and perfect blond curls falling into thick, curly sideburns tapering off in a cropped beard. He had charm, but it was not false like the paint on his servant's faces. It was quite warm, inviting, magnetic. He suddenly realized why Hadrian liked Lucius so much.

"I have been remiss in my attention to you." A smile crept across the young aristocrat's lips. "Leave me," he said abruptly to his servants, all of whom bowed and retreated, including the parasol carrier who seemed most hurt by the dismissal.

Lucius held out his hand to Antinous in an invitation to stand. The youth took it reluctantly, and flinched slightly when his former rival linked their arms together in a gesture of intimate friendship. Yet seconds later, the captivating charisma of the senator put Antinous at ease.

"He calls you 'Kynegiskos,' does he not?" Lucius asked as they began sauntering along the bank. Antinous blushed as his companion casually glanced at his pleated linen skirt then at his bare chest. After a satisfied smile, Lucius resumed his attention to the landscape.

"Yes, my lord." Antinous could smell the exotic perfume the older man wore and noticed a touch of rouge on his lips.

"Oh, stop with the formalities, my little hunter. We're brothers, you and I, bonded by our love for our emperor. Please, I insist you call me Lucius. And I shall call you Ant. I don't think your Greek sobriquet quite trips off my tongue."

"All right ... Lucius," Antinous said hesitantly.

Lucius smirked. "You're afraid of me."

Antinous turned sharply to his companion. "No!" he cried. But his flushed countenance betrayed his true feelings.

Lucius chuckled softly. "I'm not your enemy, Ant. Believe me, I do know what it is like to be in his arms, to feel his protective strength surrounding me." He sighed. "And I know what it is like to move on from such a connection when it is finished." He leaned in to his new friend. "I also know you to be extraordinarily special in Graeculus's life. He is in love with you like no other person living or dead."

Antinous stared blankly at his feet.

"Stay close to him, he needs your protection more than he thinks."

The youth looked up. "Because he is ill?"

"Yes," Lucius said haltingly. "But also because his enemies surround him, and in places you might not think, his own household even. Since Nerva, our emperors have had a tradition of adopting their heirs. This has proven to be most favorable for Rome, I think. Trajan was a good general, Graeculus talented as well. They had no blood connection. But this mean those related by blood may be angered." He eyed his companion. "You do not want to be emperor, boy, do you?"

"Zeus's Thunder, no!" Antinous exclaimed.

"That's the right answer," Lucius chuckled. "Of course you are here for his amusement and pleasure. To be truthful, I'm not quite sure what *I* am doing here. I would never turn down an opportunity to travel to such an exotic place as Egypt, and with the emperor himself, no less." He looked around at the landscape. "Such a pleasant clime for one's health," he sighed. "But I wonder if he is testing me to see if I would be a good successor. At least the gossips seem to think I am here to stake my claim to his throne."

Antinous looked away toward the river, uncomfortable at the revelation.

"Ah, I see you do not want to be included in politics. But if you are to be among his intimate *amici*, you will find that this is necessary. Even the empress Sabina must watch her back. But don't worry, you will not have to establish your own nexus. I will relay all that I know of his rivals and enemies. One learns quite a bit at societies' diversions."

Antinous smiled back. "Thank you, Lucius." He crooked his head at his new ally. "Does Graeculus know you are doing this?"

"No! And you are never to tell him," Lucius warned. "This is a secret between you and me." Once again, he stopped and stared out at the view, then chortled to himself before affectionately tousling the youth's curls.

Antinous beamed. The delightful gesture was like an older brother playing with his younger sibling. He decided at that moment that he liked Lucius very much; he had never had a brother.

Lucius continued. "As his good friends it is up to us to protect him. I only wish I could somehow bolster his health until this successor business is secured. Like give him the remaining years of my own dissolute, useless life." Lucius chuckled darkly. He looked at Antinous and smiled. "And I wish the two of you a long and happy life together. I would like to think he will not give you up because you start to grow whiskers." He chucked the younger man's chin.

"I would like to think so as well. I can't imagine living without him," Antinous choked on his words a little.

Lucius patted his arm. "We'll find a way to deal with that, don't worry," he said softly. "Perhaps the veneer of a wife and children will deflect rumors," he suggested.

"You think I should marry?" Antinous was incredulous.

"Only for him, for the two of you. A meaningless marriage, to a girl from your hometown perhaps." Lucius sighed. "Of course I'm still fodder for the gossip mill despite my Plautia and our little one."

"Perhaps it is the matching servants that riles your critics?"

Lucius guffawed loudly. "You are too much, little hunter!" He put his arm around his comrade's shoulders and drew in a bolstering breath. "Now, about protecting our mutual friend, Ant. We will start with Julius Servianus, the emperor's brother-in-law, and his snotty little grandson Pedianus Fuscus. Neither is ever to be trusted."

Lucius was wonderful, and they had talked for hours, eventually letting the painted and costumed entourage entertain them. Antinous was happy he had found an ally with the senator and was convinced of the importance of knowing what was going on around the emperor, while not necessarily being involved in intrigue. They had parted the best of friends.

But surely his Graeculus was finished with his city planners and architects by now. It was time to seek him out and tell his lover of his new companion. Antinous was certain Hadrian would be delighted.

Antinous decided to take the long way back to the canals where their barges were docked. From the banks of the river he walked through the center of the town, pleased to hear Greek spoken amongst the locals. He walked passed the baths where he and Hadrian had enjoyed cleansing massages that morning. Remembering his lover's brawny, muscular body being kneaded and rubbed aroused him into further thoughts about his glorious Graeculus.

"Antinous! What a surprise to see you here."

The friendly voice was familiar. He glanced up from his reverie. It was the empress Sabina with her personal entourage.

"My lady," the youth said with reverence and bowed.

"Oh, don't be silly," she scolded lightheartedly. Her eyes swept up and down his half-clad body. She blushed briefly. "You should probably just call me Vibia. That's what he calls me."

Of course, *he* meant their shared lover. It was the second time in an afternoon that Antinous realized he was not simply the emperor's lover, but a part of the emperor's life. A very special and intimate part.

"Thank you, Vibia," Antinous replied, still bowing.

She dismissed her attendants to follow at a distance, then affectionately took the youth's arm. They continued walking.

"I simply do not know how to thank you for how you have changed my husband. He is so much more vibrant, invigorated. It is amazing. I credit you for making this change in him." She looked up at him, satisfaction mixed with pride, and squeezed his arm in hers. "You know, he is to make a big announcement when we get to the site of Hadrianopolis. He won't tell me what it is, but I think it has to do with the succession." She stopped and turned toward him. "He's finally settled into his role as emperor. I really have you to thank."

They had wandered into an enclosed garden, secreted from the street by a high wall. Slightly uncomfortable with their intimate situation, Antinous glanced around him. The empress's attendants were nowhere to be seen. The two were utterly alone.

Sabina, however, seemed to be oblivious to their seclusion. She gave him the most heartfelt smile, then did the most amazing thing.

She kissed him. On the lips.

He had never kissed a woman before. Her lips were soft, with no prickly hair on the cheeks surrounding. Antinous suddenly wanted more of the new feeling. She was compliant, did not resist. She let him take control. He delved deeper, seeking more mysteries of her mouth, her tongue following not leading, her soft humming moans encouraging. His hands wandered across her back, down her sides, feeling the soft pliant flesh under her stola, a body that was yielding in places where on a man they would be firm – her breasts, her buttocks, her belly. Their warm wet kiss and her surrendering body were surprisingly arousing. Antinous felt himself grow hard, a response he had never had with a woman, a physical reaction he assumed was impossible with anyone other than a man. He wanted more than the kiss, he wanted his whole body to possess Sabina, to feel her warm and wet around more than just his tongue.

He lifted her slightly and pressed her against the stone wall, then pulled up the hem of her garments. She was bare underneath.

"Antinous?" she breathed with confused excitement.

He said nothing, instead used his fingers to answer. He drew his hand along her soft thigh, then explored between her legs, finding the desired orifice surrounded by folds of heated moist flesh. He probed inside watching her face melt into wantonness. The passage was pliant, not tight, but her muscles flexed in response to his touch. His curiosity was piqued. He had to have her, be inside her. He lifted his linen skirt.

He was astonished by the ease in which his hard cock slid into the passage and how deeply he could go with very little effort. As Sabina clutched at him, he felt her channel grip then pulsate around him. As he pulled out, her body demanded he stay in; as he pushed in, her body opened in welcome.

"Why have I denied myself this pleasure?" he murmured, not really wanting an answer. He was too lost now in the rhythm of the union of man and woman. He felt the familiar climb to the peak and knew that the culmination would be the same for this very different journey.

Sabina let out a clipped yelp when his final demanding thrust slammed against the wall of her cervix. Antinous savored every last moment as he emptied his sperm inside her. The empress did not protest knowing no man's seed would live in her desolate womb.

She pressed her forehead against his, panting from the excitement of the encounter.

Antinous swallowed hard. Were these the desires of a conventional Roman man? It couldn't possibly be so. Didn't the emperor Hadrian, himself a grown man, love him, want him, *him* Antinous, another man? He knew could never live without his Graeculus…

But hadn't Lucius talked of having a wife, giving her children, the trappings of a typical aristocratic Roman male? When his friend had mentioned it, it seemed such a foreign idea. Now he wasn't so sure. If making love to a woman were anything like this, it was not so repugnant. No, it was very exciting.

"I could get used to this," he said out loud, unwittingly.

"Yes," Sabina agreed softly. "You could. For him." Her tone conveyed the sympathy she felt about their dilemma.

Yes, Antinous agreed to himself, he could. And because of that he and his Graeculus could continue their love affair without anyone suspecting.

"I'd do anything for him," he said.

Egypt, Hermopolis Magna, 24 October 130

They landed at Hermopolis Magna, an ancient resort on the west bank of the river, a few days before the festival of the Nile and the festival of Osiris. This was the city of the Egyptian Hermes, known locally as Thoth. Hadrian and Antinous had shared a private moment remembering that the youth had been called Hermes by the high priestess during their initiation into the Eleusinian Mysteries. "It is your city," said the emperor running his fingers through his lover's glorious curls as they approached the docks.

Antinous had giggled at that. To have a city in honor of oneself was beyond comprehension. Only emperors and gods did such things.

The festival of the Nile fell on the 22nd of October, and two days later was commemorated the drowning and resurrection of the god Osiris. Of course, that meant the Egyptians celebrated for several days before and after. It seemed to the imperial Roman party that the Egyptians were dedicating, honoring, or rejoicing something every day along their fertile river. The beautifully clement weather probably lent to the festive nature of the native people.

Because the god and his myth were so important to the Egyptian livelihood, the Osiris festival was more solemn, at least at the start. The entire cycle of the Osiris story was re-enacted at locations throughout the city: the betrayal by his brother Set, the searching of his coffin by his sister-wife Isis, his dismemberment and drowning in the Nile, the reconstructing of his body, the reunion for one night of husband and wife, his apotheosis as lord of the underworld. Through it all, the inhabitants of the city had jeered, cried, and gloried in their god.

And then on the 24th of October they had simply celebrated, from morning until night. This year, however, was marked by a certain anxiety. They celebrated their god and their river every year, but when the god did not act in their favor, the citizens of Hermopolis were subdued and reflective.

From the perspective of their Roman visitors, they did not appear as such. The colorful banners and costumes during the day and the flaming, noisy spectacles as night fell did not reflect the despondency of a people uneasy with their agricultural future. No, it was a joyous celebration that beckoned everyone in the imperial party.

Sabina giggled as Zuester ran his hand along the open edge of her wrap-around dress.

"Certainly no god on Olympus approves of such wanton attire, my lady," he murmured seductively.

She pressed against his body. "Venus instructed my seamstress, my dear."

"Diana must be quarreling with Venus then. For our fair huntress would not allow the Empress of Rome to be such easy prey in man's pursuit." His hand slid in further.

They were on the imperial quay walking toward the night displays of fire at the Osiris festival when Zuester was inspired to seduce his lover before joining the crowds. They had both imbibed perhaps a bit too much Egyptian honey beer.

But not so much that Zuester wasn't capable of taking his empress in the improper manner he had in mind: out in the open air, against a barge, from behind.

They thought they had seen Lucius leave already with his entourage. At least they saw the entourage leave the aristocrat's barge, and Lucius did not travel anywhere without his own spectacle. Zuester took Sabina's hand and pulled her onto the deck of the boat, elaborately decorated and painted like the owner's servants.

A sleepy guard popped his head out of the curtained entry annex, clearly startled by the noise on the deck outside. He quickly bowed to the empress and her well-known paramour. She dismissed him with a wave of her hand, and he retreated to the quay above.

Zuester wrapped his arms around her shoulders. "Do you want that I should take you out in the open on the deck with the guard watching?"

As drunk as she was, Sabina had not completely lost her wits about her. "No. In the entryway."

"All right. But I'm leaving the curtains open, so he can hear you."

They went inside, immediately noticing the curtains to the main cabin were open and the doors had been left ajar. The crack between the double doors was enough to see the room inside was brilliantly lit, too much so for an unoccupied space. Lucius might be extravagant, but he was not so stupid as to leave blazing oil lamps alight in a wooden boat.

Overtaken by curiosity, the lovers peered inside. Sabina had to clamp a palm over her mouth to stifle her gasp of excitement.

Lucius, wearing only an Egyptian pleated linen skirt, carried a cedar paddle as he circled around his parasol carrier. The completely nude servant was tied chest-down onto a padded wooden bench, his head turned away from his hidden audience, his pale bottom exposed and lifted up, his genitals hanging through a hole in the bench. Every so often Lucius bobbed his head toward that of his servant, speaking inaudible commands and challenges, hitting the paddle lightly against his own hand in a threatening and exciting way.

Sabina could not take her eyes off the aristocrat. He was utterly depilated, his mass of blond curls and thick beard contrasting sharply with his hairless muscular chest and strong arms. When his sleek pectorals and biceps flexed in preparation to strike his servant, she felt herself grow wet. Her husband, she had to admit, had very good taste in lovers.

Lucius smacked the paddle against the white buttocks before him, turning the skin bright pink. He then gently smoothed his palm against the inflamed flesh, further assuring his servant with sweet words that the pain would dissipate.

The empress ran her hand along the edge of her dress, searching for the opening, and when she found it, her fingers delved into her own inflamed flesh.

Until Zuester grabbed her hand and pulled it to her back, holding it there emphatically. His own hand wandered inside her dress to pet her moisture. She tensed at first against his determination, then relaxed to watch the display in the next room.

Lucius landed another cruel blow to the bound youth. This time the servant's body shook as if he were speaking, pleading. Lucius leaned into the boy's ear, his expression and lips questioning the young man.

The servant nodded his head.

Lucius knelt at the side of the bench. With one hand he grabbed the servant's engorged cock, with his other he swung the paddle up, then crashed it down. The servant jerked from the force and cried out.

Besides the slapping of the paddle, it was the only audible sound from the decorated room.

Lucius pumped his servant's eager cock. The paddling became less frequent but the subduing words were poured out in a constant stream against the parasol carrier's turned-up ear.

Until one final brutal swat. The servant screamed and shot his seed onto the rug beneath them. Lucius continued to cruelly milk his bound playmate until the youth squirmed and cried out one more time.

The wail brought Sabina back to reality. She spit on her free palm, then reached under Zuester's tunic and grabbed his utterly engorged cock. The force of her grip sent him jostling against her.

She flashed him a mock scolding look.

Lucius untied his servant, gently rubbing and kissing the marks where the ropes had been, then helped the stiff youth stretch back to standing, tenderly massaging his muscles. The two stood face to face, Lucius speaking honeyed words to the doe-eyed youth before he took him in a devastatingly passionate kiss.

The youth wrapped his arms around the neck of his master, as Lucius stripped the skirt from his body. His magnificent prick bounced as the fabric brushed along its length, revealing the senator was also depilated down below.

Sabina gasped a loud moan.

Zuester clamped his hand on her mouth.

Lucius looked up at the doorway. He had heard.

Zuester watched in mortified panic as Lucius marched to the door and flung it open.

Sabina and Zuester fell into the room and onto the feet of their host.

"Well, well, well, what have we here?" The senator's eyes twinkled at the empress, her dress in revealing disarray. He held out his hand.

Sabina availed herself of his help and stood up, her eyes never leaving those of her husband's former lover, but clearly wanting to look elsewhere on his body. Zuester got up on his own, shaking his head at the smitten empress.

Still holding her hand, Lucius brought it to his lips. His whisper-light kiss was accompanied by a delicate touch with the tip of his tongue. Sabina shivered in lascivious anticipation.

"I presume you have been at my door for a while. Did you like what you saw?" The blond aristocrat addressed this to the both of them, his eyes skating across the slight tenting of Zuester's tunic.

The secretary blushed.

Sabina shuffled unsteadily on her feet. "We were on our way to the fire festival," she drawled defensively.

Lucius howled with laughter. "Well, you made a wrong turn, I should think." He leaned in to her. "And now I've caught you," he murmured, his lips brushing against her ear. He turned to his servant. "You may go, Stefanus. Wash and tend to your wounds. I will call on you shortly."

Once their game had clearly ended, the embarrassed servant had dressed and stood in the corner with downcast eyes. With his master's leave he quickly fled to the depths of the boat.

Sabina watched him go, then looked up at Lucius. She wet her lips. "What are you going to do to us?" she asked, unable to conceal her curious excitement.

Lucius was still very close to her, his breath hot on her cheek. "I remain unsatisfied, madam. I intend to satisfy myself."

His hands sought and found the tie holding her dress. He pulled the bow, then slid the diaphanous silk off her shoulders. The dress floated to the floor, revealing her beautifully feminine and utterly nude form.

Lucius cupped a breast.

Zuester stepped forward, then stopped when Lucius shot him a friendly – and mischievous – warning look.

The young aristocrat continued to explore the woman before him with his eyes and hands. "It is a shame your husband prefers men when he has such an exquisite wife."

Sabina's breaths came in panting huffs, her nipples hardened, not against the cool night air, but against the practiced touch of the libertine senator. He flicked playfully at the erect peaks.

"How will you satisfy yourself?" she inquired with sultry lewdness.

"Just like you were treated to a performance, I demand a show for my private amusement."

Until that moment, Zuester hadn't realized such an idea would still be so alarming. He paled, his body stiffened.

Lucius noticed.

Releasing Sabina, the senator sauntered over to the secretary, his face softening with concern, his eyes sparking with realization. He caressed Zuester's shoulder with a gentle hand, sliding it delicately down the Dacian's bare arm to tangle with his fingers. Unexpectedly titillated, Zuester felt his heart thump, his cock throb, his apprehensions melt. Lucius made empathy for his dark past appealingly erotic.

The aristocrat wrapped both hands around Zuester's waist and pulled his body close. They were matched in height, their eyes meeting at the same level. Zuester cast his downward to gaze at Lucius's plump, red lips, licking his own in anticipation. Lucius smiled, then tilted his head and leaned in, taking Zuester in a deep kiss. The Dacian flinched, unaware that he harbored a needful hunger for the senator, until Lucius's demanding tongue teased it out of him.

Zuester softened under the expert seduction. It was the first time he had ever kissed another man from desire and not from fear. It was glorious.

Lucius parted tenderly. "Don't worry, my friend," he whispered, trailing gentle pecks along the secretary's jaw. "A game, nothing more. It will be her willing body that will satisfy both our pleasures. I'm sure you don't mind."

The politician exuded charisma, which in any other man might be suspect. In Lucius, however, it was genuine and warm and very persuasive. Zuester smiled conspiratorially. It had been his secret fantasy to share Vibia. The young, attractive, sexually-experienced senator was just the man.

"Zuester," Sabina pouted, bounding over to the embracing men. "C'mon. It'll be fun." She took his hand, clearly still feeling the freeing effects of the night's earlier imbibing.

Awaiting his orders, Zuester raised an eyebrow at Lucius.

"Remove his clothing," the senator commanded the empress.

She did as told, with perhaps a bit too much enthusiasm. The two men shared a smile while Sabina worked clumsily on Zuester's sandals.

Lucius indicated the bench from the previous performance. "Sit," he instructed Zuester.

The Dacian perched himself on the comfortably padded plank.

Lucius strolled over and playfully tugged at Zuester's cock enlivening it further from its semi-hard state. He drew in a sharp breath as he glared longingly at the Dacian. "Suck him," the senator ordered Sabina, a slight quiver to his voice.

The empress got on her knees and took her lover's prick in her mouth. Zuester rolled his head back in ecstasy at her practiced tongue. She knew precisely what he wanted and how he wanted it.

Lucius looked down on the scene with amusement and delight, then knelt behind Sabina. His fingers delved between her thighs, a grin spreading across his face when he found what he wanted. "Mount him," he breathed into her ear. "Like a hetaera. And fuck him slowly."

Sabina eagerly straddled her lover and began to ride him as directed. Zuester touched her cheek inviting a kiss. She bent over him.

"Does he taste like me?" she teased.

"Let's see."

Briefly lost to each other, they did not notice Lucius oiling up his own magnificent member as he stood behind them. The moment Sabina felt the senator's presence, she wiggled her butt provocatively while continuing to move up and down on Zuester.

Yet Lucius had another plan. He caught Zuester's eye and indicated the Dacian should push Sabina off. She complained terribly until Lucius grabbed her wrist, forcibly turning her around.

"I want to see you while you take your pleasure," the senator said, his voice dripping with seduction.

"Oh, yes," she agreed.

She mounted Zuester, this time with her back to him, and once again rode him, taunting Lucius with her movements. The senator stepped closer, and she threaded her fingers through his hair, pulling his face to hers.

"Kiss me," she said.

He did. While she was distracted he pulled over a chair and hiked up a leg onto the seat.

"My lady," he intoned, "I want you to stop for just a moment while I position myself."

Zuester stretched to get a better view of the scene, his cock still fully embedded inside Sabina. The empress regarded the senator curiously at first, then in utter amazement as she watched him position his prick right above Zuester's.

Lucius's penetration of her was slow and deliberate, his eyes scrutinizing every minute reaction on her shameless face. Zuester felt Sabina's body tremble as she tried to catch her breath against the carnal assault, and felt the slick hardness slide along his sensitive shaft. The act was not new to him, but the captivating man made it feel like the first time.

"Move against me," commanded Lucius to Sabina.

She held on to the sides of the bench and thrust her hips up. As she moved her body toward Lucius, Zuester groaned beneath her. She was so wonderfully tight, and Lucius so wonderfully...*there*.

"Let's see how we can increase our enjoyment of the empress, hmmm, Zuester?" the senator taunted.

"Yes, please," the Dacian moaned.

Holding Sabina's gaze, Lucius licked his thumb then pressed it against her clit. "When was the last time you were double fucked like this, my lady?"

Sabina's jaw fell open in absolute ecstasy. "Never," she managed.

"Never?" he pressed harder.

Sabina screamed her orgasm, bucking up against Lucius's hips and clenching the two cocks together inside her.

"Gods of my father!" Zuester cried. The oiled cock rubbing against his was already too much. Now the passage was tighter, taking him to the brink.

Lucius grabbed Sabina's hair and pulled hard, forcing her to look up at him. "We're going to fuck you like you've never been fucked before, my queen," he murmured, his voice dripping with lust. "We're going to come inside you, my little whore."

Sabina climaxed again with a needful wail.

"Hold on, my lady," Lucius said hoarsely, pushing her back to lie on top of the Dacian.

Trying to gain purchase, Sabina clung to the sides of the bench. Zuester wrapped his arms around her waist to steady her.

"Now!" the senator commanded to the secretary beneath him.

Both men thrust simultaneously into the deliciously snug channel, Lucius howling with ecstatic laughter, Zuester groaning blasphemies. Approaching his peak, the secretary wanted more. He drew his hands up Sabina's torso, fondling her breasts, causing her to writhe on top of him. When he cruelly pinched her nipples, she came with a shriek.

That was enough to send him over the edge. Zuester bucked up, wondering if Lucius could feel him come, could feel the liquid heat pouring over both their cocks…

And then Lucius came, and he knew. He felt the other man's length twitch as he emptied himself inside the empress, felt a new friction as both pricks were bathed in the double emission.

"Oh, gods," the Dacian gasped.

Lucius looked down at Zuester, flashing him a satisfied grin. The men laughed in the shared delight.

"Oh, you two are monstrous! Out!" Sabina struggled against her defilers, now slack from release.

Effusing gentlemanly charm, Lucius helped the empress to her feet, and offered her a robe. He tossed a towel to his accomplice.

"What a lovely diversion," remarked Lucius impishly. He chucked Sabina's chin. "Are we still on for the festival?"

Antinous wandered alone to the Osiris festival, enlivened by his earlier encounter with his Graeculus. They had just made love in their new favorite way: face-to-face with Hadrian on bottom accepting Antinous's nourishment to his body. Afterwards, the emperor had protested that he was too tired to go out that evening, and had sent his beloved off with a tender kiss.

The crowds were dense and did not notice who he was, or they did not care. It did not matter, in fact, it was refreshing to be an unknown, inconspicuous. Religious festivals seemed to be the great equalizer, giving a chance for everyone to celebrate their gods and their own felicity. Antinous looked at the crowd, noticing the imperial party was convening unaffectedly amongst the common citizens. The empress Sabina embraced her Zuester, kissing him incautiously while Mindia and Balbilla chattered away next to them. The boy Fuscus was distracted by a display of fire jugglers. Antinous's new friend Lucius stood amongst his liveried staff with his arms draped across his parasol carrier's body. Both were smiling broadly, at each other and at the crowd around them. Lucius saw Antinous and waved, inviting the youth over to join them. Antinous smiled and shook his head. He was in a mood to watch the festival alone. He loved his friends, and was happy they were so contented, but at that moment he wanted to wallow in his own particular euphoria.

He was in love and was secure in the knowledge that he was loved.

He was so lost in his own thoughts he did not see the Parthian priest Sanabares approach him.

"My lord, Antinous," said the priest. "That is correct, is it not?"

"My lord Sanabares," responded the lad, bowing. "I am simply Antinous."

"Very good. Antinous, then." The priest walked comfortably amongst the people, nodding and smiling as they waved and touched him. From the designs on his robe they recognized him as a priest of the god Re, the father of Osiris. He seemed heartened by the attention.

"You are here in Hermopolis rather than Heliopolis, my lord?" queried Antinous. "That is quite a ways away, is it not?"

"Yes, yes. The festivities are better here," he confessed. "Somewhat more exuberant and not so dour as that other city. But don't tell my colleagues." He winked.

Antinous smiled at the joke. "Of course not."

The priest moved closer. "Antinous, I have wanted to speak with you, alone. It seems like this might be the only opportunity." It was said in Greek.

Antinous was slightly befuddled by this pronouncement and in his native language. Why would this priest want to speak to him of all people? "All right," he said. "Let us take the opportunity now." Antinous also spoke in Greek.

"Very good. It is about the emperor Hadrian. I know the two of you are good friends."

The youth's interest was utterly peaked. "Yes, we are good friends," was all he would allow.

They had been walking amongst and through the admiring crowd, Sanabares politely declining offering after offering. When they arrived at an altar of Re, the priest stopped and made his obeisance, then began walking toward the temple of Thoth, a hypostyle hall decorated with painted ibises and hieroglyphs, and bid the youth join him. Astounded by the massive scale of the edifice, Antinous walked a bit behind his host. Cauldrons of fire lit their way as they entered the building.

The priest nodded to the few other magi present, and led Antinous into a small chamber made even smaller by a daunting wooden table in the center. Sanabares went to a shelf and pulled down a box. "I have seen the emperor's astrological chart," he said placing the box on the table. "From the stars, it shows that he has only seven, perhaps eight, years left to live."

"Are you certain of this?" Antinous had not realized that Sanabares was a practiced magus.

The priest opened the box and took out a scroll. "I have run the chart several times," he said as he smoothed the papyrus out before them. "The result is the same." He pointed to an area of the chart with a symbol of a lion. "Leo at this juncture represents illness to the heart and chest." He glanced at the youth. "I understand he has trouble breathing at times." When Antinous did not respond, the magus continued. "But the result always shows Mercury in retrograde, which indicates uncertainty, and its position here indicates an uncertainty surrounding his death. Of course this means that the fate of the emperor can be changed with the right circumstances."

Antinous was taken aback at the priest's words as he tried to make sense of the incomprehensible chart laid out on the table. He loved his Hadrian. In seven or eight years his Graeculus would be in his sixties, but he himself would only be twenty-seven or twenty-eight. That was far too young to live the rest of his life without his one true love.

As if reading his mind, the priest said, "you are a young man. In seven or eight years hence you will still be a young man. What will you do without your emperor?"

Antinous did not want to hear such things. "There will certainly be another emperor of Rome."

"Of course, of course, my lad. I am simply thinking of your special relationship with this emperor."

"I don't know what you mean. In seven or eight years, I'll be concerning myself with my wife and children."

The priest laughed. "You cannot hide your relationship from us, son. You think we do not know the true nature of your friendship with the emperor of Rome? I am telling you that in seven or eight years the emperor Hadrian will no longer live. You'll be thrown out of the palace on your own. No one will take in the disgraced former lover of the dead Hadrian, even if you have a wife and child. How will you ever support a family?"

Antinous considered this, his thoughts eventually ending at Lucius. "The new emperor will take me in."

Sanabares laughed again. "And do you know who this new emperor will be?" he asked incredulously.

"No," Antinous said hesitatingly. Despite the respect and goodness of the priest amongst the people of Hermopolis, the youth realized he should not divulge any information he might have about that matter. "But I am sure it will be an ally of the emperor Hadrian."

"Of course," was the answer. The priest opened a concealed compartment at the bottom of the box and took out first a glass bottle filled with an amber liquid, then the silver condu from Heliopolis.

"That is Pachrates's cup, is it not?"

"It is the condu of the priests of Re, yes. We all use its dream-enhancing properties to experience revelations. Pachrates can appear in his subject's dreams, as I am sure you well know from a story your emperor related to you."

Antinous nodded. Hadrian had told him of the magician's appearance in his dream while the youth lay at his side and suspected nothing.

The magus smiled. "I myself can see into the future, but I need to be connected with the subject in order to do so. You are a conduit to the emperor's heart. Through you I can see into his future."

"Me?"

"Yes, you, precisely because of your special connection. With me as your guide into the future we will see what is this uncertainty shown on his astrological chart. Together we will more clearly see his destiny and may be able to change the future. This is the magic of the condu."

The priest turned the top of the condu and removed it from the cup. He poured some of the amber liquid into the cup then held it above his head reciting words foreign to the youth's ears.

"Now place your hand on my heart as I drink. In this way we will begin the connection."

Antinous did as the priest ordered, pressing his palm against the priest's chest, feeling the calm beating under the robe, feeling him swallow the liquid.

The priest poured another draught of the liquid into the condu. Again he held the cup above his head and recited an incantation. This time Antinous distinctly heard his own name amongst the words.

"I will do the same now. I will place my hand on your heart as you drink."

Antinous took the cup and drank as the priest held his hand against his chest. The liquid was at first sour, then sweet, then bitter. At the priest's nod he drank the entire contents of the condu, then placed the empty cup on the table.

"Very good." The magus rewound the scroll and placed it and the condu and bottle back into the box. He returned the box to the shelf. "Now we go to the river."

The words felt thick and loud to Antinous. He wasn't quite sure why, but going to the river seemed like a very good idea at that moment.

He followed Sanabares to the back of the temple where they exited down a short flight of steps. The river was not far off. The walk to the bank was somewhat deserted except for a few furtive lovers amongst clumps of palm trees. A small boat with a tiny cabin was tied to the shore waiting for them.

They stepped inside the boat. The priest motioned Antinous into the cabin, where he sat on a cushioned bench as the magus untied the boat and pushed off the shore. The youth heard a few quick strokes of a paddle to set them on their course before the priest stepped into the cabin. They were traveling back north, drifting with the flow of the river.

"Now, young Antinous, I have told you that the chart shows uncertainty in the final years of Hadrian. Let us join hands. A vision will come to us about how to confront this uncertainty."

Antinous took the hands of the priest in his and closed his eyes. The gentle rocking of the boat was lolling. He felt himself drifting, not into sleep, but into a trance or perhaps a dream.

"The transference of youthful vigor as prescribed by Pachrates is not working as planned. I see your emperor still struggling. Do you see him?"

Antinous saw nothing but wavy lines of color behind his eyelids. He opened his eyes. The priest was still before him, but everything about him was somehow brighter, more brilliant.

"I do not see."

"Ah, this sometimes happens. I see what you are meant to see," explained the priest. The magus squeezed his eyes shut, then began chanting. The words were like gibberish to Antinous, but their deep tones resonated inside him.

The priest opened his eyes and stared straight at the youth. "Osiris demands an offering. When he has his offering he will grant the requested number of years to the emperor."

"An offering?"

"There is an aspect of our god Osiris that we did not tell you back in Heliopolis. With the proper respects, he will transfer the years of the offerant to the intended person, until the years match. There will be no need to imagine a future without your emperor; you will live as long as he. The god has spoken to me. Osiris needs to know who is praying. Osiris will restore the health of the emperor once he receives your prayer."

"How shall I pray?"

"You will need to step into the water where you will meet with the god face to face. He will ask you who is the intended recipient of your years. You will tell him it is the emperor Hadrian."

"I have to go into the water?" This did not appeal to the youth at that moment. He had begun to feel a chill throughout his body.

"That is where our god lives."

"Oh." The idea of transferring his years to bolster those of his lover was confusing to Antinous. As he was trying to wade through the math involved, of when it was they would die together, a thought occurred to him. "How do we know that Osiris will honor the plea for a Roman man?"

"But this has been done in Rome! Even the grandfather of one of your traveling party knew about this. The astrologer Balbillus once advised Nero to have a substitute die for him to extend his life. Surely the granddaughter, Julia Balbilla, has also recommended your emperor do as such?"

"The lady Balbilla has said nothing of this. Everyone knows the emperor is set against human sacrifice."

"This is not human sacrifice!" The magus smiled. "I am not asking you to give your life for your emperor, just half of your remaining years to extend his. I have already communicated this to Osiris. He awaits your direct appeal."

Antinous felt confused again. "Where is he?"

"In the water," the priest reminded. He stood and pulled Antinous up with him. "Let us go outside to see."

The exited the small cabin. They had drifted with the current a short distance away from Hermopolis Magna. Antinous could still see the torches and fire light from the festivities. But around them the night was pitch black, only the stars above shining down.

The priest stood at the end of the boat and beckoned to Antinous. "Sit on the edge first. Get your feet wet. The god will know you are coming."

Antinous felt heavy, his limbs stiff and unwieldy. His head, however, felt light. With some effort and help from the magus, he sat on the edge of the boat, his feet dangling off the side, his toes touching the cool water. It seemed so far away.

"I can't..." he protested weakly.

"Yes, you can. For your emperor, your lover."

Antinous looked down at the black water. He would do anything for his Graeculus.

He wasn't sure if he jumped by himself or if the priest helped him, but suddenly he was in the water. His thin linen tunic felt heavy, billowing up to the surface, then soaking up water and tugging him under.

"All the way," instructed the priest. "Your head must be under. Osiris must see you in his world."

Antinous ducked under the cold water. He opened his eyes, but all was darkness. There was no god. How long would he have to remain like this? The water began to feel crushing against his skin. His tunic was like lead. He tried to tear it off in a panicked frenzy, only making himself dizzy.

Still nothing happened. There was no god.

He tried to swim back to the top, but something was holding him down, something small but insistent against his head. He thrashed about, trying to tear off the weight, but his arms would not cooperate. He screamed, but there was no sound. There was only water. Water rushing through his ears, in his mouth, down his throat. Where was the god? Where was Osiris?

Graeculus, my Graeculus, where are you?

He couldn't breathe, his limbs felt weak. He closed his eyes.

Graeculus, I love you...I will love you forever...I'm so sorry...

Then all was blackness.

Egypt, Hermopolis Magna, 25 October 130

"He fell into the Nile."

It was all the emperor could say.

Zuester had just heard the news and had run into the emperor's barge. Hadrian was standing at his window, looking out over the cruel river that had sucked the breath out of his beloved and the joy out of his life.

Sabina lay on the bed shaking with sobs.

It was incomprehensible that one so vibrant, so full of joy, so innocent, so much a part of their lives was gone. Forever.

When Hadrian had woken up alone, he had launched a search for his favorite. By chance a fisherman had pulled the pale and bloated body out of the river by the small village of Hir-wer on the east bank. The gold of the boy's girdle suggested he was not a denizen of one of the reed-and-mud huts, but a guest of the emperor. The imperial authorities had been informed. The emperor's initial shock had turned into denial until he saw the body. Despite trying to hide his emotions, everyone knew the emperor was devastated.

Zuester went to the bed and touched Sabina's shoulder. She sat up and flung her arms around his neck.

"I saw him, I saw him last night," she tried to whisper, her voice croaking in pain. "At the festival. Lucius too. Oh, gods, why have they taken him from us?"

There was nothing for him to do, there on the emperor's barge. Zuester knew he would be much more useful in whatever official capacity he was needed for. There would need to be an investigation of sorts. "Vibia, I'll return later. Look after your husband."

"Yes, of course," she said softly, wiping her eyes. "He is desolate. I know I cannot leave him alone for fear he might wish to join his beloved." She stood and joined Hadrian at the window. Her presence enlivened him for a moment and he followed her to the bench where they sat before the view of the Nile.

Inquiring amongst the praetorians and officials, Zuester discovered word of the youth's death had spread like wildfire amongst the Egyptian people along the river. But it wasn't the scandalous gossip of the emperor's boy-lover drowning himself in a fit of romantic despair that Zuester had feared. No, it was quite different.

Antinous, the beloved of the god-emperor Hadrianus Olympius, had sacrificed himself for the Egyptian people, had sacrificed himself to Osiris, had sacrificed himself to bring the inundation to their Nile.

But not only that, the favorite had sacrificed himself for the well-being of the emperor, to strengthen Hadrian's health, to extend the life of the god who walked among them.

Zuester went to the small fishing village to see with his own eyes.

Already hundreds of people had gathered at Hir-wer before a makeshift shrine of stone and palms surrounded by metal pots containing small offertory fires. The people stood at a slight distance, bowing and praying quietly. The bloated body of Antinous lay shrouded on top of the shrine, attended by a priest who sprinkled it with perfume.

Zuester gingerly approached a man dressed in the more sophisticated clothing of the citizens of Hermopolis across the water. He seemed fascinated and happy, but not as deeply mired in spiritual ecstasy as those about him.

"Can you tell me what it is the people are praying for?" he asked in Greek.

The man recognized Zuester's clothing as Roman, his signet ring as that of an imperial official. "Yes, my lord," he responded in kind. "They are thanking the blessed Antinous for sacrificing himself to appease the god Osiris who will bring the flood again." He pointed to the priest with the censer and another who was tending the flames in the metal pots. "They are the priests of Osiris. When a person drowns in the Nile their body is considered sanctified and only such priests are allowed to touch the corpse. They were called immediately when the fisherman found the body." He bowed his head to Zuester in respect. "The Nile is our lifeblood, my lord. This demonstration before you shows how important it is to us, our lives, our wealth, our place here in Egypt. That one of your own gave up his life for us is intensely moving and inspiring. The emperor will be praised along with his beloved."

"Thank you, sir," Zuester said as he pulled back to the edge of the crowd. The people were now chanting "Antinous, Osiris" all around him.

A boy, perhaps thirteen or fourteen, appeared at his side. He too was dressed not as an inhabitant of Hir-wer, but of Hermopolis. He looked up at Zuester and smiled. Zuester smiled back.

"I saw him, my lord," the boy said quietly in Greek.

Zuester felt a chill of alarm tear up his spine. He placed his arm around the shoulders of the child and led him just enough away from the crowd so no one would hear their conversation.

"What is your name, son?"

"Zoilus."

"You are Greek-speaking?"

"I live just across the river, sir." The boy pointed.

"Yes, of course. And what do you mean by you 'saw him'?"

"I was there amongst the reeds." He pointed to a clump of reeds on a high bank over-looking the spot where Antinous's body had been found.

"And what were you doing there, may I ask?" Zuester felt it best to drag all the details out before he got to the heart of the matter.

"It was best to see the fire spectacles of the Osiris festival. My mama does not want me near fire so I had to find a high place to watch it. There were spinning wheels and juggling."

Yes, there were. Very distracting to all present, Zuester mused with a heavy heart.

"I have a raft I made with reeds all by myself," said Zoilus. "I can go back and forth across the river with it when the water is low like it has been."

Zuester looked at the water. It flowed sluggishly around a sharp bend, which, he could only imagine, would be quite treacherous during the flood season.

"So, you were sitting on the bank, in the dark, watching the fire displays, and then what happened?"

"I heard a noise in the water, like a boat noise."

Not being a river person, Zuester needed more information than that.

"Like when the boat sloshes in the water. It is not like a bird or a fish. It is a boat noise."

"All right. What did you do next?"

"Well, I thought it might be my papa, so I hid in the reeds then looked to see who it was. It wasn't my Pa."

"What did you see?"

"It was a boat with a small cabin in the middle," the boy said thoughtfully. "There were people talking in the cabin. They were speaking Greek, so I could understand. I was still afraid it was my Pa, so I moved a little down the bank so I could hear better. I still couldn't hear much, but I knew it wasn't my Pa."

"What did you hear?"

"Well, like I said, not much really. But there were two voices. One was a nice man. One was a man with a foreign accent. Like yours."

Zuester did not like the implication that foreigners were not nice, but he was dealing with a child. "So the priest spoke Greek with a foreign accent. Was it the same accent as mine?"

"No, it was different. Like someone from the orient."

So, a man from the east beyond Egypt. "All right. Were you able to make out any of what the nice man and the foreigner said to each other?"

"Well, they weren't very loud. I think the nice man was made to sacrifice himself to Osiris to prolong the emperor's life. At least that is what it sounded like. He sounded scared though."

Zuester caught the sob in his throat. *Poor Antinous!* "Was he pushed into the water?"

"I don't think so. It sounded like he sort of fell in from the side. There was not a very big splash at first."

Another chill crept across Zuester's back. "What do you mean 'at first'?"

"He started splashing after he fell in. That's what it sounded like. I really couldn't see very well. It was really dark down there on the water."

"Was there any sort of cry out for help?" Zuester did not really want to know the answer.

"No. Just the splashing."

The Dacian could only imagine that Antinous had been held by force under the water. The horror of it made his skin crawl.

"And no one suspected you were there?" he asked the boy. He didn't need to inquire as to why the boy did not run for help; his mother and father were clearly the more immediate threats.

"Not a one, sir. I even saw the other man leave."

"You did?" This was very good news. "Could you describe the man?"

"He was dressed like a priest of Re. You know, the father of Osiris."

Zuester knew very well who Re was and what a priest of Re dressed like. He also knew an easterner who spoke Greek and was such a priest. What the Parthian priest Sanabares was doing so far south in Hermopolis, he did not know, but he would send agents to inquire about the priest's whereabouts last night.

Zuester fished in his purse for a coin and pulled out a silver denarius with the emperor on one side, and Fortuna on the reverse. It seemed the goddess had had a hand in leading the boy to him.

The boy took it, wide-eyed. He had clearly never seen such a thing. Zuester patted the boy on the shoulders, then watched him run away.

He would also have to send his men running if he wanted to catch up with Sanabares. No doubt the malefactor was long gone by now.

Egypt, Hermopolis Magna, end of October 130

Sabina slid her leg across the delicate linen sheet covering the mattress of her husband's bed. She couldn't remember the last time they had slept together before last night. He needed her now, needed an old friend and a comforting lover. Still, there was a moroseness she couldn't quite reach. The depths of his sorrow for the loss of the love of his life were unfathomable.

She heard a commotion in the next room, and propped herself up on her elbows to hear better.

Hadrian stormed in, closely followed by Lucius and Zuester. The emperor glanced at his wife who had grabbed the sheet and clutched it to her nude body.

"Don't worry, Vibia. There's nothing any one of us hasn't already seen."

Sabina blushed and shot a questioning glance at Lucius who smirked and shrugged his shoulders as he slumped into a chair. Of course her husband knew about her newly embarked upon affair with the senator. The emperor made it his job to know such things.

Hadrian grabbed a robe laid artfully across a bench and tossed it to her. "You should be part of this discussion." He was upset, but not at her.

"What's going on?" she asked as she got out of bed and dressed, glad her body could be a brief visual respite to the sorrow-laden occupants of the chamber.

"Antinous was led to his death by a nefarious priest," explained Zuester. "We think the same priest we met in Heliopolis."

"Pachrates? The one with the crocodile?" She looked over at her agitated husband who had begun to pace.

"No, no," Zuester said. "A Parthian."

"A Parthian?" Sabina turned to her husband. "Are we at war again?"

Lucius spoke first. "We're not sure who did this and why. Rome still has many enemies, my lady, even while we are not at war."

"But who would be an enemy to Antinous?" Sabina's voice shook as she said his name.

"He was a substitute for the real target," said Lucius.

"Like you once were, Vibia," reminded Zuester.

Sabina's hand shot to her mouth in horror.

"He had been convinced somehow that his death would prolong the emperor's life," explained the Dacian.

"He drowned himself for *my* benefit?" exclaimed Hadrian, still incredulous at the presumed motivation. "What possible benefit could I acquire from his death?" The sharp edge to his voice was tempered with the pain of loss.

"Clearly he had been under the influence of something, a spell, a narcotic perhaps." Zuester shook his head. "I cannot believe he did such a foolish thing with a sound mind."

"Well," drawled Lucius, "there is the belief amongst the Roman people that one may sacrifice oneself, with proper rituals and prayers of course, and thereby extend the life of another. I think Caligula availed himself of that. Surely you know this, Graeculus."

"Antinous was Greek," the emperor said succinctly.

Lucius was undeterred by his ex-lover's churlish response. "Perhaps they have something similar in Greece."

Hadrian ignored him. "Where are we with finding this Parthian, Sanabares?" he asked Zuester.

"I've put the *frumentarii* on the job."

Hadrian grunted. "They'll find him." Sabina knew her husband had not wanted to re-establish Trajan's special force of secret police, but throughout his reign he had found them quite enterprising and useful.

The emperor looked around at his friends, his eyes stopping at his wife. "We've all been too incautious. Vibia, especially you. I don't want you without a guard. Our enemies are still in our midst."

"Yes, Graeculus," she responded dutifully. She liked her personal guard, there would be no problem keeping them close by.

"And Lucius, I want some muscle in that entourage of yours."

"Yes, Graeculus," the senator responded mimicking Sabina.

The emperor turned to his secretary. "If they think he is a god, then I shall make him one."

"Sir?" Zuester responded dully.

"I will found a cult in honor of my favorite who died to prolong my life and to bring the floods to Egypt."

Lucius smiled. "Of course. The Nile god has always desired human sacrifice. Antinous gave up his life out of intense love for his emperor-god and the emperor-god is simply returning the favor, as a god may."

Hadrian shot him a perturbed look.

"Darling, I've fucked you. I can't possibly believe you're a god, no matter what the Greeks say."

Ever the official, Zuester began to plan the proposal. "Didn't the priestess of Demeter equate Antinous with Hermes in your initiation?"

"Yes," Hadrian responded, intrigued by his secretary's train of thought.

"And the people have been calling him 'Antinous-Osiris'. They both have powers over the world of the dead."

Lucius brightened at the idea. "He'll be a savior. Give people hope of life after death. Just like how he has sustained life on the Nile."

"And we'll have turned his death to our benefit," remarked Zuester. "Thereby conquering death brought about by our enemies. It may instill anxiety in their ranks."

Hadrian chuckled, the first time in days. "I wonder what he would have thought of all of this. My darling boy."

Sabina went to her husband. "He would be proud of you for being strong." She said, her fingers playfully dancing across his chest. "It's what attracted him to you in the first place." Her hands smoothed along his thick shoulders to his muscled arms. "Your virility, your manliness, your authority."

Hadrian gazed with admiration at his wife. "Thank you, Vibia." He pulled her to him and took her in a passionate kiss, his massive hands wandering possessively and protectively over her body as she melted into him. For a moment the two were lost to each other.

Hadrian pulled back but still held his wife against him. "And that, Lucius, is how you flatter your emperor."

"Considering how the Senate despises you, Graeculus," Lucius responded, his legs open, one draped provocatively over the arm of the chair, "I should think you would want to flatter a senator once in a while."

The emperor laughed. He took his wife by the hand and led her to the bed where they sat down. She nuzzled against his robust chest as he placed an arm around her shoulders.

"Vibia," he said gently. "I was going to make an announcement at the founding of Hadrianopolis. It is not something that will be happening now…now that I've lost my Kynegiskos. But, I wanted you to know—" He stopped.

"What, Graeculus? What is it?"

"I was going to officially make Antinous a consort—"

Lucius abruptly stirred in his chair.

"—so he could remain at my side, live in the palace with us, with me. Your position, of course, would have remained unchanged."

"Consort?" she asked a little confused. "I thought you were going to name your successor."

"No, no," the emperor shook his head. "But I would have made it clear that the position of consort was merely a private one. Given that my boy was becoming a man, I was worried he would feel he had to leave me. I even teased him that he would have to take his own boy-lover soon." Hadrian appeared distant for a moment, remembering the exchange, and suddenly regretting it. He looked up at his friends bringing himself back to the present. "Egypt seemed like the appropriate place to make such an announcement."

"The land of sister-wives, and all that," Lucius said brashly.

"I thought it a revolutionary idea, really," commented Zuester, deflecting a potentially harsh exchange between the former lovers.

Sabina turned to him. "You knew?"

"Yes. In fact I've been putting the final touches on the emperor's speech." He glanced at Lucius. "We had to make it palatable to the Senate and other politicians."

"Don't look at me! I, for one, would not have objected!" Lucius protested petulantly. "I have it on good authority that the lad was not interested in meddling in politics. Seems to be the trend in imperial wives these days." He raised an eyebrow at Sabina.

"Yes, Antinous and I would have had a grand time shopping and reading poetry, my lord," she said curtly to the handsome aristocrat. She turned to Hadrian. "You think the patricians and the military and the colonial administrators would have made a fuss?"

"Well," said Zuester, "we don't think it would have caused too great a stir considering that Antinous was Greek and not Roman. The idea fit in well with the emperor's Panhellenic policies, as well."

"Did Antinous know this?" Sabina asked her husband.

"No," he said sullenly. "I regret I did not tell him now."

"How would that have changed anything?" she inquired tenderly.

"I don't know…I don't know." Hadrian pulled her more closely to him. "Maybe he wouldn't have been so unguarded had he known his future with me was assured."

"Graeculus, you cannot blame yourself for what happened." The gracious, heartfelt words were from Lucius.

"Thank you, my friend," replied Hadrian softly. "But I cannot stop thinking about what would have happened 'if'. It plagues me. I fear it will continue to plague me for the rest of my days."

"Don't, love," Sabina admonished while she cuddled against her husband.

Hadrian kissed her hair and sighed. Then, once again shaking himself free of mourning and remorse he drew in a deep breath.

"I have another pronouncement," he declared. "And this one Zuester doesn't know about yet." He nodded affectionately at his secretary. "After the incredible out-pouring of emotion toward my Antinous by the Egyptian people, I have decided to forgo founding Hadrianopolis—"

Sabina gasped.

"—and instead found the city of Antinoopolis. It will be built near where my Kynegiskos died, and will be the center of his new cult."

All present looked at the emperor then at each other.

"What a wonderful idea, Graeculus," Sabina praised.

"Yes, magnificent scheme, Graeculus," admitted Lucius. "And politically astute. Once again harmonizing quite nicely with your Panhellenism policies. A city for the Greek favorite of the Roman emperor, the boy who saved the Egyptian people."

"Thank you," Hadrian said, clearly quite proud of himself.

"Well, then, let's get working on the plans, my lord emperor," Zuester said heartily. "We will make it a fitting memory of our dear friend."

Egypt, along the Nile, the end of October 130

Sanabares was lucky the Nile flowed northwards, in the direction he wanted to go. Despite the lack of rains, the river was still mighty but quite a bit easier to navigate than it might otherwise have been. Especially when one traversed the country during the night.

When he left Hermopolis Magna, he had, at first, gotten by quite well. As a priest of Re he was most welcome in every temple, and any house. He was well-fed and comfortably put up. But one day, after a few days of such travels, by complete chance he overheard a conversation in a market. The Roman guard was looking for a priest of Re, and, not only that, the priest was a foreigner, an easterner. In that instant, the Parthian realized they were looking for him.

He wasn't quite certain why the Romans would be looking for him. Surely he had not led anyone at the Temple of Thoth – the only place he could think where he might have been seen with the youth Antinous – to believe he meant harm to the young man. Antinous had accompanied him of his own free will, even eagerly. And certainly there was absolutely nothing to link him to the boy's drowning. It was surely too far from where the two had last been seen.

For a second, Sanabares entertained the notion that the guard was looking for him for another reason entirely. Perhaps the emperor needed a personal spiritual guide? Such a notion was quickly driven out of his head. There would have been proclamations requesting his presence, not shushed gossip at a market stall.

He needed to act, to change his identity, to put on a different accent, have a new story. Perhaps with his dark hair and tanned skin he could pass himself off as Sicilian. Why, that island was a crossroads of a mish-mash of cultures. Anyone could look like anything there!

But then there were his clothes…

His youth misspent in thievery had taught him a few useful things, one of them being that a bath house was the perfect place to get a new outfit. This came with one caveat: that such a theft could be done provided one could distract the *capsarii*, the slaves who looked after customers' clothes at the baths. Sanabares still had his purse and it was mostly full. Bribery might be risky if a slave bragged about to whom he had just given his master's toga. And he might have to approach more than one slave if any refused to cooperate. No, better to simply not involve anyone face to face.

So, at the men's bath house at Alabastronpolis, he tossed a few coins into the changing room. As the slaves present were mystified and enthralled by the sudden gift from the gods, Sanabares quickly grabbed the most innocuous clothes he could find, choosing from among only the obvious ones hanging by hooks and not the unknown attire stored in the niches. After changing, he felt it best to submerge and bury his own priestly garb in the Nile. One needed to cover one's tracks thoroughly.

Now that he was undercover, he traveled more quickly, more cautiously, gaining most of his ground at night. He really only needed to continue his covert efforts until Alexandria. There he personally knew allies of princess Roedogune. They would transport him safely to her at Ctesiphon to make his report.

His report…

Because of the urgent distractions of the last few days, he hadn't much thought about what it was he was going to tell her highness. The boy Antinous had only become the target when it became very clear that access to the emperor himself would be difficult, especially since Sanabares was told he had to act alone. Killing the youth had been surprisingly easy, given the intense connection he had with the Roman emperor. Certainly the loss of this youth would send Hadrian plunging into an abyss of anguished mourning? Perhaps he would, or could be convinced to, retreat for a length of time during his bereavement. Perhaps the princess could act when this window of opportunity was opened.

And despite that he had not accomplished the stated goal of his mission, he was quite pleased with what he had been able to accomplish. He only needed to convey this satisfaction to the princess. Eventually, she would understand, he was sure of that.

Sanabares could not wait until he got to Alexandria where the whores were plentiful and cheap. He really needed a woman. Even a boy would do.

Egypt, Thebes, 19 November 130

Zuester had decided to not go with the imperial party that morning to hear the Colossus of Memnon sing. The enormous desert statue of the Ethiopian ally of the Trojans was known to emit a noise much like a lyre being plucked but only at dawn and only to some people. While a fascinating experience to be sure, Zuester was utterly exhausted from the activity of the last few weeks. The stress of the sorrow from the death of Antinous, then working non-stop on first the investigation of the youth's death, then the founding of his city, had taken quite a toll on the Dacian. While he was himself far more energetic in his middling years than the emperor was in his own, every once in a while, and getting more frequently now, he found he needed a break. Most of the imperial entourage had left before dawn that morning. They would not be back for a few hours. Zuester had even allowed his own servants to go with the emperor and empress. A few decided to stay behind with him; they were exhausted as well.

Sabina, of course, had whimpered and pouted. Zuester promised he would go with her and Balbilla the next day. But today, today he just wanted to sleep in and visit the bath house.

He found it a most favorable choice. Zuester had paid his own guardsmen additional wages to be particularly vigilant and alert so he himself did not need to be. They barred his bedroom door after Sabina had left. Later, at the bath house, they intimidated any who sought to converse with the emperor's secretary. Zuester wanted simply to relax, to sit in the warm water undisturbed by political matters, to enjoy the physical nature of exercise, the strigil, and massage, and not be bothered with intellectual concerns, except, perhaps, some poetry. Besides, because of the emperor's visit, the bath house had been cleaned, a surprisingly irregular and very welcome event.

He had saved the massage until almost last, between sitting in the dry heat of the *laconicum* and the final refreshing plunge into the bath of the *frigidarium*. He looked forward to other people attending to his body's needs, manipulating his tired limbs, and rejuvenating his aching muscles.

The slave motioned for him to follow after having been sufficiently heated in the *laconicum*. The massage room, down the corridor, was tastefully decorated with gray-veined white marble revetment on the walls and a simple black-and-white geometric mosaic on the floor. The room was heated, not so much as the *laconicum*, but enough so that the muscles would remain warmed. His skin already having been scraped of cleansing oil, sweat, and dirt, he was now looking forward to his treatment with perfumed unguents.

The low massage divan was cushioned and covered in heated towels. Zuester lay on his back, feeling his body melt into the soft couch, letting his limbs loosen. Four masseurs – for he had plenty of money for such – were to work on him, one for each arm, one for each leg. Every muscle and ligament, from his shoulders to his fingers, his thighs to his toes, was kneaded, pounded, and stretched, at first very gently to awaken the limbs and joints to the sensations, then with force and vigor. By the time he was told to turn over, his body felt more alive than ever.

It was time to perform the same manipulations on his back and buttocks. Only two masseurs needed to work on him then and they repeated their same performance. The relaxing warmth, the intoxicating fragrance, and the pampering touch made him drift off, his eyes barely registering two hunched old men carrying stacks of towels into the room before his lids finally closed in much needed slumber.

He jerked awake when he felt fingers massaging along the crack in his buttocks and exploring his thighs near his balls. He jumped and turned around. The two women before him giggled like little girls, quite unbecoming for the middle-aged Sabina and her more mature friend Balbilla.

"Vibia!" he scolded. "How did you get in here?" He looked around. The space was empty except for the three of them, the door to the chamber closed. The robes and towels of what he had thought were old towel-carriers were discarded on a bench along the wall.

"The Empress of Rome may do anything she wants," responded Balbilla. The transparency of the cloth covering her body left little to the imagination. Despite her years, her womanly form was beautiful and elegant.

Seeing her body reminded him of his own nakedness. His hand quickly covered his crotch.

"Now, now, young man, you shouldn't hide yourself," the older woman said, gently pressing her warm palm on his thigh. "You have a very fine body. You should really show it off."

"Yes, darling, like Lucius does sometimes," said Sabina biting her lower lip and drawing a finger down his chest.

Balbilla laughed. "My dear Vibia, I think Lucius exhibits himself entirely for your benefit."

Sabina blushed. She too was wearing a sheer dress, the fabric tenting at the excited nipples perched on her firm breasts. From the nudging against his hand on his crotch, he knew he was no longer flaccid.

"Zuester, love, we're here to give you some extra attention. You deserve to be treated well after all the hard work you've done for my husband. Balbilla has some special talents she would like to share with you."

"Yes, Zuester, it would be my pleasure," agreed Balbilla seductively. "You just need to lie on your back." Her hands skated along his slick thighs until her thumbs touched the hand covering his maleness. "Let us do all the work."

At that, Zuester was rock hard. Although slightly embarrassed, he did not want to say "no".

He lay back onto the couch, revealing his excitement to Sabina's overjoyed amusement.

"Bend your legs," instructed Balbilla while she helped him into position. "Good, now open them." She smoothed his inner thighs as he dropped his knees. He was utterly exposed.

Sabina kissed him on the lips. "Relax, love." Her fingers lightly touched his face. "Close your eyes." She placed a cool, damp folded towel over his eyes.

"Lift up," came further instruction from Balbilla, her hand insinuating itself between his body and the couch. When he lifted his buttocks she placed a small stack of towels under him. "Now down," she said, gently pressing on his hips. "That's better." She never once touched any part of him that could be considered indecent, but, oh, how he wanted her to.

Two hands rubbed his already slick torso, cupping his pectorals, then sliding down his sides to his abdomen where they stayed and drew slow curves and circles. *Vibia.* He knew her touch and she knew how to touch him.

Two more hands slid down his opened inner thighs, gently rubbing and kneading the tender flesh as they worked their way toward his hips. *Balbilla.* She knew what she was doing, and her expert touch was sensual and exciting.

This was a very different experience from the pounding and manipulation of the earlier masseurs. Zuester felt his body relax like it had when those men had worked on him, but his mind remained energized and alert. He would not sleep through this.

Balbilla poured warmed oil on the juncture where his left thigh met his hip, steering its course to under his testicles, where she massaged it in, alternating between light swooping strokes and gentle pressure. The warm oil flowed in an easy, unbroken stream as the fingers between his legs became bolder, circling his anus, but not quite touching the opening.

It was excruciatingly pleasurable and Zuester wanted more.

With penetrating warmth, the hands on his abdomen rested on his belly then teased the flesh skirting his genitals. He twitched his cock in invitation to touch, but to no avail.

A finger had broached the puckered orifice of his anus, pressing through the willing flesh as oil lubricated its entrance. Unwittingly, Zuester flexed the aperture, begging to be invaded. The finger slid in languidly, drawing in more lubrication. Zuester felt his muscles at first tighten in surprise, then welcome the sensual intrusion.

The finger continued to penetrate and move inside him, until—

"Oh!"

His chest contracted with a jolting exhale, his belly suffused with heat, his head swarmed with pleasure. It was a mini crisis: wonderfully delightful but somehow incomplete.

"Looks like I've found it," said Balbilla with a gentle laugh.

The exquisite sensations began again, driving him toward a peak, but stopping just short of culmination. Every muscle in his body tensed, struggling against the force preventing him from his climax, trying to achieve it in defiance of the outside control.

It was useless effort. His body was not his own. Every time he thought he would be taken over the edge, he rolled back down to the place he began.

"Vibia?" he pleaded, whining for her help. He needed relief. He reached for his prick.

"Shh, shh." Her hot breath fanned on his cheek as she pulled his hands away from his own stimulation. "Let go, my love. We'll take you there." She gently guided his arms and hands to his sides, stroking and patting them into place.

New sensations circled his anus, teasing the swollen, sensitive rim with the promise of a larger invasion. Zuester groaned as the wave crested but did not crash inside him.

His body jerked when he felt a warm wet towel on his cock. He knew he was hard, but didn't know how much until that moment. Sabina was tenderly cleaning his shaft, which could only mean one thing…

When she drew his prick into her hot, moist mouth he exhaled heartily, as if he had been holding his breath for days. He rocked his hips to her rhythm in wanton approval.

But this was not like any oral stimulation he had ever had. Sensations swelled and flowed, taking him to the brink, then bringing him back down. He had never wanted to come so badly. And yet, he never wanted the agonizing ecstasy to end.

"You want to come, don't you?" Balbilla taunted.

"Yes, yes, please," Zuester groaned.

"All right then, it's time now. Come on," she coaxed drolly.

His body sensed it was time, simultaneously tensing and relaxing, forcing the peak to arrive while all along climbing to the apex of its own accord. Heat flushed his skin, his lungs sucked in air, his fingers and toes tingled with expectation. Energy balled up in his belly, every sensation focused on the mouth on his cock and the new pleasure within.

And then he exploded, his body freeing itself from the smothering control of another. He screamed, he laughed, he flailed in delicious abandon. And then he calmed, lying on the table panting, exhausted.

Sabina took off the damp towel on his eyes and kissed his lips. She tasted salty and sour. His taste.

"Gods of Olympus, that was wonderful," he murmured. He looked up at the sensual, mature woman still between his legs. "Thank you."

Balbilla smiled. "I will make sure Vibia knows how to take you on the same journey."

Sabina helped him sit up. "But first, tomorrow we will take you to hear Memnon sing. I cannot guarantee it will be as exciting as this, but you will enjoy it."

Egypt, Thebes, 20 November 130

It had been a very bad omen. Memnon had not sung for the emperor yesterday. "He has something very important to tell you, husband," Sabina had consoled. "He wanted to be certain that you paid attention when he did speak. That's what Balbilla said and you should believe her." On the return journey, Hadrian had sat dumbfounded in the carriage alongside his wife, holding her hand. When she had given him a squeeze he had tried to look cheerful. She knew he was sorely disappointed. "Tomorrow, Graeculus. We'll try again tomorrow," she had said.

Later that day, he had consulted the local priests at Thebes who had said the very same thing. Either both were right or both were obsequious sycophants. It didn't matter really. He would go to the damned statue that morning and wait for it to sing.

Sabina had left almost an hour ago. He knew because she had slept with him that night. Zuester hadn't seemed to mind. The Dacian had been spending a lot of time with Lucius of late. Of course, when Sabina herself wasn't enjoying the senator's talents in bed.

The emperor sat alone in his carriage, watching the hazy darkness that hung over the landscape just before dawn. He perked up when he saw them, the two gigantic statues of seated men, temple guards, probably, or possibly two pharaohs, rather than the Ethiopian king Memnon with an unknown twin. They faced the Nile river, and sat on the edge where the fertile plain met the desert.

The carriage pulled up behind the colossi and Sabina came running up to greet him, Balbilla close behind. Zuester held back briefly with Lucius and his entourage before joining the emperor. The senator smiled and waved.

"You are just in time, Graeculus," said Sabina gleefully. "The sun is about to warm the stone. Come, Julia Balbilla will recite a prayer-poem so the king will speak to you."

His wife's enthusiasm was infectious. Perhaps today the king would speak with him, king to king. They walked between the two statues, Hadrian's height only reaching to the top of the stone platform on which each colossus was positioned. Sabina held her breath and her husband's hand as Balbilla exhorted the statue to sing to *Hadrianus Augustus.*

As the sun rose in the east it shone its light onto the faces of the two colossi. Hadrian looked up at the north statue, his features exaggerated in the long rays. Then, as if the statue wanted to acknowledge the presence of the emperor and keep him there, a quiet high-pitched sound was heard. Sabina held on to Hadrian's arm in excitement.

"He speaks, husband. He speaks to you."

Hadrian glanced over at Zuester who was just as amazed as he himself was. Zuester caught his eye, and understood what his master wanted.

"Vibia, Balbilla, let us leave the emperor alone with his counterpart. They should have a private conversation." Zuester gathered the women with him and they left the emperor alone between the two statues.

The second time the colossus sang, it was a clear tone, like from a bronze bell, long and sustained, then wavered in the breeze. Hadrian turned, looking to see if it was a trick coming from behind him. It was not. He was truly alone.

The third time the statue sang, Hadrian fell to his knees.

"Oh lord Memnon, Ethiopian king and Trojan hero, hear my greeting. You who were hoped to be Troy's savior know my sorrow, for my loss has become Egypt's saving."

"I am truly sorry, Graeculus."

Hadrian stood and swung around toward the voice behind him, his hand on his hilt. He dropped to his knees when he saw the glorious spirit of his beloved, his Antinous—

"My Kynegiskos!" he said hoarsely.

"Don't," said the youth, overcome with affection. "Do not fall to your knees before me. I am but a memory, you are a god." He futilely offered his non-corporeal hand for the emperor to stand. Hadrian tried to grasp the ghostly fingers, tears streaming down his face when he realized it was not meant to be.

"I failed you, my love. I should have been there with you, to watch over you, to guard you from harm's way."

"You cannot change what has already happened, Graeculus, no matter what you think or say or wish." The ghostly figure of the youth began to pace but no dust kicked up in its path. "It is I who has regrets, regrets that I cannot grow old in your arms, regrets that I cannot stand by your side, opposite the lady Sabina—"

"You knew?"

"I know now. I know everything now." Antinous grinned as he looked deep into his lover's eyes. "Your reticence to seduce me at first was endearing."

Hadrian chuckled and felt himself blush. "I regret I did not make my move earlier."

The ghost's smile became a melancholy countenance. "What is done is done, my love. You cannot change the past, but you can affect the future."

"How? You see all, what should I do?"

"Proclaim our love, Graeculus. Proclaim our love as everlasting, transcending the short lives we have on this earth, transcending the borders of Rome. Encourage the understanding of our love. I died because I loved you. I would die for you again and again. I will never cease loving you, my Graeculus."

"And I will love you forever, my Kynegiskos." Hadrian's voice choked with emotion.

Antinous held out his hands and Hadrian his, both men wishing the touch were physical.

Then slowly, before the emperor's eyes, the ghostly body of his one true love Antinous faded, his youthful form replace by a bright light, which receded into the distance. Hadrian stood alone, tears in his eyes, his heart held in the balance with sorrow and joy.

Shouts from beyond the statues shattered the emperor's reverie.

"Look, a star!" a servant exclaimed running to get a better view.

"It just appeared!" called out another.

Hadrian walked out from between the colossi to join the commotion. Sabina took his arm.

"You've been crying," she said with alarm. "What did the statue say to you, Graeculus?"

"It was not Memnon who spoke. It was Antinous, my Kynegiskos. I saw him."

"Antinous came to you?" Sabina whispered incredulously.

They stopped and looked up at the star which had just appeared in the early morning sky. Hadrian felt the muscles of his heart clench but it was not accompanied by the usual shortness of breath. Instead he was filled with the inspiration to turn his love's words into action.

"It is he," he said to his wife. "He has become a beacon proclaiming our love for all the world to see."

Athens, Imperial villa, end of October 131

Zuester read back the proclamation to the Senate and People of Rome as dictated by Hadrian:

"The city of Antinoopolis, located on the east bank of the Nile opposite Hermopolis Magna, will be subdivided into ten phylai, or political districts, and each phylae will further be divided into five demoi, or neighborhoods. As is traditional in Greek cities, the phylai represent kinship or familial groups. In Antinoopolis this will be no different; the ten phylai will represent the heritage of the youth Antinous, the favorite and beloved of the emperor Hadrian, a young man the emperor held in great regard, like he would any member of his family. In his city the phylai will be named for Nerva, the adoptive father of Trajan; Trajan the adoptive father of Hadrian; Hadrian, the god-emperor and friend to the youth Antinous; Aelius, the family name of the emperor Hadrian; Paulina, the beloved and mourned sister of the emperor Hadrian; Sabina, the steadfast and faithful wife of the emperor Hadrian; Matidia, the beloved mother-in-law of the emperor Hadrian; Athens, the city where the Eleusinian initiation begins; Sebasteios, the Greek word for Augustus, which befits the emperor Hadrian; and Osirios-Antinous, the epithet of the youth become god."

Zuester stopped and looked up. "Shall I read the part about the *demoi*?"

"No, no. I trust that it is quite satisfactory." Hadrian grunted. "I hope my detractors notice my memorialization of Paulina. Especially Servianus and his whiny brat of a grandson, Fuscus."

"I've heard complaints that you've not founded a cult in her name and instead have given that honor to your – forgive me, Graeculus – *paidika*."

Hadrian glanced up from the papers on his desk and raised an eyebrow. "I don't fucking care what people say about my relationship to my Kynegiskos. That is none of their business. Besides, his cult is enjoying huge success, is it not?"

"Yes, my lord." Zuester could never stop calling his superior by the honorific. "We have already established centers in Bithynion, Tarsos, Eleusis, Mantineia, Argos, and Corinth. Plus, we've just established the Antinoeia games in Athens. And that does not even take into account the numerous spontaneous shrines and temples along the Nile in Egypt."

"No, no, it does not." Hadrian stared pensively into space. "Read the other proclamation, the one that states our efforts in Egypt were not in vain."

"Yes, Caesar," responded Zuester. He shuffled through the scrolls before him until he found what he was looking for.

"Osiris, the god of the river Nile, the life-blood of the Egyptian people, graciously accepted the sacrifice of the beauteous youth Antinous, beloved of the Roman emperor Hadrian. After two years of drought, the inundation of the fertile plain was almost higher than any year before, and its rise has caused the blossoming and cultivation of abundant and flourishing crops. Because of the sacrifice, the lives of the people along the river have once again been restored."

"Yes," said Hadrian thoughtfully. "My beloved died so that others might live. He shall be remembered for this sacrifice always."

PART FOUR:
TEMPUS HIBERNUM

Rome, Quirinalis Collis, May 132

His grandmother had just been insulted by what the emperor thought was an honor. A district named for her in the city of his boy-lover, his *paidika*? How was this supposed to be honorable in the slightest? Aelia Domitia Paulina deserved the titles Diva and Augusta, deserved to be revered by the Romans as a goddess with new temples and gladiator games, not to be under the shitting ass in the latrine of the emperor's fuck-boy.

Fuscus shook the cup with the dice and said a quick prayer before rolling.

"One should not gamble while one is upset, young man," came a sonorous whisper in his right ear.

The boy had lost, and he had lost big. That was what had made him so vulnerable.

Bestia was completely aware of who the boy was. Pedanius Fuscus was the grandson of the consul Julius Servianus and none other than the emperor Hadrian's grand-nephew. By default the lad was also the emperor's closest male relative and presumed successor.

Except he was not acting like a successor should. He was sulking and drunk. Plus he had willingly taken a ride in a stranger's carriage to an unknown location.

Stupid git.

And, as he was clearly not among the emperor's inner circle of *amici*, he was utterly unaware of who Sextus Quintilius Bestia was. That made things so much easier, especially given the merchant's unique appearance.

It had been difficult to establish himself back in Rome, but Rome was where Bestia needed to be, where he thrived, where he lived, and where he loved to live. No other backwater in the far too extensive empire would do, and he had been in every damned last one. Rome was *it*.

Unfortunately, in order for him to be there, he had to assume an identity and change his appearance. The identity was not difficult. Only so many praenomen to choose from; mix it up with a "rare" nomen and cognomen, and one had what one was looking for. And thus, Numerius Calvius Africanus – "Calvius" for short – had been born.

The appearance had been difficult. The scar that marred his face could not be hidden without effort; nor could the particular color of his eyes. He had lost quite a bit of weight on the run, and he was determined to maintain that shape. Only his hair and beard could easily be changed, and thus, some witch with henna had created a freak of nature.

Or so he thought every time he looked in the mirror. The red simply did not become his complexion. He reminded himself that this is what Calvius, the chief servant of the reclusive man who recently purchased the extensive villa on the Quirinal Hill, looked like.

And Fuscus had fallen for every bit of it.

It was dark when they arrived at the villa, Bestia thanked the gods for that. Fuscus had no time to look around before he was drawn into the labyrinthine assemblage of rooms, atriums, and corridors, to the private theater, where he would be treated to exotic exhibitions. The master of the house, Calvius had told the heir-apparent, loved to show off the talents of his slaves to his new friends. It started every new relationship off on a good foot, so to speak.

"Wine?" Bestia offered his guest. "We make a honeyed variety on our estates." He called his wine-bearer.

Fuscus stared as two utterly nude and spectacularly beautiful girls appeared before him. One offered him a golden cup, the other poured the sweet liquor. Bestia had to remind the gaping boy to drink.

"If you would like, they may be your companions on the couch," tempted Bestia.

Fuscus brightened at that. "Really?"

The girls took their place on either side of the youth, each placing a delicate hand on his thighs. Fuscus sighed.

Bestia laughed. "Before the show for which this villa is well-known, I would like to offer another exhibition." The merchant wanted to get some information from the boy. He had learned about the lad's predilection for astrology, of course what member of the imperial family did not put stock in such augury? Bestia found that a very good astrologer could definitely offer useful insights into one's future; however, for himself, he believed there were multiple paths toward a predetermined event in one's future and, with sufficient enterprise and money, one could control the outcome. The alignment of the stars often meant several futures were possible. One just needed to choose the right one.

Wine cup in one hand, the other draped on a girl's shoulder, Fuscus sat against the silk pillows on the couch in the small theater looking like he belonged there. "So what do you have to show me, Calvius?" he asked, impatience edging his voice.

Bestia snapped his fingers and a cowering slave appeared. "The astrologer," he directed.

"An astrologer?" the boy complained as he watched the slave leave. "I have my own, thank you very much. I don't need yours."

"Oh, but you do. You have a Roman astrologer, correct?"

"Yes. The best."

"No, no, my new friend. The best astrologers are from the east, the magi who follow Zoroaster. You will see."

Fuscus was unimpressed and went back to brooding in his wine cup and playing with the girls' breasts. A soft rustling made him look up. His jaw dropped.

The magus, a giant of a man dressed in robes of blood red and deep indigo silk brocaded and dotted with jewels with a matching tall cylindrical hat, stood before him. His long beard and elegant curls were streaked with silver hinting at his vast experience. He had with him a small entourage, similarly dressed. It was as if the group had simply appeared from the air as they had barely made a sound when they came in.

"Good evening, magus," greeted Bestia. "This is Pedanius Fuscus. He is a member of the royal household and is skeptical of your abilities." He stepped back into the darkness.

The magus laughed, a deep, bass laugh. "Well, we will have to prove you wrong, young man," he said in a booming voice. He waved his hands about and said a few words in a guttural tongue. His entourage snapped into action.

A square folding table was set out and a large, backless folding chair set behind it, opposite Fuscus's couch. Next to the chair was placed a lectern and a low table onto which were placed, respectively, a bound scroll and a pen-and-ink set. A richly-dressed servant unrolled a blank chart onto the taller table, while other servants moved into place to hold the large sheet of papyrus down. When the busying about of the servants had calmed and all seemed to be in place, the magus sat on the folding chair, his robes elegantly draped behind him.

He leaned in and looked at Fuscus with kohl-rimmed eyes. "What is the date of your birth, young sire?"

"On the eighth day before the ides of Aprilis, in the year of the consuls Publilius Celsus and Clodius Crispinus. The noble Trajan was emperor," he added with a touch of defiance.

"Very good." The magus turned to the scroll at the lectern and unwrapped and unrolled it. As he searched through the tables and charts, he made notations on the large chart on the table. He looked up at Fuscus. "You are nineteen, then? And of senatorial rank."

Alarm briefly flitted across his face before Fuscus tamped it down. "You can tell that from the scroll?"

"Yes and from knowing a little about your ways, such as your clothing, my son." The magus snapped his fingers and a servant appeared with a small sueded bundle in his hand, then unrolled it before his master, revealing sets of dice sitting amidst the fur lining. The magus looked at the sets of dice, looked up at Fuscus, then chose three twelve-sided pairs each in a different color.

He began rolling each pair in succession, first the black, then the red, then the green, after each roll consulting the scroll on the lectern. After a few rounds of this he stared at Fuscus, examining his face.

"You have lost someone close. You are very upset about this."

"Yes, I—"

"Let me see your hands." The magus indicated that Fuscus should hold his hands on the table.

Fuscus handed his cup to a girl then did as told reluctantly.

The magus took each hand in one of his and closed his eyes. "You've lost both your mother and grandmother. Your grandmother feels dishonor has come to the family." He opened his eyes and stared at the boy again, releasing his hands.

"I—"

The magus ignored Fuscus with a wave and went back to the scroll and chart and dice. Finally, he stopped and looked at the chart before him, inspecting it, and nodding his head.

"You are very strong with imperial ties, perhaps to ascend the throne yourself one day. There are some impediments to this future, however—"

"Impediments?"

The magus was not pleased to have been interrupted. "Yes. You have blood ties and are meant for the throne. But there is another without this tie, someone young, or perhaps merely youthful. Someone who has been in the good graces of the emperor all his life, and loved greatly by the emperor. Someone who had a special relationship with the emperor when he was a boy."

"Lucius," Fuscus grumbled.

"Ah, so you know this person, this Lucius."

"Yes. He is one of the emperor's fuck-boys, or was, at least."

The magus raised an eyebrow at the crude phrase. "I also see an untimely death where the throne is concerned."

Fuscus's eyes widened. "Lucius?"

"Perhaps, if you so choose to fulfill that prophecy."

"I can choose my future?" Fuscus had gone back to drinking his wine and pawing at the girls.

The magus chuckled in his deep tone. "Yes, my son. The stars give us many paths to one destination, and sometimes many outcomes from one path. To fulfill your destination correctly, you must choose wisely."

"What does it say about my life?" he asked excitedly. "How long will I live?"

The magus studied the chart. "You have a grandfather, yes? Very old?"

"Yes, my grandfather is eighty-five."

"I see that you and your grandfather will share the same years."

"So, I will live as long as he does?" He was impatient.

"Yes," responded the magus.

Fuscus sat back and swallowed more wine. "When am I to inherit the throne?"

The magus examined the chart once more. "I see an emptiness where the throne is concerned in five years."

The lad was quite animated at that revelation. "You mean that's when Hadrian will die?"

"He will die at that time, yes."

Fuscus let loose a maniacal howl.

The magus glanced at Bestia, then turned back to the boy. "I see you do not like your emperor."

Fuscus scowled at the astrologer. "He never held a funeral for his own sister, my grandmother, and yet he made his damned fuck-boy a god – with his own cult!" His voice grew louder, more emotional, with every word he spoke. "He's never shown me, his own relative, any favor, never took me under his wing. I'm his bloody heir! I deserve to be treated like the emperor I shall one day be!"

Bestia stepped forward. "Yes, Fuscus. You speak the truth." He placed a hand on the youth's shoulder. "Thank you, magus, for your wonderful insight. Perhaps you would like to interpret some of these signs to my scribe for the youth's later perusal?"

The magus nodded. "Yes, my lord, I will do so." He once again snapped his fingers and waved his hands. The entourage swiftly packed the tools and furniture and exited the theater.

Ignoring the activity around him, Fuscus preoccupied himself with fondling and kissing the girls on the couch.

Bestia knew it was time for the second part of the evening. "How about some entertainment, now that you can relax knowing your future is assured?"

"I can have more than the girls, Calvius?"

"Yes," Bestia chuckled. He knew he needed something exciting yet palatable to his guest. That generally meant no animals. Bestia had found, in the past, people were a little put off by sexual congress shared by animals and people. As Bestia himself loved such displays, he was really not sure why his guests did not. So, he had long ago decided the best approach was a menu from which his guests could choose. He snapped for a servant.

A nude boy appeared with a list of exhibits.

Bestia held out the menu to Fuscus. "And what would you like to see tonight?" he asked solicitously.

Fuscus gaped at the choices, grunting and laughing. "Ordinarily the girl with the dog. That sounds spectacular." His slurred speech revealed his growing drunken state. "But tonight, I would like this one." He pointed to an item.

Bestia was more than happy to comply with the request.

"Except I want it to be a bearded man – an old bearded man – and I want him to be restrained quite uncomfortably."

Bestia grinned with understanding then whispered instructions to the nude boy.

"I will leave you to your enjoyment, my friend," Bestia said. "The girls are at your disposal."

Fuscus beamed at his host. "Thank you, Calvius." He quickly glanced at the girls. "Anything?" he asked the merchant.

"Anything," was the answer.

Bestia slid into the shadows to observe the lad unnoticed.

Of course, like any young man, Fuscus ordered one girl to suck his cock. The other he kissed while fingering her eager cunt.

The lighting in the stage pit focused on a man strung up in a swing contraption, his legs spread open, his limbs restrained. He was middle-aged, brawny, and bearded – the slave who most closely resembled the emperor Hadrian that Bestia could think of on such short notice.

Fuscus held the girl's head to his crotch as he gazed with expectation at the stage. A dozen naked youths, none older than his own age of nineteen, streamed in, each one in spectacular form, each one magnificently erect. They circled the old man and pumped their cocks.

"Yes," Fuscus hissed.

One youth shoved his cock in the old man's mouth, holding him harshly by his curly hair, and slamming his hips against his jaw. The others continued their rhythmic pumping.

"Suck my cock, ass-fucker!" Fuscus inelegantly pressed the girl's head into his crotch. Bestia heard choking sounds emanating from her tender throat.

In the pit, another youth covered his fist in pig fat, and without warning, jammed it into the anus of the man in the swing.

The old man screamed in pain against the cock in his mouth.

Fuscus laughed.

The other youths continued their rhythmic pumping.

The youth between the old man's legs pulled his fist out, wiped the fat on the old man's stomach, then rammed his cock in the well-lubricated anus. He slammed against the man's ass, driving himself to climax.

The other youths continued pumping their cocks, their muscles tensing, their expressions slackening.

Fuscus licked his lips. He had removed his hand from the girl's head and instead was rocking his hips against her face. "Yes...do it..." he growled.

Two at once, then three, then eight, then ten cocks came, jetting their hot ejaculate onto the old man in the swing, most aiming for his face. The youth with his cock in the man's mouth pulled out only slightly, covering the man's beard with his milky fluid.

Fuscus howled with glee, hitting the couch with a fist. He stared at the pit, rage glinting in his eyes.

The youth in the man's ass stifled a cry then abruptly pulled his cock out. At that, the youth at the man's mouth swung the man around half-way. Now placed at the man's head, the youth shoved his fat and feces-covered prick into the old man's mouth. He grunted his climax holding the old man's head in place as he emptied himself into the man's throat.

Fuscus tore the girl off his crotch, then leapt up, his face twisted with rage, and ran into the pit.

Bestia started, then held back.

"You ass-fucker! May the Hounds of Hell rip you to shreds!" Fuscus screamed.

The youths in the pit stepped back, stunned.

The man in the swing struggled, unsure what to expect. Fuscus slammed his cock in the man's anus.

"Ass-fucker! Ass-fucker!" the boy shrieked as he rammed himself into the man, gripping his thighs cruelly. "How does it feel to get fucked by one of your own?!"

Bestia motioned to one of his servants. The boy was crazed and he did not want to lose one of his best and most seasoned performers. He watched the pit nervously.

Fuscus drove relentlessly into the man's ass, snarling expletives. At the brink of climax, Fuscus grabbed a dagger hidden in his boot. As he came, he held the dagger above the heart of the shocked man in the swing.

"Die imperial fucker!"

Bestia's servant was just in time.

On his mark, the dozen youths grappled Fuscus to the ground as the servant grabbed the knife. Fuscus groaned then crumpled in an exhausted heap.

Bestia knew he could have had Fuscus arrested for attempting to murder one of his slaves, but he wouldn't. The boy was far too useful to him free and alive. The brat would have no problem getting himself killed down the line, anyway. The merchant had his guards take the boy away. They would drop him somewhere on the Palatine Hill where Bestia had other agents to escort the drunken lad to the imperial residence.

After the incident, his slaves calmed and back in their cells, Bestia sat with Sanabares – the magus from earlier that evening – reviewing the lad's chart.

"Is Lucius the rival Fuscus thinks he is?"

"No. There is another, someone much younger. A boy. A child not more than ten, I believe. I will admit I sincerely do not know how he will fit into the imperial succession. And I see signs indicating 'truthfulness' or 'trustworthiness'."

Bestia racked his brain. The only imperial child he could think of was Marcus Annius Verus. His lips curled when he remembered Marcus's nickname was "Verissimus" – "most truthful".

"And," continued Sanabares, "the sister of Hadrian, Paulina, seems to have resigned herself to not being deified. Something about a poor choice of husband had consigned her to the ranks of undignified mortals." He eyed Bestia. "So her soul conveyed to me."

Bestia glanced at the chart and the scribe's notes one last time before ordering a servant to roll it up and send it to Fuscus at the imperial palace.

"Thank you, Sanabares, my friend," the merchant said as he handed the astrologer a pouch filled with gold. "You have been quite convincing and helpful in setting my plans into motion."

"At your service, my lord Bestia, or should I say Calvius?" the magus responded, bowing. He turned to leave, but stopped. "The princess Roedogune awaits her chair, my lord," he said. He smiled and bowed once again, then left.

Bestia had almost quite forgotten his promise to the Parthian court.

Tibur, Hadrian's villa, July 136

Sabina had instructed the two *ostiarii* guarding the entryway to direct the expected visitor to her garden first, and she would personally escort him to the emperor herself. She waited nervously, pacing, her heart thumping a little too loudly in her head.

And when she saw him approach, she knew she blushed.

"Lucius!"

He grinned ear-to-ear at seeing her flustered like a schoolgirl. "My lady," he said taking her hands. "So good to see you."

"It's been a long time."

"It has."

"You look well," she said trying to keep her voice under control. He looked the same, of course: handsome, fashionable, exuding his usual natural charm and sensuality. The thrill of his touch sent shivers through her. They had not been alone since their return to Rome a few years ago, after a very exciting affair in the East.

"As do you, my lady."

She could stand it no longer. "Kiss me, Lucius," she commanded with a pout.

"With pleasure."

He pulled her to him, wrapping his arms around her waist, his fingers skirting the top of her buttocks. He dipped his head to her neck and shoulder, breathing in her perfume. Sabina clung to his strong shoulders for dear life, feeling heat build in her belly and pulse wantonly between her legs. When the tip of his tongue brushed under her ear, she let out a little whimper. His lips fluttered, whispering lewd orisons, as they traveled along her cheek and jaw. He pulled her closer, pressing his hard body to melt into her soft curves, his hands coursing possessively down the cleft of her bottom.

And then his mouth covered hers, their tongues tangling in mutual ravenous need. He tasted, delved more deeply, trying desperately to satisfy a desire that had burned within him for far too long. She slackened in his arms, willing him to take control, letting him explore her with lustful fingers and libidinous tongue.

When he had had his fill, Lucius pulled back, unslaked hunger still flickering in his eyes.

"How long are you here for?" she panted.

"A few days."

"Your wife?"

"No. I'm alone."

"Pity," she said, smoothing his shoulders. "I like Plautia."

"Wicked woman," he scolded.

They both knew they were expected by the emperor and that they would have to continue their reunion another time.

"Come," she said. "My husband is waiting for you."

Sabina took his arm and they walked along colonnaded breezeways, chatting mostly about court gossip and current events. At the door to the imperial office, the empress nodded a greeting to the guardsman who let them in.

Hadrian sat at one end of a long table, Zuester and a young secretarial attendant along the side, papers and ink, wax tablets and styli positioned before them.

Sabina watched the color drain from Lucius's face the moment he saw the emperor. The younger man had been warned, but, she found, no warning could prepare one for the reality.

Hadrian was ill, an illness that had ravaged his body, rendering him gaunt and frail. He still kept up appearances with curled hair and trimmed beard, but had decided against dye, leaving him totally gray. He looked far older than his sixty years.

"Graeculus!" Lucius ran to the emperor and fell to his knees.

Sabina motioned for the door to be closed and guarded, and took her seat behind Zuester.

Hadrian patted Lucius's head tenderly. "Get up, fool," he admonished with a smirk.

Lucius stood, tears wetting his lashes, and took a deep breath. He glanced around dumbly for a chair, found one behind him, and sat.

"Lucius, before you ask, the doctors are doing everything they possibly can." Hadrian's breathing was labored. "But I am obviously dying. And you are here for a reason." He turned to his secretary. "Zuester?"

The Dacian glanced up. "Hello Lucius, good to see you." Sabina caught a twinkle in his eye for his fascinating rival.

"Yes, it is, old friend," responded the senator.

Zuester turned his attention to a document in front of him. "I have before me the terms of succession. You have been chosen Hadrian's heir, but with certain conditions."

"Yes, of course. I understand completely."

Sabina noticed Lucius did not exhibit surprise at the announcement. From his experience in the Senate, he was trained to be polite and professional when needed. And he must have realized that this moment was one of those times.

"You have been chosen *consul ordinarius* for this year and have served as expected in that office," Zuester continued, summarizing the declaration. "You have also fulfilled the emperor's wish that your daughter, Ceionia Fabia, be betrothed to Marcus Annius Verus. These accomplishments are testaments of your loyalty to the emperor. Now you have been chosen heir and will be formally adopted by the emperor as Lucius Aelius Caesar—" Zuester pointed to a sheaf of documents "—but you must agree to further conditions.

"First, you must serve in the army—"

Sabina watched Lucius as he heard this news. He showed no reaction. *Good boy*, she thought.

"—at Carnuntum on the Danube as governor of Pannonia Inferior and Pannonia Superior. The term of this service will be for at least one year. Second, when you return from your military service, you will deliver a speech to the Senate detailing the remaining terms of the succession. These are that you will adopt Marcus Annius Verus as your heir and successor alongside your own son Lucius Ceionius Commodus."

Lucius continued to sit stoically, waiting for the rest.

Zuester looked at him. "'These are the terms of the agreement'," he recited.

Sabina observed Lucius exhale imperceptibly.

Hadrian broke the silence. "I want a man of peace, not one with an extensive military career. But to appease the army, I need you to experience field life."

"Yes, Caesar."

"I don't want familial jealousy. Marcus will rule jointly with your Commodus. There is some precedence for this. Both boys are far too young to be even considered now. They will have age and experience when your time has expired."

Hadrian's tone was conversational. It appeared the formalities had ceased.

"I may live to be ninety, Graeculus," said Lucius. "Like your brother-in-law, Servianus."

Hadrian grunted. "I doubt it. Your penchant for wild parties and other excesses points to a well-lived but short life. Besides, I've consulted your horoscope. You'll not have Servianus's years."

Lucius appeared shocked, but only for a moment. "Why Marcus?" he asked quietly.

"He's honest, intelligent, honorable. Your Commodus is only five, Lucius. I don't want to exclude him, but I don't know anything about him." Hadrian took a moment to catch his breath. "Really what I am trying to do here is prevent Fuscus from claiming any right whatsoever. And Servianus. The gods know that conniving scoundrel is unfit to rule as well."

"If anyone is unfit to rule, Graeculus, you know it is me," responded Lucius.

"Yes, well, we've had libertines before. The army usually kills them," remarked Hadrian with a grin. "That is why I want you in their good graces. Plus, you have far better relations with the Senate than I ever could have had. An emperor needs to be able to work with the Senate."

"The Senate appreciates all you've done, Caesar," Lucius said genuinely. "You've secured all of our borders, there are no more wars to wage. Even the Jews have ceased revolting in Judaea."

"My policy of Panhellenism may not hold. You will have more revolts."

"I will have your able generals to advise me, my lord."

Hadrian's colorless eyes brightened. "I think we have our man, Zuester. Let's get these documents in order."

As the three men hammered out the details, Sabina contemplated her life with each one of them. She still shared Hadrian's bed, but only as a sleeping companion when he was not in pain. She loved him deeply, and after thirty-six years of marriage, still felt joy swell her heart at the thought of him.

Zuester, of course, steadfast and unjealous, remained her lover. He lived with her, having given up his own suite of rooms at both the palace in Rome and the villa in Tibur. She watched him writing furiously, supervising his attendant, and smiled with pride.

Lucius was a new toy, one she hadn't played with for a few years, but for whom her enthusiasm persisted. And now he was to be Caesar. She would still share the emperor's bed when Hadrian was gone, she realized. There would just be a different emperor in it.

* * * * *

Zuester lay alone on the over-sized dining couch in the mosaic-covered grotto at the end of the Canopus. Water softly cascaded down the sides of the vaulted shell, feeding into an elaborate system of canals encircling and flowing under the tiny island upon which the couch was placed, burbling out to the long pool that stood as a symbol of the Nile river. Zuester's torch and oil lamp had long gone out; he amused himself by staring up at the stars, or down along the edges of the pool at the nude statues of heroes and gods bathed in moonlight.

He heard footsteps to his left but did not turn. He had expected him.

"He re-dedicated this to Antinous, you know," said Zuester. "It's just one of the many places devoted to his memory."

"Yes. A lovely memorial befitting a beautiful boy," said Lucius behind him.

"Come, sit." Zuester patted the space next to him.

Lucius slipped his torch in a stand and lay down next to his friend, looking up at the dazzling summer night sky. "How is the empress?" he asked.

Zuester smiled thinking about her sensual, sleeping form. "She was tired so she went to bed early."

"Your bed?" Lucius moved closer.

"Hers, really, I suppose. But, yes, our bed." Zuester glanced at his friend in the dark. "Don't worry. She'll be in your bed soon enough."

Lucius chuckled. "You are lucky to be with the woman you love. My wife and I are agreeable to each other, but certainly not in love. It is the unfortunate consequence of most political marriages."

Zuester shifted a little toward Lucius. "What were the politics behind your union?"

"My wife's father, Avidius Nigrinus, was once in service to Trajan," sighed Lucius, bored by the topic. "Rumor has it that he tried to assassinate Hadrian upon his assumption of the throne. For that Hadrian supposedly had him killed. The truth is that Hadrian did not want to kill my father-in-law, but his agents acted on their own accord. My marriage to the daughter of Graeculus's purported enemy is meant to bring Avidius Nigrinus back into the good graces of the imperial family."

"Ah," remarked Zuester. "Complicated, isn't it?"

Lucius chuckled. "Marriage is, sometimes." He moved closer.

"So, Pannonia…have you ever been?"

"Gods of Olympus, no! Not very glamorous or exotic." Lucius turned to Zuester. "Oh, sorry. You're from there or something, right?"

"Or something," Zuester laughed. "I'm from Dacia. That's a little to the east of where you're going."

Lucius shifted again until the two men were almost touching. "What's it like?"

Zuester felt a thrill at his friend's closeness. "When are you leaving?"

"This fall."

"Not the best time of year to go. It will be cold soon enough. The snow in winter will be beautiful."

"I've never seen snow up close before."

Zuester laughed. "I will admit it is much more enjoyable when one is a mischievous boy. The cold and wet can just be annoying for adults."

There was a brief silence.

"Zuester," Lucius began tentatively. "I'm scared." He reached for the Dacian's hand.

A flush of anticipation coursed through Zuester at the senator's touch. "Don't be. You'll have experienced people all around you."

"Not about Pannonia in the winter."

"Oh."

Lucius took a deep breath. "I've never been around military men, I'm certain I won't fit in, or worse, will do something stupid." He pressed his body against Zuester's. "I'm not really sure I'm up to the task of being emperor, even. Sometimes I feel weak."

Zuester put his arm around his friend and pulled him close, breathing in his exotic, arousing scent.

"My Stefanus, my parasol carrier in Egypt, died recently. I sometimes fear I have whatever disease killed him. I pray to my family gods every day to protect me."

"Do you feel sick?"

"No, and the doctors find nothing wrong with me. I'm really just afraid." Lucius looked at the stars trying to calm his anguish. "I guess I want them to find something," he confided. "Zuester, it's not me he wants. He wants his little Marcus, his Verissimus, to rule. But he is far too young."

"I know," Zuester sighed. "I've been working with him on the succession documents for weeks." He caressed Lucius's shoulder. "He has confidence in you, too. He would not have chosen you if he did not."

"I suppose." Lucius wrapped his arm around Zuester's waist and hugged him. "Zusc," he finally asked, "How did you come to leave Dacia?"

"I was sold into slavery during the wars and brought to Rome."

"Oh," said Lucius after a brief silence. "I had never thought about that."

"About what?"

"We just assume slaves are war booty, barbarians with little intelligence. Certainly not people like you."

"Thank you, Lucius. I think." Zuester laughed.

"So how did you end up with this lot?" Lucius asked, flicking his hand to indicate the sprawling villa.

"I escaped from my original master."

"That's criminal is it not? I could have you arrested." The senator snuggled deeper in the crook of the freedman's arm.

"I suppose, except my new master was one of your colleagues. A senator who made it look like he acquired me legitimately. After my manumission, the emperor Trajan requested I serve the imperial household."

"Why did you escape the first master?"

"I was made to do things I did not want to do."

"We're all made to do that, my friend," Lucius said bitterly.

"Yes, true. But if you refused Hadrian he would probably not have you whipped and killed."

"No," agreed Lucius soberly. "Did you see many of your friends die?"

"Yes, well, I mean, they just disappeared and we never saw them again, really. In that sort of environment it was difficult to form attachments."

"What did your master make you do that was so abhorrent?"

"The worst was sexual congress with animals in front of a drunk, screaming crowd under the threat of the lash."

Lucius drew back, completely appalled. "Oh, gods of Olympus! I'm so sorry, Zuester, I simply had no idea."

"When one is a slave one's body is not in one's own control."

Lucius sought and took Zuester's hand, squeezing it.

"The best one can do is keep one's wits about one," Zuester continued. "To be vigilant, to not give in to despair."

"To always have hope that things will change. Like Pandora's box."

"Yes, precisely."

"Thank you, my friend," sighed Lucius. "If you can endure such a horrific ordeal, then I may at the very least spend a winter in the northern provinces. At least I do know there is hope at the end."

Zuester looked down at the younger man pressed against his body, and brushed an errant blond curl from his forehead, his finger trailing along his cheek to the whiskers on his jaw. Lucius gazed up expectantly, licking his lips. Impulsively, Zuester bent forward and kissed his friend on the mouth.

The kiss was tender at first, a simple act of comforting a beleaguered companion. Soon, though, a craving long buried flickered inside Zuester and flare into need. From his companion's frantic pawing, he knew the passion to be mutual, both realizing their feelings for the other were so much more than friendship, so much more than innocent consolation. They tore at each other with lust and desire, until Lucius pushed himself from under Zuester to straddle him.

"Make love to me, Zuester," he panted lasciviously.

Zuester wanted nothing less. Still he tensed. "Lucius," he confessed hesitantly. "I've never been with a man, or a boy, well...*willingly.*"

"Never?" the senator asked incredulously.

"Never."

"Do you *want* to be with me?" It was obviously an effort for Lucius to calm his excited breaths.

"Oh yes," Zuester averred, sucking in his lower lip. "I do. Very much so."

"Top or bottom?" Lucius's eyes were wide with anticipation.

Zuester laughed. He threaded his fingers through the blond curls hovering over him. "Bottom."

Lucius beamed at that, then nibbled on his lip. "But you're older, it goes against convention."

"But you're to be emperor," Zuester countered. "I am a mere freedman."

"Not just any freedman. You're you."

Zuester grinned. He pulled his friend's face to his for a deep kiss. "Fuck me, Lucius."

The senator swallowed hard then looked around nervously for the oil lamp he thought he had seen when he arrived.

"Here." Zuester reached for it on his right and presented it to his seducer.

Lucius looked down bashfully. "I'm usually more confident than this. What are you doing to me?"

"I'm not doing anything, my lord."

"Don't call me that, freedman," Lucius teased.

Zuester chuckled and unwrapped Lucius's summer mantle, then worked on the golden girdle of his tunic. "I take it you've wanted this for a while?"

"Since our time in Egypt." Lucius helped with the linen wrapped around his groin. "You intrigue me."

"What about me intrigues you?" Zuester worked on his own underwear, pulling the cloth free.

"You're Vibia's, you're exotic—"

"Exotic?!"

"Dacian can be exotic."

Zuester was quite amused.

"You're a good friend to Graeculus, and I want to know you better," Lucius pulled off his tunic, his smooth, hairless athletic form mirroring the idealized sculptures lining the pool nearby. His eager cock bobbed between them.

Marveling at the perfection before him, Zuester stroked the lean muscles of his friend's abdomen, then drew his hands along the strong thighs. Lucius's hard body, in glorious shape at thirty-five, was that of a man, not a boy. Why the emperor desired boys when he could have this in his bed, mystified the Dacian.

"I want to see you too."

Zuester glanced up at his lover's hungry eyes. "Of course." He struggled with his tunic until Lucius helped him.

Now both nude, they took turns stroking and staring, Lucius playfully tugging on Zuester's chest hair, the Dacian marveling at his companion's hairless sac. They knew it was wrong, two adult men in sexual congress, but neither concerned himself with convention at that moment. They simply wanted to share mutual ecstasy.

Lucius grabbed his cock, his eyes directing Zuester's attention to the lubrication of the erect member, massaging the shaft up and down, taunting his lover.

Zuester reached for his own cock, but Lucius stilled his hand.

"No. Let me."

Zuester sunk into the cushions as the senator took him deep into his mouth, his skillful tongue bringing him to full hardness. He flinched ecstatically when he felt the back of his throat squeeze him. "Gods, oh, gods," he murmured.

As he sucked and licked, Lucius teasingly tickled the cleft of Zuester's butt before finding his intended target. Zuester clenched at the intimate invasion, then groaned and sighed as the deep sensual massage took him gently to the peak, suspended him there for a moment, then gently brought him back down.

Lucius lifted his head and smiled. "Now for something more." He carefully pulled his fingers out and displayed his eager prick.

Zuester licked his lips in anticipation and watched as Lucius slowly penetrated him, inch by deliberate inch. He used his breathing to relax against the pain, glancing up at Lucius to watch his face, marking every reaction.

"Is it good, Zuse?"

Zuester felt stuffed, stretched, delirious. "Take me," he murmured.

As he gently pushed in and out of the tight passage, Lucius grabbed Zuester's now languid cock, pulling and pumping it once more to excitation. He bent forward and kissed his friend's gaping mouth, thrusting his tongue inside in rhythm to his prick's motions below.

Zuester's hands and fingers danced frantically across Lucius's back, wanting to feel everything at once. Lucius's mouth moved down, nibbling and licking Zuester's neck, all the while still furiously pumping his slick cock.

"It's wonderful, is it not?" The senator's breath was hot against a nipple.

"Yes, oh gods, yes." Zuester's head lolled against the cushions.

Approaching his own peak, Lucius forgot all about delicacy and slammed into Zuester's arse, cruelly squeezing and pulling the cock between their bodies. Zuester gasped at the delicious violence, feeling his own climax surge forth, hover, then burst sparkling like the star-filled sky above them. He spurted warm jets onto his torso as Lucius milked him dry.

Lucius bent over his lover, sweating, panting. "You want me to stay inside you or come on your belly?"

"I want to feel you hot inside me."

With a clipped cry, Lucius thrust one last time, holding his body steady as his cock spasmed deep inside Zuester. He collapsed on top, breathless, his heart pounding against Zuester's chest. Zuester wrapped his arms tightly around him and kissed his hair.

"That was wonderful," he whispered.

"Zuse, you'll stay with me when I'm emperor, right?"

"I'll remain at court as long as you need me, Lucius."

Rome, Quirinalis Collis, October 136

"I'm his bloody grandnephew! What is that bloody ass-fucker thinking?!"

Servianus watched Fuscus pace in Calvius's audience hall, trying to make sense of the news that Lucius Ceionius Commodus – "another boy-fucker" – had just been chosen the emperor Hadrian's heir and successor.

In his eighty-nine years, Servianus had witnessed a great many machinations amongst the Roman aristocracy. The Flavians were the worst. All three had lived and ruled, but Domitian achieved the throne surrounded by rumors he had murdered his own brother Titus. Nerva had begun the now accepted custom of "adopting" heirs, men with no blood connection to the emperor. In the case of Trajan, Hadrian even, Servianus had to admit, the men were chosen for their deeds and service to the empire. Lucius Ceionius Commodus was an unremarkable senator whose only distinction was that he had once sucked Hadrian's cock.

Fuscus himself was of senatorial rank. He was young, true, but he lived in the imperial household, had been exposed to politics beyond what any other mere senator would ever have seen, even if that senator had once fucked the emperor. If Hadrian had felt a more experienced man should be appointed heir as a placeholder to Fuscus, then clearly Servianus would have been that man.

Servianus was suspicious of Calvius, the man Fuscus called "friend," a mere freedman steward, his odd appearance seemingly covering up secrets in plain sight. However, Calvius had information that surprised the old man with its depth and veracity. The steward could definitely be useful. And, as they had been promised a show of epic eroticism, he was at least willing to socialize with the man for the evening. Fuscus definitely needed to let off steam. The boy was angry, and well he should be. Hadrian had made a huge mistake.

And Hadrian would pay.

* * * * *

Bestia regarded the old man and his grandson. He did feel a certain privilege in the presence of Julius Ursus Servianus, a man so old he had lived through more than a dozen emperors and pretenders. Bestia chuckled to himself. Several of those rulers rose and fell in one year alone. That was how unstable the empire could be, and how unstable it could be made to be. Now that the merchant had two imperial guests, he was optimistic that future instability was at hand.

He had to be very careful in the entertainments for the evening. He did not want to induce rage in the boy Fuscus again, which meant no bloodletting, no exclusively male displays, and nothing that reminded the boy of Hadrian or Lucius. On the other hand, Bestia wanted to impress the old man. Servianus must have seen quite a bit in his time. However, the merchant reminded himself, while the former governor had lived under the deranged Nero, he had missed the debauched Tiberius entirely.

And Fuscus had mentioned he enjoyed displays with animals.

Bestia had arranged a pantomime of sorts, a story of a cuckold who discovers his wife with another man. He rarely did story-based entertainments as his sex slaves were horrible actors. However, most likely such a diversion would distract and engage the boy Fuscus enough that Bestia and Servianus could have a more useful conversation.

A nude pair walked onto the stage, the woman a lithe but well-endowed blond, the man well-muscled and dark. He pulled her to a bed, where she straddled him and they frantically copulated, smiling and laughing.

Bestia glanced at Fuscus. The boy was already entranced with the performance. However, it was difficult to glean emotional response from the craggy face of the old Roman, but he appeared to be amused, if only slightly, by the scene before him. He sipped his wine casually and adjusted his clothes a bit, then watched with perhaps feigned interest. Fuscus, however, had shamelessly grabbed the nearest servant and had pushed the nude girl to her knees to suck his cock.

"Not so fast!" the youth complained. The girl slowed to a languid pace.

A man with a body like a gladiator accompanied by several similarly built men, walked onto the stage. He reacted to the couple by forcibly pulling the woman off the dark-haired man. They argued – which involved the gladiator shoving his fingers up the woman's cunt as she struggled – while the gladiatorial gang grabbed her lover. One penetrated him violently from behind as another jerked his cock savagely. In an instant he came, his spent body tossed aside as the crew turned to the woman.

"Excellent show, Calvius," remarked Servianus as he watched briefly. He turned his attention to the merchant, unflinchingly holding his eyes. "My grandson says you are willing to support us in our efforts against the emperor. His choice of Commodus is disastrous."

"Have you voiced your objections to your brother-in-law?"

Servianus cackled his disagreement. "Hadrian has never sought my counsel and would never listen to unsolicited advice. He's an arrogant, pig-headed fool."

The woman on stage was being held down by the gang of gladiators, her legs spread wide as the leader brought out a mastiff. Fuscus let out a whoop of appreciation as the dog penetrated the woman amidst her screams.

"Well, it was a question that needed to be answered before we could continue," admitted Bestia. "What is your preferred strategy? Kill Lucius first then Hadrian? Or kill Hadrian then Lucius? With proper planning, it would not be impossible to commit both acts at the same time."

"You get to the point rather quickly, do you not?" A cool smirk flitted across the old man's face. "Do you have agents in Pannonia?"

"Yes, in both Superior and Inferior," responded the merchant proudly.

"Lucius will be heavily guarded, the emperor has made sure of that. Plus he will be surrounded by the army. Soldiers are known for picking their own emperors. If Lucius is successfully assassinated, we may be stuck with someone just as incompetent or even more so. We don't want to risk such an event."

Clearly the old man had thought this through. "So what is your proposal?"

The dog ejaculated a mess on the woman's thighs, which the woman's dark-haired lover was forced to lick up. Fuscus howled in laughter at the defilement. A gladiator carried the woman, weakened by her debasement, to the bed and tossed her on the mattress. One by one the gang members penetrated her in the ass, each pulling out as he came, spewing seed on her abused body.

"Wait until Lucius has returned from his governorship and is ensconced back in Rome. There will be a lull of imprudent carelessness after the seeming victory of his tenure. We will strike when their guard is down."

"You are willing to wait that long?"

"You mean do I have that long to wait?" the old governor laughed. "I am a man of many years, Calvius, but I am in vigorous health." He eyed his grandson. "Fuscus is restless, but he needs to learn patience and a bit more about politics before he can take power. We need that year for him, as well." Servianus glanced briefly at the disgraceful scene on the stage below before studying his gold wine cup. He looked Bestia straight in his eyes once again. "What's in it for you?" he asked with a crooked eyebrow.

"Uncertainty always yields higher prices for goods, especially luxury items. We have well-established connections in the east where such goods are best made."

"But Fuscus will immediately be placed on the throne. There will be no uncertainty or instability."

"The mere act of assassination causes instability," the merchant responded calmly. "A change of power always ushers in uncertainty. Some businesses thrive on instability and uncertainty."

"And when we have established our power beyond a shadow of a doubt?"

"Some affairs require the constancy of security," Bestia chuckled. "And some business," he said indicating the entertainment below, "will endure no matter what the political climate."

Tibur, Hadrian's villa, August 137

"With Lucius in Pannonia this summer, the Villa seems awfully quiet."

Sabina tugged at her summer frock, straightening and smoothing the fabric aimlessly as she lay at Zuester's side on the courtyard couch. Her cap sleeve dropped down to her arm and Zuester nipped playfully at her uncovered shoulder.

"It's not like you've ever spent much time with him here. Your memory of him has become overblown and embellished, I fear."

Sabina sighed. Her infatuation with the aristocrat had become more pronounced since he had been appointed heir. "I can't get enough of him," she pouted before she caught Zuester's teasing smile. "And you can't either, you cad."

Sabina goosed her lover at the waist hoping to subdue him with tickling. Instead, he fought back with pokes and pinches of his own and had her under him in moments, pinning her against the cushion. As always, she gave in too easily.

"It's a good thing I have you, then, isn't it? I can't get enough of you ever, Vibia."

Zuester kissed the empress, relaxing against her as she melted into the soft couch. Her hands played in his hair as she let his lips and tongue torment and arouse her.

"What do you expect he's doing right now?" she taunted her lover.

"Masturbating on a Pannonian hillside in the summer sun while dreaming of you."

"Or you. He likes you quite a bit."

Zuester nuzzled his nose in the crook of Sabina's neck. "Yes, I know. I'm spectacularly flattered. I like him quite a bit too."

"Well, then, what can we do to satisfy our mutual fantasy? I've my agate dildo in my room..."

"Hmm...." Zuester moaned as he kissed his empress's luscious mouth.

"We'll pretend you are in the middle...between the two of us..."

"I want to feel a real cock in my arse..."

"I'll blindfold you," offered Sabina.

"We'll both be blindfolded and think of him.'

"And then we'll write to him telling him…"

"He'll probably demand to be returned to Rome instantly."

Sabina giggled. She enjoyed that she and Zuester finally shared a lover.

The sound of sandals clicking against the tiled yard accompanied by clinking metal brought them back to reality.

"Ah, refreshment," said Sabina. "And right on time. I'll need nourishment for later." She poked Zuester's chest indicating he should get up, then reached for a deep red cherry from a bowl.

Zuester grabbed her hand to stop her. He looked up at the servants present. "Who prepared the food?"

"I did, my lord," said a middle-aged man.

"Ah, Eutyches. And you tasted the wine?"

"Of course, my lord."

"Very good." Zuester picked up a cherry and licked the skin. Tasting nothing unusual, he popped the fruit in his mouth and ate the rich, juicy flesh.

Sabina crossed her arms impatiently.

Zuester held up the clean pit and showed it to the empress. "Everything seems fine, my love." He turned to the servant. "Thank you Eutyches. As always your impeccable efforts are appreciated."

The servant bowed and motioned for the other slaves to take their places along the corridor.

Sabina held Zuester's eyes as she ate a cherry. "He's become distrustful of everything and everyone. I hate it."

"With all you've been through, the emperor has far too many reasons why he should protect you." Zuester poured wine in twin cups. "I, for one, applaud his efforts."

"It's not like he has to worry about Lucius wanting the throne earlier than expected."

Zuester tasted the wine in both their cups before handing one to Sabina. "The choice of Lucius was unpopular, Vibia. You know that. Hadrian is seen as not having had all his faculties when he made that decision."

"Yes, yes, I know. People don't know his grand plan yet. Once they do, they'll see their emperor as the astute leader he always was."

"Of course. And you, my love, know your food has always been tasted before you ate it, your rooms always searched before you inhabited them. It is what has always been done for the entire royal household."

"It's just so obvious now. A damnable reminder that our enemies are always present. I find it stressful." She snuggled against Zuester's chest. "I can only rest at night when you hold me in bed. But really just barely."

The freedman wrapped his arms around the empress, then moved his body until she was seated between his legs. "Let go, Vibia. I have you."

Sabina let her muscles relax and release as she nestled against her lover.

"Yes, yes, good," Zuester said gently. "Now weren't we just talking about what we were going to do when Lucius returns?"

Rome, Quirinalis Collis, October 137

"It will be difficult to penetrate through the ranks of slaves, freedmen, and guards, my lord Fuscus. The emperor is well protected at every turn."

Pedanius Fuscus paced impatiently in Calvius's office, eyeing the steward with suspicion. The stupid freedman did not seem to understand. Even his own grandfather sat silently in a corner shaking his head in defeat.

"I am a member of the imperial household myself, you fool!" Fuscus exclaimed. "I have access to the emperor! I can do whatever I bloody well please!"

"Are you sure about that, son?" asked Calvius of his guest.

Fuscus rounded on the steward. "What do you mean by that, freedman?" he shot angrily.

Calvius remained cool. "I mean no insult, but you must admit you do not seem to be in the emperor's favor. He passed you over for the succession. You, who are his only blood relation."

"You think he will deny me a private audience? Do you think he harbors suspicions against me?"

"He has always been suspicious of me, Fuscus," admitted Servianus quietly. "He may now try to protect himself against you as well. Don't expect to be granted any familial privileges."

"Damn you old man for ruining it for me!" Fuscus was livid. "The astrologer predicted I was to be emperor, I was to rule." He leaned toward his grandfather. "And I am to live as long as you, old man," he snarled.

"Then Rome will be bankrupt by the time you die, Fuscus," Servianus said sourly.

Fuscus thumped his fist on the steward's desk. "Not one of you will support me?"

Calvius sighed. "I have spies in the palace who will have information regarding movements and schedules. Plus, I can supply you with well-trained fighters who can act as simple household slaves. That is the most I can do. My own master cannot afford too many failed ventures."

Fuscus glared at the steward, then sighed. If that was all he was going to get, he would take it. He turned to Servianus. "You will not support me, grandfather?"

"I cannot," he sighed, frustration apparent in the response.

"Then when I am emperor, you must be content with retirement in one of your villas. I will allow you to retain just the one."

Servianus glared at his grandson and shook his head. He remained silent.

"Well," Calvius broke in dispersing the familial rancor, "Fuscus my lad, let me know your plans when you have figured them out."

"Thank you, Calvius," he said not looking at the servant but instead at his grandfather. "It is good to have support."

Rome, Imperial Palace, November 137

"I miss him, Zuester."

Zuester supervised the staff in Hadrian's apartment as they scurried about dressing and attending to their master. The emperor was feeling better that day and wished to take some exercise. Zuester wanted to ensure his friend was warmly dressed before heading outside.

"You mean your Kynegiskos, my lord?"

They spoke in Greek. None of the staff knew Greek and the two enjoyed conversing in relative confidence.

"I wonder what he would be doing at this moment."

"Lying on your bed, complaining about the cold, and wondering what crazy notion has compelled you to go out of doors."

Hadrian laughed. "Yes, yes, I suppose he would be acting like an old housewife by now."

Zuester smiled. "Enough," he said in Latin. The servants stepped back.

"Am I ready?" Hadrian also turned to Latin.

There was a commotion in the apartment's reception chamber. Zuester and Hadrian locked eyes. "Wait," the freedman said. "I'll investigate." Zuester instructed the attendants to guard their master until he returned.

The small reception room was filled with servants dressed in matching uniforms. For the briefest of seconds, Zuester thought – hoped really – it was Lucius returned from Pannonia. But something was off. The servants were too gruff and rough looking, not delicate and prettified. A shrill voice informed Zuester of what was going on.

"I demand to see my grand uncle! I will wait no longer!"

It was Pedanius Fuscus with an entourage of what could only be considered henchmen. The emperor's own guard had wisely decided to prevent the young man's entrance into his elder relative's apartment. *Castor and Pollux!* It was the moment they had all feared. Zuester had to keep his wits about him.

"You there," the young aristocrat called out to the Dacian. "You're his secretary. Let me in to see him. *Now.*"

"Good morning, my lord," said Zuester calmly. "As you are aware that your grand uncle is not a well man, I must inquire as to his health this morning with regards to accepting visitors."

"You're here," Fuscus said snidely.

"My lord?"

"You're visiting him, are you not? And you're just a servant. I'm his sister's grandson."

"Yes, my lord. The emperor and I discuss his business appointments every day as a matter of course. I do not know if he is holding audience today or not. We were just about to go over this when I heard you come in. If you will be patient for just one moment, I will see when the emperor will be available."

"He is available right now," came the impertinent response.

"Yes, my lord, as you say. Please, let me check in with the emperor for a moment. Please, wait here."

Zuester motioned to the Praetorians to secure the entrance to the inner rooms, then returned to the bedroom as quickly as he could without revealing his distress. Hadrian stared and waited for an answer.

"Melo and Micus!" Zuester barked pointing to two young and strong servants. "Come with me."

The youths responded immediately, joining the secretary at Hadrian's side.

"You will follow your emperor and do what he says. It is very important. A matter of life and death. You must protect and defend him. Do you understand?"

"Yes, my lord," the two answered in unison.

Zuester turned to a concerned Hadrian. "Graeculus," he began in Greek. "Pedanius Fuscus is asserting his power—"

"Oh, gods of Olympus—"

"He won't have thought to occupy Vibia's quarters. Go to her room immediately. Use the passage. Once there, tell Melo to alert the Praetorians. Micus will protect you. Do not leave until I myself come to get you."

"Zuester—"

"Go. Now. My lord." Zuester bowed briefly, then motioned to the remaining servants to exit the bedroom. The private passage had been continually kept a secret and Zuester intended to keep it that way. Melo and Micus were fiercely loyal and could be trusted to preserve such an important confidence.

Fuscus began yelling from the reception room.

Zuester knew he needed to stall to allow Hadrian time for his escape. "Opis," he called to a dark-haired youth who immediately appeared. "Announce to Pedanius Fuscus that the emperor will see him presently. Go." He gave the servant a light but encouraging nudge.

Such an announcement from a mere bedchamber attendant, a most inappropriate source of information, might distract the aristocrat enough.

The ensuing ruckus was exactly what Zuester had hoped and what he needed. He went to the reception room, taking two well-muscled attendants with him.

Opis was struggling between a couple of Fuscus's brawny escorts who held him fast.

"My lord!" Zuester called out. "What appears to be the problem?"

"How dare you insult me by sending this fuck-boy to do your job!" Fuscus snarled.

"I apologize," the secretary intoned, bowing deeply. "I think my command was misunderstood. Please, let me discipline him in my own way." He held out an arm in supplication.

Fuscus nodded to his men who released the terrified servant. The youth fled into the apartment.

"I will wait no longer, Dacian."

"Yes, my lord. I mean, no, my lord," Zuester purposefully stammered. "The emperor needed time to make himself presentable. With his illness, he has to keep up appearances even with such an intimate member of the family."

"I don't give a fuck what he looks like. I need to speak with him. Now."

"Yes, yes." Zuester knew if he drew Fuscus into the apartment there would be no means for the aristocrat to escape, especially once the entrance was blocked by Praetorians. "Come this way," he said, motioning with his hand.

Fuscus followed. Once in the bedroom he looked around. "Where is he?"

Zuester said nothing.

Fuscus rounded on the secretary. "*Where is he?*" he screamed grabbing Zuester by the shoulders.

Shouts and the clash of knives could be heard coming from the reception area.

Fuscus released the secretary and turned toward the clamor. "What in Hades is going on?" he howled.

The Praetorians spilled forth into the bedroom and descended upon him instantly.

Zuester pressed himself against a wall, trying to steady his breath. He looked down at his hand. He was shaking.

"My own flesh and blood," Hadrian murmured. "Trajan and Plotina warned me about this." He slumped over on the edge of the bed, his face in his hands.

"Shh, shh, love," Sabina calmed, stroking his back gently.

"Graeculus, Vibia?"

The couple jumped. Neither had heard Zuester come in.

"Zuester!" Sabina leapt up and ran to him. "What happened?"

The Dacian let out a tremulous breath. "I don't want to alarm the household just yet, in case the conspiracy runs deep. I want you two to remain here. No one is to know the emperor's whereabouts."

"Is he alive?" Hadrian was hoarse.

"Yes, yes. We'll keep him for questioning. Most of the men he brought with him were murdered. It's quite a mess." Zuester smiled weakly.

The emperor snorted at the dark humor. "Servianus?"

"I've made inquiries. No one is sure where he is, but he is not in the palace. I've sent guardsmen to find and secure him."

"Interview them separately. See if Fuscus and his grandfather implicate each other."

"Yes sir." Zuester glanced back and forth between the emperor and empress. "I've put extra guards at Vibia's door—"

"Oh, gods above!" Sabina cried quietly.

"—I'll return when I have a better handle on the situation. Then you both should make a public appearance. We will announce the emperor is alive and well."

"Lucius!" Hadrian exclaimed.

"I'll send a message as quickly as I can." Zuester bent down and kissed Sabina on the forehead. "Just know that you are both safe and secure."

Tibur, Servianus's villa, November 137

Bestia paced frantically along the tessellated floor of Servianus's retiring room. He wanted so much to hit someone, something, anything. The slave girl he had forced into submission the minute after he heard the news of Fuscus's failed coup had screamed in such agony he had had to stop. Too many of his men – his property – had died already that day. He could not afford to injure another, least not an exquisite expert in fellatio.

Through it all, Servianus, wisely, had remained hunkered down in his villa. He had disagreed with his grandson's plot and had conveniently excused himself to his country villa – a bit odd so late in the year, but the Romans had a habit of accepting the eccentricities of their elder statesmen. As Fuscus's closest relative, he had been placed under house arrest, of course, after the incident. But as he had been nowhere near the palace and insisted on his innocence, he retained the many privileges of his status. It seemed no one could, or dared, touch the old man.

After he had heard the news, Bestia needed a change of location. He showed up uninvited at the old man's villa. His presence, however, had been expected.

"That damnable fool!" Bestia hit his fists against unseen objects in the air. "He should have waited. A month or two from now he would have owned the world!"

"You're taking this rather harshly, Calvius." Servianus was calm, controlled, drinking his wine as if it were just another evening symposium.

"I can't suffer fools who get my men murdered! And for nothing!"

"Slaves are easily replaced. And what do you mean by 'your' men? I thought they were your employer's men."

Bestia eyed Servianus long and hard. He knew he would have to come clean if he were to retain the trust and confidence of his best contact in the emperor's inner circle. "I *am* my employer. I'm not Numerius Calvius Africanus. I am Sextus Quintilius Bestia. My cousin was Caius Calpurnius Crassus Frugi Licinianus, exiled by Trajan and assassinated by Hadrian."

"Hounds of Hell," Servianus whistled through his teeth as he stared at his visitor. "You're a Frugi? Your family has been at odds with emperors for decades."

"Unfortunately, whoever has occupied the palace was not intelligent enough to recognize talent."

"But they did recognize ambition, my friend." Servianus relaxed against the couch cushions. "I think you might be a distant cousin to the empress Sabina herself." He took a draught of wine.

"I have heard the same. Perhaps it is true, but, as the bastard son of a gladiator and a high-born lady, I am doomed to never reveal my true familial connection."

"Ah."

Bestia sucked in a long breath and exhaled loudly. "That bloody grandson of yours should have waited! Someone should have taught him a little patience."

"Don't try to implicate me in my grandson's failings. Many have encouraged him. Including, as I recall, an astrologer of yours who suggested the boy might one day rule."

"Are all the members of the imperial house weak-willed, easily-swayed imbeciles?"

"Just the stupid ones."

"I don't need him," Bestia concluded out of the blue.

"'No, you don't. Even if you did you would have to do without. He's been arrested and not allowed to have visitors on his tiny island. I, at least, am allowed company, despite my own house arrest."

"I don't need you either."

"I doubt that."

"I can prove it."

Servianus turned serious. "Calvius, or Bestia rather, please do not act rashly. Like you just said, we've had enough death for a while."

It was the wrong thing for the old man to say. At that moment, Bestia did not want to follow orders from anyone. And he especially did not need a member of the imperial family telling him what to do.

He could very easily do quite a bit of damage all on his own. He would remind the emperor what it was like to lose a loved and admired relation.

Tibur, Hadrian's villa, mid-December 137

"I came as soon as I could."

In the darkened room, Hadrian looked up when he heard Lucius speak to the German guardsmen at Sabina's door. The dim light of the hallway revealed the brawny pair of sentinels were both trying unsuccessfully to conceal their profound sorrow. They somberly let the heir to the throne into the bedroom. Lucius had only returned to Rome hours before and now was met with the grim reality that was the empire.

The unbelievable had happened. Sabina was dying. She had been poisoned. No one knew how or who, but clearly the select, trusted members of the imperial staff had let their defenses down for the briefest of moments, long enough for an infiltrator to act. But they were not to blame; most of the household had become complacent after the coup attempt by Fuscus. It just seemed that the threats to the emperor and empress had passed.

Lucius, himself pale with a coughing sickness contracted during his assignment in Pannonia, entered and looked around. He caught Hadrian's eye, nodded, and took a seat next to Mindia, her body shaking with silent sobs. When Lucius spied Zuester, Hadrian watched as the shock of realization finally registered on the heir's face. The Dacian lay curled up at Sabina's feet, his grief-stricken form an immobile heap shrouded in the darkness.

Hadrian sat on the mattress at his wife's side. Seeing Lucius made him remember the vibrant woman who once shared the senator's bed, with no compunction or jealousy from himself or Zuester, loving each man as she did in her own way. The emperor's tears began to fall uncontrollably.

Sabina stirred. She reached up and touched her husband's cheek. "The emperor does not cry."

Hadrian took her hand in his and kissed her palm. "I would relinquish the title if I could but have you back alive. Vibia, you are my soul."

"I thought that honor fell to Antinous," she said weakly.

Hadrian smiled. "He was my heart. You are a part of me that is much deeper." His eyes penetrated hers. "A part of me that is much darker. You are part of my true self."

Sabina smiled feebly. "Graeculus, I'm tired. I must sleep now."

He knew if he let her close her eyes he would never see her alive again, hold her warm flesh against his body, hear her scold and tease him. He fought to hold back fresh tears. "Yes, of course, my love. I will be right here beside you when you wake up."

Her head sagged against the pillow. "Good night, husband. I'll pass along your love to Antinous when I see him.

A cold chill traversed down Hadrian's spine. "Yes, love, I would like that very much."

He lay down beside her and enveloped her in his arms. He stayed awake long enough to feel the life leave her, then cried himself to sleep.

Rome, Quirinalis Collis, late December 137

The failed coup had only been a setback. The murder of Sabina had been a victory. With one simple act, Bestia had proven he was still a force to be reckoned with, that the emperor could not afford to become complacent. Hadrian would be hyper-aware now. The palace would be a quagmire of suspicion and protracted protocol. The reminder that enemies still abounded would create a little push toward paranoia.

Bestia let his shoulders sink into the luxurious cushions of the couch and watched the bouncing breasts of the slave girl riding him. He smiled at the view of beautifully round orbs of pale flesh topped by delicate pink tips rising and falling to the rhythm of the cunt squeezing his needful cock. An obsidian-haired girl sat under the edge of the couch sucking his pendulous balls, expertly avoiding the enthusiastic butt of her companion.

It had been the paranoia of Domitian that had led him to an early grave and had the Senate damning his memory afterwards. Hadrian's grave was overdue; when the time came an official *damnatio* would undo all the good he thought he had accomplished. Pax Hadriana would be remembered as a reign of terror. All because his final acts as an old man would be spurred on by hate and anger, not duty and paternalism.

The enthusiasm of the girl riding him was flagging as she fatigued. It took Bestia a little longer now to reach an excited state, and much more time to achieve his culmination. Luckily he had a bevy of beauties at his beck and call.

"Off," he commanded. "Another."

A waiting slave girl mounted him, her long hair the deep brown of autumn chestnuts. She was young and tight, and exclusively used for his pleasure. But perhaps if she were tighter…

"Afer!" Bestia called out to one of his large African guards.

The young man immediately stepped forward.

"Fuck her in the ass."

Without hesitation, Afer positioned himself behind the brown-haired girl, oiled himself, then slowly pressed in.

A guttural groan escaped Bestia's throat as he felt her cunt tighten with the new invasion.

Forced to move away with the crowded conditions at the foot of the couch, the black-haired girl sucking his balls now let her nimble fingers and hands stimulate her master. The oil dripping from the African's massive cock lubricated her ministrations. She pulled and squeezed with every slam of the brown-haired girl's cunt.

Bestia sighed. Pleasures like these made all the miseries and impediments of life worth it.

Yet it was the plots and intrigues that created the miseries and impediments that were so utterly thrilling to him. Could the tight, squeezing cunt and the torturous ball-play compete with the thought that the murder of the empress was only the beginning of the end? Next could be that damned Lucius, and of course the idiotic embarrassment named Fuscus tucked away in exile. What about Servianus? Ha! The old man wouldn't see it coming. Then, of course, Hadrian himself. With no one in line for the succession, the Senate would be in turmoil, pandemonium would break out in the streets. Perhaps there would be calls to restore the Republic...

The slaps of Afer's vicious slamming against the pale ass of the brown-haired girl became louder, rousing Bestia from his momentary reverie. He was hard as iron and on the brink of climax. The girl riding his cock was limp with exhaustion, her cunt no longer a match for his rod, but the temptress massaging his scrotum had slithered an oiled finger into his anus to torment his prostate. She kept him on edge. *Gods above*, she was good.

Caught up in a sexual frenzy, Afer spanked the brown-haired girl unmercifully, her cries causing her cunt to twitch. Finally, screaming his climax, the African came, cruelly gripping the ass of the panting girl.

It was the signal Bestia's wicked black-haired siren was waiting for. Her magic fingers took him to the brink, held him there, then let him go as she deftly crushed his balls. Bestia howled his climax unwittingly.

"Fascinating performance of stamina for a man of your years."

Bestia threw off the slave girl still mounted on top of him and turned toward the familiar voice.

Sanabares stood just inside the doorway of his sitting room leaning against a wall.

"How in Hades did you get in here?" the merchant bellowed.

"I told one of your guards that if he did not let me in the future of his master was in jeopardy." The magus smiled. "So easily convinced. Such loyalty."

"Such weakness," Bestia grumbled. With a wave of a hand he dismissed the slaves servicing him, indicating the black-haired girl should wait for him in his bedroom. As he rose, he tugged his tunic into its proper place.

"I should have you killed," he said to the astrologer. The Parthian was dressed in the manner of a Roman citizen just returned from the Orient, not in his usual terrifying garb. Really Bestia should have the guardsmen at his apartment killed.

"You won't."

"Hmmpf." The merchant paced, bracing himself against whatever miseries and impediments the magus was going to lay at his feet. "Why are you here? I didn't send for you."

"No," said the Parthian as he sat uninvited. "But someone else sent me here. Someone to whom you made a promise nine years ago. A promise that has not yet been fulfilled."

"Who?"

"The Princess Roedogune."

Jupiter's balls! The Throne!

Bestia had not heard that name since, well he wasn't quite sure, but it was years ago. He hadn't completely forgotten about his promise to find the *sella regia*, but he had secretly hoped the Parthians had.

"My lady would like to know your progress in obtaining this important symbol of our ancient heritage."

"It has been difficult," Bestia deflected.

"Yes. Clearly." Sanabares did not seem convinced.

Bestia glared at his intruder. "I have spent the intervening years strengthening my imperial contacts," he retorted churlishly. "I now have the ability to find the treasure. It has been well hidden and very few people are apprised of its whereabouts."

"Is that what I should report back to my lady?"

"She will have it at the beginning of our new year."

"Ah," snorted the astrologer, disbelieving. "You will be well rewarded once we have the throne safe in Parthia. Well rewarded, so it will be worth your while, merchant." He raised an eyebrow. "Otherwise, please keep in mind that my lady's anger knows no bounds."

Bestia stared in anger as the astrologer left. When he thought he was far enough away, he breathed a sigh of relief.

Servianus. He would know. Good thing he hadn't killed him yet.

Tibur, Servianus's villa, late December 137

"Last I spoke with you, you said you didn't need me," said Servianus snidely. "And yet, here you are."

Bestia looked away briefly, then met the old man's eyes full on. "I didn't need you. I committed the act against the empress on my own."

"Yes. Poor Sabina. She really didn't deserve that. Her marriage to Hadrian was suffering enough for one lifetime."

Bestia could only guess that Servianus made such a statement because of his own hatred of the emperor. Almost everyone in the imperial inner circle knew husband and wife actually got along well enough – for a married couple. He plopped down on a couch in Servianus's retiring room.

"Have some wine, Bestia."

The merchant begrudgingly took the proffered cup, then drank the contents down. Servianus could always be counted on for having some of the best vintages.

"Now, why are you here?"

"I need your help."

"Ha! I knew it! Now, that wasn't as hard as you thought it would be, was it?"

"No." Bestia refilled his cup. "I need to know the whereabouts of the *sella regia*," he said matter-of-factly before downing the wine once again.

"The *sella regia*? The Parthian throne?"

"Yes."

"Whatever for?"

"Let's just say I made a deal with the Parthian court."

"And you intend to return it to them?"

"That is the idea, yes."

"Hmmmm." Servianus pondered this situation for what was to Bestia far too long. Either the old man knew where it was or he didn't.

"Do you know where it is?"

"I do."

"And…?"

"I need you to do something in return."

Bestia was expecting this. "What?"

"Since you have proved yourself so effective at imperial assassination, I need you to kill Lucius Ceionius Commodus."

"Hadrian's heir?"

"The same. And I need you to do this very quickly. He is giving his acceptance speech before the Senate on New Year's day. I don't want him to give that speech."

"Meaning you don't want him to inherit the empire."

"No, no. That doesn't concern me actually. He's rather sickly. It's a lung ailment; he coughs up blood. I suspect I'll outlive him. It is the contents of the speech I do not want revealed."

Bestia was perplexed. "Interesting reason to kill a man. Why not slip him another speech?"

Servianus laughed at what he considered a very droll joke. "No, no. He already knows the contents of the speech." The old man examined Bestia quizzically. "You don't really understand, do you? Of course not, why should you." He sighed impatiently. "Lucius will be detailing the succession of the empire for the next generation, maybe more. The Senate will think him very clever and will agree to the succession on the spot. I need a little upset. I need to rattle Hadrian a bit. He may see reason and finally choose his own brother-in-law as heir."

Bestia snorted. "I doubt that very much Servianus. I mean no disrespect, but he has passed you over for succession for twenty years now."

"I think he can be convinced. He has very few choices. Most, if not all, of his intimates and family are unwilling, unqualified, or dead. I suppose he could look beyond the court—"

"Like what he did with Lucius."

"Well no. Lucius was part of his entourage at one point, a very frivolous part indeed, but the two connected philosophically. People have wondered about the choice of Lucius, but not I. It makes very good sense." Servianus sipped his wine. "Anyway, Hadrian is a very sick man. Once Lucius is gone and his plans fall through he will be very desperate. Very desperate indeed."

Bestia thought about his own desperation. "And the throne? The *sella regia*?"

"If Lucius dies on time, it will be delivered to your house in Rome."

"Thank you, Servianus."

Rome, Imperial Palace, 31 December 137

"'… my responsibility in accepting this great honor is to name my own successors…' Oh, that sounds horrible, does it not?" Lucius fretted. He turned to his companion. "Zuse, what do you think?"

"I think you should stop worrying and come to bed. Everyone will know you didn't write the speech. It's formal and boring. Not at all like you. Stop driving yourself mad with details and come to me."

Zuester lay on Lucius's bed in the heir's apartment. The two had inexorably resumed their love affair after the death of Sabina. Each needed the other, and once in the other's arms, realized how very much indeed.

"Ugh! I am so…nervous." Lucius paced to match his words. "I'm never nervous."

Zuester patted the silk-covered bedspread. "Well, then, let me relieve your tension, Caesar," he smiled.

"Gods above, I hate when you call me that! Sounds so…so *official*. What are you going to call me when I'm emperor?"

"'Your eminence,' probably."

"Humph," Lucius pouted. He sat grumpily on the mattress.

Zuester scrambled over and wrapped his arms around his lover, slipping his hands under the silk robe to stroke the muscles of the depilated chest. "You'll be fine, love. You're always fine. You're charismatic and handsome and the Senate loves you. Just be yourself." He pecked Lucius's shoulder, then licked and nipped and breathed in the scented flesh.

"You're too good to me, Zuse." Lucius turned around to face the Dacian, cupping his bearded cheek, searching the depths of his eyes. "I burn for you terribly. This sickness…I hate it, not being able to be with you completely. The gods know I want to kiss you so badly it's driving me mad."

"I too, Lucius."

"Damn Eros and his arrows!"

Zuester pulled the senator to him until the men lay on the mattress side-by-side, face-to-face. "Don't damn love, darling. Damn the sickness." He tugged at Lucius's robe, allowing his hands to wander around to the naked back, gliding across the smooth skin.

"Damn Stefanus," Lucius muttered as he nuzzled against Zuester's neck.

"Damn Pannonia," Zuester responded, his fingers tangling in his lover's luxurious blond curls.

"If I could, I would kiss you so innocently, so tenderly…our flushed, sensitive skin barely touching." Lucius tapped a finger to Zuester's smile. "No wetness… but, only just at first. My rapacious tongue would quickly grow restless." The senator drew a caressing line around his lover's open mouth. "Driven by lascivious need, it would insinuate itself ever so gently between your closed lips. Ah, but you have needs of your own, and an encouraging moan would cause my unruly tongue to thrust its velvety tip deep inside you, forcing you to open wide, open willingly for my sensual invasion. Our mouths would tangle in their mutual lust, trying to slake a desire so strong it could only be quenched by our joining as one."

Zuester grinned. "Damn you. Now I'm hard as a rock."

Lucius gently opened Zuester's robe and pressed their nude bodies together. "Me too. What should we do about it?" he teased, feeling the heat grow between them.

"Hmmm," the Dacian kissed his lover's neck. "Will I still be able to tie you up once you're emperor of Rome?" he squeezed Lucius's butt, then tickled the ridge between the cheeks.

"I think I'll need to consult the Senate about that." Lucius pressed his hips against Zuester's, mingling their cocks.

"I can still suck you, you know," Zuester provoked, his sonorous voice sending a thrill through the senator. "Sickness or no, emperor or not."

Lucius lifted his lover's face to meet his. Zuester's expression changed when their eyes met.

"Lucius, what's wrong? It's frustrating, I know, but we can still be together."

Lucius blinked back budding tears. "Zuse, I want you to fuck me. I want you to come inside me." He drew his fingers across the secretary's shoulder to his arm, delighting in the soft, dark hair. His attention returned to the face he loved so well. "I want you to give me your energy."

"My energy?" Zuester queried, nonplussed.

"When Graeculus was sick in Egypt, he let Antinous do so. An astrologer said that the energy of the healthy would help heal the sick."

"Did Graeculus feel it worked?"

"Yes, he did. Then, at least. He was restored after the journey."

"Yes, but Antinous also drown himself on the emperor's behalf."

The senator started at that. "Zuse, I would never—"

"Lucius, I know. I know you would not ask such a thing of me. I only wonder if it was the intimacy or the sacrifice that was the cure."

"I'm willing to try the intimacy remedy," Lucius grinned and bit his lip.

Zuester raised an eyebrow. "Scurrilous rogue. All right, I'll be happy to fuck you, like the doctor ordered."

Lucius laughed and rolled onto his back. "Did you ever sleep with Graeculus?" he suddenly asked.

Zuester threw his lover a curious look. "No."

It was not the answer the heir was expecting. "No?!"

A smirk twitched on the Dacian's lips. "No."

"Never?" Lucius was incredulous. "How come?"

"The desire was not there, I think. A great deal of respect, but no attraction. We're better as friends."

"Too bad. He's quite good, you know."

"Yes, I've heard," Zuester laughed and pounced on the younger man, straddling and pinning him to the bed. "But I'm better."

Every pore on Lucius's skin tingled in anticipation. The heat between Zuester's legs spread through him at the point of contact, jolting his cock to full stand. The Dacian leered seductively at his conquest.

"Caelius!" Zuester called out without looking up.

The young servant appeared instantly from the next room. "My lord?"

"Bring that jug of oil and the lamp from that table there," the secretary ordered, pointing to Lucius's desk.

The servant did as commanded, obviously trying hard not to look at the utterly provocative sight of the two partially-clad men, one of whom was in a most unseemly position for one about to be named emperor. Two free, adult men should never be in such a position. However, Caelius remained at the bedside, awaiting the next directive.

Zuester ground his hips against Lucius. The senator snickered. They loved tormenting the palace staff.

The servant blushed crimson.

"You may go," said Zuester. "And we are not to be disturbed until it is time for your master's medicine."

Caelius fled.

Zuester stripped off his robe revealing his down-covered athletic form. Lucius loved the gray hair scattered amongst the dark brown. He drew his hand up the Dacian's belly to his chest, grabbing strands between his fingers and pulling his lover to meet him.

Their faces hovered apart, each longing to kiss the other, each keeping regret at bay.

Zuester grabbed the still-burning lamp and placed the flame under the jug of oil, swirling the contents carefully. Satisfied, with his task, he blew out the lamp and placed it on the floor, then poured oil on Lucius's belly.

The warm liquid was soothing, Zuester's delicate touch exciting. The Dacian coaxed the oil to Lucius's hard shaft, the course made easy by the lack of hair at his groin. Lucius sucked in air when Zuester's fingers curled around his erection.

He groaned an exhale when Zuester slowly stroked up and down, thoroughly coating his cock.

The Dacian held his eyes as he poured oil into his palm, then masturbated his own throbbing erection. When Zuester grabbed both cocks, his hand spanning the double circumference, Lucius had to look. The sight of the glistening shafts rubbing together was magnificent, and the voluptuous feeling sent a wave of desire surging within him.

"Fuck me, Zuse."

Delight flickered briefly across the secretary's face before once again assuming his role as the superior. He poured oil on his lover's sac, gently massaging and enlivening the stones, then poured more oil along the ridge underneath. His slick fingers slid inside Lucius's pulsating, puckered hole.

The senator relaxed into the invasion, rocking his hips in encouragement.

His eager yearning was apparent to his partner. Zuester removed his fingers and, with exquisite deliberateness, inserted the head of his cock.

Lucius melted against the bed.

Zuester pushed in more. Lucius could feel his own muscles welcome the intruder, feel his passage flex and relax. Zuester proceeded undaunted, sliding through the first tight ring and beyond until he broached the second. The pain was exquisite. Lucius's palm went to his cock.

"Not yet." Zuester stilled his hand.

And then the Dacian pulled out and slammed in with such force Lucius let out a little cry.

Zuester continued his forceful battering, his body bent over the senator, his dark curls shaking with the violence of his thrusts, holding Lucius's blue eyes with his own, the brown irises turned to a lustful black.

"Now."

Lucius grabbed his longing prick, matching his fist's rhythm to his lover's pounding pulse. Their excited breaths mingled, the scent of raw masculinity mixed with sweet exotic cologne as sweat dripped from the lovers' brows. The Dacian dropped his head to the pillow next to the senator, his dark brown hair dancing with golden blond curls, as each drove on to his own rapturous culmination.

"I'm going to explode…" Zuester growled.

"Deeper, Zuse," Lucius pleaded frantically. "As far as you can. Please." The senator was on the brink as well.

At the moment of climax, Zuester pinned Lucius to the bed gaining traction as he buried himself to the hilt, slamming his hips until they could go no further, trying to extend his prick as if it would stretch beyond the physical boundary. Reaching the precipice of pleasure, he came with all his might deep inside his lover's body. The intensity of his groaning howl spurred Lucius to climax, his seed jetting hot onto his hairless chest.

Zuester collapsed in a heap alongside his partner. "And does Caesar feel rejuvenated?" he panted.

Lucius stared up at the gilded ceiling. "Very much so," he grinned.

Zuester sat propped against the pillows while Lucius dozed, comfortably nestled in the crook of his arm. The secretary gently fondled his lover's soft blond curls, twisting the silky strands through his fingers, then leaned over to breathe in their sweet fragrance, pleasure pulsing through him as he relived the earlier intimacy.

Lucius stirred, burrowing against the Dacian as he woke. "I love you, Zuse." There was a hint of desperation in his voice.

"And I, you." Zuester pulled the senator more closely to him and kissed his golden hair. "Lucius, darling, don't fret," he said quietly.

"We can't sustain this you know."

Zuester said nothing. He was content to be in the moment, knowing tomorrow everything would change. He knew all too well their affair would have to come to an end.

"I suppose we can continue as long as Graeculus is alive," Lucius concluded.

Zuester adjusted himself to press more closely against the senator's nude body. "I'm a foreigner and you're a Roman. A freeman and a citizen. There is nothing untoward about that."

"I never think of you as a foreigner. And I never think of you as a former slave," he said tracing the branding scar on Zuester's back. "But, anyway, you are older than I. *That* simply goes against convention. The emperor must not have an older man as his lover."

"There would be riots," Zuester remarked drolly.

"Yes, and there must not be a war while I am alive. Marcus and little Lucius can have all the wars they like." Lucius turned his face up to his bedmate. "You shall take a wife and have children," he pronounced.

"Children! At my age?"

"You are not so old you cannot have children! Why you are a man in his prime." Lucius flattened his palm against the manly chest. "A very young wife. One who will please you in bed." He stroked Zuester's satisfied cock. "And I know just the girl."

"Oh?"

"She's a bedchamber maid to my wife. You'll like her. Red hair like Vibia. And she's Dacian."

"Dacian? Are you sure she's not Pannonian?" Zuester teased.

"Oh you mock, my friend, but after spending a year in that quadrant of the empire forsaken by all gods I assure you I can tell a Dacian from a Pannonian from a German from a Gaul. I can even suss out a Briton if I put my mind to it."

Zuester laughed. He loved their playful banter. Lucius, despite his status, made him feel so comfortable. Even if they stopped sleeping with each other, he knew they would always remain friends.

"Yes, I will have Plautia make the introductions," Lucius continued. "You'll forget me in no time."

"I very much doubt that." Zuester kissed the top of his lover's head and gave him a reassuring hug.

Lucius sighed, and on his exhale he coughed, a reminder of the sickness that both knew would eventually kill him.

From behind the curtains to the bedroom Caelius called out. "My lord, the doctor is here."

"And just in time," Lucius said dryly. "Send him in," he commanded.

The doctor shuffled in, his head slightly lowered in deference and his aged body conveying just the correct amount of obsequiousness.

"My lord," the doctor greeted, bowing a little more deeply.

"Doctor, you are very much welcome here," said Lucius as he put on his robe. "You are my protector. There is no need for such ceremony."

"Thank you, my lord." The doctor looked up from his bow and blushed at the sight of the Dacian getting out of the senator's bed, utterly nude.

Zuester quickly covered himself with a tunic draped over a nearby chair. Indeed, his affair with the heir to the empire was a little scandalous to some.

The doctor snapped orders to his assistants. A measured draught of a clear liquid was poured into a glass goblet. The drink was offered to Lucius, who took it and drank.

"My medicine," he said to Zuester as he returned the goblet to the servant's tray, "is tasteless. I sometimes wonder if I am being treated at all."

"Oh!" cried the doctor. "Sire, you must know that I have prepared the medicine specifically for your condition. It will help the lungs relax."

"Yes, yes, of course. I was only joking."

But the doctor continued as if he did not hear, his voice tinged with urgency. "It is carefully measured. Only the precise amount can be given to you. Too little, it does nothing. Too much and you could die."

Lucius touched a hand to the doctor's trembling arm. "Thank you, sir, for you concern and assistance. I do so very much appreciate your efforts to prolong my life. I want you to know that I am making the most of my last years." He flashed a smile at Zuester. "The emperor also thanks you."

"The emperor?" The doctor was wide-eyed with delight and disbelief.

"Emperor Hadrian himself."

The doctor bowed. "Thank you, sire."

Lucius glanced around at the waiting servants. "Will someone bring me my wine?" He returned his attention to Zuester. "I should like to review my speech and the protocols before I dine. I'm having my final dinner as a common man with my wife and children."

"No one could ever call you common, Lucius darling." It drove Zuester crazy that they could not interact physically when they were in the company of attendants and staff. Knowing Lucius was nude under his robe inflamed him, that all he had to do was slip his hand inside the silk to touch the smooth skin...

A youth dressed in the uniform of the senator's serving staff entered the bedroom with a tray. "Your wine, sire."

"Thank you, Rufus." Lucius filled his golden cup and brought it to his lips.

Horrified, Zuester grabbed the cup. "You know better than that, my lord." He smelled the wine, took a sip, swished the liquid in his mouth, swallowed, then waited almost a full minute. "All right. You may drink." He handed the vessel back to the senator.

"I hardly understand why you think I'm going to watch you die before me," Lucius scolded under his breath before he took a long draught from the approved cup. "Have a servant do that next time."

"Yes, Caesar," Zuester smirked.

Lucius brushed passed the secretary, their fingers touching briefly, as he went to his desk. He picked up the papyrus with the speech and paced impatiently.

The doctor shuffled.

The senator looked up. "Doctor? Is there something else?"

"I have orders to perform a physical examination, sire. Tonight," he explained nervously. "Before the ceremony tomorrow."

"Oh, very well." Lucius put down the speech and sauntered over to the doctor and his assistant.

He never quite made it.

"Oh, gods!" he cried, then doubled over and vomited blood.

"Lucius!" Zuester's heart clenched as ran to his lover, reaching him before anyone else. Instinctively, he dropped to his knees to catch the collapsing senator. Lucius struggled to breathe while Zuester settled his heaving body against his legs on the floor.

"Darling," Zuester said with a trembling whisper, trying to keep his panic at bay. "I have you, I have you," he consoled as he bent down over the senator's forehead crinkled with worry.

The doctor only stared, his hand over his mouth, while his young assistant stood dumbfounded, distress puffing his wet cheeks.

"These are the effects of too much of the medicine!" the doctor cried. "Someone has poisoned the wine." He pointed to the golden cup.

"Zuse?" Lucius choked, confusion and fear in his eyes.

"Shh, shh, love." Zuester wrapped his arms around his friend and squeezed his eyes shut to beat back his tears. "I couldn't tell...I couldn't tell...the medicine had no taste...it tasted like wine...only wine..." He rocked back and forth, his head pounding with despair, hugging his lover, desperately hoping against hope that what had just happened did not just happen. Yet, he could feel the life slowly draining from Lucius's body, vibrant and joyous only moments before. He looked up at the doctor.

"Is there nothing you can do?" he pleaded.

The old man was clearly repelled by the sight before him, as if he had never before seen death. "No, my lord. There is nothing," he trembled in his hysteria.

Lucius was weakening, his body getting heavier as he slumped further to the ground. Zuester knew there was no time for propriety.

"I love you, Lucius. I love you, forever." The tears fell uncontrollably, wetting the beautiful blond curls. "Oh, gods! Why are you taking him!" he wailed.

Lucius stirred once more against him. "Zuse..." he started weakly. He struggled to lift his head, as if seeing something before him. "Vibia?" he said hoarsely. He squinted. "Stefanus?"

Zuester watched as his lover's blue eyes froze, still reflecting a mixture of confusion and realization.

Rome, Imperial Palace, 1 January 138

From the window in his private office in the palace, Hadrian looked out onto the cityscape that was Rome. The activities of life seemed to go on as if the tragedy had not happened.

"What next?" came the ragged voice of his secretary.

Hadrian did not turn toward the voice. Every little movement agonized him. Simply standing was painful, but it was a temporary relief from sitting. "We cannot mourn officially until after the New Year's celebration. The gods must be satisfied."

"They are not satisfied enough?!"

Hadrian understood Zuester's outburst. If his body would have allowed it, he would be grieving as well. But his failing health meant it was simply too painful to cry.

"We will hold the funeral in a week's time. I also want to proceed with the deification of Vibia."

"Yes, of course. The gods must rejoice that they have her as well."

Bitterness. Hadrian understood that emotion all too well. He, unfortunately, also empathized with the sudden surges of sadness, the feeling of loss and emptiness, the loneliness and isolation of despair. Zuester had been through far too much in the past two months. His devotion to both Sabina and Lucius was profound. While Hadrian knew he himself had been the target of the attacks, it had been Zuester who had suffered the most.

Perhaps if he discussed things other than death. "I will meet with my advisors about the succession. It is imperative we choose another as soon as possible. I need a man of peace," the emperor mused. "Someone competent, well-liked, uncontroversial. Someone who will agree to a pre-established succession after his own death—" Hadrian stopped short. He hadn't meant to remind them of their current situation.

"Oh gods, oh gods, oh gods..."

The plaintive sobbing of his secretary moved him immensely. He walked with effort to the younger man who sat at the desk, his head cradled in his hands, his fingers woven through his hair looking as if they were ready to pull the strands out at the roots. Hadrian lay a comforting hand on Zuester's shoulder. The Dacian reached up, gripping him, needing the human contact. Hadrian leaned in a little, smelling Lucius's favorite fragrance in the secretary's curls.

"It was I who first gave him that perfume, almost twenty years ago. Frivolous and seductive. It seemed to suit him so perfectly."

"It does suit him...did." Zuester haltingly sucked in air. "So vital one minute, then the next..." he trailed off, his voice a mess of choking sobs.

"Go," Hadrian ordered. "Go to his room, sleep in his bed. Mourn him, remember him. There is no one to support you this time, like how he did you after Vibia died. You need to take time to grieve."

"But—"

"Hush. I can manage without you. I have a legion of secretaries, and at least a dozen of your apprentices are almost as good as you. I will be in good hands."

Zuester stirred in his chair and looked up at his emperor. "He said her name, you know. He called out to Vibia and to his dead servant. It was the last thing he said."

Hadrian pursed his lips to keep the tears at bay. "Then he is well-cared for in the afterlife." He sat, which was now a relief from standing. "I never thought I would outlive them. Either of them. All of them," he reflected quietly.

"No, my lord." The Dacian had reached a sudden calmness, his body probably weary of sorrow.

Hadrian reached out his palm. "Zuester?"

The secretary placed his hand on the one outstretched before him. "Yes, my lord?"

"After you have mourned your lover, you must find who did this." He kept his voice very low to prevent any spies from hearing. "You must find the villain and kill him. I suggest you begin with that good for nothing Fuscus and his treacherous grandfather. Neither need live beyond their usefulness. I give you leave to execute the criminals after you have extracted what you need from them."

"Yes, my lord."

Tibur, Servianus's villa, mid-January 138

No one had barred the way for Zuester and the six Praetorians when they entered Servianus's extensive villa. In fact, the guards posted there pointed out the way to find the old man. He sat calmly in his study, a fire blazing in a stove to ward off winter's chill, and merely glanced up at the imperial retinue.

"I didn't expect to see you so soon after Commodus's death."

Servianus's tone carried all the arrogance Zuester had expected. What he had not foreseen was the sense of accomplishment conveyed.

"I am strongly motivated to find his assassin, consul," replied the secretary.

"Of course you are," said the former governor, his voice dripping with insinuation. "Well, it was not I. I was here during the event." He relaxed further against his couch.

"Yes," Zuester smirked. "But perhaps one of your subordinates was present?"

"I hardly think so!" Servianus snorted at the notion. "My staff has been reduced to such a ridiculously pitiful level, I can spare no one. Furthermore, my outside contacts are limited since my sudden and unwarranted exile."

"Unwarranted?"

"I had absolutely nothing to do with Fuscus's plot. He acted against my wishes. I have been saying that since the failed scheme was executed."

"Speaking of which, he has been executed."

"Fuscus?" Servianus seemed surprised, there was even a flash of regret in his expression.

"Yes. For treason. He made it clear that he had no involvement with the later assassinations, however."

"And neither did I."

"Then you too are no longer useful to us." Zuester nodded his head toward the Praetorians and flicked his hand at Servianus. "Guards."

The six men moved in unison toward the old man.

Despite his ninety years, Servianus jumped out of his chaise. "What is the meaning of this?"

"Bad things keep happening while you are alive, consul." Zuester pulled a scroll from under his pallium. "And, besides, we have a list of your visitors since your exile and some time before. We will easily be able to ascertain whether or not you were actually involved in any of the recent tragedies through personal interviews with your associates."

"Nonsense!" Servianus's voice was a bit too loud, and a bit too nervous. "The emperor needs me."

"Whatever for?" Now it was Zuester's turn to exhibit composed arrogance.

"His options are really very few," Servianus countered, trying very hard to sound confident. "He has no relations except myself. He has no more allies. There is simply no one else left to rule. And he is a very sick man. I've got thirty years on him and I am in wonderful health."

"There are plenty of men who wish to rule Rome. I would not concern myself with that." Zuester once again waved a hand at the guardsmen.

Three men rushed the old man, holding his struggling form as a fourth stripped him of his winter mantle. Another guard drew his sword and waited for instructions.

"Am I not at least to be given the honorable choice?" Servianus screamed.

"Suicide?" queried Zuester calmly. He motioned for the guard to release their prisoner.

"I do not deserve to be humiliated in this way, to be slaughtered as a defeated enemy! There has been no public trial; how am I to defend my honor? I am, after all, a member of the imperial family. It is not simply *my* honor which is at stake but that of the whole bloodline. The emperor has already defiled his own sister by not honoring her death." Servianus spat on the ground. "He didn't even hold games in her memory."

Zuester had been expecting just such a reaction. "Your property?"

"Yes, yes, take it. It seems I have outlived all my heirs except Hadrian anyway."

"All right," Zuester paced thoughtfully. "I will allow suicide. On one condition."

Servianus shook his head in disgust. "Which is?"

"I want one name."

"Just one?" the consul said in mock surprise.

"There have been far too many attacks directed against Hadrian, even before he was emperor. This is personal. Someone has been involved since the beginning."

Servianus regarded the Dacian curiously. "You're very clever, you know. Far too clever for your own good."

Zuester raised an eyebrow. "Well?"

Servianus threw up his hands in defeat. "You want Sextus Quintilius Bestia, otherwise known as Numerius Calvius Africanus in that scroll of yours," he pointed at the list of visitors. "He's a Frugi, and, continuing in their familial tradition, has caused quite a bit of upset to the imperial household. My steward can help you with his whereabouts."

"Thank you, consul," Zuester said with a bow. He motioned to a Praetorian who handed Servianus his sword, then turned to leave the room.

"Give my regards to my brother-in-law, young man."

Zuester turned back to face the consul. "You've lived a good life, have you not?" Zuester said. "And a long one."

"Indeed I have."

"As a philosopher once said, the wise man will live as long as he ought, not as long as he can." Zuester bowed. "Good day, consul." He turned and left.

Tibur, Hadrian's villa, end of February 138

Zuester rolled over in bed, then smiled to himself when he remembered the beautiful girl at his side. Lucius had been right; the red-haired Dacian maid was very much to his liking, her voluptuous body so utterly responsive she almost made him forget his past loves.

Almost.

He pulled her sated, sleeping form to him and buried his face in her perfumed tresses. He wasn't quite sure if he was in love with her yet or not, their affair was too recent to know for sure. He knew what love was, knew from Vibia and Lucius. For now, though, he was content to be with his Thaedra. She made him quite happy.

She let out a little sighing moan as she shifted alongside him, her fleshy thighs pressing against his, enlivening his cock. It was too soon to renew their love-making, for him anyway. At nineteen she was seemingly ready at all times, in any place. He had to admit, he loved that about her.

Love.

Hadrian's newly chosen adopted son and successor, Aurelius Antoninus, was apparently deeply in love with his wife of over twenty years, Faustina. The emperor had even inquired after this one day when the heir came to visit him at the Tibur villa.

"You are married, are you not, Antoninus?"

"I am, Caesar."

"And do you love your wife?"

"Very much so, sire," the mild-mannered man had blushed to his gray roots.

"Ah, yes, I *see* that you do." Hadrian had looked quite pleased. "And," he had added covertly, "what about your enemies? Have there been attempts on your life?"

Antoninus had started at this. "No, my lord! I may have critics amongst the Senate but no one who would wish to kill me, or I them for that matter."

"Very good, very good," Hadrian had chuckled. "Then I shall pass along a word of advice from my predecessor. If you are to succeed in this business of empire, you must continue to love. The ability to love is the first step in being considered trustworthy. Let the world know you love your wife. Then the world will know it can put its trust in you as their leader."

Aurelius Antoninus had looked confused, but had accepted the advice as the words of a sick, dying man who lived amidst calumnious politicians. Zuester had smiled as the heir simply nodded his head in acquiescence.

Yes, love.

Hadrian loved and trusted the youth Marcus as the grandson he never had. Now named Marcus Aurelius Verus, he had been formally adopted by Aurelius Antoninus and officially designated an heir to the empire. In the quiet, meditative boy Hadrian no doubt saw a reflection of himself, one who was intelligent and philosophical, who would eventually lead an empire based on considered policies and the benefit of Rome, not the aggrandizement of the self via wasteful war.

Hadrian himself was leaving an empire at a tentative peace held together by the philosophy of Panhellenism. He had not wavered in his belief of its validity and truth.

Thaedra stirred at Zuester's side once again. His hands were now perfectly placed to cup her generous breasts. The soft, buoyant flesh taunted him to stroke and knead, but he resisted. He did not want to wake her just yet. His insomnia shouldn't disturb both of them. Distracted by worries and thoughts, his palms and fingers instinctively curved around the plump orbs before him.

Down the hall, the emperor slept. Now completely crippled by pain, Hadrian had holed himself up in his villa. His days consisted of badgering his staff to put him out of his misery and handing the terrified servants various implements of death, alternating with the far more calming diversion of writing his memoirs. Sometimes while at his desk, Hadrian would sit in utter silence, his eyes glazed over in thought, then suddenly burble out in quiet chuckles and grins. Zuester was certain he had been remembering his beloved Antinous, his Kynegiskos. He one day listed the altars and temples accorded to the dead youth across the empire, a reminder that the cult, like the emperor's love for the boy, had endured.

Love, true love, would last forever. Zuester knew that from feeling the profound emotion in his heart every day for the friends of his past, hoping for the feeling to extend to the companions of his present.

Thaedra had not been a virgin – there were few of those in Rome – but she had been inexperienced. For the first time in his life, Zuester had had to teach a lover. It had been peculiar at first, but he quickly grew to enjoy instructing such an eager and willing pupil, one who wished to practice at every opportunity. The very thought of it excited him. He pulled her closer, thrilling as his fingers skirted her nipples.

She had been quite a distraction from his duties, which were easily covered by his numerous assistants. The emperor had found it positively endearing that his steadfast and reliable middle-aged advisor had been caught up in the confusion and impulsiveness of passion and desire. But he understood; Hadrian had been Zuester's age when he himself had fallen in love with one so many years his junior.

Zuester sighed. Unfortunately, one important duty had remained unfinished, a task no assistant could perform.

He had to kill the merchant Sextus Quintilius Bestia.

It was a task delayed by his current distractions. Zuester truly wanted to kill the man. He knew precisely who the villain was, although surely Bestia himself had no idea who Zuester had once been and who he was now. Zuester was going to savor the surprise. The man had brutally attacked then murdered his precious Vibia, killed the innocent Antinous, assassinated the promising Lucius, and probably incited the foolish Fuscus. There had been numerous attempts against Hadrian, some of which surely were the merchant's doing. Seeing him squirm and beg for his life was going to be quite satisfying. Zuester grinned so widely his body moved.

Thaedra stirred against him. "Zuse?" she said sleepily.

"Shh, sweet. Did I wake you?"

"No." She smiled the most alluring smile. "I felt your hands touch me. So exciting." She nuzzled against him. "I think my body misses you."

He felt himself grow hard.

She knitted her brow at him. "You look preoccupied. What are you thinking about?"

The thought of his unfinished business with Bestia found its way back into his head. He sighed again.

"You worry too much, love," she scolded.

Indeed, in the space of a second, the evidence of his desire had softened.

Thaedra wrapped her hands around his cock and gently stroked it. "I think I have an idea of how to stop you from worrying."

She moved underneath the bed covers and slid down his body. Her touch was delicate and fluid, almost masterful. She stroked his shaft reverently, then took him fully into her mouth.

"Gods above!" Zuester groaned, rocking his hips in encouragement. This was most definitely the best way to distract him from his worries.

Rome, Quirinalis Collis, April 138

Bestia stuffed the lengths of silk and the gold jewelry alongside the ivory statuette of Venus. He didn't need much but whatever he brought had to be useful or sellable and very definitely portable. As only his most trusted servant, Segomaros, would be accompanying him he would have to pack lightly.

After Servianus's death, Bestia had frantically contacted every one of their mutual associates, hoping against hope that the consul had left a message for him. But it was all for naught. Servianus had forsaken him, the old man had not kept his promise.

The Parthian throne had never been recovered.

He had waited four months after the death of Lucius Ceionius Commodus, had thought perhaps Servianus had indeed sent word to have the throne delivered to the merchant, that it might take some time if the jewel-encrusted chair was in some far flung corner of the empire. But nothing. And no one knew anything about such a thing. It was a disaster. Any day now the Parthians would be after him.

Bestia checked and double-checked the documents before resealing them. Letters of *commendatio*, professions of familial lineage, commercial licenses, declarations of provenance and authenticity for the *objets*, all under various aliases, from various officials real and imagined, cleverly interweaving falsehood with truth, would have to be transported close to his person. His traveling satchel had long sat unused. Its many concealed compartments would be useful now.

He had his suspicions that the Parthians were already on his tail. He couldn't walk through the market place without thinking those dressed in foreign garb were watching him, whispering behind his back, sending hand signals to counterparts in neighboring stalls. Were they simply waiting for the right time, when Bestia might slip up so they could catch him unaware?

At his age the idea of travel had lost its romance, especially travel not of his own choosing. As it was up to him now to find the *sella regia,* he would need the most useful information. His best contacts were in Rome. He sat with an exhausted thud on his bed. Why did he need to leave Rome? He had contacts across the empire, he could simply gather information like he always had…

Except this time the enemy was after him. They knew where he was, could attack at any moment…

No, he said to himself, he was panicking, not thinking clearly. He needed to calm down and concentrate on the problem logically: Where would such a treasure be kept? Who would have such information?

Did he really think the answer would be in Rome?

Bestia considered that last thought for a moment. The throne had been captured in the east during Trajan's war there. Trajan died only a year and a half later. Hadrian had acceded to the role of emperor far too quickly and ended the Parthian campaign abruptly. Would he have thought about something as inconsequential to Rome as the *sella regia*? As far as Hadrian had been concerned, his empire was in chaos; he was back in Rome in less than a year having ended the Parthian campaign begun by his predecessor. Why would he have brought the throne with him?

Wouldn't it still be in the east? Perhaps Antioch. Bestia had lots of contacts in Antioch. He knew he had to go there and he knew it had to be now.

"Master?" The servant's soft voice startled him from his thoughts.

"What is it, Segomaros?"

"There has been activity near the villa. Soldiers and such."

They had to leave immediately. Bestia was packed, but he was not, he had to admit, emotionally ready. He stood and draped his satchel across his chest. "Take my bag," he instructed.

"Yes, my lord." Segomaros leapt into action and padded behind his master along the labyrinthine route to the rear exit near the servants quarters.

They had delayed too long.

Bestia opened the door only to find a phalanx of Roman soldiers blocking his way.

Somewhere deep inside him he felt relief that it wasn't the Parthians.

The soldiers parted for a small group of Praetorians who guarded a middle-aged man wearing a tunic and cloak of the finest fabric known in Rome. He had no jewelry except a signet ring with a laurel wreath. *Subtle, but understood.* The man was some sort of imperial official, but not a military man. Perhaps a secretary or other advisor.

"Going somewhere?" the official asked sardonically.

"I have business in Antioch." *What else could he say?* There was still the remote possibility that this Roman could help him.

"I hardly think so." The secretary motioned for the soldiers to push further into the villa, grabbing Bestia by the arms and dragging him into the kitchen atrium. Twisting his ear, they forced him to kneel on the tiles.

"Who are you?" Bestia demanded with irritation.

"You don't recognize me?" There was a touch of anger in the official's voice.

"No. Should I?" He searched the face of the man, but could not bring up a memory of ever having met him.

"A good merchant remembers all costly and valuable transactions. However, it has been thirty years since I was last in this house. You were a fool to return here after all you have done."

If this man was going to be cagey, then so was he. "What is it that I am supposed to have done?"

"Crimes against the emperor and the imperial household."

"What crimes?" Bestia tried to sound incredulous.

"Attempts on the emperor's life, attacks on the empress, the murder of Antinous, the murder of Lucius Ceionius Commodus, the attempt to overthrow the emperor Hadrian." The secretary stopped and narrowed his eyes. "Should I go on?"

Bestia shook his head in disgust. "Do you have proof of these alleged crimes?"

"The empress gave me a description after your second attack on her. I knew right away who you were," he raised an eyebrow, "from personal experience. The consul Julius Ursus Servianus implicated you in the murder of Commodus. I have recently made acquaintance with Parthian diplomats who offered several stories of how you have threatened the emperor and his household, resorting, ultimately, to murder."

Bestia exhaled. The Parthians had ratted him out. But he remained curious as to who the man before him was. "How is it that you know me?"

"I carry your mark."

"*My slave?!*" Bestia was incensed. "Escaped no doubt." He spat on the ground before the man. "You are my property. You have no power over me. I should have you killed."

"Ah, but as so many of your transactions were illegitimate, I'm fairly certain your purchase of my person was highly irregular." The official circled around the merchant still kneeling on the floor. "My manumission, however, was done with the utmost care to legal detail." He spat on Bestia's face, then smiled when his prisoner winced. "I serve the emperor now. No other."

"Fool."

The official smiled. "Gavros!"

A brawny soldier immediately appeared at attention at the official's side. "Yes, my lord?"

"Round up all slaves in this house. Gather them in the main court. Go," he waved his hand.

The soldier took a few of his comrades to carry out his orders.

Despite his slender athleticism, the official loomed large above Bestia as he paced calmly, eyeing his captive, smirking and shaking his head in disapprobation. The fine lines on his face and the gray in his hair did not detract from his handsome features. He must have been chosen for his good looks many decades ago, and that could only mean one thing: He had been a performer in Bestia's sexual extravaganzas. He must have become the emperor's *puer* after his escape, and discarded from the bedroom when he got too old.

The secretary removed a scroll from beneath his pallium, then snapped for a guard who brought forth a portable desk with parchment, pen, and ink.

The secretary smiled. "You will free your slaves before you die."

"What? I will not!"

Bestia had no time to react as his toga and tunic were ripped off his body and a flagrum lashed across his bared back, the jagged metal barbs tearing at his flesh. He felt blood flow in slow rivulets down his tender skin.

The official grabbed the merchant by his beard forcing him to look into the rich brown eyes flashing with anger. "You will do as I say," he hissed. "I know some tortures give you far too much pleasure, so I will restrict my men to the kind that simply hurt." He opened the scroll to the bottom and pushed the inked pen into Bestia's hand. "You will sign your last will and testament manumitting and providing for all of your slaves and giving all of your remaining possessions to the emperor." He narrowed his eyes. "Then we will put the will into effect by killing you."

Had he really been beaten this time? Bestia tried to collect his thoughts, shrinking slightly at the sight of a soldier at the ready to scourge him again. He looked over at Segomaros cowering as he was held fast by a burly guard. The boy paled when he met Bestia's eyes.

The official noticed.

"What is your name, son?" he asked gently.

"Segomaros, sir."

"That's a Gaulish name, is it not?"

The servant beamed. "Yes, sir, it is."

"Do you enjoy living in Rome? Do you miss your family in Gaul?"

"Rome is very exciting, sir. But I would like to see my mother again."

The official cleared his throat, as if suppressing an emotion long thought dead. "You will get your wish, Segomaros. Do you know which hand your master uses to write?"

"The right, sir."

"Then he will not need his left."

The official flicked his wrist again and two Praetorians sprang into action, one grabbing Bestia's left arm, exposing the hand, while the other stood poised with his sword.

"Wait!" Bestia screamed, trying desperately to free himself from the guard's strong grasp. "What are you doing?"

"Perhaps my methods of persuasion are unfamiliar to you," the official sneered contemptuously.

"All right, all right. I'll sign." It was resignation rather than defeat. He was too old and tired to argue.

The Praetorian released him as the portable desk was shoved under his face. He signed, then let out a long exhale. *What was next?*

The secretary rolled up the scroll. "I offer my gratitude for your cooperation." He turned to Segomaros and bowed slightly. "Yours as well. You may go. My guard will escort you." He motioned and spoke to a soldier to take the boy to the main courtyard where the other slaves were waiting. The official turned to Bestia, his countenance twitching with contempt. "I really see no reason to prolong this encounter."

Bestia looked around frantically. Instinctively he struggled as he was pulled up from the tiles and held fast by a Praetorian at each arm. "Is this to be an extra-judicial execution?" he cried. "What about a trial? I deserve to be heard! The emperor is not himself blameless!"

The official raised an eyebrow. "No, there is to be no trial." He paced thoughtfully. "Hearing a commotion in your villa as we passed, my guard and I came to investigate only to discover your body, the perpetrators having fled. We then found your generous final testament, recently signed." The official stopped before Bestia with a satisfied smile. "Members of your family, the Crassi Frugi Liciniani have been at odds with Rome's emperors for one hundred years, since the days of Claudius," he proclaimed. "Despite your bastard status, you have chosen to follow in the footsteps of your aristocratic forebears. I was surprised to discover that among your ancestors were the two *triumviri* Pompey and Crassus." The smile grew slightly wider. "Which leads me to decide upon the nature of your death. As befits your heritage and your imperial pretensions, I will give you a suitable execution. The former imperial secretary Suetonius wrote in his biography of Julius Caesar," the official leaned in a little, "the third member of the triumvirate," he hissed with emphasis, "that the dictator was assassinated by three and twenty wounds." The smile turned smug. "I will leave it to my guards to decide where, precisely, to stab you."

Bay of Naples, Baiae, 10 July 138

A cooling breeze blew in to the atrium from the bay below, filling the villa with much-needed fresh air. The warmth of summer had turned stagnant in the imperial household as all waited for the emperor to die.

It had been a long time coming, months filled with Hadrian's agonizing pain and his anguished cries. More than once Zuester had been ordered by Hadrian himself to kill his master, and more than once the loyal secretary had refused. He had even taken a knife away during a futile attempt at suicide.

Moving to the summer palace had proven to be a brilliant idea. Distracted by stunning vistas and new routines, and removed from the reminders of his lost beloved – the statues and busts, the memorial fountains and gardens – Hadrian became a changed man. Perhaps, Zuester mused to himself, it was because the emperor knew he was finally dying.

They sat together, secretary and emperor, lover and husband, friend and friend. Servants moved slowly or not at all so as not to disturb their master. The officials of the emperor's inner circle conferred quietly in a corner. The emperor-elect, Aurelius Antoninus, stood facing out at the magnificent view, his wife Faustina veiled in mourning attire at his side.

Hadrian stirred in his bed. "Zuester," he said weakly. "They're all gone."

"Yes, Caesar."

"My Vibia…Lucius…my favorite, my love Antinous, my Kynegiskos. Lives lost needlessly."

"It was not to be expected."

It should have been me."

"Don't say such things, sire. You escaped death several times. The gods held you in their favor."

"I loved each one of them. Is it fair that a man should lose everything he loves?"

"No, Graeculus." Zuester placed the emperor's hand on his.

The use of the familiar name put a smile on Hadrian's lips. "But you're still here."

"Yes, my lord."

"What will you do?"

"Retire to your Tiburtine villa as you have allowed in your will."

"Yes, of course. I remember. And what will you do in my villa?"

Zuester chuckled at the emperor's prying. It had been both a fault and an asset that Hadrian concerned himself so much with the details of the lives of those around him. "Well," he began, "I will look after your papers as you have directed. And, I will be busy with my family. I have made Thaedra my wife. She carries my child."

"Wife? Good, very good. And pregnant? Already you have forgotten your old lovers."

"I will never forget them, like you never forgot them."

"And what will you name your progeny?"

"Lucius Hadrianus if a boy, Sabina Antinoë if a girl."

"It will be a son. I feel it."

"Thank you, my lord."

"And, at least, you will have someone to support you when you mourn my loss."

Zuester recognized it as a very weak attempt at humor on the emperor's part. "Yes, Graeculus."

Hadrian shifted in his bed, futilely trying to get comfortable. "Zuester," he said softly, "you have been with the imperial household for how many years?"

"Almost twenty-five, Caesar."

"And in those twenty-five years have I ever called you 'friend'?"

Zuester started and swallowed hard. "I don't know, my lord. But you needn't ever have said it."

"Yes, yes; stop being polite. Now that I am leaving you, I should say it. You have been more than a servant, more than a secretary and advisor. You have been my friend, my *amicus*, and I am thankful for such loyalty and unwavering affection."

Zuester felt his heart tighten in a joyful pang, and when he inhaled he knew he would not be able to stop the tears. He let them flow without restraint. "Thank you, my lord. That means a great deal to me."

"It means a great deal to me that you were there for Vibia, as well. She was deeply in love with you, and I don't think she could have found a better man." Hadrian gave a feeble squeeze to Zuester's hand. "Now, call those waiting over. I should address my councilors one last time."

Zuester gathered the officials in attendance and the emperor-elect to Hadrian's bedside. Some looked a bit frightened, a few had been crying. Aurelius Antoninus was stoic, fully cognizant as to what was about to befall him.

"I honor all of you for your service and sound advice over the years. Of my eminent *amici*, those of you who remain are most capable and trustworthy. I hope that the new emperor will take that under consideration when he needs council of his own."

The men collectively nodded their heads and uttered scattered words of gratitude.

Hadrian turned as well as his body allowed toward Aurelius Antoninus. "The Senate never really liked me, you know that. Had I had a natural-born son, most likely they would have fought to prevent his succession. But adoption allows the best to be chosen. Having you as my heir ensures they will, at the very least, not abolish the imperial throne. I leave a vigorous yet well-defined empire, an empire at peace."

Aurelius Antoninus bowed. "Thank you, Caesar. I am grateful for your confidence."

Hadrian pressed against the pillows. "I think I shall rest now," he said with a grunt. "You may all go."

The councilors shuffled off knowing full well that the emperor's last breath was imminent.

Hadrian glanced painfully around him. "Zuester?" he called meekly.

The Dacian stood before his master instantly. "I am here, my lord."

"Good. Stay with me."

"I will stay with you Graeculus, old friend," Zuester said quietly, once again taking the emperor's hand in his own.

"I've had premonitions of this day, you know. Of my death." The emperor's voice was growing weaker, but Zuester knew he wanted to speak, so he encouraged the conversation.

"Such as what?"

"A lion, lunging for me much like what happened to my poor Kynegiskos."

"I remember the incident. But your favorite survived, and virtually unharmed."

"Would that I were as lucky." Hadrian drew in an uncomfortable breath. "But my body has long been dead, my poor little soul rattling around in this broken shell of a man." His exhale was ragged. "I release it now, to wander, to play, to joke, but I wonder if it has forgotten how to enjoy these amusements."

"I think your Kynegiskos will remind you."

"Will I see him again?" The emperor looked at his secretary sounding hopeful, as if he were now eager to die.

"Yes." Zuester tried to keep the tears as bay as he gently squeezed the hand of his emperor. He realized he had spent half his life in the service of the imperial household. But now, everyone he had known, everyone he had been close to was gone. At times he felt this immensely, wanting to tell Lucius a joke, to argue philosophy with Hadrian, to spy on Fuscus, to sense the jealousy of Suetonius, to make love to Vibia. Would the new emperor have any need for him, he wondered? Perhaps not. It did not matter. He had a new life ahead of him, a family to care for and a small apartment near the library of the extensive Tibur villa. Once his mourning had subsided, Zuester knew he would be very happy.

Zuester felt Hadrian's fingers go limp. And then the emperor was gone.

FINALE:
TEMPUS AETERNITATIS

Hadrian drew in a deep breath and immediately realized one thing: It didn't hurt. It didn't hurt to breathe, it didn't hurt to move, it didn't hurt to exist. In fact, he had to admit, he felt great.

He had quite forgotten what it was like to live without pain.

He moved his limbs, twisted his torso, noticed his body was that of a man in his prime, dressed in the garb of an unarmored soldier. He looked around and saw only mist and fog. He recognized his surroundings; he had been there once before. He chuckled to himself. The goddess Aphrodite Urania had been with him then.

This time, he knew, it was different, it was real, it was permanent. Yet, he couldn't recall having crossed the river Styx, couldn't recall having patted Cerberus on the head, couldn't recall his judgment by Minos, Aeacus, and Rhadamanthus. But perhaps he had already imbibed of the waters of forgetfulness from the river Lethe.

One thing Hadrian did know, could feel and sense: He was in paradise.

He waited, wondering what one does exactly in paradise, when out of the obscuring whiteness a figure approached. Youthful from the gait, dressed in a simple tunic, slender, tall, blond...

"Kynegiskos!"

Hadrian ran to his beloved, enfolding him in his arms.

"I knew you would come eventually, Graeculus," Antinous said with a playful grin.

His beloved was as the last time he saw him, an athletic youth of twenty. Antinous smiled as his eyes skimmed over the figure of his love, in awe of the handsome, robust man before him.

"You are as the first time I met you," Antinous sighed.

Hadrian grinned. "I remember it well, my little hunter." He embraced him once again, their bodies melding comfortably as they used to. "My Kynegiskos, my love," he repeated, scattering kisses over the youth's face and neck. He threaded his fingers through the golden curls and pressed his lips against the succulent mouth, feeling a now-remembered thrill course through his veins.

Lost in their passion, their limbs entwined as they fell back into the clouds, tumbling, letting the mist cradled them.

"I've missed you, Graeculus. My body has certainly missed you," Antinous smiled, "but my mind as well."

"We used to talk for hours."

The youth's face brightened. "Yes!"

Hadrian caressed his lover's smooth cheek. "I'm here now. No more waiting, love." He grasped the hem of Antinous's tunic and drew it up, marveling at the sculpted musculature revealed inch by inch. "The gods know I have been longing for you every day of my life since I lost you. Now they grant my prayer." Impatient, he pulled the garment off, sucking in a sharp breath at the magnificent sight. His hands coursed along the taut flesh as Antinous moaned encouragements.

The soft laughter of a woman stilled Hadrian's hands. He looked up but saw nothing.

"I see you are finally made a god."

Hadrian turned around to face the familiar feminine voice. In the glowing light he discerned two figures: a woman in a long stola of diaphanous gold, and a man in a sheer white tunic.

"Or perhaps we must still wait for the good emperor, the pious Aurelius Antoninus to insist on your deification," the woman continued. "The Senate never really liked you Graeculus, my love."

Hadrian squinted into the light as the mist and clouds lifted to reveal the couple more clearly. He grinned broadly at his new companions.

"Vibia! Lucius! I...I...never thought..." He trailed off, overcome, joyful emotion choking him.

"We've not been waiting as long as Antinous," said Sabina, wrapping her arms around Lucius. She, too, was as she had been in her youth, a lithe figure with buoyant breasts. "But, don't worry, we've been keeping him in good spirits." She blew the nude youth a kiss.

Lucius laughed at Hadrian's bewildered reaction, then bent down and kissed Sabina fully on the mouth. His hands wandered over her body tugging at the filmy fabric that seemed to float over her flesh.

"Tsk, tsk. What will Zuester think when he arrives?" Hadrian teased.

"Zuester has a good thirty years before we'll see him," replied his wife.

"Which means I only have to share you with two for the moment," murmured Lucius, preoccupied with tickling and kneading the empress's supple figure.

Titillated at the sight, Hadrian's skin prickled then flushed with warm desire, energizing his newly rejuvenated flesh. He wanted them both. And he still wanted the naked youth lying beneath him. He hadn't lusted for such sport for decades. Now he couldn't quite figure out why he ever gave up the erotic games.

He turned around and pulled his lover to him, kissing him deeply while he wrapped his fingers around the youth's erect cock. Antinous moved his hips in encouragement, his hands gripping Hadrian's shoulders for purchase. When the emperor reached for his own prick, Antinous pulled back.

"No, Graeculus. Not yet," he said, although his tone suggested his unwillingness to stop.

Hadrian looked perplexed. "Why not?"

Antinous's lips twitched with a mischievous curl. He glanced over at Sabina and Lucius, then returned his focus to Hadrian.

"Vibia," he called. "Remember when our emperor initiated us into the Eleusinian Mysteries?

Sabina laughed. "Yes, yes I do."

"We should return the favor, so to speak." He faced Hadrian but still spoke to the empress. "Initiate Graeculus into the ways of paradise."

"Whatever sort of initiation might I need?" Hadrian said uneasily as a smirking Sabina sauntered over to him.

She drew her fingers across his chest and laughed when he jumped back into Antinous's arms. "We're not here to frighten you, love," she said, placing her palm reassuringly where she had touched him. "But this *is* your first time in Elysium—"

"It is not," Hadrian responded categorically.

"Really?" his wife was incredulous.

"I had a vision on a mountain. Aphrodite Urania was there." He cupped her face and bent down to meet it. "I made love to you," he said duskily.

Sabina blushed before regaining her composure. "Not like this you haven't."

Suddenly, the light of heaven disappeared and darkness engulfed him.

The shock made him stumble. He swung around, reaching out in search of his vanished friends. His eyes tried to discern his surroundings, but he was unable to see beyond his own body. He was naked.

For one instant he thought he had been tricked by the gods, that his final destination was instead Hades.

Until he heard Sabina giggling.

He looked in the direction he thought it might be coming from, and waited. Like the light of candles and lamps illuminating a cavernous temple, the darkness lifted slowly, revealing an exotic, luxurious space, similar to his barge in Egypt or the palace at Antioch. Amidst pillows and clouds sprawled the emperor's three lovers, also nude, Lucius delicately caressing a compliant Sabina, Antinous sitting off to the side. The youth held out his hand in invitation and Hadrian went to him.

The two men embraced once again, their mouths seeking to slake the thirst of desirous need, plunging to sensual depths the emperor had never before encountered. Hadrian felt consumed by Antinous's passion, and struggled desperately to keep pace with the assault of pleasure, finding himself swirling in a vortex of oblivion, to a depth where the youth would subsume his master, body and soul. Determined to maintain his sense of self, Hadrian clung to every shred of his own desire. He dug his fingers and palms against the musculature of his lover's back, compelling himself to feel every sinew, every ridge and ripple of flesh and bone. Soon, a flush of energy surged through him, sensations magnified, encouraging him to grip harder, convincing him he was climbing toward the precipice of the abyss. Emboldened, he moved his hands lower to feel the youth's taut butt, then further to grab his strong thighs, his cock enlivening in anticipation. Antinous thrashed against him, challenging his lover's resolve. Caught in a battle of wills, confusion beset the emperor. Hadrian grasped the heated flesh, trying to reign in the youthful lust, to tame it to match his own mature desire. But the harder he clenched, the more the youth struggled and could not be contained. Hadrian felt himself slip back into the void. Exhausted and defeated, he relented, relaxing his grip. Suddenly, an explosion of sensation scorched his skin, expelling the lovers beyond the tenebrous chasm. He felt his own self fully, yet at the same time felt Antinous wholly: his body, his mind, his emotions, his deeply-felt love and longing for the emperor. Sensations, dreams, desires were shared completely, their origins indistinct. The two men had become one.

Hadrian drew back in amazement. "I feel it, I feel it my love. We are…truly equals." He pulled Antinous to him. "This is what could have been."

Antinous grinned excitedly. "Yes, what could have been, and what it is now. What it is like here." He stroked the masculine chest before him, combing the dark hair with his fingers. "Let me, Graeculus," he said softly. He looked up beseechingly at Hadrian's gray eyes. "Let me take you. You'll see, it doesn't matter up here. The conventions of our old lives below do not matter here."

"I see that things are very different," the emperor murmured, gently raking the blond curls. "I would very much like you to have me in any way you desire."

Antinous brushed kisses along Hadrian's chest and shoulders while his hands trailed across the down-covered flesh of his abdomen. He slowly moved until he was behind, then pressed his chest into Hadrian's back, feeling their breaths merge into one rhythm.

Hadrian now regarded Sabina and Lucius, who had been watching the scene before them, smiling while playfully pawing at each other. "Come, Lucius," the empress said with a mischievous grin. "Let us join in the festivities."

Holding Hadrian's eyes, Sabina sashayed over to her husband, her perfect breasts swaying gently with her movements. The emperor felt his cock twitch. Sabina's lips curled triumphantly at the sight.

"I don't think Antinous would mind if you had a little distraction while he takes his pleasure," she said pressing her hand to Hadrian's chest, before drawing her fingers downward to play with his erection.

Antinous laughed.

Sabina dropped to her knees and teasingly flicked her tongue against the bulbous tip before taking the entire shaft into her mouth.

Hadrian groaned.

Antinous positioned his prick. "You want me," he sighed admiring the flexing orifice, then pushed in as far as he could.

"Gods of Olympus!" Hadrian exclaimed in surprise, grasping the air for purchase but feeling secured by the mists of heaven. He had expected the usual erotic pain of invasion, yet instead felt a pleasure verging on the orgiastic.

"I told you things are different here."

As Sabina continued her sensual assault below, Antinous licked and nipped the muscles of his lover's back, moaning as he slowly slid in and out. Hadrian reached around to press his hands against the youth's firm butt, encouraging his rhythmic movement.

Still, the emperor wanted more, wanted to feel the soft curves of his wife, wanted to hear her moans mingle with Antinous's panting breaths. Hadrian grabbed a handful of her luxuriant red hair and pulled her to standing.

"I can't remember the last time we made love, Vibia," he said, his hand cupping her mons, his fingers finding her slick and wet.

"Nor can I, husband," she responded seductively, rubbing against him.

Hadrian nudged her thighs apart with his knee. Lucius approached and took his position behind Sabina, steadying her as the emperor hesitated a moment then thrust inside to match the tempo of the ravishment behind him.

The double delight sent a shock wave of pleasure shuddering through him. It was the first time for such an indulgence, an act the hierarchical proprieties of Roman society denied him in life. Experiencing it now, he had no idea what purpose such a restriction served. Pressed between both lovers at once was positively, mind-numbingly wondrous.

Hadrian set the pace, played with the rhythm, alternating his thrusts with those of Antinous. The youth hugged him, his arms wrapped lovingly around his waist, his fingers straying at times to pinch his nipples. Sabina clung to him, her gripping hands mirroring the clenching of her passage. Hadrian buried his face against her shoulder as he gently kneaded her pliant curves.

So engrossed, the emperor did not notice Lucius moving behind her. Seconds later, Sabina jerked forward with a laughing cry. Her cunt squeezed as tight as a virgin's.

To her utter delight, Lucius was fucking her in the ass. And Hadrian could feel every glorious movement.

He exchanged smiles with his old lover, then bent forward to take him in a devastatingly deep kiss.

Now joined with all three, every erogenous zone was attended, every nerve ending pulsed with erotic delectation. Familiar feelings surfaced, sensations similar to those experienced by the emperor's mortal flesh, but somehow tinged with a difference, not strange and unwelcome, but new and enticing. The sensual intertwining of multiple bodies was no simple, playful game. Hadrian's earlier unearthly kiss with Antinous showed there was so much more. He stopped trying to feel, stopped trying to act, and let go of his grasp of the current reality. As a new flush of sensation washed over him, Hadrian became fully cognizant not just of the erotic delights stimulating his body, but of a strong and deep emotion, an emotion that in corporeal life was fugitive, diminishing a little with every day, but in Elysium was intensely experienced. It was beyond the ecstasy the Celestial Aphrodite had shown him. This love, perfect and true, encompassed not only all that *he* could and did ever love, but all that the four intimate friends ever loved. It flowed through their united bodies and minds, intensifying their carnal pleasures.

Their bodies moved in rhythmic unison, increasing in cadence, all striving for the same destination. Each felt the others' libidinous hunger magnify their own, felt the swell of shared desire. They were all rushing to the same inexorable release.

Hadrian leaned his head back onto the crook of Antinous's shoulder. "Can we…all at once?" he asked between panting breaths.

Antinous understood exactly what his lover meant. "We can indeed, Graeculus."

"Then we shall," Hadrian decided, or had they all decided at once? It was difficult to determine.

But no matter. The tangle of limbs wound more tightly in the frenzy of movement, coiling once more before exploding in an ecstatic fervor. Each voice cried out in joy, holding a sustained note before accepting that, for the moment, their lascivious needs had been slaked.

The release had been magnificent. Hadrian began to laugh in sheer joy. Understanding his lover's reaction, Antinous gave him a squeeze and grinned against his back. Lucius joined with the emperor's infectious laughter. Sabina giggled.

Hadrian looked down at her, meeting her eyes with his own. He threaded his fingers through her vibrant red hair, and studied her face. She had been the one constant for most of his life. His Vibia, his wife, his soul. Through the plots and intrigues, the numerous affairs however long or brief, had he truly shown his appreciation to this most tolerant woman?

"Vibia, in life, did I ever tell you I loved you?"

"Yes, husband, you did," she said smiling broadly. "More than once."

"I'm sure it was not enough, so I'm telling you again. I love you."

She slid her hands around his neck and stood on tiptoe to give him a soft peck on the lips. "And I love you, too," she murmured gently. "Forever."

About the Author

Regina Kammer is a librarian, an art historian, and an award-winning, international best-selling, multi-published writer of provocative historical romance and contemporary romance with a touch of history. Her short stories and novels make history sexier, whether the era is Roman, Byzantine, Viking, American Revolution, or Victorian. She's even sexed up contemporary settings, Steampunk, and Greco-Roman mythology. She has been published by Cleis Press, Go Deeper Press, Ellora's Cave, House of Erotica, Story Ink, Loose Id, The Naughty Literati, and her own imprint, Viridium Press. She began writing historical fiction with romantic elements during National Novel Writing Month 2006, switching to erotica when all her characters suddenly demanded to have sex.

Keep up with Regina
Check out her website: https://reginakammer.com/
Never miss a new release! Subscribe to *Kammerotica News*:
https://reginakammer.com/newsletter/

Historical erotic romance by Regina

Victorian
The Pleasure Device (Harwell Heirs Book 1)
Disobedience By Design (Harwell Heirs Book 2)
Where Destiny Plays (Harwell Heirs Book 3)
The Westerman Affair (Art & Discipline Book 1)
The Demonstration
The Invitation
Disputed Boundaries (Stories from the San Juan Islands)

American Revolution
The General's Wife: An American Revolutionary Tale
Winter Interlude: An American Revolutionary Novelette
On the Eighteenth of January, '78; or, A Night At Valley Forge

Ancient World
Hadrian and Sabina: A Love Story
Ancient Shorts: An Ancient World Romance Collection

Steampunk
One Cheek Or Two? (Ockham Steam-Works Laboratory Chronicles 1)
Delia's Heartthrob (Ockham Steam-Works Laboratory Chronicles 2)
Swing Follies (Ockham Steam-Works Laboratory Chronicles 3)